Clare Morrall was born in Exeter and now lives in Birmingham. She works as a music teacher, and has two daughters. *Astonishing Splashes of Colour*, her first novel, was published in 2003 by Tindal Street Press and was short-listed for the Man Booker Prize. She has since published four novels: *Natural Flights of the Human Mind*, *The Language of* Others, *The Man Who Disappeared*, which was a TV Book Club Summer read in 2010, and *The Roundabout Man*. Her sixth novel, *After the Bombing*, is published by Sceptre in 2014.

Clare Morrall

SCEPTRE

First published in Great Britain in 2003 by Tindal Street Press Ltd

This edition published in 2013 by Sceptre
An imprint of Hodder & Stoughton
An Hachette UK company

2

A CIP catalogue record for this title is available from the British Library

ISBN 9781444780314

Printed and bound by CPI Group (UK) Ltd, Croydon, CR0 4YY

Hodder & Stoughton policy is to use papers that are natural, renewable
and recyclable products and made from wood grown in sustainable forests.
The logging and manufacturing processes are expected to conform to the
environmental regulations of the country of origin.

Hodder & Stoughton Ltd
338 Euston Road
London NW1 3BH

www.sceptrebooks.com

For Alex and Heather

Acknowledgements

I would like to thank the following:

Jackie Gay, Emma Hargrave, Penny Rendall and Tindal Street Press for all their help and support;

Chris Morgan, Pauline Morgan, Gina Standring (without whom there would be twice as many adverbs in this novel), Jeff Phelps, Dorothy Hunt and Joel Lane for their many valuable words of criticism and belief;

Terry, Yvonne, Anna, Simon and Nicholas Gateley for their generosity in giving me space in their house.

'For Neverland is always more or less an island, with astonishing splashes of colour here and there'

from *Peter Pan*, J.M. Barrie

1

The Flash of my Skirt

At 3.15 every weekday afternoon, I become anonymous in a crowd of parents and child-minders congregating outside the school gates. To me, waiting for children to come out of school is a quintessential act of motherhood. I see the mums – and the occasional dads – as yellow people. Yellow as the sun, a daffodil, the submarine. But why do we teach children to paint the sun yellow? It's a deception. The sun is white-hot, brilliant, impossible to see with the naked eye, so why do we confuse brightness with yellow?

The people outside the school gates are yellow because of their optimism. There's a picture in my mind of morning in a kitchen, the sun shining past yellow gingham curtains on to a wooden table, where the children sit and eat breakfast. Their arms are firm and round, their hair still tangled from sleep. They eat Coco Pops, drink milk and ask for chocolate biscuits in their lunchboxes. It's the morning of their lives, and their mums are reliving that morning with them.

After six weeks of waiting, I'm beginning to recognize individuals, to separate them from the all-embracing yellow mass. They smile with recognition when I arrive now and nearly include me in their conversations. I don't say anything, but I like to listen.

A few days ago, I was later than usual and only managed to reach the school gates as the children were already coming out. I dashed in, nearly fell over someone's push-chair, and collided with another girl. I've seen her before: an au pair, who picks up a boy and a girl.

'Sorry,' I said, several times, to everyone.

The girl straightened up and smiled. 'Is all right,' she said.

I smiled back.

'I am Hélène,' she said awkwardly. 'What is your name?'

'Kitty,' I said eventually, because I couldn't think of a suitable alternative.

Now when we meet, we speak to each other.

''ello, Kitty,' she says.

'Hello, Hélène,' I say.

'Is a lovely day.'

'Yes, it's very warm.'

'I forgot to put washing out.'

'Oh dear.'

Our conversations are distinctly limited – short sentences with one subject, one verb. Nothing sensational, nothing important. I like the pointlessness of it all. The feeling that you are skimming the surface only, whizzing along on water skis, not thinking about what might happen if you take a wrong turning away from the boat. I like this simple belief, the sense of going on indefinitely, without ever falling off.

'Where do you come from?' I ask Hélène one day. I'm no good with accents.

'France.'

'Oh,' I say, 'France.' I have only been to France once, when I was sixteen, on a school trip. I was sick both ways on the ferry, once on some steps, so everybody who came down afterwards slipped on it. I felt responsible, but there was nothing I could do to stop people using the stairs.

Another mother is standing close to us with a toddler in a pushchair. The boy is wearing a yellow and black striped hat with a pompom on it, and his little fat cheeks are a brilliant red. He is holding a packet of Wotsits and trying to cram them into his mouth as quickly as possible. His head bobs up and down, so that he looks like a bumble bee about to take off.

'Jeremy, darling,' says his mother, 'finish eating one before starting on the next.' He contemplates her instructions for five seconds and then continues to stuff them in at the same rate as before.

She turns to Hélène. 'What part of France?'

Hélène looks pleased to be asked. 'Brittany.'

James would know it. He used to go to France every summer. Holidays with his parents.

One of Hélène's children comes out of school, wearing an unzipped red anorak and a rucksack on his back in the shape of a very green alligator. The alligator's scaly feet reach round him from the back and its grinning row of teeth open and shut from behind as he walks.

''ello, Toby,' says Hélène.

'Have we got Smarties today?' he demands in a clear, firm tone. He talks to Hélène with a slight arrogance.

Hélène produces a packet of chocolate buttons.

'But I don't like them. I only like Smarties.'

'Good,' she says and puts the buttons back in her bag.

He hesitates. 'OK then,' he says with a sigh, wandering off to chat to his friends with the buttons in his pocket. His straight blond hair flops over his eyes. If he were mine, I'd have taken him to a barber ages ago.

Hélène turns to me. 'We walk home together? You know my way?'

'No. I live in the opposite direction to you.'

'Then you come with me to park for a little while? Children play on swings?'

She is obviously lonely. It must be so hard to come to Birmingham from the French countryside. How does she

11

understand the accent, or find out the bus fares and have the right change ready?

'I have to get back,' I say. 'My husband will be expecting me.'

She smiles and pretends not to mind. I watch her walk miserably away with her two children and wish I could help her, although I know I can't. She chose the wrong person. The yellow is changing. I can feel it becoming overripe – the sharp smell of dying daffodils, the sting and taste of vomit.

When I walk home, I remember being met from school by my brothers, twenty-five years ago. It was never my father – too busy, too many socks to wash, too many shirts to iron. I never knew which brother it would be. Adrian, Jake and Martin, the twins, or Paul. I was always so pleased to see them. Paul, the youngest, was ten years older than me, and it made me feel special to be met by a teenage brother, a nearly-man. None of them looked alike, but my memory produces a composite brother. I don't have a clear picture of him. I remember only the joy of seeing him there.

'Kitty!' this composite brother would call, and I'd feel important as I walked away with him, my empty lunchbox rattling in my plain brown shoulder bag.

They all called me Kitty, my brothers and my father. It used to be Katy, but we had a cat once and when anyone called Kitty, I came running. They often tell people this joke; each time they tell it, it expands and becomes more vivid, so I have the whole story in my head now. The cat was black, they tell me, black as my hair, with white whiskers and blue eyes. I often try to remember him, and sometimes I almost can, but it's like a poster flashing past when you're on the train – there, but too fast to catch.

The cat got run over and died, so I moved along and took its place.

We had an older sister once, too, who I never knew.

Dinah. She ran away before I was born, so I took her place as well. I'm good at filling gaps.

A few days later, Hélène approaches me again outside the school. 'Kitty?'

I smile at her, but there's a smell of danger in the situation, so I don't say anything.

'Will you need to 'urry after school?'

She's rehearsed this speech, trying to get her tenses right.

'I'm always in a hurry,' I say.

'I am wondering . . .'

I wait, feeling my stomach churning. I should learn to listen to my stomach. It seldom makes a mistake.

'Perhaps I can walk a little way 'ome with you? I want to make friends. I have no friends in Birmingham . . .' She has difficulty with Birmingham. She divides the three syllables precisely, but loses the 'h' in 'ham'. Her voice tails away.

'I don't think so. You'd have to wait ages for me. Henry's always late out.'

'I don't mind. Children are 'appy with Smarties.'

I'm running out of excuses.

The children are pouring out now, all on top of each other, shouting, running, arguing. Henry is not among them. Henry my baby, who never comes when I want him. Eventually, there's only me and Hélène left. Even the teachers are leaving in their cars.

'Your son is very late,' she says. Her children are walking along the low wall at the entrance with their arms stretched out. Toby is faster than his sister and keeps nudging her along from behind, trying to hurry her up.

'Stop, Toby,' says Hélène. 'You 'ave accident.'

They ignore her.

'He likes to help with the library,' I say cheerfully.

'I wait,' she says. 'Is nice to have someone to talk to.'

No, I think. I don't want anyone with me.

We wait another five minutes.

'Look,' I say. 'I'll go in and find him. You go ahead, and we'll walk together another time.'

But she sits down on the end of the small wall. 'I wait,' she says.

I walk towards the school. Just before I reach the main doors, I look back and see she's still there, slumped on the wall, ignoring the children. I see Toby push his sister over and hear her wails as I enter the building. There's nothing I can do about it.

Inside, the corridor is lined with photographs of children in a play. Henry and Gretel – no, Hansel, not Henry. There's one of the gingerbread house, which has giant Smarties down one wall and liquorice allsorts down another. The roof is made up of huge chocolate fingers. There are several photographs of the witch, crouched under a black cape. The girl's face is all screwed up behind her glasses; she is clearly enjoying the challenge. I stop for some time and examine a picture of Hansel and Gretel, holding hands, alone in the woods. They are in a single spotlight, surrounded by darkness, so they look very small. Their eyes are very big and round and frightened. You can see that they are lost.

Further on, there are pieces of writing, pinned up on a purple background. 'My Best Friend' is the title, and under the writing they have drawn a picture of their best friend.

The name Henry Woodall catches my eye and I stop to read it.

My best friend is Richard Jenkins. He is in my class at school, but he has a wheelchair so we push him every-where. I wish I had a wheelchair. It must be really good fun –

'Can I help you?'

I jump and turn round, to find myself facing a woman with a stern, authoritative face. 'I'm sorry,' I say. 'I was

14

looking for my nephew, but I think I must have missed him.'

She is tall, older than me, and she wears an olive crinkled cotton dress that reaches nearly to her ankles, with a loose beige cardigan over the top. I am convinced that she is the headmistress.

'Everybody's gone,' she says. 'What's the child's name?'

'Henry,' I say. 'Henry Woodall.'

'Oh, yes.' She allows a brief smile to drift across her face. Henry must be a character. Just like my Henry. 'I saw him leaving with Tony Perkins' mother. Were they expecting you to pick him up?'

'Not exactly. I said I would try to be here in time if I could.'

'I see. Another time, it would be helpful for us to have a letter from his mother explaining the situation. I am sure you can appreciate that we have to be careful these days.'

I nod. 'Of course,' I say.

'You know the way out?'

I nod again and turn towards the main entrance. Once I reach the double doors, I look back to check she's gone. Then I race up another corridor in the opposite direction, hoping there's no one else in the building. There must be a back way out. My heartbeat thuds in my ears, booms, thunders. I run past rows of empty pegs, infant toilets, unoccupied classrooms. There'll be cleaners round every corner.

A fire door: THIS DOOR MUST BE KEPT CLOSED.

I would close it if I could. This is an emergency. The caretaker's bound to see it later.

The playground has a gate on the far side. I make myself slow down and walk towards it. Holding my breath, tensed for the inevitable challenge. Nothing happens. I reach the gate and go through it.

Then I run again and I can't stop. I run and run, along

unknown streets. Pelican crossings without waiting for the green man. Groups of mothers with pushchairs. Clusters of small shops. I can't go on. I slump against a lamp post, gasping, a stitch in my side, until I can breathe more easily. There's a raw, scraped feeling in my chest. After a while, I set off again and walk, slowly and delicately, until I find a bus stop. I'll catch a bus into town and then another out in the opposite direction. Back to my anonymity.

As I step on the bus, I remember Hélène waiting outside the school. I wonder if she'll go in and look for me. Guilt bubbles up and fills my chest. She picked the wrong person.

So much for yellow.

I don't always go home. There are places in Birmingham where you don't have to speak to people. You can stay all day in Rackhams, using their loos, riding the escalators, eating a sandwich, drinking a cup of coffee in their rooftop restaurant. I try on clothes I couldn't possibly afford, and experiment with the perfume testers all down my arm until the smells run into each other. I've spent an entire day going up the escalators to the top floor and then down to the basement, turning in physical circles to try and calm the circular motion of my mind, where every revolution seems to overlap with the next.

The Central Library is open until eight o'clock in the evenings. I sit at a desk and put a book and paper and pencil in front of me. Then I pretend to work, turning a page occasionally, jotting down strange comments in case anyone is watching me: Chapter 3 – where is she? Character development weak. Does James know Henry?

I stay out all night after the yellow collapses. I go to Rackhams until six p.m., the library till eight and then I walk up and down Broad Street until the lights come on, as if I'm going to Symphony Hall. I wander amongst the groups of people going to a concert or the theatre. I stand in front of the three-headed fountain, watching my feet get wet from the spray. I check my watch frequently, as if I'm meeting someone, look past people, searching the distance. I join the crowds having coffee in the intervals, then pretend to be part of the groups going home after the performance. I get on buses and go to Bearwood, King's Norton, Hall Green. Halfway along the route, I get off and go back into the city centre.

I think only about me not thinking. There is a lightness inside me that makes me believe I could float if I tried hard enough. I like this non-thinking, this sensation of not being part of myself.

Music spills from the open doors of Brannigans and

Ronnie Scott's. Occasionally people speak to me, but I'm surrounded by a vast bubble of silence and they're so far away that they hardly exist. Figments of someone else's imagination.

Two boys who look about sixteen, who've been drinking too much: 'Hello, darling.'

'Want to come with us? We could show you a thing or two.'

They collapse against each other, hysterical with laughter. I walk on past as if they don't exist.

Then the cold, dark time when everyone goes home and the nightclubs shut up. Couples pile into taxis. I wait in a bus queue with a group of young people who shriek and laugh. I don't believe in their happiness; they are acting it out, trying to convince themselves. I get on the bus with them and watch them fall into an uneasy silence. I get off after a twenty-minute ride as we approach Weoley Castle Square, cross the road and wait for another bus to go back into town.

'You're out late tonight,' says the bus driver as I put my fare into the machine. He's the one with a jagged scar on his left cheek, who never smiles. It bothers me that we're losing our anonymity.

I keep moving now. Only the homeless are left in their doorways. I am not homeless; just hopeless. I walk and walk and walk.

When the sun rises, I'm still walking. There is a greyness just before dawn. A paleness without colour. This is the reality. The daytime colour is a façade, a coat of paint splashed on to fool us into thinking the world is genuine.

Then the sun rises amongst the fragmented clouds. The buildings around me grow pink and splendid – concrete suddenly glows and I'm surrounded by beautiful blocks of offices, flats, hotels, which shimmer in sympathy with each other. Then pink turns to yellow and I remember that I can't go and meet Henry any more, so I go to a bus stop and wait for a bus to take me home.

After climbing the three flights of stairs, I pause for a moment in front of James' door. But there's no sign of life, so I get out my key and go into my flat. He won't know that I've been out all night.

There is safety in my flat, where I am surrounded by colours and objects that mean something to me – my Cézanne poster collection, my GCSE artwork, my wall-hanging of multi-coloured scarves. There is also a small number of my father's unsuccessful paintings, which I especially like because they are rejects: a line is not straight, a blue is too vivid, or Dennis the agent just doesn't like them. It pleases me to see what my father doesn't wish to be seen, these poor abandoned creations, the part of him that isn't perfect. Like his days in the RAF. I can see through him because I know about his medals and his secret flawed world.

James and I are married, not divorced, or even separated. We live next door to each other.

My brother, Martin, who is a long-distance lorry driver, has put several shelves on the walls, between the pictures. When he's home, he does these things for me lovingly but imperfectly; the shelves slope slightly. Every three weeks, my china jugs edge their way down to the left and congregate in groups. Eventually I put them back in position, so they can start their journey all over again. I have collected jugs since I was eleven, brought from all over the world by Adrian, my oldest brother, who travels more stylishly than Martin when promoting his books. He never forgets me – he always finds something new, a vivid combination of colours, a satisfying curve. I like to take them down and hold them, smoothing my hands over their glaze, knowing each one through my fingers.

Underneath the china shelves are bookshelves, which are completely inadequate. My books fill every blank space, pouring out of the shelves, creeping along the narrow hall in piles, spilling into the bathroom, sitting on top of the television, tottering off the top of the fridge.

This is why I exist, to read books, children's books. Not picture books, but stories for children who can read. I review them (I have impressive credentials: Adrian Wellington, the novelist, is my brother) in various newspapers and I read them for agents and the children's library. I type out a two-page report or a one-page review, intended to be neat, but actually full of pencilled corrections and new, exciting thoughts which occur to me too late. I put it in an envelope, and then start on the next book.

So this is my life. I sit or lie and read and read and read. My head is full of bullies, wicked stepfathers, catastrophes on Betelgeuse, successful mothers who leave fathers in charge of the children. Children who run away from home, children who live at the top of a tower block, children with no friends.

But in the end – and I can't help seeing this as failure – I am only a consumer. I eat up other people's ideas and have no serious impact on anyone.

Perhaps my mother was a consumer. Perhaps I am like her.

My father bought 32 Tennyson Drive with money he had inherited after the war, when it was surrounded by similar houses. In the last thirty years, the others were first divided up into bedsits and then demolished. New houses have been built, neo-classical and detached, with double garages fronted by block-paving drives. Now number 32 doesn't fit. It looks tired and dishevelled, the window frames rotting, the gutters rusting. A delinquent child, it exaggerates its failings in a bid for attention.

My father sometimes talks about modernizing the house, but I don't want any changes. It's exactly right as it is – the place where my memories always end up. Every time I step through the front door, I am filled again with the experience of my brothers when they were big and I was small. Their willingness to play with me.

We often played sardines, a version of hide and seek, where one person hides and everyone who finds him joins him, until there is one person searching alone. I remember hiding first, alone in a tin trunk where we kept dressing-up clothes. I could hear approaching footsteps, see a crack of light as Paul looked in. I crept into myself, stopped breathing, willed myself invisible.

'No,' he called cheerfully to someone and I heard the footsteps move away.

Then suddenly he was back, silent in his slippers, leaping in beside me and pulling the lid down carefully.

But Jake returned, not fooled by Paul's trick.

We squeezed together in the darkness. I could hear Paul's watch ticking – was he calculating even then, his mathematical brain analysing the odds of remaining hidden against the ticking away of the seconds? Jake was breathing through his mouth, his blocked-up nose whistling gently in time with a tune in his head. The dressing-up clothes smelled old and musty. They were all men's clothes: velvet dinner jackets, tartan waistcoats, a spotty bow-tie. How did we all get into that tiny space? It doesn't seem possible now.

Then there was dodgems, another version of hide and seek, where the one hiding keeps on the move, doubling back to occupy spaces already searched.

Brushing through the cobwebs, we crawled under beds, inside wardrobes, crouched motionless on a high mantelpiece, hidden by the dingy gloom of forty-watt light bulbs.

There were so many hiding places, so many unused rooms. Furniture was piled redundantly into corners: wicker chairs, camp beds, chairs with holes instead of cushions to sit on. Cupboards were built into the walls, with crumbling plaster at the back, their doors hanging loose from broken hinges. There were huge cardboard boxes, trunks, piles of newspapers. We hid underneath tables, squeezed up against bare floorboards, mingled with the dust of generations.

We discussed tactics. Adrian, of course, giving instructions: 'Paul, start in the old bathroom. Kitty, go to the other end in the green toilet. Martin can try the bedrooms. If I stand here, I'll see him move. He'll have to come this way eventually.'

The green toilet: dark with bottle-green lino curled at the edges. The walls were hidden by my father's failed portraits. Eyes watched your every move, wherever you were in the room. Jake, small and slippery, moving rhythmically, sneaked out behind me. I heard the air move, the floorboards creak, and I missed him.

'Adrian!' I shrieked. 'He's out, he's coming your way.'

He had us turning in circles, falling over each other, catching us out each time.

But we cornered him, cut off his escape routes, and suddenly there he was, between us, trapped in the middle of an upstairs corridor. A last-minute leap to a landing halfway down a flight of stairs, but we jumped after him and caught him. We piled on top of each other, breathing heavily, the air full of sweat and dust, as we emerged from the half-lit secret places of the house.

Sardines again. I was the last one, unable to find them, stumbling through empty corridors, an edge of panic working its way up from my legs. I thought they had all gone, and started to whimper, believing I'd been left to wander for ever alone.

I tried to call them. 'Jake. Where are you? Paul, I give up.'

I stopped to listen. A creak, a moved foot, a stifled cough. The sounds came from nowhere and everywhere, memories of previous occupants, their silent traces drawn in the dust.

And then I found them, my four brothers cramped up in the linen cupboard, standing on each other's feet, cobwebs in their hair. I slid the door back and it jammed, but I had seen their shoes, the reflection of Martin's eyes in the dark, the paleness of Adrian's hand.

'Found you!' I yelled. They all came tumbling out, and everything was all right.

Do I remember this correctly? Did these brothers who were half men drag themselves away from their records and girlfriends and their cricket lists of England v. the Rest of the World to come and play with a little sister?

Have I embroidered my memories? Perhaps the experience of one occasion has multiplied into dozens of new memories, each developing a life of its own.

They live such respectable lives now. Adrian and Jake are both married, Adrian has children. Jake's wife, Suzy, is a bank manager. You can't get more respectable than that. It's difficult to believe that they were ever boys, stalking each other through the endless spaces of our home, playing children's games with such conviction.

My father's studio is on the second floor, built into the eaves, with a huge window that looks out over the rooftops and treetops of Edgbaston.

This is where I went to talk to him on the day, seven years ago, when I had committed myself to buying the flat. I was twenty-five; it was my first major decision. I should have told him earlier, but I knew he wouldn't want me to go, so I kept putting it off, waiting for the right moment. I crept in and found him standing, half-facing his easel, working on another picture of the sea – a red fishing boat rocking up and down in the blue-green swell, a seagull perched on its prow, the boat straining against its anchor. He spent much of the time looking out of the window, apparently gaining inspiration from the Birmingham landscape, where the leaves became the sea and the magpies became seagulls.

His paintings are full of colour. He can create Mediterranean light from memory – or possibly imagination, since he has not been there in my lifetime. With a sweep of the brush he produces palm trees, balconies, plants in terracotta pots, washing on a line, blue, waveless seas. Has he ever been there? I don't know. If I ask him, his answers are vague; I'm never sure what he's telling me. Perhaps he doesn't need to have seen it. Maybe his head is so full of vivid colours that they just spill out of him, splashing down on the paper, jumping around until they settle, forming their own images and patterns.

He started to teach me when I was three. He set up a small easel next to his, where I painfully tried to draw. I must have been a great disappointment to him.

'Never mind the shape, Kitty,' he said. 'Throw on the paint, the colours, mix them up. Bold and strong.'

I learned to love colour. Or maybe it was already programmed. A tiny genetic thread, a map guiding me down a certain road, the scenic route, handed down from him to me.

On the day I went to tell him about the flat, I stood for a while, watching him paint. He wore a grey overall that was streaked with decades of paint, predominantly red. As far as I knew it had never been washed and probably never would be. It was a work of art in its own right. He wore, as always, a crimson bow-tie underneath.

'Kitty!' he said.

He always did that. He knew I was there without looking.

'How did you know it was me?' I asked.

He turned around, peered at me over the top of his glasses and smiled. 'Work it out for yourself.'

I found this unsettling. He seemed to be suggesting that I knew the answer, but was too blind to see it. I hoped he meant that my silence wasn't as effective as I thought. I didn't like to think that he could just sense my presence, or hear my thoughts.

'I brought you a cup of coffee,' I said, placing it on the window sill. I ran my hand over the red and black throw that Adrian's wife, Lesley, had given him a few years ago to smarten up the sofa. He showed his contempt for this by using it as another convenient surface to wipe surplus paint off his brushes. There didn't seem to be any wet patches, so I sat down cautiously, nursing my mug of coffee. I slipped off my shoes and drew my legs up underneath me, wriggling a bit to avoid the broken spring.

He was muttering to himself all the time. 'If you have a red boat, the red must be reflected into the sea. Can't understand why people don't see this. Think Turner, I say to them, he knew how to put in every colour in the world . . .' He was attacking a section of his sea, slapping on reds and purples and blacks and stirring them together. 'No *Swallows and Amazons* today? Not flying off to Neverland?'

'Don't mock,' I said. 'I don't read them for pleasure.'

'Rubbish,' he said. 'You wouldn't do it if you didn't like it.'

I took a sip of my coffee, burning my tongue. 'When's Martin due back?' I asked.

He didn't seem to be listening, absorbed once again by the contours of the red boat.

'Tomorrow,' he said after a while. 'He was hoping to catch the six a.m. ferry from Boulogne.'

I was glad he would be back soon. I always missed him. Martin's a safe person, with a slow careful manner that manages to soften my father's edginess.

'Bother,' said my father, throwing his paintbrush down on the floor. He picked up another, bigger brush and painted a wide black cross over the entire picture. 'There,' he said and reached for his coffee.

This used to alarm me. Many times when I was younger, I felt that it was me who had driven him to these acts of destruction. Now I knew it was all for show. He would paint it out tomorrow and the picture would become stronger, with more depth.

Once a month, a man called Dennis comes and takes his pictures away. When I was little, I thought Dennis was stealing the pictures. I hated him coming, because I could feel the life draining away from my father, as if it was his blood going with Dennis. It always took several days for him to accept the loss. During that time, he would perform great feats of endurance – shopping, cooking in batches for the freezer, washing and ironing curtains. The house lost its neglected feel and started to shine with energy and polish. We all became sharper, funnier, more willing to help.

Then, gradually, he'd be drawn back to the studio, spending longer and longer hours there while the house drowned in dust, we ran out of underwear and baked beans on toast became our daily meal.

Now I know that Dennis is his agent. He sells my father's

paintings to restaurants, managers of large businesses, fast food outlets, libraries, schools. All over Britain, my father's pictures look down on people and bring unexpected relief to their cold, grey world. Curiously, he only ever puts his signature on the back – Guy Wellington, large and ornate – and remains anonymous to the general public.

He thinks he is a misunderstood genius, while Adrian thinks he has a mediocre talent, earning money but not acclaim. Paul, Martin and Jake refuse to comment, and I'm uncertain. My opinion seems to depend on my mood. There are flashes of brilliance, but at the same time, I can see evidence of his showmanship everywhere: flamboyance, exaggeration; ultimately a con trick.

I took a breath. There was no easy way to say this. 'I've found a flat,' I said.

He didn't react. But I watched his body tense and his breathing become even. His reaction was a carefully calculated non-reaction.

'I thought I'd get Martin to move my things in his lorry.'

'Bought or rented?' he said.

I hesitated. It had taken me a long time to reach this decision. 'Bought,' I said, and a wild exhilaration rushed through me. I'd done it, made an adult decision in an adult world. I'd filled out forms on my own, been to speak to my bank manager, to mortgage lenders, and made an informed decision, all without any help from my family.

My father put the coffee down and went back to his painting. 'Nice of you to let me know in advance,' he said quietly.

'I wanted to make the decision on my own,' I said, a little too loudly. 'I'm telling you now – you're the first to know now that it's definite. It's not far from here. I can come and see you all the time.'

'Oh no,' he said in a hard tight voice. 'There wouldn't be any point in moving if you did that.'

I'd known he would be hurt. I wanted to go up and put my arms around him, but that wasn't the way we behaved.

He was stabbing at the painting. 'Well,' he said, 'you seem to have got it sorted. Congratulations.'

I wanted to tell him that it was difficult for me too, that I knew he liked to have me around. 'You keep me young,' he often said. But he was seventy, and I couldn't keep him young for ever. I was unable to say any of this, because he wouldn't hear the words. So it hung unsaid in the air between us. I wanted to put my hand out to break through its barrier, but I didn't know how to. You can't just start to communicate if you've never managed it before. Neither of us had the language.

He was slapping huge wodges of red paint on to his picture – on the boat, in the sea, in the sky. I waited to see if he wanted to say anything else, but he didn't, so I stood up, my legs trembling with uncertainty.

'Yes, off you go,' he said viciously. 'You'd better start packing.'

'I won't be far away,' I said again. 'I'll be back all the time.'

'Don't bother,' he said, and jabbed his paintbrush so hard it went through the canvas. He looked at it in surprise. 'Now look what you've made me do,' he said and his face was genuinely puzzled.

I knew it was not a major disaster – he worked fast and could easily reproduce the same work tomorrow – but I felt bad anyway as I slipped out of the room. I didn't make him do that, I told myself firmly.

As I climbed down the stairs to my bedroom, an idea came to me. I would ask for the painting later, when he had reproduced it, and hang it in my new living room, where the hole in the canvas would greet me every morning.

In bed that night, I listened as my father clattered repeatedly up and down the stairs, watched the late-night film at full volume and threw books at the giant stuffed panda that stood in the corner of the living room. Paul had won the panda at the shooting gallery on the pier at Weston-Super-Mare three years ago, but his smart girlfriend of the time had not been interested in cuddly toys. The books were cookery books that my father kept buying and never consulted. I lay still in bed and pretended that I was asleep and didn't care.

Martin came home in time for breakfast, just as I was pouring the tea and my father was putting bread into the toaster. Our usual routine. Cornflakes on the table, fetch our own plates and cutlery, nothing to say to each other, because my father won't talk in the morning. I wondered if he would have breakfast at all after I left. Did he only do it for me?

A shadow cut out the early sunshine for a few seconds; Martin was parking the lorry on the drive under the mulberry trees. I happily took another mug out of the cupboard. It had a picture of Winnie the Pooh clutching a large blue balloon that was floating into the sky. I'd bought it for Martin a few years ago, because there was something about Pooh Bear's bewildered face – trying to remain unconcerned, but actually terrified – that reminded me of Martin. He was very fond of it. The handle had fallen off some time last year, and he was so upset that I stuck it back on again with Superglue.

The front door opened and Martin ambled in, stopping to hang his anorak on the pegs behind the door and remove his shoes, replacing them with the ancient pair of sheepskin slippers that he seems to have worn for the whole of my life.

'Morning,' he said with his usual amiable smile. 'What's for breakfast?'

Neither of us answered because breakfast was always exactly the same.

We sat down together, but didn't speak. I might have talked, but my father's early morning silence was too uncomfortable to break. Martin occasionally made a comment if there was a major disaster impending – 'Why is the toast burning?' or 'Why is there water dripping through the ceiling?' He was always ready to talk if anyone wanted him to, but no one ever responded.

We didn't leave breakfast things out for Paul. Nobody knew when he was going to get out of bed, or even if he was in. Sometimes he disappeared for weeks at a time, and then just turned up for lunch when we'd almost forgotten about him.

My father finished his toast, put his plate and knife in the dishwasher and went off with his cup of tea to start painting. He wasn't angry any more. This was quite normal. He never seems to hold to any important viewpoint for long. The heat of his fury grows stronger throughout the day – we've learned to keep out of his way, so he can direct it at inanimate objects: he likes to throw plates and hurl furniture around – then the fury goes out overnight.

'No,' he'll say, as if he's really perplexed. 'I wasn't angry. Not at all. I'm never angry.'

Sometimes I think that he hasn't grown up. He paints all his emotions on the surface, like a customized jacket, and when he gets bored with them he throws the jacket away and finds another. But are they real emotions, or just what he thinks we expect? How can you tell?

I sat watching Martin eat, spreading butter on his toast so that it was the same thickness all over, including the corners. Then he lifted it up and demolished half of the slice with one enormous bite. It hardly seemed worth all that trouble.

He saw me watching him and smiled slowly. 'Rough crossing this morning,' he said at last.

I leaned across the table. 'Martin, I've bought a flat.' I couldn't help it, the excitement was still with me. I had to tell him.

He chewed thoughtfully. 'So you're going to leave us?'

I loved his calm acceptance. 'Can you take my stuff to the flat – in your lorry?'

'Of course. When?'

'Saturday. I want to move on Saturday.' The excitement was spilling out of me. 'It's not far – only one bedroom – wonderful view. It's just right for me –'

'Fine,' he said and lifted his cup for a large gulp of tea. 'Good for you.'

Paul was home by Friday evening, looking tired and unshaven. Dad had phoned him – how did he know where he was? – and he wanted to help, he said. Things hadn't worked out with Jody. He needed an excuse to come home.

I couldn't remember which one Jody was.

'Was she the one who shaved her eyebrows?' said my father. 'Purple fingernails?'

Paul thought for a minute and seemed unsure. 'No,' he said eventually. 'That was Jenny. You've muddled Jenny and Jody.'

'Well, as long as you know which is which,' said Dad.

'Doesn't matter,' said Paul. 'I'm not likely to see either of them again.'

He's a researcher, working from home, spending hours at a desk, thinking, calculating, inventing. I've lost track of his girlfriends. Immaculately dressed women under thirty-five, in linen suits and straw hats, their bobbed hair ending in razor-sharp edges. They must be impressed by his brain. I can't see what else they see in him. I suppose he's exciting at the beginning, when he buys them flowers and meets them from work, openly adoring them. They end up feeling neglected when his latest project takes him over and his mind can only focus on numbers and equations. When each affair ends, he goes through a denial stage, then he falls desperately in love with the next woman and all his old girlfriends become intimate friends with each other. They are happy to talk to him for hours on the phone, letting him pour out his feelings about someone else. Perhaps they feel safe once they know his love has moved on, and his romantic demands are falling on someone else's shoulders.

There wasn't really much to take, I realized on Saturday morning. Paul and Martin carried my bed downstairs, my MFI wardrobes, my stereo, my boxes of books. I watched them load up all my possessions and they looked small and insignificant in the enormous darkness of the lorry. My father stood with me.

'You need more furniture, Kitty. Come with me. We can do better than this,' he said, leading me back to the house. We went into the kitchen and he emptied piles of cutlery out of the rickety drawers. 'We don't need all this. Take them, take them.'

He opened more drawers and cupboards, producing saucepans, frying pans, plates, dishes, bowls. There were so many they filled the table.

'Boxes,' he shouted out of the front door to Paul and Martin. 'Go down to Tesco's and fetch some boxes.'

He was enjoying himself, rooting through cupboards that hadn't been opened for years. 'Come on,' he said. 'Help yourself. You need chairs, a table, sofa, cushions, curtains.'

I picked up the knives he'd put out – old knives that had lived for many years, cooked in the dishwasher, old, warped, used. I loved them all.

He stopped suddenly. 'But you need a cooker, a fridge.' He ran his hand through his hair and looked appalled.

'What are we going to do? We should have thought of this ages ago.'

Did he really think I was so incapable? 'I'm going to buy them, Dad. I'm earning money.'

He looked amazed, then relieved. 'That's all right then. You can come and eat with us to start with – until you get your own cooker.'

'Yes,' I said. 'Of course.'

Paul and Martin came back with the boxes and we started piling in everything we had found. Paul picked up each item reluctantly and with distaste. 'You can't take these, Kitty,' he said. 'They're disgusting, a load of junk.'

'No,' I said with surprise. 'They're lovely. When you use them, you think of all the hands that have held them, all the mouths that have eaten off them. Years of memory, decades of history that most people have forgotten.'

Paul raised an eyebrow. 'You've been reading too many books.'

'You shouldn't criticize what you use,' I said and scowled at him. Yes, everything needed to be cleaned – I would do that when I was settled – but I thought he was being unkind. He'd lived with these things all his life. He could have moved into a home of his own somewhere, but he chose to stay here amongst our broken rubbish.

He looked back at me, cool and impersonal, unmoved by my irritation. I've never been able to penetrate his thoughts.

'Stop arguing and carry these out to the lorry,' said my father. 'Then get Martin and you can take out the sofa – the blue and yellow and red one.'

'Dad,' I said, 'you don't want to give me that. It's been there for years. It's part of the house.'

He laughed uproariously. I could see that he was beginning to get over-excited. 'So what? It was your mother's. Take it. She would want you to have it.'

'Oh, Dad,' I said and could feel tears forming. That was

the first time he had ever mentioned my mother in the context of our home. Never mind that the sofa was decades old, losing stuffing through a hole in the back, one corner resting on a *Chambers Concise Dictionary*.

So we left 32 Tennyson Drive in a convoy. Martin and I went in the lorry, Dad followed in the Volvo and Paul drove behind in his metallic-blue sports car. We were high up in the lorry, and when I looked back I could still see the house behind the wall. The mulberry trees looked wet and miserable in the autumn dampness and our house seemed to be sinking into the mud, settling into its history and our history, refusing to acknowledge the forward movement of time.

We unloaded the furniture into my new flat, carrying everything up three flights of stairs. No one came out of the other flats to greet us or welcome me. We arranged the rooms, hung the curtains and put the china into cupboards.

Then we all went back to 32 Tennyson Drive for lunch. Dad stirred the sweet and sour sauce into the frying pan and muttered lists to himself. He was going through all the things that were needed to set up a home, happy to keep talking even if no one was listening. The subject matter was unimportant.

'Potato peeler,' he said dramatically, turning round to face me. 'I bet you haven't got one.'

Now I have a potato peeler and a cooker and a fridge. Am I richer for the accumulation of objects? Have they changed me? I don't go home very often. I have James instead.

I don't feel grown-up any more. Somehow since my move, my marriage, my loss, I seem to have gone backwards. I feel as if I'm the pet again, little, without forward drive, dependent on others. I find myself wanting to ask permission before I do anything:

Can I go to bed now?

Am I allowed to use the cooker?

Is it all right if I finish the book tomorrow?

Shall I turn the light off?

I make myself some toast, look for orange juice in the fridge and find there isn't any. I fill a glass with water from the tap and gulp everything down, not because I am hungry or thirsty, but because I think I should.

The telephone rings and makes me jump, but I don't answer it. Perhaps the school has discovered who I am, perhaps it's Hélène.

When it stops ringing, I set the answer machine. Then I lie down on my sofa and go to sleep.

My dreams don't refresh me. I wake up exhausted. If I try to remember the dreams, it's like stepping into an alien existence, a world that is parallel to reality, but sinister and twisted, with shapes that expand and distort like a Salvador Dali painting.

I dream in colours, astonishing, shimmering, clashing colours. So many shades. Not just red, but crimson, vermilion, scarlet, rose. There are not enough names for the colours in my dreams. I wake up longing for visual silence, looking for a small dark place where there is no light.

*

'Kitty, it's James. Are you there?'

Why does he have to tell me who it is? I know his voice. I've been married to him for five years.

'I know you're there, because the answer machine wasn't on when I rang last night –'

Very clever. Why didn't I think of that? I stay on the sofa. I don't want to talk.

'Pick up the phone, Kitty.'

He sounds so sad, but I'm not sure if I believe him. He likes his space as much as I like mine. Perhaps he phones because he feels he ought to. Perhaps he secretly hopes I won't answer, but needs to convince himself that he doesn't.

I nearly leap up to answer the phone, to go next door, but I don't. I know he will be happy playing on the computer on his own.

I know he won't come round unless I ask him.

'I'll try later, Kitty. I'm at home if you want me.'

The phone rings every hour. He doesn't say anything. He just waits. I wish he would do something positive. I wish he would use his key, rush in and find me on the sofa, sweep me up in his arms.

But he won't, because if he did, he wouldn't be James.

James moved into the building six months after me. His presence announced itself with a great deal of banging that started at eight in the morning and ended at six o'clock. I thought he might be paying workmen, but there was never any evidence of this. No vans outside, no men in overalls on the stairs. At first I was irritated by the noise, and several times found myself on the landing, poised to knock on his door. But my anger always subsided as I raised my fist and I would shrink hurriedly back into my flat, hoping he wouldn't come out and catch me. And, gradually, the hammering became part of my background, so when he wasn't doing anything, the building felt empty, too silent.

We started with a smile on the stairs. He was very polite, and always waited at the top or bottom of a flight of steps when he saw me coming. If he got caught in the middle, he would flatten himself against the wall to let me past. I found his appearance unsettling. I seemed to tower above him. I thought that I should be standing aside as *he* limped up the stairs, a traditional dwarf in a modern setting.

James is five years older than me, and he is not handsome. He's not exactly ugly either, at least not in a traditional, Rumpelstiltskin sense, but his shape is out of proportion. He is not ergonomic. His body is a normal size, but he has unusually short legs and a large head, made even bigger by his bouncing, curly black hair. He walks with a limp, because one leg is slightly shorter than the other. His parents tried to do something about it when he was younger, but he refused to submit to painful operations, preferring to assert himself mentally if not physically. School was difficult, he says, where status depends on sporting ability. He describes it as a formative experience. Now he marches around lopsidedly and faces the world aggressively. Demanding, confronting, refusing to be treated as an outcast. He prefers to make himself an outcast voluntarily – not to be pushed into it by people who take exception to his appearance.

One day I came into the block just behind him. I followed him up the first flight and he was waiting for me at the top.

'Hello,' he said. 'I'm James. And you are?'

'Kitty,' I said nervously.

'Hello, Kitty,' he said. He looked less alarming once we were on the same level, and his face was more comfortable, more lived in than I expected.

We went up the next flight of stairs with me in front, trying to turn round occasionally and smile, in case he thought I was ignoring him. We went up the third flight side by side; it was a bit of a squash, but not impossible.

'I've just moved in opposite you,' he said.

'Yes,' I said. 'I know.'

'I haven't seen any other tenants,' he said. 'Do they exist?'

'They're all elderly. They hardly ever go out.'

'That explains it then. We're the only ones still in the living world.'

I thought he was being unfair. 'They're quite sweet,' I said. 'Miss Newman on the second floor invites me for morning coffee sometimes. It's very polite, with doilies and slices of fruit cake.' It sounded as if I was mocking. I didn't know how to explain to him that I liked old people. I like the wrinkles, the trembling hands, the unsequenced memories. I often take the conversations home with me and fit them with previous bits of information, linking them like a jigsaw.

'That's a good idea,' he said.

I seemed to have missed an essential part of the conversation. This happens sometimes, a loss of concentration, my mind wandering elsewhere. I blinked at him, and tried to work out how much taller I was than him. Maybe only two inches. I kept thinking of Snow White. But I don't have ruby lips, I thought, although my hair is almost black as ebony.

'Coffee,' he said.

'Oh.' I wasn't sure if he was inviting me to his flat, my flat, or a café somewhere. 'All right.' I followed nervously as he led the way to his front door.

James opened the door and we stepped on to a wooden floor in his narrow hall. The wood gave off a feeling of light and space which I liked then, when I first saw it.

'Did you do this yourself?' I asked, although I knew the answer already.

'Yes. You can buy it from Ikea. It's very easy to fit.'

But noisy, I thought as I tried to walk on the soles of my

feet. James just seemed to glide across it, lurching on his uneven legs, but somehow making no sound. He led the way into his lounge and I stood in the doorway, blinking with surprise.

'Is anything wrong?' he asked.

'No,' I said. 'It's just –' How could I explain my reaction? There was nothing to react to. More wooden floor, bare white walls with no pictures. Two white leather chairs with metal arms, and a hi-fi in one corner on a cupboard with pine louvred doors – presumably where he kept the CDs. Under the window was a computer desk; disks were stored neatly in a series of labelled boxes on two wooden shelves beside it. The ceiling lights had been changed to groups of spotlights and there were two angular lamps, one on the computer desk and one tall standard lamp between the chairs. That was all. Nothing else in the entire room. It was alarmingly colourless. I thought I would lose myself with all this space round me.

'Where are the books?' I said.

He looked confused and I liked the way his eyes creased uncertainly. 'I have some books in my bedroom,' he said eventually.

I didn't think I would ask to see the bedroom, books or no books. 'Is this room the same size as mine?' I said, and my voice seemed to get lost in the emptiness. I tried to compare the length of his walls with mine, the position of the window, but it was like comparing an elephant to a piece of rhubarb. Where do you start? How can you compare two things that have no point of contact, where their whole structure is different? His room didn't feel alive to me. My flat is small and cluttered, but living, throbbing with colour and evidence of me. His is huge and empty, like a barren plain, its boundaries far beyond my sight.

'Would you like to sit down while I make the coffee?' he said.

39

'No,' I said. 'I'll come into the kitchen with you.'

But his kitchen was no better. The cupboard doors were stainless steel mirrors and the tops gleaming white, so every surface shone. It gave me a slightly dizzy feeling. There was nothing out of place, not a crumb fallen carelessly to the floor, not a half-eaten apple left on the side, not a stray tea-leaf in the sink. This was not a kitchen where you would make scones, or sit and chatter with friends.

I sat on one of the tubular metal stools and watched his meticulous coffee-making. It was as if he counted every granule as he put it into the filter.

'You're very tidy,' I said.

He stopped measuring and looked up at me. A faint flush was creeping up his face. He smiled in a lopsided way. 'I'm sorry,' he said. 'I'm too tidy, aren't I?'

Something about that crooked smile and gentle flush caught me in my throat. 'Well,' I said, desperate to cancel my last comment, 'it's a good thing someone is. If the world was inhabited by people like me, everyone would be buried in mountains of their past. I lose my shoes, my door-key and my diary, which tells me where I have forgotten to go.'

He laughed. 'I was brought up in a tidy house,' he said, 'and taught to fold everything neatly and put it away. I think it's more genetic than anything.'

'A family obsession?'

He nodded. 'They're both doctors – surgeons. They can tie knots with one hand, sew things together meticulously. They've declared war on germs. I think they sometimes got muddled when I was a child and thought I was a germ too.'

I thought he might want me to laugh about this with him, but his eyes remained still. I could feel his sadness over his germ-free childhood.

'Are you a doctor too?'

'No. That was my act of rebellion. They wanted me to study medicine, but I chose computing instead – as far as possible in the other direction.' He hesitated. 'My programs are almost alive to me. I'm not sure you could say quite the same about their patients – they're very keen on research and figures. They don't say a lot about the people.'

I had a vision of him working on his computer, wearing a white coat like his parents.

'My job's easier,' he said. 'I can throw a computer away if it's not worth saving. They don't have that option.' He pulled out a tray and took two china mugs out from behind their stainless steel protection. 'What do you think of the flat? Do you like it?'

'Is it finished?' I said.

He nodded vigorously as he poured out the coffee without spilling a drop. 'Yes. Every room is exactly as I wanted it.'

So. No pictures waiting to be hung, no big colourful sofa waiting to be delivered. 'Are all the rooms the same?' I asked, knowing the answer already.

'More or less. I'm comfortable here.'

'Don't you think it's a bit – boring?' I found myself saying this before I could stop it. His crooked smile had affected me and I wanted to know if he was as honest as he seemed.

He looked genuinely surprised. 'No, I find it very calm.'

I looked around and from the safety of my stool I could see what he meant. There was nothing here that could crowd in on you, nothing to distract you. The reflecting surfaces of the kitchen only reflected each other. Somehow we made no impression on them.

'There is nothing here to give you nightmares,' he said surprisingly. 'Nothing threatening.'

I wasn't so sure about that. I have nightmares where I'm

wandering through an empty building, on and on, thinking I've found a way out, except that every room I go into is the same as the last, so I become afraid that I'll catch up with myself if I keep going any longer. I see the dust still flying from the person I'm following and the person I'm following is me. If I go fast enough I'll see the flash of my skirt as it disappears round a corner.

'What do your parents think of the flat?' I asked.

'Well, they quite like it – I think.'

I began to feel quite fond of his parents. Did they know he was blaming them for his hang-ups? They must be reasonable people, even if they did spend their days cutting and stitching up people's insides. 'What do they think about your job?'

He smiled again, and I suddenly realized that he was nervous. I'd never met anyone who was nervous of me. My throat was catching, my insides squeezing.

'They can't really say much. I'm quite good at it all, and I do earn a ridiculous amount of money.'

So the bare surroundings were a deception. He was trying to give the impression of coolness when really he was just the same as everyone else. Nervous, anxious to make a good impression, still insecure enough to blush. I decided that I liked him. Or I would like what was underneath the bare, ordered part of him, if I could find it.

We took our coffee into the lounge and sat on the two leather seats. I held my mug with both hands, but I could feel a trembling inside, working its way up to my arms, that would make me spill it, even when I was trying not to.

'Put it on the floor,' he said. He leaned over, took the coffee and placed it at the side of my chair.

'I always spill things,' I said. 'Another of my bad habits.'

'Do you think I need a coffee table?' he asked.

Yes! I wanted to shout. A coffee table, a red and blue Kashmir rug, curtains splashed with birds of paradise, a television, bookshelves cluttered with old copies of *Amateur Photography*, postcards from around the world, unpaid gas bills, posters of steam trains . . .

'Well,' I said slowly. 'What do you think?'

He relaxed in his chair and sipped the coffee. 'I didn't want one, because I thought it might feel too crowded. But I can see it might be useful. You're the first person to visit me.'

'Really?' I couldn't decide which bit to follow up. The need for a coffee table, or his absence of friends. 'But your parents have been here.'

'Well – no, not really. They came and looked around it when I was thinking about buying, but they haven't been here since. They'll know what it looks like. My last place was the same.'

'The same? Exactly the same?'

He moved his head uncomfortably, as if his neck was hurting. Was I pushing him too far? 'Not exactly. The furniture was the same, but the rooms are bigger here and the windows are better. There is far more light here. I like the light.'

I felt a rush of pleasure and understanding pass between us. 'Yes,' I said. 'I like the light too. As much as possible.' I looked around again and saw the space in a different way. The wooden floor reflected the light filtering through the white gauze curtains.

I felt exhilarated. 'Yes, of course,' I said. 'I didn't see the light before.'

He looked puzzled. 'But isn't that the first thing you see?'

'No. You see emptiness first and it takes time to recognize that the emptiness is full of light.'

I felt embarrassed about my own flat. I had wanted light in my home, but had cancelled it out with my clutter. Moving restlessly, I knocked over the coffee with my foot. I leapt to my feet in panic. 'I'm sorry. I'm sorry –'

He stood up. 'It's all right. Don't move. I'll go and fetch a cloth.'

He went out and came back again, calmly efficient with a bowl of water and a cloth.

'I'll do it,' I said. 'I'm really sorry.'

He flashed the lopsided smile that I was beginning to like. 'It's no problem.' He knelt down and wiped it up.

'I'm your first visitor and I mess it up.'

He wrung out the cloth and spoke with sincerity. 'I need someone like you to bring a bit of chaos into my life.' He stood up with the bowl. 'Can I make you some more coffee?'

'No,' I said. 'I have to go home. I have work to do.'

I thought he might protest, but he didn't. 'We both of us work at home, then?'

I nodded. 'I'm sorry. I'm a bit behind schedule.' I started edging towards the door.

'Thank you for coming,' he said. 'I was beginning to think we would never speak.'

Another gentle flush was creeping up his cheeks.

I felt guilty about spoiling everything. 'Next time, you'll have to come and have coffee with me.'

'I'd be delighted,' he said.

My insides squeezed again, a thrill of pleasure at his formality.

2

The Lost Boys

I'm dreaming that my father's house is on fire. He and I are trying to wake Martin, who is wrapped up in his duvet like a hibernating bear.

'Is Paul at home?' I shout.

'How would I know?' my father says. He starts rolling Martin from side to side in his bed. But he's too heavy and we can't rouse him. The approaching fire engine's siren wails in the distance.

I wake up sweating and realize the phone is ringing. The room is light with sun, but I can't remember if it's summer or winter, so I don't know how early it is. I lean over to look at the clock, but my eyes won't focus. As I try to work out where the fire is, the answer machine comes on.

'Kitty! It's Adrian.'

A panic seizes me. The fire's at Adrian's house. Emily and Rosie are trapped. I grab the phone. 'Adrian, what's happened?'

'Nothing. Aren't you up yet? It's nine fifteen.'

I have a theory that Adrian doesn't write his books at all. He keeps a wild genius locked up in his office, who throws out brilliant ideas and phrases that Adrian writes down and organizes. Adrian starts his day in the same way every morning. Up at 8.00, breakfast at 8.30, start work at 9.30. How can such a conventional man have an imagination and make up stories?

'Of course I'm up.'

'You don't sound it.'

'Don't I? Well, I haven't spoken to anyone this morning, that's all.'

'Could you babysit on Friday night? Lesley has a parents' night and I'm off to London. Not sure what time I'll be back.'

'OK,' I say.

'Will James mind? He can come with you if you want.'

'Can you afford to feed us both?' This is a joke.

'Yes,' he says. He doesn't like to discuss his income. 'I can't see a problem.'

Of course there's a problem. I'm not quite sure if James and I are friends. It's at least four days since we last spoke to each other. I've turned off the answer machine, so now he's stopped phoning. But Adrian doesn't know this.

'You could bring your work with you – the girls go to bed quite early.'

I know what time the girls go to bed. I've been baby-sitting since they were born. 'I said, OK.' I don't know why he goes through this guilt thing every time he asks. He knows I love Emily and Rosie.

'Right. Can you be here by five thirty? Lesley has to go out by five forty-five.'

'Fine,' I say.

The children are like butterflies. They're playing hopscotch up and down the front path, waiting for me to come. Emily is five and Rosie three, and they dance fluidly over the slabs, darting around each other while the afternoon sun catches their blond hair. Rosie has a red balloon she's brought home from a party and it floats lazily behind her as she jumps. They move so fast that the brightness of their hair whirls behind them, while their giggles echo through the warm air. Flashes of red and yellow from the balloon and their hair, blue and cerise from their dresses spin chaotically. They are only still for a second, giving a brief glimpse of their intricate patterns before they fly away again.

Lesley goes to considerable trouble to dress them in different clothes; she wants them to develop individual characters and not be identified as sisters. But they conspire behind her back. They like the same colours, the same styles. They're given chances to find their own paths, their own shapes, but they're not interested. They operate together and won't be separated. Two halves of a whole, two wings of the same butterfly.

Emily sees me first. 'Kitty!' she cries, and throws herself at me. Rosie looks up and echoes Emily. I wrap my arms around both of them.

'Have you brought the books?' asks Rosie.

Of course I have. My nieces love books, holding them, handling them, having them, and I'm here to supply them, even though they're outside my specialist age-group.

'Yes, I've brought the books,' I say, disentangling myself. I've brought the tickets as well, but they don't know about that yet.

Lesley is checking over lists of pupils when I enter the house. She looks up at me and smiles. 'Hello, Kitty. It's good of you to come at such short notice.'

'You know I'll always come.'

'I thought you might bring James.'

'He's busy,' I say, 'and he loves his computer too much. He takes it to bed with him – it gives him a feeling of safety.'

I can say these things to Lesley, because she doesn't listen properly. I like to say bizarre things to her every now and again as a test. She fails every time.

She stands up and pushes her piles of notes into a briefcase. She is taller than me and slimmer, more tanned, and her hair is blond. I think she puts a rinse in it. Nobody of her age has hair that yellow.

She looks at me closely. 'Is everything all right, Kitty?'

'Of course,' I say. But she can't have heard what I said. She would say something more specific.

Lesley makes me nervous. She's very capable and knows what she wants. She never shouts at the girls, but reasons with them. She's older than most of the parents of their friends. But she doesn't mind. She controls her own destiny. 'Follow me,' she says and marches off with her nose in the air. Everyone follows. It's expected, inconceivable that anyone should disobey. She was born to be a headmistress. She just needs to listen more and then she'll be ready for promotion.

'I've left the school phone number if there is an emergency.' She gives the girls a kiss and hug. 'Year 9,' she says to me and grimaces. 'Hard work.'

Then she's gone. The car door slams, the engine starts, the car pulls out of the drive.

'Right,' I say to the girls. 'Tonight we have a treat.'

They laugh because they don't know what I am talking about, but they can see it's going to be fun.

'Tea first,' I say, 'and then wait and see.'

Emily and Rosie live in a pink house. A house made for winter, with drawn curtains and chairs pulled up close to the gas log-fire. Everything in the house is pleasant and new. It smells new, as if Adrian wants to cancel out the years growing up in our old, second-hand home. There is a heather-pink carpet in the lounge, smooth and restful, and the curtains swirl with shades of pink. They have modern lighting, spotlights behind cheese plants, shaded lights in alcoves, uplights that cast pale ovals on the ceiling. I turn all the lights on when I am there in the evening, but it's not enough. There's a dinginess in this soft lighting that troubles me. As if they want to bury the colour and make believe it's not there. It makes me uncomfortable, gives me a queasiness inside. But I like the pink.

Emily dodges round me as I make tea. I nearly fall over her every time I turn round. 'Emily, why don't you sit down for a while?'

'All right,' she says, but she hovers on the corner of a chair, her plump legs restless, twitching, ready to leap off at any minute.

'What's Rosie doing?' I ask.

'She's upstairs playing with her Barbie dolls.' She sounds contemptuous.

'You don't like Barbie?'

'Mummy says it's impossible for someone with her statistics to exist.'

Emily knows everything. She recently lectured her teacher about the facts of life. I gather the teacher didn't mind too much, but would have preferred less detail. Lesley was dismissive. 'What's the point in making up stories? The earlier they know all about it, the less alarming it becomes.'

I prepare the meal that Lesley has left for us: tuna salad, baked potatoes, cold beans, french dressing with plenty of olive oil; nothing that could contaminate the children. But I have cheated and brought them some chocolate. I often do this, and I have to swear them to secrecy.

Emily is off her chair again. 'Mummy says I can help you make the tea,' she says.

'Right,' I say, putting her back on the chair. 'You sit down there and grate the cheese.'

She stays for a bit, singing to herself. 'Down it goes. Out come the wiggly worms. Hello, worms, what did you do today? I bet you didn't have to do spellings. Our spellings are easy-peasy. Everyone can do them – what, why, who and things like that.' She looks up. 'Is your treat chocolate, Kitty?'

'No,' I say as I get the baked potatoes out of the oven.

'Oh,' says Emily.

'Better than that.'

'What then?'

'I'm not going to tell you, otherwise it wouldn't be a surprise.'

'It would still be a surprise to Rosie even if I knew what it was.'

'No,' I say. 'Wait and see.'

I call Rosie, who comes obediently downstairs with a Barbie dressed in luminous pink. Every time I see Rosie, I curl up inside and have to fight the urge to pick her up and squeeze and squeeze. She was born three years ago. She could have been my baby.

We sit at the table and eat our tuna salad and baked potatoes. When we've finished I give them their chocolate. Emily eats it slowly and carefully. She sucks it for the long-term flavour. She still manages to talk as she sucks. 'Mummy would be really cross if she saw me eating this,' she says and giggles, her laugh escaping from her as if by mistake, rich, but casual, her little shoulders shaking with pleasure.

Rosie eats hers faster, stuffing it in until her mouth is bulging. Then she sits chewing, her eyes shining with anticipation.

I put the plates in the dishwasher. They're both watching me. 'Right,' I say. 'Coats on. Something exciting is going to happen now. We're going to go – Wait and see, wait and see –'

Dressing them for outdoors is time-consuming: coats, scarves, gloves, socks, shoes. Nothing goes on easily. They struggle to put the gloves on themselves, and put fingers in the thumb holes, two fingers into another hole, so their little fists stick out, clenched at the centre, with distorted fingers flailing. They have lovely hats which tie under the chin, with a bobble dangling down at the back, blue for

Rosie, pink for Emily, to match their coats, but they swap and change and make themselves a mixture of pinks and blues.

'Where are we going?' says Emily.

'Wait and see,' I say again.

Buses change their nature once it's dark outside – the warmth and light draw you in while the world outside is hostile and unknown. People sit silently side by side in their individual bubbles as always, but they no longer seem so unconnected.

When we stand to get off, the woman opposite smiles at me. 'What beautiful children,' she says.

'Thank you,' I say and glow inside.

We're going to the theatre to see *Peter Pan*. I've decided that Rosie is old enough to concentrate now. I haven't told Adrian or Lesley about this because I want the treat to be exclusively mine, so that whenever they think of *Peter Pan* later in life, they'll remember the mystery and excitement that led up to it. I want it to be a happy memory of a gift from me. Adrian is away for the night, Lesley will be late back from her parents' evening. This is my treat. I'll introduce the children to Tinker Bell, flying, the lost boys. When Lesley comes home I will tell her where we've been. She might complain, but I don't care. The time I spend with the girls is its own reward.

The Alexandra Theatre is swarming with parents and bright-eyed, excited children. I walk cautiously into the crowd, carrying Rosie in my arms and holding Emily's hand. Emily hangs back unwillingly.

'Come on, Emily,' I say cheerfully. 'You're going to love this.'

But she resists me, pulling on my hand. 'Did Mummy say it's all right?' she asks.

'Oh, yes,' I say, almost believing it myself. 'You don't

think I'd make you do something without telling Mummy, do you?'

'Why didn't she tell us then?'

'It was a surprise. I told you that, didn't I?'

Emily frowns, but comes with me. I want to buy a programme, but there are so many people round the counter that I'm nervous about holding on to both girls. I look around for somewhere safe to leave them and decide they can stand by one of the pillars. I put Rosie down. 'Now just hold hands and stay together there. I won't be long.'

I fight my way through the crush and buy two programmes, but when I return to where I think I left the girls, I can't see them. My stomach lurches painfully and I look around in panic. I approach a couple standing by a pillar. 'Have you seen my girls, my two girls?' I'm talking too fast. I try to slow down. 'I left them here, two blonde girls, very pretty –'

The couple look concerned. 'Where did you leave them?'

'Here, they were just here and I told them not to move –' I am going to cry. I can feel it all rising inside me. The woman puts a hand on my arm. 'I'm sure they can't be far away. Just stand here for a few seconds and look round slowly.'

The man turns to me. He's elderly, with a neat beard. 'Would that be them there? Two pretty blonde girls?' He has a kind voice. I turn to look and there they are, holding hands, still with their gloves and hats on, looking over at me.

I dash over to them. 'Where have you been? I told you not to move.'

'We didn't,' says Emily indignantly. 'We stayed here all the time.'

I count the pillars from the entrance. They are by the sixth pillar and I was sure they had been by the seventh.

52

I have a sudden vision of myself when I was very young. I'd been told to hold my mother's skirt so that she could have her arms free for the shopping. I remember the skirt – purple, crinkly material, with broderie anglaise along the hem and bell-like tassels hanging down from the waist. I know I didn't let go of the skirt, but I looked up suddenly and there was a complete stranger above me. I don't know how I reacted. I suppose I screamed. This is one of my very few memories of my mother.

I turn to thank the couple, but they've gone. I bend down to Emily, who looks frightened. 'I'm sorry,' I say as gently as I can. 'I must have made a mistake. Let's go and find our seats.'

Our seats are right at the top of the theatre on the third level. I hold on to Rosie and Emily very tightly as we edge our way along the row, trying not to look down.

'What are these?' says Rosie when we've sat down.

'Opera glasses. Look at the programme.'

'What are they for?'

'They're binoculars so you can see the people on the stage more easily.'

I hope there won't be too much high flying, because we're sitting so far up that we won't see it. The top half of the stage is completely out of sight.

Emily is struggling with the opera glasses. 'I can't get them out.'

'You need 20p.'

'Have you got 20p, Kitty?'

'And me,' says Rosie.

I open my purse and find that I only have one 20p piece. I give it to Emily and Rosie's face crumples, ready to burst out in jealousy.

'Excuse me,' I say to the man sitting next to Rosie. 'I don't suppose you have a 20p piece for my change?'

He obligingly finds one and hands it over amiably.

They settle down with their opera glasses, standing up and leaning over to see the audience sitting below us.

'Sit down,' I say, 'otherwise the people behind us won't be able to see.'

They sit back for two seconds and then jump up again. I sigh, but know they will sit still when it starts.

The lights dim.

'Sit down,' I say. 'It's going to start now.'

'Kitty,' says Rosie urgently. 'I want to go to the toilet.'

Our trip to the toilets has not made us popular. Everyone has to stand to let us through, so the people behind can't see either. Nobody says anything, but I can feel their hostility. I can't see their irritation, because I'm too embarrassed to look at their faces, but I know it's there. I whisper 'sorry' as I stumble over their shoes, guiding the children in front of me, trying to persuade Rosie to move faster. We finally settle back in our seats and I breathe slowly and deeply, forcing myself to sit very still. I wait for the sweat of embarrassment to cool and dry.

'Is that a real dog?' whispers Emily almost immediately after we get back.

I nod.

'How do they get the dog to do what they want?'

I try to ignore her.

'Kitty!' she whispers more loudly.

'Shh.' I put a finger to my lips and shake my head.

'How?'

'I'll tell you later,' I whisper into her ear.

She nods and sits back, and for a while we have some peace.

'They're flying!' Rosie announces with delight.

'Shh.'

'How do they do that?' asks Emily.

'Shh,' I say.

'Kitty! How do they do that?'

'Magic,' I whisper.

'There's no such thing as magic.' Her whisper is gradually turning into a normal speaking voice.

'Shh.'

People are shushing all around us. I close my eyes and try to work out which people we are irritating most. But the shh is a whisper without a mouth, a manifestation of annoyance without a source. It comes from nowhere and everywhere and circles us, and there's no doubt about where it's aimed.

For a time, everyone quietens down. Then Emily starts to use the opera glasses. Rosie sees her and tries to do the same. She slips off her seat, which tilts backwards with a thump, and stands looking at the stage. Neither girl is talking – they are becoming interested in the play – and I allow myself to relax very carefully.

I feel a nudge from behind. I assume someone has moved a foot, so I ignore it.

'Excuse me.'

I turn round and a man is bending towards me. 'Do you think your daughter could sit back? My wife can't see.'

'Rosie,' I whisper. 'Sit down. They can't see from behind.'

'Shh.'

The first act continues and the girls start to concentrate better. I knew they were old enough to enjoy it. Why shouldn't they whisper a bit? Everyone knows that children never sit still. Surely it's the people round us who are at fault. Why have they come without children to watch a children's play? Perhaps they're lost boys themselves who have never grown up and need to keep reliving their childhood, thinking they'll discover what's missing from their lives. They could try to be more tolerant and find pleasure in watching children enjoy themselves. I'd like to suggest this to them in the interval, but I know I won't, because I can understand the reasons they'll give for being here and wanting to listen in peace. We're grown-ups. We come here to remind ourselves of this and remember our lost youth. We've paid good money for these seats and we'd like to enjoy the play. There are matinées for young children. The other children who come to this performance are older and well behaved, used to coming to the theatre.

They're right, I think sadly. I shouldn't have brought them. I only see Emily and Rosie once or twice a week and it's not enough. How do I know when they're old enough? How can you tell?

A heavy weight settles on me as I see the future stretching ahead of me, with no clear way of finding out how children develop and change. I've lost it all. There's nowhere for me to go.

'Kitty!' Rosie is at my ear. 'What's the fairy called?'

'Tinker Bell.'

'Shh.'

As the lights come on in the interval, I turn round and apologize to everyone in earshot. They nod and smile politely and say they don't mind at all, but someone must be lying. Shushing doesn't create itself. There are no invisible machines under the seats, producing the first furious shh that then feeds off itself and multiplies. There has to be a human source. I can't guess from their faces or their manner who was most annoyed. They all seem pleasant.

We go down to the entrance and wait in a long queue for ice-creams. Emily is very excited about Peter Pan, and Rosie is excited about the ice-creams.

'What can we have, Kitty?'

'Whatever you want.'

'But what is there?'

I show them the pictures of what is available. Emily wants a Cornetto and Rosie wants an orange ice-lolly. When we reach the counter, they only have tubs.

'Strawberry, chocolate or plain?' says the woman.

'What flavour do you want?' I ask the girls.

'Orange,' says Rosie.

'I want a Cornetto,' says Emily.

'Two chocolate, please,' I say.

I can't believe how expensive they are.

'I want an ice-lolly,' says Rosie, starting to cry. She is looking flushed and tired, and for a moment I wonder if I should give up and take them home. But then I remember that they'd enjoyed the first act once they'd quietened down. I was right to bring them. I open the tub and scoop out some chocolate ice-cream.

'Open wide,' I say and pop it into Rosie's mouth quickly, before she has time to change her mind. The bell rings for the end of the interval.

'Quick,' I say. 'Does anyone want to go to the toilet?'

'No,' says Rosie and swallows her mouthful.

'Yes, please,' says Emily. 'What shall I do with my tub?'

'I'll hold it while you go.'

Emily is much easier than Rosie. She can go in the toilet on her own and flush it afterwards. She comes out and washes her hands slowly in the pink washbasins. 'Nice toilets,' she says to me as we go back.

We reach our seats just in time and I can almost hear everybody sigh in disappointment when they see us returning. I settle the girls down, one on each side, eating their ice-cream. They are silent for some time and I begin to relax.

'Kitty! I've spilt my ice-cream.'

I rummage in my bag for a tissue. Somebody pokes me in the shoulder. I turn round and the woman from behind hands me a wodge of tissues. 'Thank you,' I whisper, and manage to wipe most of the ice-cream from Rosie's front.

We relax into our seats and I think of the people sitting around us. They probably have their own children, much older than Emily and Rosie, and know what to expect of them. I'll never know what they know, even with Emily and Rosie. I'll always over-estimate or under-estimate their development, because I'm not there every day, giving them breakfast, talking to them, listening to them, reading to them every night. I only know children in books, having adventures, discovering things, thinking things, but because they don't breathe or talk they can never be real. It's not the same as living with the same children and watching them grow.

I think about the lost boys and realize that I'm one of them, not the people round me. I grew up without a mother. I'm lost and nobody can guide me back to the right place, because there's nobody who can give me what I most want.

'Kitty,' hisses Emily. 'Rosie's gone to sleep.'

I take the ice-cream out of Rosie's relaxed hands, wipe her face gently and lower her head on to my lap. I eat her ice-cream slowly and resist the urge to cover her with kisses.

We don't realize that we haven't got Rosie's coat until we're at the bus stop, the bus already approaching.

'Kitty!' Emily tugs at my sleeve. Rosie is lying on my shoulder, still half-asleep, and my arms are aching with her weight.

'Wait till we get on the bus.'

'Rosie's coat!'

'Can you hold it until we're on the bus?' The change is ready in my hand.

'We haven't got Rosie's coat. It's in the theatre.'

My right foot is on the step and I look at Emily irritably. 'Of course we've got it – it's under my arm.'

'No it isn't.'

She's right. We haven't got it. I pause in the middle of the step and try to think.

'What's it going to be?' says the driver. 'On or off?'

I look at him. I am strongly tempted to get on anyway. 'Sorry,' I say. 'We've lost a coat.'

He smiles, quite friendly. 'The next bus is in thirty minutes.'

'Thanks,' I say.

We trudge back. It's ten o'clock and the theatre might be locked. I can't think about Lesley getting home before us. Ten o'clock isn't late. We can be home by eleven o'clock. I've known Lesley be later than that.

The doors to the theatre are still open, so I tell Emily and Rosie to stand by the door, while I go up to where we were sitting. I look back at them. Rosie is still half-asleep and Emily is trying to hold her hand. They have trouble fitting their hands together.

I run up the steps to the upper circle. Cleaners are moving between the rows, vacuuming, picking up rubbish. They haven't reached our row yet. I race to the top. Two steps at a time. A pink sleeve dangles over the seat in front. Rosie's coat, ice-cream stains down one side. I grab it. I don't look at the cleaners.

When I come back downstairs, there's a man talking to Rosie and Emily, crouching down so that his face is on their level. He is a young man in jeans and a red check shirt and there is something vaguely familiar about him.

'. . . put a glove over my hand, like this . . .'

Children talking to strangers. Children disappearing mysteriously. I rush forward.

'Kitty,' says Rosie as she sees me. 'There's my coat.' I grab her hand firmly, and take Emily's in the other.

'Hi,' says the man, straightening up. He has curly hair and open, easy eyes.

'Girls, you shouldn't be talking to a stranger,' I say. This is one thing I do know about children.

'He isn't a stranger,' says Emily indignantly. 'He's Captain Hook.'

That must be why he looked familiar, but I can't see it when I study him more closely.

'I thought they looked lost,' he says.

'Well, they're not,' I say.

'It's Captain Hook,' says Emily again. 'He's all right.'

'That's not the point,' I say. 'You don't know him. You mustn't talk to someone you don't know.'

The man spreads his arms defencelessly. 'Sorry. You're quite right.'

'I know,' I say. I take the girls by the hand, tuck Rosie's coat under my elbow and march them to the door.

'Kitty,' wails Emily. 'He was nice.'

'You don't know that,' I say. Just before going through the door, I look back and he is standing watching us, not annoyed, a pleasant smile on his face. It's true, he does look nice. But you can't take chances on people. It's safer to assume they're hostile.

The bus is late, more than thirty minutes after the previous one. We stand at the stop in silence. I keep looking at my watch and calculating what time we will get home. How long will it take to put them to bed? A cold solid lump is slowly gathering inside me. I'm just beginning to tell myself not to look at my watch again when the bus turns a corner and rolls slowly towards us, reassuring and familiar.

'Here it is,' says Emily. 'Buses are good, aren't they? When you miss one, another one comes instead.' They're not used to buses.

We climb on, pay and sit near the front. I am trying not to worry about time, but I can't think of anything else. What time will Lesley's parents' evening finish? She might stay talking until they lock up, but I don't know what time that would be. How long does it take to drive home?

The girls sit hunched next to me, silent and miserable, knowing they can't talk to me, feeling my worry, afraid to break into it.

Emily tries once. 'Kitty –'

'What?' My voice is flat and unfriendly.

'Nothing.'

I feel guilty. 'Nearly there,' I say in a semi-cheerful voice, which sounds unreal, even to me.

They don't reply.

The bus stops a few hundred yards from their house. We climb down. I suddenly feel extremely tired and forget what I was worrying about. The girls hold hands with each other and I walk behind.

A police car passes us and stops. I immediately feel as if I've committed a crime, but surely there's nothing illegal about going to *Peter Pan*. We are allowed to be out after ten p.m. with children, aren't we?

A policeman gets out and approaches us. He's enormous, towering above us as he puts his cap on. We stop walking and look at him.

'What does he want, Kitty?' says Emily. She pushes backwards into me for safety. Rosie starts to cry.

'Would you be Katherine Maitland?' he says in a deep, serious voice.

I nod. My mind starts racing. How does he know? Has someone told him about the girls being too young for the theatre, or about leaving Rosie's coat behind? Is it something else? I can't remember, but I feel as if there's something I've forgotten.

'And these are your nieces, Emily and Rose?'

I nod. There doesn't seem to be anything to say. Emily and Rosie huddle close to me.

'We've been looking for you,' he says. He goes back to

the car and speaks to his colleague. Then he beckons us over. 'We've just radioed through to let them know that we've found you. Jump in. We'll run you home.'

Obediently, we climb in the back of the car and drive to Adrian's house. Lesley is waiting for us on the pavement. She pulls the girls out, hugging them. I climb out awkwardly and make my mouth smile at her. The light spills from her open front door on to the pavement.

'We've been to the theatre,' cries Emily. 'We've seen *Peter Pan*.'

'Flying,' mutters Rosie in a very tired voice.

Lesley tries to pick them both up at once and kisses them repeatedly. I have never seen her so demonstrative before. She looks oddly unwell.

'Did your parents' night finish early?' I ask, not at all sure of the time.

She looks at me and her face seems to close up. 'I came home early. I had a headache,' she says in a curiously cold voice.

'Oh,' I say.

We stand looking at each other and I know I'm in trouble. In the half-light she apparently sees me better than I can see her. I'm frozen in the glaring spotlight of her disapproval.

'Why don't we run you home?' says the policeman. 'Then you can sort it out tomorrow.'

'Thank you,' I say and climb into the car. I can see Lesley taking the girls into their pink house. A neat little house with a place for everyone, where they live and grow together, where they know they belong. The front door closes. I sit in the back on my own, feeling as if I'm about to cry, and look for a tissue in my bag. There are three tickets next to the tissues. Train tickets to Edinburgh – one adult and two children. I don't really know why they're there.

Jake's porch is big. Indoor plants grow dark-green and rich in the heat of the sun through the windows and with water from Suzy's loving hand, but they never look hysterical or out of control. Suzy has style. The plants know exactly how big they're allowed to grow, how wide their glossy leaves can become. There is room for two white wicker chairs with bright, tapestry cushions. It is more a conservatory than a porch, where Suzy and Jake could sit and watch the passing traffic. But I'm sure they don't. The chairs are like the plants, part of a design, a testimony to Suzy's good taste.

I'm surprised to find that the outside door is open. I step in. I'm tempted to move the chairs together to make a bed, and my whole body aches at the thought of lying down. But I'd prefer not to meet the postman or the milkman at six o'clock in the morning. I couldn't bear the thought of being watched while I'm asleep.

I knock gently and step back from the door to see if there are any lights on inside. It's not easy to tell because the windows have heavy metal shutters. Suzy, the bank manager, knows about security.

There's a light on inside, but I suspect it's a night-light, intended as a deterrent to burglars, not a welcome for me.

It's after midnight, but you can't tell with Jake. He could be fast asleep – tucked up by a mothering Suzy – or he could be sitting up all night with the television, nursing his insomnia. Paul reckons that this is the result of a guilty conscience, but he hasn't yet produced a good reason for the guilt.

I step to the side of the porch, out of reach of their security light. The night is never black in Birmingham, so just beyond light is the darkest place to be and the most comforting.

I am cold, chilled from inside. I go back, lift the knocker

and tap very gently. He won't hear it if he's asleep, but he might if he is lying awake – unless he's watching a horror film. Panic bubbles up inside me and I struggle to stop myself crying. I'm afraid. I don't know what to do. I need sanctuary. I wish Jake would just appear.

I listen intently to the silence that is not really silent at all. I can hear my heart beating, a rustle in the hedge, a car in the distance – and another noise, a shuffle from inside the house. I hold my breath and hope it isn't Suzy.

Someone is on the other side of the door. I hear a light switch, a footstep and then nothing.

'Who is it?'

I start to shake with relief. 'Jake? It's me – Kitty.' My teeth are chattering. I don't know if he can hear me. I can hardly hear myself.

He pulls back the bolts, the mortise lock and finally the Yale lock. The door eases open and I see Jake's tangled hair, his waxy face, his eyes dark and not well.

'Can I come in? I won't make any noise.' Please, Jake, let me in.

The door opens wider and I step through. Jake shuts it behind me and rolls the locks back. Then he turns. I can only see the paleness of his face in the dark.

'Go in the living room,' he whispers. I tiptoe in, wondering if he will follow me, or just go back to bed.

The door closes, then there is a click and the light comes on. I stand blinking, unable to see anything in the sudden brightness.

'What are you doing here, Kitty?'

I try to focus my eyes. Jake is wearing a pale pink chenille dressing gown. 'Why are you wearing Suzy's dressing gown?'

He doesn't bother to look. I worry about how silly he will feel when he realizes he is decorated with pink roses. First floor, Ladies' Separates and Lingerie at Marks & Spencer.

He sighs and bends to light the gas fire. 'They're after you,' he says. 'Adrian phoned earlier to see if you were here.' He sits heavily on the sofa by the fire, looking cold.

I move a chair closer to the fire and curl myself up on it. I can't stop my teeth chattering.

'I know,' I say, feeling more miserable than I did before. 'Why do you think I came here?'

He smiles at me, and I feel easier. Jake's great strength is that he's good in a crisis. He can rise above the temperatures and tonsillitis and infected in-growing toenails and become wise and serious and supportive.

'Did I wake you?'

'No, I wasn't asleep.'

I silently bless his insomnia. 'I didn't know where to go.'

'Home to face the music, I should think.'

I smile feebly and watch the flames of the fire. They are a clever invention, these pretend-coal fires. You have to study them for a long time before you realize that the flames are not random, but follow a meticulously organized pattern. And even then, you can't be absolutely sure.

I haven't talked to James for several days.

Jake stops smiling. 'Kitty, what were you thinking of, taking the girls out without telling anyone? I assume they're at home now?'

I can't look him in the eye. I study the carpet instead. It's a neutral beige, calm and spotless, made from natural fibres so that it won't aggravate Jake's allergies. Much too hard-wearing for Jake and Suzy who live in a bubble of cleanness and never spill anything. 'We forgot Rosie's coat. It would have been all right if we hadn't had to go back.'

'You can't just go off with children like that. They're too young.'

What does he know about children and the age they do things?

'Where did you take them?' The tone of his voice is casual, but the loudness gives away his eagerness to know.

'*Peter Pan.*'

He nods knowledgeably, either trying to tell me that he knows *Peter Pan*, or that he considers it to be a wise choice.

There is a plate of Quality Street on the coffee table. Suzy always leaves eatable temptations around. I think she likes to show everyone that she can exercise restraint, that she doesn't eat nice things whenever she sees them. I take a toffee and unwrap it. As I chew, I want to throw the paper into the fire, but remember at the last minute that it isn't a real fire. I screw it up in my hand, then open it out carefully on my knees, smoothing out the creases, folding it perfectly and folding it again.

'Did I wake Suzy?' I ask eventually.

Jake sighs. 'No, I don't think so. She's had a tummy upset during the day, but she's a lot better now, thank goodness.'

'Was she sick?'

'Yes, very.'

We sit in silence. I don't really want to talk to Jake. I came here because I needed somewhere to go, and I didn't want to stay out all night again. There's a deep coldness inside my stomach which is spreading upwards and outwards. The heat of the fire can't reach me.

The train tickets flash into my mind: little white cards, neatly printed, sitting in my bag next to the purse.

Where did they come from?

Did I put them there?

Why?

'Is there anything on the telly?'

'Does James know what's going on?'

I shake my head. 'Well, I suppose he does now. No doubt Adrian will have phoned.'

He nods and takes a coffee cream.

'It's a good thing somebody likes coffee creams,' I say.

'I don't like them. I just eat them because nobody else wants them.'

We munch together and the pile of Quality Street diminishes. Suzy will know I've been when she gets up tomorrow because I always sit down and eat the lot. I hope she feels too ill to notice.

'Anyway,' I say, 'Adrian isn't even in Birmingham. He went to London.'

Jake coughs. I can hear the phlegm in his chest. 'No. He came home – he had to walk out of a major awards ceremony.'

'Whatever for?'

'Lesley phoned him on his mobile. She thought the children had been abducted. People think like that, you know, if their children aren't where they should be.'

'They weren't in any danger,' I say.

'But how would Adrian know? The three of you could have been murdered.'

'I wrote a note,' I say and stop. 'Actually, I think I might have forgotten.' My eyes shift away from his gaze. I'm not very good at lying.

'Quite.'

'Lesley wasn't supposed to come home so early. I was going to tell her all about it once the children were safely in bed.'

He picks out all the coffee creams and lines them up on the arm of the sofa. He starts eating them one by one, folding the papers neatly and throwing them into the wastepaper bin. Not one of them misses.

I snatch a handful of sweets irritably. I can't bear to watch his neatness, his precision. I start to stuff the sweets in my mouth, not waiting to finish one before starting the next.

'You'll have to face them tomorrow,' he says mildly. 'You can't hide for ever.'

I shrug. 'Don't worry. I'll be gone before you get up.'

We have nothing to say to each other. I know he won't push me too far. Like, 'Is it to do with the baby?' He won't be able to ask me that, because he knows I can't answer.

'I'll get to bed, then,' he says. He stands up in his pink dressing gown and coughs again. It doesn't sound good. 'Help yourself if you want to make a drink. Only –'

'Yes?'

'Try to be quiet. Suzy needs a good sleep.'

'By the way,' I say, 'the porch door is unlocked.'

He stops at the door, about to say something, but changes his mind. I pick up the remote control and put on BBC2. It's the Open University. They're having a discussion on cloning.

'Sleep well,' I say. 'You can count babies to help you nod off.'

He's gone. I only said that because I knew he wouldn't hear it.

I listen to an earnest woman with glasses on a chain round her neck, and a younger man wearing a white coat with a pager in the pocket. Scientist or doctor? I wonder. They talk with great conviction, but they don't agree. I'm beginning to warm up. My eyes are suddenly heavy and aching. I huddle down into the chair, lean my head on the cushion and try to concentrate on cloning.

I wake with a jerk, and my neck cracks with the movement. The telly is still on, but I can't work out what they're talking about. The faces are blurred, the words incomprehensible.

I was dreaming about babies all over the place – in beds, on chairs, in prams. There is nowhere to sit because everywhere is full of babies. They are gurgling, sleeping, screaming. In the second before I wake, I realize that I am one of them, and open my mouth to scream, to prove it. I wake up at that precise moment, feeling stiff and ill.

I look at my watch. It's 5.30. Time to go home, before anyone guesses where I am.

A group of suited men on the television are talking in a foreign language. I leaf rapidly through the *Radio Times*, wanting to know what it is. Russian. No wonder I can't understand them.

I turn off the television and get up. My legs are very stiff and I nearly fall over, my right foot tingling with pins and needles. I jump up and down on it until it starts to work again.

When I turn the light off, I can still see – it's no longer dark outside. Going into the hall, I move very carefully so that I don't wake anyone, but just before I open the front door I hear a movement behind me. I turn round, expecting Jake, and find myself confronting Suzy.

'Oh,' I say in alarm and put my hand over my mouth.

She looks strangely unfocused. 'Kitty,' she says. 'What are you doing here?'

'Well,' I say, and I haven't a thought in my head. 'I was just passing . . .'

She stares, but her intense concentration is not directed at me, but on some internal dilemma. I've never seen her before in nightclothes, her face pale without make-up, her hair greasy and ragged.

'Oh –' she groans suddenly and races away into the kitchen.

As I unlock the front door, I can hear her retching into the sink. I shut the door behind me, trying not to hear her being sick. I know about this – being sick all day. She doesn't have a tummy upset, she's pregnant. I recognize the look.

My legs are heavy, as if I'm trying to run in water, and it feels as if they're not moving at all. I'm not sure I can manage to get home.

*

I hesitate outside my flat door, uncertain where to go. Home or to James? Where would Adrian expect to find me? My flat? I wouldn't let him in and he wouldn't have a key. He might go to James and ask him to let him in. Would James do it? I'm not sure. Hovering agonizingly, I consider going to visit Miss Newman on the floor below. She'll invite me in for cake and tea. This is unrealistic. It's too early for cake.

I move from one door to the other, incapable of making a decision.

The decision is made for me as James' door opens and Adrian comes out.

'Ah, there you are, Kitty,' he says, as if it is normal for him to be coming out of James' flat at 6.30 in the morning.

'Yes,' I say and look at my feet. My shoes are covered in mud.

'We need a talk,' he says, and he sounds like an all-knowing headmaster, a benevolent father, a big brother.

James comes out behind him. They're both fully dressed, but crumpled.

'Kitty!' he says, coming towards me. He sounds pleased to see me, but I'm probably misreading him. He comes over and puts an arm round me. 'Kitty,' he says again, and I lean against him. He is pleasingly warm and soft. 'Thank goodness you're all right.'

I feel not very all right at all. My legs are stiff, my neck hurts, I have a tummy ache and I can't remember where I left my bag with my purse and key in it. This strikes me as hilarious, because I wouldn't have been able to get into my house anyway. I fight back a wave of giggles that threatens to ripple through me. I can imagine Adrian's response to that. 'Laughter is not appropriate.'

Adrian leads the way and they guide me into James' flat. I want to say, 'I can walk, you know,' but what I actually say is, 'Suzy's pregnant.'

*

There's a smell of burning toast, and James dashes out, leaving me alone with Adrian. This is unfair. James is married to me and I'm partly his responsibility – even if he'd prefer not to be involved. I'm more important than toast.

Adrian paces up and down, putting his hands in his pockets and taking them out again. There's a dark stubble on his face and his brown eyes seem more hollow than usual. I have never seen him genuinely agitated before, and watching him makes me breathe too fast. My head starts to swim and I wish he would stop.

'I really think, Kitty . . .' he says and slows down.

His shoes are hard and noisy on the wooden floor. I worry about Miss Newman downstairs. She will be woken up with all the noise. If I wait until Adrian goes, I could slip down and see her. She might be ready for tea and cakes by then.

He tries again. 'Why didn't you say something? It seems so – so –'

James comes back into the room. 'Go home,' he says to Adrian. 'We all need some sleep. I'll ring this evening.'

Amazingly, Adrian turns and goes out of the door. He rarely takes James seriously, so I wait for him to change his mind and come back to finish his argument. But the front door closes behind him.

I sit on the sofa and wait. Everything around me is unnaturally bright and hard-edged. Then James is in my line of vision. He has done it again, walked across his floor without a sound. I look up at his face, waiting for the questions, but none comes. He sits down beside me, but doesn't touch me.

Does he know about the train tickets? I start to sweat. Has he found out? Did I tell him?

'Come to bed,' he says gently. 'We'll talk later.'

Obediently, I get up and follow him into the bedroom. We undress and climb in under the double duvet. We lie side by side, neither of us moving. After a while, his body grows warm and heavy and his breathing becomes even. Poor James. He must be exhausted after his sleepless night. I move closer to catch his warmth.

But every time I close my eyes, a tangle of colours races across my mind. Butterflies dancing in the wind, crocodiles, dark green glossy plants, cloned Peter Pans talking Russian, Suzy carrying five babies together, all laughing and being sick down her smart pink suit.

I jerk my eyes open. I don't want to sleep. It's too exhausting. I can't think about the last twenty-four hours, so I think about my mother instead.

She died when I was three, so if she miraculously appeared now, resurrected, I wouldn't recognize her. When I dream of her, she's real. I see her long dark hair and the necklaces of beads that I played with as a baby. I don't know how much is memory and how much imagination. The dream is not a nightmare, it has only comfort in it, but I lose it too fast when I wake, and I lie alone with a terrible pain inside me, a hole that will never be filled. I can't decide which is worse, to not have a mother, or to not have children. An empty space in both directions. No backwards, no forwards.

She died in a car crash, but nobody will tell me anything about it. Whenever I ask, an enormous vagueness descends. I would like more detail. Whose fault was it? Was she driving? Was there anyone else in the car? I need an end before I can go back to the beginning.

My brothers rarely talk about her, as if they've all agreed to forget. Unlike me, they have a memory of her being there for their childhood, but they can't seem to translate that into a physical description. Sometimes I think they all knew a different person.

When I was about twelve, I tried to find out more about her and pushed my brothers for some details.

Paul's mother is tall with short hair. 'She liked gardening and her nails were always black with soil. She only talked to us for a bit at mealtimes, and even then she started looking through the window again, thinking about the garden.' He can only describe her outside, pruning, raking the leaves, designing a herb garden.

'She sang in the garden,' he said once. 'I could hear her sometimes, after I'd gone to bed, when there was still some light left outside. I think she went on gardening in the dark, with a torch.'

'What did she sing?' I asked.

He looked confused. 'I don't know. I couldn't hear the words.'

'"A Hard Day's Night"? Or "Penny Lane"?' I discovered the Beatles records in the lounge when I was eight, and played them over and over until I knew all the words. My mother always sings them in my dreams.

But Paul shook his head. 'No, of course not. She was too old for that. We were the Beatles fans. She sang –' He stopped and tried to think. 'I don't know – folk songs, I suppose. "Greensleeves", "The Ash Grove", and things like that.'

I was disappointed, and certain that he was wrong. He was only twelve when she died.

Martin's mother is small, like me, and her hair is straight and long. He thinks she was blonde, but he's not quite sure. In several of the black and white photographs in the wedding album, the light falls on her hair from the side and it looks blond. I think Martin only remembers her from the photographs.

He finds it even harder to remember what she was like. I asked him about her soon after I talked to Paul. Martin had to deliver 500 boxes of crisps to Newcastle, and I was allowed to go with him because it was the Christmas holidays and he could be there and back in one day.

'No,' he said, leaning on one of the tyres he had been examining, 'I don't remember her singing.'

The cold of the early morning surrounded us. I put my gloved hands into my pockets and snuggled into my scarf. Martin's breath came out slowly in huge milky clouds. I wished he would hurry up and get into the cab where we could warm up, so I didn't say any more.

Twenty miles later, Martin decided to continue. 'I remember she had a brown dress covered with tiny white daisies. She wore it a lot.'

I waited for more, but nothing came. Martin, who had known her for fourteen years, had only a tenuous grasp on her image. I know nothing of her brown, daisy dress. It is nowhere in the wardrobe of my memory, so it must have worn out before she even thought of me.

Jake's mother is just a presence, with no physical details at all. He remembers her only in connection with his violin playing: 'She always came to my concerts, even when I was small.'

If he talks about her now, he gazes mysteriously into the distance. I don't believe in this. He's thinking about how he should look when remembering a tragedy. 'At least, I think she did.'

I can't understand all this uncertainty. I can remember more detail than anyone else and I was only three when she died. Don't any of my brothers have dreams?

Jake has occasionally offered more information. 'She often used to play the piano for me,' he announced in the middle of another conversation. 'I'd forgotten that. Extraordinary.'

It didn't surprise me. Jake doesn't play with other people, he plays for them. When Jake is playing, he thinks of Jake, and he'd expect the accompaniment to be there. But I like the idea of my mother playing the piano. 'Did she sing?' I asked.

He looked vague. 'I don't really know.'

'Didn't you ever realize you belonged to a family?'

'What do you mean?'

'Well, if you can't remember your mother, there isn't much hope for brothers and sisters, is there?'

'Mmm,' he says. 'That's interesting.'

I think he'd have preferred to be an only child.

I've always expected Adrian to have more to tell, since he's a writer and should be interested in details. He was sixteen when she died, and his first novel was published when he was twenty-three. He must have written something about her, but he denies it. I'm sure he's not telling me everything – perhaps from some brotherly motive of sparing my feelings. He likes to think he's responsible.

He occasionally produces details in passing and, for a time when I was younger, I used to hang around him so that I could gather information. He must have found me intensely irritating, however, because he was always busy. 'Later, Kitty, later,' he would say, flapping his hands at me. 'Not now.' He'll regret it one day, when his biographer interviews me about his early life. I shall be entirely truthful.

'She had long hair. Then she had it cut. Then she grew it again,' he said in answer to my question, giving the only logical explanation for her ever-changing appearance.

'Did she sing?'

'I don't remember. Oh yes – I think she sang in the bath. And nursery rhymes. I remember "Little Bo-Peep".'

'Did she sing in the garden?'

He looked surprised. 'I've no idea. I never went out there. We weren't keen on her gardening, because she sometimes forgot to cook the supper. I suppose she might have sung outside. Does it matter?'

Of course it does. I've a right to know about my mother. 'You were there, you should be able to describe her.'

'Yes,' he said. 'But I don't seem to have a very clear picture of her any more.'

Why's he so vague? Is he trying to hide something from me?

I like to think of my mother in the garden, growing and creating things with her fingers, refusing to conform to a wifely image. I'm glad she didn't like cooking. I've always assumed she was calm and good-natured, but more recently I've realized that she and my father must have had rows. Nobody could live with him and not have rows.

'She argued a lot with Dinah,' Adrian added unexpectedly. 'It was a relief when they went and shouted in the garden. I imagine that's why Dinah ran away.'

Dinah left when she was fifteen. There's very little information about her either. The men have apparently erased them both as an irrelevance. No time for women.

Nobody ever mentions the accident.

When I asked Adrian about it, he looked amazed. 'Well, I don't remember –'

'You must remember what happened.'

He looked almost distressed – unusual in Adrian. 'Dad didn't give us many details. He was very upset – wouldn't talk about it.'

As if my father wanted her removed from their lives. Cleaned up, swept away, all gone as quickly and neatly as possible.

I find my brothers' lack of interest astonishing. They've closed their minds down, shut the door, moved on. But then they never talk to each other, so I suppose it would be difficult to get the memories stirred up and moving. It's a good thing I talk to them. They might forget the others exist.

None of them give any indication that they missed her,

but I don't believe them. I think she had long and short hair; she was tall and short; she sang in the garden – folk songs to herself, nursery rhymes to the boys and Beatles songs to me. I think she held us all on her lap, even Dinah, one at a time and loved us all. Nobody can remember because she did it so well that the memories have become lost in the inner contentment of a happy childhood. I think that the others dream of her occasionally, but forget when they wake up.

I would have given Henry that inner contentment. I would have learned how to sing for him.

My mother loved the garden, which has grown wild and strong in her absence. I think it was the conflict between her and Dinah that led to Dinah's leaving.

My father gives me stories about my mother, but only of the time before they married. He never talks about her as a mother, or even a wife, as if he is still angry with her for dying and can only see her in the context of a fairy-story beginning. Even now, when I'm thirty-two, he tells me the same stories, but he muddles and embroiders them.

'No,' I say, 'that isn't right!'

He stops painting, or ironing, and looks up at me with a strange, affectionate smile. 'Oh dear,' he says. 'Wrong again.'

He met my mother, Margaret, in 1945. His parents had both died in the bombing in London, and he never talks about his part in the war. I once found some medals in an old shoebox in the attic, and brought them down immediately.

'What are these, Dad?'

He was making an apple crumble at the time, and turned to look, his fingers in the bowl of flour and margarine. He saw the medals and his hands became still in the bread-crumbs. The apples sizzled urgently in a saucepan, but he ignored them. His fierce energy drained away, and he looked different – smaller. 'Where did you find those?' he asked.

'In the attic. Are they yours?'

He muttered something and leaned over to stir the apples, turning his back on me.

'Were you in the RAF?' This was exciting to me. We were doing the Second World War in History.

'It was a long time ago,' he said quietly.

'Can I take them into school? For my project?'

There was a pause. 'If you want to. Put them back when you've finished.'

I looked at his silent back for a long time. He was fifty-five, and I was ten, old enough to feel his discomfort. Something wasn't right.

I put them back in the attic, replaced the lid and pretended that I had never seen them. Neither of us spoke of it again.

After the war, and whatever he did in it, he decided to explore the coast of Britain, he says. 'I made sketches, looked for shapes and patterns in the sand, pebbles and shells. I liked the depths and shallows in the sea, the storms and the stillness. I always wanted to be an artist, so this was my inspiration.' I have seen his collection of sketches from that period, and although they are fascinating, there aren't many.

'It's all in here,' he says solemnly whenever I ask, tapping the side of his head.

I was scornful then, but now accept that he did store it all somewhere in his mind. Where else does he get ideas for his paintings? A perfectly formed pebble, rubbed smooth by the sea, saturated with colours that shimmer and change as you look at it. A sea that always surprises, a restless gull. I picture him as a young man, standing on the edge of the ocean, watching the pebbles roll in and out, seeing things that others can't see and recording them for later use.

While he was roaming the seashore, my mother was studying at Exeter University. According to my father, when she was waiting for first year exam results, she and a group of friends went on the train to Exmouth. They walked from the station to the beach and took their shoes off as soon as they reached the sand dunes.

Margaret and two young men raced across the hot beach, over the hard, tightly packed sand at the water's edge and into the sea. The men stopped to roll up their trousers, but my mother pulled up her skirt higher than her knees and waded in, shrieking with delight at the coldness of the water. My father was standing at the edge with his feet just in the water, wearing shorts and holding his sandals in his right hand. On his back was a rucksack containing all his worldly belongings. His hair was too long, creeping down his neck towards his shoulders, and he was tanned and fit. There were torn patches on his shorts, which had been cut from an old pair of trousers. He describes himself and I can see him: the first hippy.

My father still takes pleasure from Margaret's appearance then. He rolls the words round in his mouth, tasting them, pulling them out of his memory, like an almost forgotten feast from the past.

'Tall, thin, alive,' he says, and pauses. 'Part of the beach, shrieking like the seagulls, her hair long and loose, flying behind her. She was waiting for me in a dress of red poppies that was too small, with her thin arms poking awkwardly out of the puffed sleeves. The angles of her elbows were sharp and hungry, her smooth skin white and unlived in, waiting to be touched. She looked innocent, as if she hadn't yet woken up. The wet edge of her skirt clung to her skinny legs, and she danced with excitement and cold.'

My father didn't take much notice of the two young men with her, or the larger group still chasing each other among the sand dunes. I'm surprised he even knew they were there.

He threw his sandals and rucksack down on the beach and rushed through the shallow waves to my mother. She saw him coming and stopped her shrieking. She stood still, alarmed by his response. She tried pulling her skirt down, but the edge started to float in the water.

'She looked like a frightened doe,' he says. 'Waiting for rescue.'

Did he really think that then? *Bambi* hadn't been made in 1945.

'I waded through the water towards her and took her by both hands. I whirled her around, and she had to follow, otherwise she'd have fallen over. She laughed, with her head leaning back so that the laugh came more clearly through her open throat, and the sound skimmed over the surface of the water. I laughed too, and we whizzed round faster and faster until we fell over.'

They stood up, both of them looking at their wet clothes and sobered by the cold shock of the sea.

'My dress,' said Margaret, suddenly nervous.

'My shirt,' he said in the same tone. They both laughed again.

'It'll dry in the sunshine,' said my father and held out a hand to her. She took it.

'My name's Guy,' said my father.

'My name's Margaret.'

My father tells this story as if it were a Hollywood film – the background a blur behind them, a Rachmaninov piano concerto swelling to fill the gap left by their silence.

'What happened to the students who came to the sea with her?' I asked once.

'I don't know,' he said.

'Weren't there other people in the sea? How did she know that you were only interested in her?'

'I don't know,' he said again.

'What happened next?'

I've wondered if what he tells is the truth. Was it really so romantic? The scene is full of detail, but no facts. Did my mother go back to the university with her friends, or did she ride off into the sunset with him? There must have been some practical matters that needed to be sorted out first.

'Then we got married,' said my father, abruptly, as if I was asking for details as the credits rolled up the screen.

Just like that. 'But did she finish her degree?' I asked. I knew the answer already, but have never been happy with it. I want it changed. 'Did she go back to the university and finish?'

He always looks puzzled when I ask this. 'No, of course not. She didn't need to. We got married.'

So. My father wants me to believe they lived happily ever after. My mother, Margaret, probably with a promising academic career ahead of her, surrendered it to get married and have six children.

The mother of my dreams is tall, thin, brown-haired, laughing in the sea. Where do I come into all this? I look through the wedding album, black and white, and my father never looks quite right. He should be full of restless energy and his fierce eyes should stare out of the photographs, somehow willing the photographer to get it right, to capture his real identity. But the very nature of a photograph – freezing him in time – misses a vital part of his personality. What we see is only half the man.

My mother looks so young and pretty next to him, her hair unfashionably long and straight. I suppose if my father was the original hippy, she was the second, fashioned out of his rib. Did she always look like that, or did he change her? Was the mother we knew the same as the university student who never finished? Do we only see half the woman in the photographs?

I have grandparents – Margaret's parents, who live in a small bungalow in Lyme Regis. I used to go and stay with them in the school holidays, because my father was always busy and my brothers were unreliable. I still occasionally go down for a weekend. They're over ninety. My grandfather sits in front of the television every day, barking with laughter at regular intervals. In the evenings I sit with him and watch programmes I never knew existed.

'Did you see that?' cries my grandfather every now and again, slapping his leg and sucking the edges of his moustache. I try to see what he is laughing at. I used to think I was too young to understand. I now think he doesn't understand either. He wants to convince himself that he is still alive, that he still has an active brain under that shiny bald dome. Sometimes he calls his wife from the kitchen. 'Mrs Harrison,' he shouts, 'come and see this.'

She comes in from the kitchen, wiping her hands on a tea-towel, and stands in front of the television for ten seconds. 'Well I never,' she says. 'Don't laugh too much, Mr Harrison – your teeth will fall out.'

For years I thought old people didn't have first names, that they were christened Mr Harrison or Mrs Harrison.

My grandmother lives in the kitchen, baking, cleaning, scrubbing the floor, constantly wiping her dishcloth over the yellow Formica tops. 'Such wonderful things you can buy today,' she says to me with pleasure. 'These tops come up lovely.'

She is very thin and pale, her skin settling in loose folds round the base of her neck. Her hands are mottled red and blue, as if she were permanently cold. She tries to feed me non-stop. 'Have another scone, dear,' she says. 'You're far too skinny. All this rationing – it's not good for you.'

She frequently thinks I'm Margaret, that she's lost fifty years somewhere and is starting again. I like this confusion. It makes me part of my mother.

There is a large black and white studio photograph of Margaret in the lounge, mounted and framed. She's sitting sideways, but her face is turned towards the camera, looking across her shoulder. She has a long pale neck and her skin is smooth and unblemished. Her dark hair is tied into the nape of her neck and she looks beautiful, like an Edwardian lady, graceful and frozen into a past that doesn't exist any more.

My grandmother tells me different stories every time she sees me looking at this picture. 'Why, that was before she went up to university. Mr Harrison and I wanted to remember how she looked when she had just grown up. You can see the innocence in her eyes.'

Or: 'After she was married. I remember they came to stay after their honeymoon and Guy – your father, dear – insisted on a portrait photograph. We thought it was too expensive, but he said he was paying. He insisted.'

Why does my father not have a copy of this picture at home? Why are the wedding photograph and album the only pictures he has of my mother?

There are photographs of my mother all over the house in Lyme Regis. At eleven, with long stick-like legs and thick dark plaits; at three, squatting on the grass picking daisies, her hair cut into a severe bob, but her eyes bright and inquisitive.

There are photographs that my father has sent of all the grandchildren and great-grandchildren, but my grandmother has trouble remembering the names. Also, several photographs of the wedding, my mother clutching a bouquet of white lilies, two friends as bridesmaids with their fashionable hair curling round tiny hats, and my grandparents as middle-aged parents, from another era, people whom I've never known. I've sat and examined this picture many times. Do I look like her? Did she want to be my mother? Did I sit on her lap and have cuddles?

'Why did my parents go and live in Birmingham when they both liked the sea so much?' I asked once.

My grandmother stopped beating her cake mixture for a few seconds and looked bemused. 'I don't know,' she said. 'I expect it was because he wanted to take her away from her university friends. They were a bit rowdy.'

This answer worries me. Was she happy? Six pregnancies. Did she want us all?

Sometimes, I think I can remember sitting on her knees, playing with her fingers as she laced them together, hearing a soft, low voice singing 'A Hard Day's Night'.

Every now and again I determine to find out more about my mother and how she died. I've made lists: are there reports in old newspapers about the crash she died in? Could I find any of her old university friends, school friends? Ask my grandparents about the funeral?

But these are big tasks and require energy and I put it off, until one day it will be too late and everyone who ever knew her will be gone. Even now, I make the lists and never do anything. There is something that makes me uneasy. I don't know what it is.

I lie next to James and think about it all. I've learned to keep it there in my mind without it becoming urgent or frustrated, but not losing it either.

Now, hearing James breathing, feeling the space around me, the calming emptiness, I feel my body grow heavy and still and I sink finally down into sleep.

James and I sit in the doctor's waiting room. I've been here before, many times, and I'm familiar with the posters about Aids, breast cancer, diabetes. I know several of them by heart.

Depression:
'Do you wake early in the morning and not get back to sleep?' (Yes.)
'Do you find it difficult to eat?' (No.)
'Do you find it difficult to talk to people?' (It depends who they are.)
'Do you find it difficult to concentrate?' (Yes.)
'Are you tired all the time?' (Yes.)
You might be depressed.
(Yes. Right.)

This is part of a deal with Adrian. If I don't go to see the doctor, he won't let me see Emily and Rosie again. Ever. He's waiting outside in his car, expecting to take us home. The engine's probably already running, in case I try to escape and he has to give chase.

When I woke up on Saturday, out of a frenetic, kaleido-scope dream, James was no longer lying next to me. I lay still for a while, trying to clear my head from the dream, dazzled and confused by its complexity, but unable to remember much.

I could hear James' voice from the other room, talking to someone on the telephone, and I realized that his voice had been in my dream and taken it over, words coming out of his mouth visibly in multi-coloured layers.

'Give us an hour.' I sat up to look at the alarm clock on the bedside table and was amazed to see that it said 7.15. That's impossible, I thought. We only came to bed at 7.00. I've been here longer than fifteen minutes.

James came into the room, pleased to find me awake.

'Hello,' he said. 'You've had a good sleep.'

For quarter of an hour, I thought. Then I saw that he'd changed his clothes, shaved, brushed his hair, and I realized I had lost twelve hours.

'You'd better get up,' he said. 'Adrian wants us to go over to Tennyson Drive by eight.'

'Wonderful,' I said. 'You're going to love that.' James and my father are like jigsaw pieces from two different puzzles. They look as if they'll fit together, but they don't.

James sat down on the edge of the bed and looked at me.

'What?' I said.

'Are you all right?'

'Of course,' I said, and swung my legs over the side of the bed so that I wasn't facing him.

'Only –'

'Yes?'

'It was a bit silly – taking the girls –'

I turned and gave him a hug. I like him to be protective. 'I know,' I said. 'I didn't think it through properly.'

He kissed me on the tip of my nose. 'Tell me next time, and then we can work on the defence together.'

'Have I got time for a bath?'

'Yes. Do you want me to go next door for some clean clothes?'

I nodded and decided to wait for him to return before running the bath. He would select the right clothes for the occasion.

'Sorry,' he said as he opened the door to go out. 'I wanted Adrian to come here, but he refused. Neutral ground, he said.'

'Not so neutral with Dad there.'

'No.' He rolled his eyes and left.

We were a bit late – we'd stopped to eat some beans on toast. Adrian's car was in the drive, white and spotlessly clean, fresh from its Saturday morning polish. James and I don't drive. We're both too scared, but we tell everyone we believe in saving the planet.

'Hello, Kitty,' said my father as we came in the front door. 'In trouble again, I hear.'

'Nothing too alarming,' said James.

My father ignored him and talked to me. 'Best to sort it out straight away. Adrian and Martin are in the lounge. Lesley has to stay at home with the children. I don't know where Paul is at the moment and Suzy's ill, so Jake is looking after her.'

Terrific. 'Have you invited all the neighbours?'

My father looked at him askance. 'I don't think it concerns them.'

'I hope you won't be joining the discussion,' said James. 'It's really none of your business.' His hair was very springy that day, as if he had deliberately antagonized it. It bushed out all round his head, making him look two inches taller than he really was. But it didn't work. My father still looked right over the top of him.

'I'd like to help,' said my father to me as he followed us into the lounge, 'but I'm too busy.'

'That's a relief,' said James.

Martin was watching a football match on the television with the sound turned down. 'Hello, Kitty, James,' he said without taking his eyes from the screen.

'An urgent commission,' said my father, 'for a new chain of restaurants – can't remember the name. There's a lot of money in it, according to Dennis.'

'Off you go then,' said James.

My father smiled at me. He's very secure in his refusal to acknowledge James, even when James works so hard to shock him into a reaction. They're like children in their rivalry. My father wants me to remain as his little girl – his last chance, I suppose, since he lost the other women in his life. And James reacts to this intrusion in his usual dogged fashion, head on, determined to resist. My father uses his silence like a weapon, hurling his arrows through the air, soundless but touched with venom. James absorbs the arrows without any discernible effort. They stand in opposite corners, counting up the score as often as possible, knowing that neither can win.

Adrian was pacing up and down already, but not making as much noise on the threadbare, dust-clogged carpet as in James' flat. Every now and again, Adrian's pacing took him across the front of the television, but Martin didn't notice. I wondered if he'd gone to sleep with his eyes open.

'Hello,' I said to Adrian.

He ignored me.

'I'll be off then,' said my father.

'Good,' said James to my father's back.

Adrian started immediately. 'Kitty, you must go to the doctor's.'

I couldn't make the connection. Did he know something I didn't? A lump on my breast, varicose veins, high blood pressure? Can you tell these things just by looking? 'Why? I thought we were going to have a row about last night.'

'Don't be facetious. We don't want to argue, but you must see that your behaviour wasn't rational.'

'James,' I said. 'He's telling me I'm mad. I'm not, am I?'

'No, you're not mad,' said James. 'Of course not, and nobody is suggesting you are, but –'

'But what?'

'We're worried about you,' said Adrian. 'We feel you're not quite yourself.'

'Have you two been talking to each other?' I said.

'Obviously,' said James, confusing me. I had expected a reasonable amount of plotting, but I thought they'd be more subtle and deny any collusion. 'We spent the whole of last night together, worrying about you.'

'Oh, yes.'

'You do realize,' said Adrian, 'that I was in the middle of an important dinner and I had to leave before the main course? I drove all the way back from London, not knowing if Emily and Rosie were even alive. Obviously my family is more important to me than an award, but it's very embarrassing. What explanation do you think I should give? My sister has behaved irresponsibly?' He paused. 'I might have won an award and not been there to collect it.'

'And did you?'

'What?'

'Win?'

'No, actually. But that's not the point.'

He couldn't be that upset if he'd found time to telephone and find out. I wanted to say this, but it seemed such an effort to open my mouth that I sat down instead, next to Martin, and wished I could go back to bed.

'I think you should give Kitty some credit for looking after the girls properly,' said James. 'They were never going to come to any harm.'

'No,' I said. 'That's right.'

'And presumably they enjoyed *Peter Pan*.'

'Yes,' I said.

'You must understand that Lesley was extremely upset.'

I thought of calm, organized, reasonable Lesley, who always knows exactly what she is doing and why. I've never seen her upset. 'It was a mistake,' I said. 'It won't happen again.'

'No,' said Adrian, standing still at last. 'It won't happen again because Lesley doesn't want you near the girls any more.'

I leapt out of my chair. 'That's not fair,' I said. 'They're my nieces.'

We stood facing each other, all of us annoyed. I looked round to see if Martin was going to join us, but he was still watching the football. He dislikes arguments. I was surprised he hadn't left the room.

'Well,' said Adrian, 'Lesley and I have talked it over and we feel that if you are going to be allowed to see the girls again, you must try to sort out why you behaved so irrationally.'

'See,' I said to James. 'He thinks I'm mad.'

'No, not mad,' said Adrian, 'just – disturbed –'

I would have leapt to my feet, but I was already standing.

'I think that's a bit strong,' said James mildly. He will never be angry when I want him to. 'She planned a treat for the girls which went wrong. That's hardly disturbed behaviour. More – foolish.'

'Yes,' I say.

'Don't forget she was out all night,' said Adrian.

'She was at Jake's,' said James.

'Yes,' I said.

'Goal!' yelled Martin, and leapt off the sofa, his arms shooting upwards. He looked at us, standing tensely in the middle of the room, grinned sheepishly and sat down.

'Yes,' said Adrian. 'It's the wrong word. I chose the wrong word.'

'Well, you're only a writer,' I said. 'You can't be expected to find the right words.'

Nobody laughed. I sat down, folded my arms and watched the television.

'What I mean,' said Adrian, 'is that you've not been yourself since – since –'

He wouldn't say it. Nobody ever does. They come dangerously close, I'm ready for them, but then they don't. It's as if there is a big hole around it and everyone is afraid of falling in. They teeter on the edge briefly, then turn round and walk away.

'Well,' said Adrian after an embarrassed pause. 'We'd like you to talk to a doctor, someone who understands you.

We're worried about you, and I'm sure James would agree with us.'

Oh no, I thought, James doesn't agree. I looked at him, but he was composing a kind, compassionate look for me, so I couldn't tell what he was thinking.

'You realize that certainly Emily and possibly Rosie have lost faith in you?'

'It was a treat,' I said. 'It was meant to be a surprise.'

'I don't know if Lesley will be able to trust you again,' said Adrian.

So here I am, trapped, back where I was three years ago.

'Katherine Maitland?' says the receptionist and points to the door on her left. James smiles encouragingly at me as I get up, and I try to look keen, to please him.

Actually, I quite like Dr Cross. She's always calm and I sometimes take some of that calmness away with me. I just don't want to be pushed into seeing her.

I used to come and see her a lot once – I'm not sure why I stopped – so it's not difficult to explain why I'm here. I tell her about Rosie and Emily, about Adrian and James, about *Peter Pan*. I don't tell her about the yellow period, or the train tickets to Edinburgh.

When I've finished talking, she sits for a while as if she's thinking hard. She is a small woman, and very neat and precise in appearance. Her words are neat too, and it's clear somehow that she knows much more than she says.

'So,' she says after a pause. 'Do you feel you acted responsibly?'

I know her well enough to understand that she wants me to think about it. 'I don't know,' I say. 'Adrian says I'm mad.'

'And what do you think?'

I think he might be right, but I don't say so. 'I don't know. I suppose I was stupid.'

How does she make me confess this? I haven't admitted it to anyone else.

'Do you think you might be depressed?'

I knew she was going to say that. 'I suppose I must be,' I say and start to cry.

She waits. She doesn't say anything. I like her stillness and eventually I stop crying. She passes me a box of tissues and I take one and blow my nose.

'Sorry,' I say.

'How would you feel about taking antidepressants again?'

I look at her. She doesn't smile. She just looks at me.

'I don't know how I feel,' I say.

'I think it might be a good idea to try them again,' she says.

'OK.' I nod. I'm afraid of where I am going, and I think she knows this.

'It's three years now since Henry died?'

There is no embarrassment with her. She just says it and I accept that she can say it. 'Three years,' I say, 'two months, and five days.'

'And it doesn't get any easier?'

'No.'

She looks down at her notes. 'It doesn't seem that long ago.'

'He would be going to nursery school by now. He would have friends –' I hear my voice disintegrating, so I stop for a few seconds and look out of the window. 'Lots of babies survive at twenty-eight weeks. I keep seeing it on the television – in the paper. Babies everywhere survive . . .'

A silence grows between us. There is something fluid and tangible about this silence. It flows through the air and seeps into me.

Eventually she moves. 'What about James? Does he talk about Henry?'

'No,' I say. 'He won't.'

She nods. 'I'm going to give you a month's supply of tablets. You know that they take two or three weeks to start working, so don't expect any sudden change, and I want you to come back and see me in three weeks' time. Make an appointment before you go. And –' she hesitates '– do you think James would come too?'

I am startled by this. 'You want us to come together?'

'Yes, if he's willing. Do you mind?'

I don't know. 'I'll ask him,' I say.

I go out and find James reading *Woman's Own*, so I sit down next to him. 'I've got to come back in three weeks, and she wants you to come too.'

'Me?' He looks alarmed. 'Why should I come?'

I shrug. Isn't it obvious? 'We have to make the appointment now.'

I wait while he goes up to the receptionist.

'Kitty,' he says as he comes back to where I am sitting, 'why do I have to go?'

'She probably thinks you're interested.'

'Of course I am. But that doesn't mean I have to go with you. You know how I feel about doctors. They remind me of my childhood.'

'Nobody's going to force you. It's up to you.' I don't want to get up and go out to Adrian in his smart car. 'Why don't we sneak out the back way?'

'But Adrian's waiting for us.'

'We could phone him on his mobile when we get home.'

James frowns. 'I don't think we should antagonize him.'

Adrian is sitting with his windows closed, and his eyes closed, listening to Bach on his CD-player. I open the door and get into the back seat. 'There,' I say. 'That's my part of the deal. Now you work on yours.'

'What did she say?' I can see his eyes watching me briefly in his mirror, before he pulls out into the passing traffic.

'She gave me a prescription and I've got to go back in three weeks.'

He nods approvingly. 'We'll stop at the chemist's on the way back then.'

We drive along in silence. James doesn't look happy.

'By the way,' says Adrian into the silence, 'I phoned Jake. Suzy isn't pregnant. She has a tummy bug.'

A knot re-ties itself inside me. I think of Suzy's sickness. I know I'm right. Why is nobody admitting it?

3

A Good Silence

The telephone wakes me from a deep sleep and I hear the answer machine: 'Kitty? It's Caroline. Where are you? I've been ringing you for days.'

I pick up the receiver and interrupt her message. 'Sorry, Caroline. I haven't been well.'

'You shouldn't cut yourself off completely. What if there was an emergency?'

'Do you mean my emergency, or someone else's emergency, which I am expected to attend?' I can't think of a single situation that could arise. I experienced my only emergency three years ago, and there's no chance of that happening again.

'Have you read the book?' Caroline does not like to be drawn into personal conversations.

'Of course.' Which book is she talking about? I hold the telephone between my chin and shoulder while I start to scrabble through a pile of manuscripts on the floor.

'What did you think?'

'About what?'

'Well – was it perceptive or was it racist?'

I hold up a manuscript in my hand, entitled *Bella the Black Beauty*. I think it sounds sexist rather than racist, but I can't remember reading it. 'I'll send you a report tomorrow.'

'Can't you tell me now?'

'No. I really think I should go through it again. I don't like making quick judgements.'

'Well, all right.' She sounds impressed by my willingness to read it again. 'But I must have it back by Friday.'

'No trouble,' I say and ring off. I don't know how long I've slept, but I'm ready for some hard work.

I dress quickly and look at myself in the mirror. Not too bad, I think, for an insomniac who has possibly been asleep for days.

The telephone rings again. I pick it up. 'Hello, James.'

There is a pause. 'Kitty? How did you know it was me?' Not, how are you? I've missed you.

'I guessed.'

'Do you want me to come over?'

'No. I'll come to you.' I know he's sighing with relief, silently, because he's always polite. He has problems with the chaos of my flat. 'Put the kettle on.'

Before leaving, I go into the bathroom and pick up the bottle of pills that Adrian made me fetch from the chemist. *Take two tablets in the morning after eating*, the label says. *Do not drive or operate machinery if drowsy. Avoid alcohol.*

I have read all this before. The sight of the pills in my hand makes me feel sick. I know what they taste like, the way they affect my mood. I sit down on the edge of the bath, trembling, my legs suddenly weak. The pills rattle in the bottle. I pour them all into my hand – small white tablets, innocent, potent, offering false hope, undermining my grief –

I pour them down the loo and flush it. Most of them float to the surface, so I wait for the cistern to fill and flush it again.

When they still refuse to go away, I scoop them up and bury them in the wastepaper basket, under the empty toilet rolls and discarded toothpaste tubes.

*

As I shut my front door behind me James' door opens, and we stand looking at each other.

'So,' he says eventually. 'Have you eaten?'

'What do you think?' He knows I forget to eat. Why does he pretend?

He puts a hand on my elbow and leads me into his flat. I wish he would stop and hold me properly, but he likes to be careful.

We go into the kitchen, which is as immaculate as it was when I first saw it. I've made no impression on his home. But then, he's made no impression on mine. I sit up straighter and feel better. His outward appearance is deceptive, anyway. He is spinning so fast that all the colours in his life overlap and blur, become white. Shiny, pure, unreal white.

'How's work?' I don't really want to know, but I would like him to start talking.

'Good. You know I've started to do some work for an American firm?'

I didn't know, but I'm not sure if that's because he hasn't told me, or because I don't listen. I nod.

'They want me to go over to New York sometime – to meet them.' He pauses. 'What do you think?'

I stare at him in amazement. As long as I have known him he has never wanted to go anywhere. I had to force him to buy tickets to Venice for our honeymoon. 'Really?' I say.

'Well, it was just a thought.'

'I think it's a brilliant thought. Can I come too?' This is a test. I want to see his reaction.

He doesn't hesitate. 'Yes, of course.' Ninety per cent for a quick response. Ten per cent off because he was too quick. He might have prepared himself in advance.

'Let's do it,' I say. 'Tomorrow.' I can read Caroline's book all night. Who cares? Why shouldn't we do something exciting?

'Tomorrow?' He looks appalled. 'I can't. I have too much work to do.'

'So? Make them wait. The world is at your feet.' I realize I'm getting a bit carried away, and try to talk more sensibly. 'Anyway, we have to stop spinning occasionally – let the colours show – like a kaleidoscope or merry-go-round – the colours blur if you go too fast – it's a spectrum. You know – white –'

He is about to drink some coffee, but he stops with the cup just under his lip. I rather hope he might spill it, but he doesn't. He puts it down again. 'What are you talking about?'

'Nothing,' I say. 'Come on. Why don't we?'

'Well . . .' I can see he is thinking about it seriously.

'What time is it?'

He looks at his watch. 'Six o'clock.'

I assume he must mean six in the evening, not six in the morning. I would like to know what day it is, but presumably I'll find this out soon. 'Let's have a Chinese takeaway and discuss our holiday. We could phone for tickets and pick them up at the airport.'

I know I'm talking too fast, but suddenly everything seems possible. When I woke up, I'd lost my sense of time. Now everything fits my mood and appetite exactly.

While James goes to fetch the food, I put plates to warm under the grill and lay the table. James likes things to be done properly. We eat more frequently in his flat than mine, because he can't relax until he has personally washed everything. I don't mind. I just invite him round when my kitchen needs cleaning and I don't feel like doing it.

While I wait for him, I read *Bella the Black Beauty*. I turn the pages very fast and I'm halfway through when James returns with sweet and sour pork, egg fried rice and barbecued spare ribs. I attack it with enormous pleasure. James is more careful and takes smaller helpings. He watches me. 'Not so fast, Kitty, you'll make yourself ill.'

'I'm all right.'

Until next time, I can hear him thinking. But there won't be a next time. There are no more mornings in my life, no more yellow – I know I can't see Emily and Rosie again. I'm moving forwards now – into the unknown . . .

We eat until we're full and leave the dishes in the kitchen while we take coffee into the lounge. I gave him a wonderful Chinese rug two years ago, brilliant gold dragons breathing flames of red and orange, which added life and movement to the room. He said he liked it and it stayed on the floor for a month. Then, one day, it was gone. He had rolled it up and hidden it, or even put it out for the dustbin lorry. I knew then, clearly, why I kept my flat. The huge emptiness of his was too much like the huge emptiness inside me.

He has, however, recently bought a coffee table, quite a nice one, in pale wood, of course. I'm frightened to put my hot coffee mug on it, in case it leaves a stain, so the table sits between our two leather chairs looking functional but unused, while our mugs sit reproachfully on the floor.

'Come on, James,' I say, pulling my feet up on to the chair. 'Let's do something crazy for once and just go. We'd be back before anybody noticed we were gone.'

He looks unhappy and sips his coffee. 'It's just –' I wait. 'I think we should be a bit more organized. Contact my people in New York, tell them when we're coming, so they can book us a hotel and find someone to show you around while I'm working.'

'I don't want anyone to show me round. Surely you'll have some time free?'

'Yes, of course. But we'll need at least a week to organize it –'

'Let's compromise. We could go in four days' time.'

He grins. 'All right. I'll ring them tomorrow and start the arrangements.'

'But don't ask for someone to show me round.'

He smiles. 'OK.'

We sit and look at each other, shocked by our daring. We are acting impetuously. We are doing something we want to do without consulting anyone else. I'm usually too scared, James is usually too careful. 'I've always wanted to go to New York,' I say.

'Adrian says it's worth going up the Empire State Building. Apparently there's a glass floor and you can look down at the whole of New York beneath your feet.'

I didn't know he talked to Adrian. I certainly didn't know he listened to him. 'We'll have to go up the Statue of Liberty.'

'I'm not sure if that's such a good idea. It's very crowded and you have to queue for a long time.'

'That's all right,' I say. 'We'll be on holiday. There won't be any rush.'

'I'll have to spend time working –'

'I know, I know. But that's all right too. We're going to do what we want to do.' I'd be happy to stay in bed, or read and wait comfortably for him.

We sit together in silence for a while. This is what I have always liked about James. We can make a good silence together. There's something between us that doesn't need words or actions. It settles around us and I can feel it now, hovering gently, ready to wrap me in its nebulous folds, like a delicate lace shawl. I want it to be like this always, something inside us meeting and holding hands, something calm and soothing and healing.

'I have to finish this book,' I say. 'I've promised Caroline I'll send it tomorrow.'

He smiles gently. This is when I love him the most, when

100

he accepts me as I am and likes me to do what I want to do. 'Of course. I'll go and wash up and then I'll do some work myself.'

He gives me some paper and pencils and lurches off into the kitchen with the coffee cups. I hear him moving around in the kitchen, washing and drying. He never leaves anything to drain. I feel a contentment that I'm always looking for but seldom reach, and then only for a few fleeting moments. I know it won't last. There are just a handful of good moments in a great long life. Like eating one good meal in a year of starvation.

We work quietly together. The sound of his clicking keys soothes me. I finish the book and jot down my immediate thoughts. I enjoyed it; the title just needs to be more sensible.

I stand up, and move towards James at his desk. He stands up at exactly the same moment and we meet in the middle of the room. This is why I married him.

I put my arms round him and lean my head on his shoulder. He holds me and strokes my hair. We go quickly to the bedroom because we're not very good standing together. I'm taller than him and the geometry isn't quite right. None of the angles or straight lines line up properly.

When I wake, the clock says seven a.m. James is lying with his back against mine, warm and relaxed. I want this moment to be with me all the time, so there is no future, so that this is my life. Everything else is illusion, a world of false colour. Perhaps if I don't move, it will go on and on and there will be no more emptiness inside me.

But there is something about my waking that wakes James, as if he catches our silence leaking away. He seems to know that I am thinking real thoughts and not dream thoughts. He rolls over and puts his face against my shoulder, his arm circling me gently, lovingly.

'Are you awake?' he whispers.

'Mmmm.'

'I wish –'

He doesn't finish because I know what he wishes. I know he wants to wake up every morning and find me there. But I can't do it. There are only certain times, when I feel right and he feels right. Then his white slows down so that all the yellows and blues and reds in his spectrum meet mine and merge, complementing the frenetic whirls of colour inside me. We look at each other and we match. Things can only work if we can share the colours out properly, evenly, between us.

'Kitty?'

'Mmm?'

'Are you taking your pills?'

The comfortable warmth between us zooms abruptly away. I push his arm off me and climb out of bed. 'I have work to do,' I say.

I get dressed with my back to him. I pick up my book and papers that he's left neatly stacked on the coffee table and I let myself out.

I don't really know why I'm crying.

We take the train to London and a taxi to Heathrow. It's hugely expensive, but James earns a lot of money and we don't often spend it. We only have hand luggage, because we don't possess any suitcases, and we couldn't find much to put in them if we did.

'We'll buy what we need,' says James. 'Everything's cheaper in New York.'

I'm very excited about going abroad. For our honeymoon, we travelled to Venice by ferry and train. I couldn't sleep on the train and spent my time trying to see out, even in the dark. We raced past places and names I'd only ever seen on a map – Paris, Geneva, Milan. I wanted to see them all and keep hold of them in case I never went there again.

We leave Birmingham barely awake, and arrive at Heathrow in the cold grey of early morning. There is a bleakness about the time, and I imagine the rest of England just waking, preparing to live through another ordinary day. We're escaping. I want to jump up and race around like a toddler, shouting with joy. It's so difficult sitting still and pretending to be patient.

We listen carefully to the announcements and follow directions. The departure lounge is full of slumbering people.

'Did I remember to turn off the central heating?'

'Yes.'

'Whose idea was it to come at this ridiculous hour?'

'Yours.'

'Do you think they really give us boiled sweets?'

'No idea.'

After a time, I realize that James isn't as excited as I am. I lean against him and pretend to doze, jumping every time there's an announcement, but James feels hard and rigid. I wonder if he's nervous about meeting the Americans.

'I'm sure they'll like you,' I mutter, but he gives no sign that he's heard me.

Finally our announcement comes and we join the group of people forming a new queue. We board a bus and get driven to our aeroplane which looks like a toy in the distance. It gets bigger and bigger until suddenly it's real, and we're making our way up the steps.

'It's very easy, isn't it?' I say to James. 'Anyone could do it.'

He doesn't answer. His face is set into an artificial expression of endurance. Someone jostles him from behind as we try to get into our seats and he stumbles forward.

It's a middle-aged man with glasses. 'Sorry,' he says kindly, offering his hand to help James to stabilize himself.

James ignores him and pushes me into the window seat, sitting down heavily next to me. I smile at the man who jostled us and he smiles back. 'Sorry,' I say, feeling my good spirits draining rapidly away.

James is white and angry. 'Don't apologize for me,' he says through tight lips.

'What's the matter?' I've never seen him like this before.

He is breathing heavily, in and out through his mouth so that I can hear it. There are trickles of sweat running down his forehead, getting caught in the creases round his mouth.

'Are you all right?'

He gives a strange, drawn-out groan and gets clumsily to his feet.

'James,' I say in alarm.

But he's gone. I'm sitting in an aeroplane bound for New York, and my husband, who's holding the tickets and passports, is not here. I feel a vibration through my seat, and I'm sure that the engines have started and we're about to leave. I leap up and grab our bags, stumbling over the legs of the people sitting next to us.

'Sorry,' I say, 'sorry,' as if it will somehow save me. 'Sorry. Only my husband – he doesn't seem to be well –'

They nod and smile, but they don't care. They have their own well-being to worry about. I reach the gangway, but he's not here. I don't know which way he's gone. People are still finding their seats, so I have to force my way through them to the exit.

I find James arguing with a stewardess. 'Let me off,' he is saying very deliberately. 'I have to get off.'

The stewardess is about six inches taller than he is, with red hair. She doesn't look pleased and is trying to bar the doorway, to push James back in.

'I'm sorry,' I say to her. 'I think we should get off.'

'Don't apologize,' says James through clenched teeth. 'Let me out, woman.'

'We can't delay the take-off,' she says.

She's still trying to look professional, but a button has popped open on her blouse and we can see her bra – black with tiny pink roses along the top. Strands of wiry, red hair are bursting out from her hair clip. Why doesn't she just let us go?

A uniformed man comes running up the steps from behind her. He's putting the end of a banana into his mouth and is still holding the skin. He chews quickly and swallows. 'What's going on?'

'Thank goodness you're here,' says the stewardess.

'We need to get off,' I say, and smile pleasantly as I discover that I can be articulate in the middle of James' crisis.

The man studies us. 'I'm your pilot,' he says. He is fiddling with the banana skin, not knowing what to do with it. He almost slips it into his pocket, but stops himself and apparently considers just dropping it on the floor.

'Let us off,' says James, his voice hard with anger.

Two identical men emerge from the passenger cabin. They're smartly dressed, very tall, very wide, very alarming. 'Do you need any help?' says one of them.

The pilot looks as taken aback as I am. 'No,' he says. 'I think we can cope.' He hesitates. 'Thank you.'

The men look at each other. 'Well, if you need us, we're sitting at the back.'

'Who are they?' says the pilot.

'No idea,' says the stewardess. She relaxes for a second, and James pushes himself to the door, his foot outstretched to reach the movable steps.

'Please can we get off?' I say.

'You can't leave,' she says. 'You have to stay with your luggage.'

'That's all right,' I say. 'I've got it here.'

'It'll be in the hold now,' says the pilot, easing himself gently between James and the exit.

'We didn't have any big luggage,' I say.

The stewardess looks at the pilot. 'Check,' he says. 'On the computer.'

'Maitland,' I say. 'James and Katherine.'

She disappears. James stands next to me, silent and rigid.

The stewardess returns. 'There isn't any luggage,' she says. She looks at the pilot. He hesitates, then nods.

'Let them go,' he says and moves aside. James runs down the steps.

I start to follow him, but the pilot catches my arm and pulls me close to him. 'They do courses,' he whispers in my ear. 'You have to confront the fear.'

I pull away from him.

The stewardess leans forward. I try not to look at her gaping blouse. 'Have you tried yoga?' she says. 'I hear it's very good.'

I fight a terrible urge to giggle, waves of laughter working their way from my stomach upwards. 'It's all right,' I say. 'He has a heart condition.' My voice is shaking with the suppressed laughter.

The stewardess steps away from me and looks offended.

'I'm sorry,' she says. 'It would have helped if we'd had prior notice.'

'That's all right,' I say, and I'm running down the steps to where James is waiting. As we stand isolated, on the edge of the runway, looking for a passing bus, the engines start on the aeroplane. We cling to each other in alarm and the noise becomes deafening. A bus stops in front of us. We climb on and join a group of Japanese tourists who have just landed.

'Is this Toronto?' a man asks us.

'No,' I say worriedly.

'Oh good,' he says, getting a French phrase book out of his pocket. He starts to read, turning the pages faster and faster.

James' tightness seems to be dissipating now that we are off the aeroplane. 'I'm sorry,' he says at last. 'I couldn't do it.'

'You should have told me you were afraid.'

'I know.' A huge sadness settles over him. 'I messed it up, didn't I?'

I put my arm through his. 'Let's have some breakfast.'

The Japanese remain on the bus when we get off, and continue towards their unknown destination. In a café, we order croissants and rolls and jam and coffee. We eat in silence for a while and I think about our empty seats flying across the Atlantic without us.

'Do you think those men were gangsters?' says James, taking a second croissant. 'Twin gangsters.'

'I don't think the pilot believed in them.'

He looks at me and we both start to giggle. 'Well,' I say, 'he was our pilot, so he should know.'

James wipes the tears from his eyes, and then starts to laugh again. 'Did you see – ?' He has to stop to try and control his voice.

'The bra?' I say. 'I hope she realizes sooner rather than later.'

We gradually calm down and the giggles subside. 'What are we going to tell people when they find we haven't gone away at all?'

'Do we have to tell them?'

I think of my father splashing paint on to his canvas, not really noticing if we're there or not; Paul, looking at us cynically, finding the whole situation hilarious; Adrian trying to make us understand that it was inevitable. 'No,' I say. 'Let's not tell them.'

'We don't have to go back home,' says James. 'We could stay in London instead.'

So that's what we do. We buy clothes and books and suitcases to put them in, and then find a hotel. We go to the Planetarium, Madame Tussaud's, the British Museum; a tour of London on an open-topped bus and a river trip up the Thames. Photographs by the Houses of Parliament, St Paul's, Westminster Abbey, postcards which we send to ourselves at home. We're like children again, doing all the treats, having fun in a way that you forget once you're an adult.

And every night before we go to bed, we talk. James talks about his fear of flying. 'I thought I could do it with you there.'

I've never before understood that I too can be needed and wanted. I've been the youngest child for so long that I've never seen myself in any other way. I like this new role.

We nearly talk about the baby. But we don't – not quite.

Then, after a week, we go home.

We decide to live in the same flat for a while, to bring back with us some of the fun we had in London.

We both try. I cook, James washes up. Then he cooks and I wash up except I don't do it carefully enough and he does it all again, wiping up immediately and organizing the china in the cupboard so that it looks like an illustration in a catalogue. The china belongs to us both, a wedding present from his parents. Royal Doulton. Delicate, fragile bone china, white with red and gold round the edges. It fits well into James' flat where it can sit untroubled by nightmares of breakage.

I try to stack my books neatly. He tries to scatter his disks carelessly on the coffee table, but even his random patterns are calculated. I have discovered that there is shape, an order in everything he does, so that when he picks them back up again, he knows immediately where they all are.

Then, one evening, he gets up and fiddles with the curtains that I have just drawn. They don't quite meet in the middle. He has to open the curtains and close them again, so that they hang symmetrically.

I watch him and a great pain opens up inside me. I get up, gathering all my books and papers in a pile. He watches me without a word.

'I think I'll go home for a bit,' I say.

He nods and walks with me to the door, picking up the pencils as I drop them. I look at him, his bouncy hair and his carefully composed face, and wonder if he feels as desolate as I do.

4

Feeding the Rhododendrons

Now that I am home, surrounded by my own silence, I can wander through the muddle of my life without trying so hard to produce a pleasing image of myself for James.

Whenever I'm on my own like this, I like to think about Dinah, my sister. She's fifteen years older than me, and doesn't even know of my existence. She ran away with the raggle-taggle gypsies.

I wonder if she left because she needed to make her own space. Like me leaving my father, and then not moving in with James.

Am I like her? Does she ever wish she could come home? It's even harder to find pictures of her than of my mother. There is just one – of all the children except me, because I hadn't been born. On the back of the frame, it says 'Summer 1963', in a clear round handwriting that I believe is my mother's. The children are listed with their ages. Five children. And then she had me. She must have loved children.

I know this photograph by heart. The three younger children are sitting on chairs at the front with Dinah and Adrian standing behind. It's rather formal. Jake, Martin and Paul have been placed close together, leaning against each other, tense with the touching they've been forced to endure. Jake and Martin are ten, and put next to each other because they are twins, although you would never know this. Martin is already much bigger than he should be at ten, and you can see the muscles in his arms and the slightly confused expression he still has today.

Jake looks like a little gnome. His face is delicately and artistically structured, framed with large, sticking-out ears, and his dark eyes stare away from the photographer, slightly feverish. He must be in the middle of a cold as he has a shiny nose.

Paul, at eight, looks healthy, and older than Jake. There is no sign of his domed forehead, or all those brains that are meant to be inside. He doesn't look clever at all. I think the photographer made a mistake and thought that Martin and Paul were the twins, and Jake the youngest. That's why he's arranged them on either side of Jake – for symmetry.

Behind, Adrian at twelve looks serious. He didn't have glasses then, and his face looks naked without their intellectual frame. He could afford contact lenses now, but presumably he prefers to cultivate the practical, sensible look that comes from wearing glasses. He has his right hand on the inside shoulder of Paul.

Dinah stands next to him, and she ought to have her left hand on Martin's shoulder. But she doesn't, and it's that one act of rebellion that fascinates me.

The boys look connected, related, by the physical contact between them. And because of this connection, you can see the family resemblance too – the slightly long noses, olive skin, the tilt of the mouth to one side and the very slightly cleft chin.

Dinah doesn't belong to them. She is standing slightly back from the others, so there is space round her, and she stares directly into the camera. She's fourteen, two years older than Adrian, and there's an independent look about her. She knows who she is, what she wants, and she won't be pushed into anything. I think often of her two hands hanging down by her sides, of the distance between her and the boys, and I realize that she is stronger and cleverer than all of them, because she makes no concessions. She won't pretend to be what she is not.

When I was fourteen, the same age as Dinah in the photograph, I decided that I needed to know more about her. I wrote 'DINAH' on the cover of an exercise book in big black letters and underneath, in brackets: '(PRIVATE. DO NOT OPEN)'.

I went to my father first. He was painting at the time, of course, but when I mentioned Dinah, he stopped abruptly and scratched his head. 'Did someone speak?' he said.

I realized I'd chosen a bad day. He didn't always like being interrupted. 'Nobody ever tells me anything,' I said.

He started painting again, without turning around. 'Dinah? Wasn't that Alice in Wonderland's cat? Do cats eat bats? Do bats eat cats?'

I tried again. 'Dad, what really happened to her?'

He ignored the question. 'There is a clear cat connection here. Cat, kittens, Kitty.'

I rose to my feet. 'Thanks a lot,' I said and slammed the door.

I went back to my room and opened the first page of my exercise book. At the top of the page, I had written 'Dad'. I found a pencil and put a diagonal line across the page.

Jake was in bed with tonsillitis. I ran down the road to buy him a newspaper and some sweets. Sherbet lemons. Pineapple chunks.

'Hello,' I said, putting the newspaper on the bed beside his mound of bedclothes, and went to open the curtains. 'It's too dark in here,' I said loudly, as if he would pay more attention to me if I raised my voice.

He rolled over and sat up, narrowing his eyes against the sudden light. The room smelled of dirty socks and sweat. I felt threatened by his germs and opened the window to give them a chance to escape.

'Kitty,' he muttered. 'Shut the window. I'm ill.'

'You're always ill,' I said, and left the window open.

I moved a chair to the bed, but not too close, then sat and looked at him. 'I'm conducting an investigation,' I said.

He looked interested. 'What into?' His black hair was greasy and lank, making his ears even more prominent than usual. His nose was red and sore, his cheeks flushed.

'Have you been taking the antibiotics?' I asked.

He nodded. 'What are you investigating? The effectiveness of antibiotics? Don't bother. Sometimes they work, sometimes they don't. What more is there to know?'

I ignored him, crossed my legs and opened my exercise book. I picked up my pencil and sat poised, rather as I thought a journalist should look. 'Dinah,' I said.

'Dinah? You're asking me about Dinah?' he said, looking baffled.

'I want you to tell me about her.'

He lay back and looked at the ceiling. 'I don't know anything about her.'

I could see he was just being lazy. 'You were twelve when she ran away. You must remember something about her.'

'She was a bully,' he said eventually, and smiled with a peculiar satisfaction.

I was taken aback by this. I had an image of her in my mind: strong, fearless, daring, but not selfish in her superiority. I saw her as higher than her brothers, cleverer than them, but guiding them occasionally out of kindness.

'She used to pick legs off spiders.'

I relaxed. Being a bully to spiders is not a desirable quality, but it's not as bad as bullying people.

'On a Saturday when we bought our sweets, she would wait until we got home and tell me to give her half of my sweets.'

I waited. 'Did you do it?'

'Of course I did. Wouldn't you give all your sweets to someone who pulls your arm behind your back and promises to break it if you don't give in? I was a musician. I couldn't take any chances.'

I looked at him with contempt. She only bullied him because he let her. 'She was only bluffing,' I said. 'She wouldn't have really done it.'

His eyes slid past me and over to the open windows. 'She would have,' he said. 'She did it to Martin.'

Now I knew he was making it all up. Martin must have been the same size as her and much stronger. But Jake looked awkward and I didn't think he'd respond well to further interrogation. I looked out of the window at the mulberry trees where the fruit was ripening into a deep black-red. We should keep silkworms, I thought: there are enough mulberry leaves to feed an army of them. We could make a fortune. 'Why did she go?' I asked.

He shrugged. 'How should I know? Her friends were more interesting than us.' He smiled tiredly. 'She was probably right. Life was much easier after she left.' He shut his eyes and sank down on his pillows. 'Do you mind, Kitty? I feel awfully tired.'

I stared at my empty book and wondered what I should write. The investigation wasn't proving very productive. I went to the door.

'Thanks for the paper,' Jake said behind me, but I didn't acknowledge him. This small glimpse of his vulnerability, his fear of Dinah, made me uncomfortable.

I found Paul at his desk. I think he was working for a Ph.D. at the time. Every time I saw him, he walked with a curious swagger, as if his mind were elsewhere, and he talked in monosyllables. There weren't many girlfriends during this period.

'Hello,' I said.

'Hi,' he said but didn't look up from his work.

'I wanted to ask you –' I was a little nervous of him.

'Yes?' He wrote down more figures.

'About Dinah.'

He looked up while still writing. 'Diana? I went out with her for a bit – last year.' His pen slipped slightly and I was worried that I'd distracted him and made his calculations go wrong.

'Not Diana. Dinah.' I was getting fed up with everyone's inability to remember her. 'Your sister.'

'Oh,' he said and wrote down '5?n(x–4y)'. 'She left years ago.'

'Exactly,' I said. 'You knew her. I didn't. She's my sister too, you know.'

'Mmm.' He frowned and it wasn't clear if he was frowning at me, at Dinah, or at his work. 'Well, I didn't really know her. She was much older than me.'

'Of course you did. She didn't leave until you were nine.'

He sat back. 'That's true. But I didn't have a lot to do with her.'

'Jake says she was a bully.'

'Did he? I don't remember.'

I breathed a sigh of relief.

'Of course she might have been and I didn't know. Don't forget, six years is a very big age-gap when you're nine. She had her own friends, and went off with them in the end.'

'Gypsies,' I said confidently.

'No, I don't think so. What makes you think that?'

I didn't know. I just thought it was gypsies. 'Where did she go then?'

'She went off with a group of hippies – into free love, I think. They had long hair and beads and didn't wear shoes. I imagine they went to live in a commune.'

'What's a commune?'

'You know, everyone living together and sharing everything, sex mainly. I shouldn't think it lasted very long.'

'Why didn't she come home then?'

'I rather think Dad told her never to return.'

This was beginning to get interesting. I liked the idea of Dad standing on the doorstep, raising his arm in anger and shouting, 'Never darken my doorstep again.'

Paul picked up his pencil again. 'I have work to do.'

'But what was she like?'

'Like? What do you mean? She was just there and then she wasn't. It was more peaceful after she left.'

I felt somehow that Paul knew more but wasn't going to tell me. I suppose it had been a difficult time when Dinah left. I was born, and mother died – big changes in a short space of time.

Adrian wasn't much more help. He had recently married Lesley, and they spent all their spare time doing DIY, first in the house, then the garden.

'I must get this next slab down,' he panted when I arrived unannounced. 'So we can lay the turf tomorrow.'

I watched from the kitchen window as he and Lesley heaved an enormous slab into position. I thought he would be the best person to tell me about Dinah, because he was closest in age.

But when he came in, he was vague. 'I don't think about Dinah very often, I'm afraid. It's so long since she went. I certainly didn't miss her at the time.'

'Jake says she was a bully.'

He shrugged. 'She didn't bully me, but then she wouldn't have, would she? I was bigger than her. There's a photograph of her, in the sitting room, all of us together. Except you, of course.'

'I know,' I said. Obviously. 'Why aren't there any others of Dinah?'

'I think Dad threw them away when she left. He was angry.'

'Was he angry with Mother too?'

'Sorry?'

'Well, there aren't any photographs of her either, are there?'

'Interesting thought.' He filled the kettle. 'I suppose he was angry with her. Leaving him on his own to cope with four children.'

'Five,' I said. He had forgotten me as a baby.

He frowned, then nodded. 'Five,' he agreed.

'Why do you think she ran away?'

'I suppose it seemed romantic at the time.'

'Was she clever?'

He looked surprised. 'I don't know. She may have been, I suppose.'

He started to make the tea. 'Look, I hardly remember her. When we were little, we played together, but it wasn't very successful because we both wanted to be in charge. Then we had different friends and only met at mealtimes. When she got older, she shouted a lot, threw things around, and one day she left. She hung around with a group of dodgy people who had a van – you know, a motor-caravan – painted pink with distorted question marks all over it in lurid colours. Rather like Salvador Dali –' The kettle boiled and he poured it into the teapot. 'Kitty, what's the matter?'

I couldn't think. My mind was racing. The question marks were green and yellow and orange and the colours went spiralling through the pink background as if they were snakes, huge and swollen and somehow disturbing. I knew the van that had taken Dinah away.

I went home to find Martin, who was ironing his shirts.

'Martin,' I said, perching on the arm of the sofa opposite

the ironing board, 'you know the van that Dinah went away in?'

He nodded absent-mindedly.

'I've seen it.'

'Mmm.'

'Listen, Martin. I know it. I've actually seen it.'

He smoothed a sleeve with his hand before ironing. 'You can't have, Kitty. You weren't born when she left.'

'I know, I know, but I've seen it.'

He didn't reply. He was guiding the iron between the buttons – very, very slowly.

'Why do I know what it looks like, Martin?' I said miserably.

He shook his head. 'I don't know. Maybe you've seen one like it. Lots of people had vans then.'

'Do you think they came back? Dinah and her friends?'

He stopped ironing and looked at me closely, apparently thinking hard. But you can't tell with Martin. Sometimes he's not thinking at all. 'No,' he said. 'They didn't come back.'

He started on the collar.

'Did she break your arm, Martin?'

He looked puzzled, but continued ironing. 'Who?'

'Dinah. Jake says she did.'

He looked at me again, vaguely puzzled. 'Well, I did break my arm, but I can't remember how it happened. We were playing, I think, on holiday near the sea, and I fell several feet off the cliff.'

'Did she twist it – your arm?'

He frowned. 'I don't know. I just remember that I had to go to hospital. Let me get on with this, Kitty. I'll talk to you later.'

But I didn't go back. I wasn't happy with my information. There was something about it all that made me uneasy. I wrote nothing in my exercise book. I kept thinking about

118

the van, and each time I did, my stomach churned, I started to sweat and felt ill.

These conversations took place a long time ago. What I really learned was not about Dinah, but about my brothers. They were completely isolated from each other – and still are. Families are supposed to have an inner closeness, a network of roots that go deep down into the soil and connect – a collective memory. What happened to the Wellington connection? Has someone dug down there below the soil with secateurs and snipped them all apart, so the plants on the surface grow independently of each other? Have they become so absorbed in their present lives that they have dismissed the past completely?

Since then, I have learned to live with the image of the kaleidoscope van without becoming so agitated, and I have gradually allowed Dinah to exist in the same shadowy place that she is in for everybody else.

I have a backlog of books to work on, so I start at the top of the pile and read and read and read. I occasionally watch myself objectively, as if from the ceiling, and wonder why I can't keep still. I'm on the move all the time, rolling over and leaning on alternate arms, sitting up, lying down, crouching, twisting, turning. Sometimes I read all night, typing up my comments as the early morning sun creeps bleakly into my cold sitting room. I don't know the time, I don't eat. Twice I sneak out in the late afternoon, furtively watching James' door, afraid he will come out and we'll have to talk. I post the completed manuscripts back with my pithy, authoritative comments, and I know it is not my opinions that come out, but some alter ego within me. An intellect without a body, a mind without emotion. Then I buy a loaf of bread from the corner shop and run back into my flat, grabbing the next manuscript from the shelf by the door and read walking around, eating bread and jam.

A third time, I leave the flat on impulse, run down one flight of stairs and knock on Miss Newman's door. As I stand there, I realize that I don't know the time of day.

The door opens and Miss Newman peers out. 'Kitty,' she says, and she seems pleased to see me. 'Come in.'

I follow her into her flat, which is overflowing with pictures and ornaments that she's collected over seventy-five years. The furniture is dark and heavy, there are twisted overgrown plants and thick curtains. An enormous wooden trunk stands in the hall, with figures of monkeys and exotic trees carved deeply into the dark, almost black wood.

'It's Indian,' she told me once. 'I was born in India and lived there for many years.'

I like to imagine her as a baby, waking and crying in the heat, a mosquito net round her bed, peacocks in the garden. She came home with the end of the Empire and never went back. She doesn't put her Indian mementos out for inspection. She keeps them all in her trunk.

'That trunk is very precious,' she says.

I long to open the lid and look.

I follow her into the kitchen. She is small and frail, her white hair thinning at the back, pink scalp showing through. It reminds me of a baby, and it surprises me to be confronted so graphically with the inevitable, circular shape of our lives. This baby must be travelling around with us, always there, lurking beneath the skin, biding its time, waiting to resurface. I would like to be a baby again. No more decisions, no need to go forward any more.

She opens a cupboard and carefully removes two cups and saucers, which she places side by side on a tray, each with a silver teaspoon. The cups and saucers are made of wafer-thin bone china, vivid with flourishes of deep pink roses on a white background and edged with gold. They are very beautiful and I know she has a whole set. She always puts a milk jug and a sugar bowl on the tray even though I don't take sugar: a social grace that she has brought with her from her pre-war generation. She places everything on the tray very slowly and with great care. She treats the china with enormous respect.

We go into her sitting room and she carries the tray because she is more careful than me. We sit opposite each other and smile.

'There,' she says, 'just a few minutes for the tea to brew.'

She makes tea properly, warming the pot, using loose tea, not teabags, keeping it warm with a tea cosy. When she pours, the water comes out eagerly in a perfect light brown arc, and the sound of it filling the cup, gurgling gently, reminds me of something – my grandparents in Lyme Regis? breakfast with my father and Martin? It makes me want to cry.

'I haven't heard you much recently,' she says. She's directly under James' flat. I often wonder what she can hear.

'No. We've both been working hard this week.'

We smile at each other. She smiles like a child, tentatively, watching for my smile first.

'So what are you doing?'

'Reading.' She never believes me.

'Well, how strange. When I was a girl, reading was considered to be a waste of time. "You're squandering your life away," my mother used to say if she found me reading.'

'It's a good thing we're more enlightened now.'

For some reason, she finds this funny and we laugh together. We have this conversation every time. I know how it starts and I know how it finishes; the routine is reassuring.

'Have some shortbread.' She hands me the plate with a doily on it and five pieces of shortbread arranged in a star shape. I take a piece and bite into it, waiting for her to start talking.

She chatters without prompting. 'We lived in the country, you know. Jack and I were courting just before he signed up. He wrote me some lovely letters – but not so many when he was flying. He was killing people, you see, and he didn't like it very much. It upset him. He came home on leave once, and they had a dance in the village hall for him. There was a theme – Dancing for Victory – and my mum fixed me up in a Union Jack dress. She swapped thirty tomatoes from our allotment for some parachute silk, and we painted the dress with red and blue crosses. It rained on the way home and the colours ran, all down my legs. But it didn't matter because I had danced with Jack. He didn't talk much when he came back . . .'

She's like a tape-recorder. You press 'play' and everything starts to come out.

'We knew how to enjoy ourselves then and we didn't need much money. Nothing to spend it on. My Jack's dead now, of course, shot down in the Battle of Britain.'

She's told me this before, many, many times, but I've recently realized that there's something wrong. If she stayed in India until the end of the Empire, she can't have been in England for the Battle of Britain. I went to the library and checked the dates in the *Encyclopedia Britannica*. I've tried to question her, to establish which event is truth and which fantasy. But she is convinced of both stories and she can produce the memories, the sights, the smells – they're locked into her memory in cinematic detail.

Miss Newman gets Jack's photograph down from the wall and holds it, gaining comfort from the physical contact. Then she passes it to me.

I look at the two of them together, each holding a bicycle, the two front wheels making a V-sign at the front of the picture. It's impossible to tell where they are – just a road and some indistinct sepia bushes in the background. She shows me this photograph each time and I know every detail, but I still like to look again. There is something satisfying about a happy memory, when everything was bright and exciting. Somewhere you can retreat to, where you know nothing will change. A place of safety, where everything is certain, the details already mapped out.

I look at Miss Newman now. She's thin and shapeless, her skin drooping slackly over her elderly bones. She covers her shapelessness with a plain silk dress which drapes flatteringly downwards, covering most of her unused body, in sympathy with her deceptive vision of the past.

In the photograph, she's lovely. Young and sweet-faced, smooth, fresh. She is smiling, wearing lipstick, her curled hair clipped up; smart, but somehow innocent. I compare her image of today with the photograph of yesterday, straining to find a resemblance in the nose, the curl of the hair, the sparkle in the eye, but failing every time. I look at Jack and wonder if he was ever as she saw him.

I hand the photograph back and she replaces it on the wall. 'I was sorting through some old letters yesterday,' she says, 'and I found the poetry that Jack wrote for me.'

She pauses and I wait. We haven't had this conversation before.

'I don't think I will show you, dear.' She lowers her eyes coyly. 'It is too private to show anyone else.'

'Of course,' I say.

'They didn't all go up willingly in the Battle of Britain,' she says. 'Jack told me that some of the young men had to be forced into their aeroplanes, crying. It wasn't like the films.'

I have heard this before.

'Of course, Jack found it difficult too, but he followed orders. He knew where his duty lay.'

I sometimes think she hesitates before she says it, as if she's pushing away a darker, more truthful picture.

'Such beautiful poetry,' she says.

If Jack had lived, his patriotism might have turned to prejudice. He might spend his time at the golf club, drinking double whiskies, fighting a rearguard action against immigration, having affairs with a succession of secretaries, and she would be trying to stay cheerful, knowing all about his indiscretions. She's better off with a memory.

'Did he write many letters?' I ask.

'Oh yes, dear. I kept everything. I've got a box full of Jack's things – his medals, other photographs. His senior officer sent them to me when he died, because he left a letter telling them what to do with his private possessions. His parents were annoyed – they thought they should have them. But I didn't give in to them. I knew his last thoughts would have been about me.' She folds her hands carefully on her lap and I catch a glimpse of that stubborn girl who wouldn't give in.

Jack's life in a box, I think, and then something occurs to

me. There could be a box with my mother's life in it some-where.

Miss Newman talks on, but I'm no longer listening. Would my father really have destroyed all traces of my mother? Maybe he has more of her hidden away. There might be a box in the attic which would reconstruct her and tell me about her.

'We never argued: there wasn't time,' says Miss Newman. 'Do you know, I remember more about that period of my life than the things I did yesterday. His mother was dying of cancer at the time, but she was still busy, organizing fêtes, running committees.'

I make myself concentrate. I imagine the cake stalls in the garden, under the marquee, the committee meetings in the village hall, Jack's mother smiling graciously as she bullied everyone into doing what she wanted. Miss Newman treasuring Jack's medals, believing he thought only of her. Don't men think of their mothers when they think they're going to die?

'They did a scan, you know. She had to lie very still and they pushed her through this machine while they looked at the pictures of her brain.'

She's gone wrong again. Muddling her own memories with *Coronation Street* or *EastEnders*. Perhaps none of her memories are correct. Does it matter if she weaves false memories with the true, embroidering the story, losing the thread in the middle, twisting it round in the wrong direction? Maybe all memories are like this, a core of truth, suffused with a golden glow, becoming more pleasurable the more they wander.

I wait a bit longer and listen to her talking. When I finally remember to look at the clock on the mantelpiece, I see that it says 8.30. A strange time to be having tea and cake, whether it is morning or evening. 'I have to get back,' I say. 'I have so much to do.'

She comes to the door with me. 'It was lovely to see you, Kitty. Do come again.'

'Thank you for the tea.'

We walk into the hall, and I fight my usual desire to open the trunk and see all her Indian life packed away. As we stand there, she remembers something. 'Wait a minute,' she says, and disappears abruptly into the kitchen. I hesitate for two seconds. Then I bend over and hastily lift the trunk lid – it is heavier than I expected – and shut it again immediately.

It's empty.

Miss Newman comes back with a tidy parcel of short-bread in a paper napkin and presses it into my hand. 'Something for later,' she says.

'Thank you,' I say.

Now I know why she talks more about Jack and less about India. She has lost her memories of India.

She stands at the door, watching me climb the stairs. 'Goodbye, Kitty.' She is waving.

I turn back and wave. I don't call out in case James hears me and comes out.

I find it difficult to settle after this. My mind, which has been leaping through the last few days, letting me read quickly and think analytically, has suddenly braked. I know why. It's the thought of finding out more of my mother's life. I like this idea of a person being contained in a box. Better than a few unidentifiable ashes in an urn. There are boxes and boxes of papers in the attic of Tennyson Drive, amongst forgotten furniture and spiders' webs. I don't like going up there, but I intend to try.

I want to go immediately, but know I should slow down and approach it cautiously. I need a time when nobody is home, which is almost impossible. I need an excuse to go up there, but I can't think of one.

The doorbell rings and makes me jump. James waits all this time to speak to me and when he finally gets here, he rings the doorbell. He has a key. He can come in any time he wants to. I wish he would learn to be spontaneous.

I open the door, and there he is looking foolish, holding a Tesco's carrier bag.

'You've got to go for your doctor's appointment,' he says. 'I thought we could eat together afterwards.'

'What do you mean, *I* have to go? I thought it was *we*?'

He coughs and looks at the floor. 'I rang up and told them I won't be coming.'

Anger rises inside me, boiling up from my stomach and branching out in all directions, making my feet, my hands, the tip of my nose throb with the desire to scream at him. 'She wants to see you too,' I say slowly, my voice shaking.

'I know,' he says.

I want to put my hands round his neck and shake him. I want to shout at him, bully him, force him to come with me. How can I face Dr Cross without him?

'Kitty –' he says.

'What?'

'I can't.' He looks up and I see that it upsets him nearly as much as it does me.

My anger fizzles like air out of a balloon, and I sag with exhaustion. 'So much for twenty-first-century enlightened man. You're not supposed to have inhibitions these days.'

He spreads his arms, too ready to surrender. 'I'm a failure. I'm sorry.'

I pull him inside the flat and put my arms round him. 'Only half a failure. At least you can cook the meal while I'm gone.'

'Don't you want me to walk you there?'

'No. I'll go on my own. I want to eat as soon as I get back.'

He follows me into the kitchen with his groceries and

looks at my rows of dirty coffee cups. He picks up a pile of books on the kitchen table and stacks them neatly, corners lined up, spines all facing in the same direction. Then he goes over to the sink and starts to run the hot water. He picks up the washing-up liquid from the window sill, squeezes it and puts it back in the cupboard under the sink. He won't start cooking until the kitchen is clean.

'What time is the appointment?' I ask.

'Half an hour's time.'

I don't know why he won't talk about Henry or even say his name. It's as if he has to be cushioned with emotional cotton wool, to protect himself from all the rage he can't touch. Real anger is too messy for him. Once it's out in the open, it can't easily be tidied away. Or maybe he's got so used to protecting me that he can't break out of the habit.

It's a good thing he came. I had no idea what day it was. But, of course, he knew that.

Dr Cross's room is tidy, like James' flat, but more occupied and attractive. There is a picture on the wall, a Matisse print of apples. The light is exactly right. The room occupies the middle condition between James' flat and mine. Normality, I suppose.

'He wouldn't come,' I say as I sit down. 'I'm sorry.'

She smiles briefly. 'No, I thought he wouldn't.'

How could she possibly know? She has never met him.

'Ask him again,' she says. 'If you can learn to talk freely to each other, about the baby, it will help you both.'

She knows how we live. She knows about our next-door flats.

'I'm going to investigate my father's attic,' I say excitedly.

She has no idea what I am talking about, so she waits for the explanation. I like this patience.

'There might be things about my mother in there some-where,' I say. 'You know, letters, photographs, clothes –' I tell her about my visit to Miss Newman and the box of Jack's life.

'How much do you remember about your mother?' she asks.

'Not much. I remember a dress – a crinkly dress – and beads.' And 'A Hard Day's Night'.

'Can you remember her smell? Her colours?'

I look up quickly. How does she know I notice colours? 'I don't know –'

'Does your father talk about her?'

'Only about the times when they first met. He's angry with her – for dying.'

'How do you know?'

'Well, Adrian, I think, told me. I've asked them all about her, but they don't say anything useful. They all seem to remember a different person.'

Dr Cross sits quietly and thinks about what I have said. She doesn't look worried or concerned. 'When did you last ask anyone?' she says.

'Oh, years ago. I was only about twelve.'

'You're an adult now. Perhaps you should try again.'

'But they don't know anything. They contradict each other.'

'I'm sure that's not true. They're older than you – they must all have memories of her. They're probably thinking about her more now that they're adults and old enough to have their own children.'

She's right. I've been relying on childhood memories. It's perfectly legitimate to look at your past when you're older.

I sit with Dr Cross for a bit longer.

'Make an appointment for next week,' she says when I go.

As I walk back home, I wonder if Miss Newman has lost the truth about Jack too. Maybe the box of his life is as empty as the trunk of India.

129

I check my watch as I leave the surgery and I'm delighted to see that it's only 3.15. There's time for a detour. I have five minutes, and I'm not sure if I'm going to make it, so I start to run.

I can see the school gates before I get there. The children are beginning to come out, so I slow down. I won't see Rosie – she goes to nursery school and is picked up separately – but I am hoping for a glimpse of Emily. I stand on the corner of the pavement watching the children. My mind jumps back to my yellow period, waiting outside the school for Henry – who wasn't there. I think of Hélène. Is she is still in England, meeting her two children every day, while Emily comes running out here in Harborne? There is an elusive fluttering sensation deep inside me that leaps perpetually out of reach whenever I try to approach it.

I recognize the child-minder who picks up Emily. Her name is Theresa and she collects several children. No welcoming mother for Emily when she comes out of school. No Lesley ready to hear the stories of the day. How can Lesley do this? How can she bear to miss any time with Emily and Rosie, and not hear everything they have to say? They must forget so much before they see her: all those thoughts that they'll never have again.

Emily comes out, skipping with another girl, hand in hand. Her hair gleams like polished gold – one moment still and dense as she pauses, the next shivering and disintegrating into a thousand glittering pieces as she dances over the paving stones.

She's nearly level with me before she sees me. She stops and opens her mouth to speak, but I shake my head and put a finger to my lips. The other girl skips ahead without her. Emily and I stand looking at each other for a few seconds. She smiles shyly, but makes no further attempt to speak.

I smile at her, and then raise my hand. I kiss my fingers, blow the kiss towards her and turn away. I don't want to see her catching up with the others, skipping away from me.

As I turn, I nearly fall over a little boy with an apple in his hand. He's stopped to examine it, moving it round in his hands as if he doesn't know what to do with it. His mother is ahead. She stops and looks back at him.

'Harry!' she calls. He ignores her, so she comes back for him. 'Come on, Henry,' she says. 'Do hurry up. Thomas is coming to play.'

I go home to James, who is an expert at producing meals at strange times. He somehow knows when I need food. He adapts to my irregular eating habits, irritated by the messiness of it all, but prepared to be tolerant.

'You look cheerful,' he says as I come in, exhilarated by my illicit contact with Emily. 'How did it go?'

For two seconds I don't know what he is talking about. Then I remember Dr Cross. 'Fine,' I say.

'Have you been taking the pills?'

I put a finger casually into his sauce and lick it. 'You should be a chef,' I say. 'You're wasted on computers.'

He moves the saucepan out of my reach. He wages war against germs as obsessively as his parents. That's one of the big advantages of being surrounded by the sterile empty spaces of his flat. There's nowhere for the germs to go. They can't creep up on you unexpectedly.

'We've got to talk about Henry,' I say suddenly, deciding that I will creep up on him unexpectedly instead.

He says nothing and stirs his sauce as if I'm not there.

'Our baby,' I say, putting my mouth close to his ear. 'In case you've forgotten him. We have to talk about the baby who never was. You are the father of a dead baby who will never grow up. We'll never have to pay a fortune for

Startrite shoes with an F fitting. He'll never read *Winnie the Pooh*, never have smelly feet, never play his music too loud, never make us watch football on TV, never struggle over simultaneous equations. He will never marry someone we don't approve of, never give us grandchildren –'

I stop. There are so many things in my head that he'll never do that I can't cope with them all. I want to stop and examine each one in detail, but I can't. It would take a lifetime to go through them all. A lifetime that will never happen.

James puts down the spoon that he is using to stir the sauce, puts a lid on the saucepan, leaving a small gap for the steam to escape, and turns the gas down. Then he puts his arm round me and leads me to the living room where I sit down heavily on my battered sofa.

'Why won't you talk about him?' I ask, and my eyes fill with tears.

He doesn't sit with me. He stands and looks out of the window at the same patterns of Edgbaston trees that can be seen from my father's studio. 'Because –'

Because you spent all those years before you met me not talking, not learning how to express yourself, hiding behind your aggression and your computer. Because you're a coward. You're stuck in the old stiff upper-lip way, however hard you try to persuade me otherwise.

'How am I supposed to have an argument when you won't speak?' I say.

He sighs and remains still. Then he turns back to the kitchen.

'How about a career move?' I shout to the empty air. 'You'd get on really well with deaf people. You could learn sign language. That would be useful.'

My father is mowing the lawn when I arrive. I go upstairs to the first floor and look out of the window on the landing. He is manifesting his usual fury with the lawn mower, swinging it round viciously, and his mouth is moving up and down as he talks to himself. I know he is reciting lists of plants. I've heard him do this many times: buddleia, potentilla, rhododendrons, ceanothus, lavender, hydrangea . . . After a while, he'll put them into alphabetical order.

The plants themselves are too big and wild, tumbling out from their beds with the wet heat of the summer, blurring the edges of the lawn. Taking over the garden. My father won't mind – there's less grass to cut.

He doesn't like gardening. Sometimes he sends Martin out to do some tidying, which Martin will do in his usual amiable way, piling up the pruned branches and having a bonfire in the evening. I used to enjoy helping him when I was younger, happy with his easy acceptance, smelling the dark, brown earth, the restful scent of the bonfire. But Martin is away on a trip to Germany, and however hard he tries, my father cannot persuade Paul to go out into the fresh air. So he has to mow the lawn. He's already let the grass grow too long and it washes up in untidy piles behind him as he moves urgently through it.

Now's my chance to go into the attic. I've brought a torch, and have some excuses ready, if anyone finds me there. A broken chair that I want to renovate, my old maths books which must be up here since they don't seem to be anywhere else, old clothes for a jumble sale.

The entry is difficult. There is a step ladder behind a lumpy mattress in an unused bedroom, which smells damp and unlived in. I extract it with some difficulty and open it up under the loft entrance. It's too short. I can push the loft cover away and place my hands on the edges of the hole, but I can't pull myself up far enough. This is puzzling. I have been up here before, a long time ago, but I can't remember how I did it.

133

'You need muscles for that, Kitty.'

Paul's voice makes me jump and I nearly fall off the ladder. I look down at him and feel the sweat of embarrassment breaking out all over me, dripping down my back.

'Paul!' I say, and notice that his hair is going thin on the top of his head. I climb back down, my legs trembling.

'Whatever are you doing?' he asks. He's holding a pile of papers and looks as if he hasn't slept all night. He often brings his research work home and gets so interested that he stays up all night. The skin on his face is patchy and loose and there are dark creases under his eyes. He looks middle aged and he's only ten years older than me.

'Well,' I say. 'I wanted to have a look in the attic.'

'Whatever for? It's full of spiders and cobwebs.'

'I can cope.'

The mower is still whirring out in the garden.

'It's full of junk.'

'But it might be interesting junk.'

He looks at me and I think he can read my mind, so I surprise myself by being honest. 'I just thought I might find out something about Mother up there. In a box –' This sounds unconvincing.

He puts down his papers on a stair and looks up into the hole of the attic. He looks at the torch that I've stuffed into my pocket. 'What do you want to know?'

'Anything.'

'You could just ask someone.'

'But nobody remembers anything.'

He sits down on the top stair and frowns. 'How do you know?'

'I've asked before, you know.'

He looks perplexed. 'When?'

'Lots of times,' I say.

He rubs his eyes. 'I don't remember you asking. Ask me now. Anything you want – I'll do my best.'

I hesitate. I am torn between the chance to go into the loft without my father's knowledge and the chance to speak to Paul, who normally only ever has half a mind available for conversation and who can disappear for months at a time. But I'm all geared up for the attic and the box of memories.

Paul looks offended and picks up his papers, making my mind up for me. 'Well, if you don't think I'm any use, I'll get on. I'm very busy at the moment.'

'No,' I said. 'I do want your help. But can I come and find you later – when I've tried the loft?'

'I'll have to see,' he says and starts to walk down the stairs. 'I might not have time then.'

'I really need your help now.'

He stops.

'Could you help me climb into the loft? It's too high for me.'

He sighs, puts down his papers and comes back. Without a word, he waves me away from the ladder and takes it down. He folds it up and then opens it in a different way so that it is one long, continuous ladder that reaches right up to the loft entrance.

I feel foolish. 'I didn't know you could do that.'

'No,' he says as he walks away again. 'That's why a world inhabited only by women wouldn't work.'

'By the way,' I say, 'did you know you were going bald on top?'

He stops again. I am expecting another insult. 'Adrian has a new book due out next week.'

'Yes. So?'

'He hasn't told you then?'

'Told me what?'

'It's semi-autobiographical. We're all given parts in the book – he's changed the names, but Lesley says you can easily tell who is who. He says we were only the starting

135

point and the characters develop into new people. But how many families do we know who grew up in an extra-large house, where the father is an artist and there are four sons: a writer, a musician, an academic and a lorry driver?'

I stare at him.

'I just thought he might put something of Mummy into this purely fictional account of his early life.'

I've never heard him say Mummy before. It's difficult to believe he still thinks of her in that way, but I suppose his relationship with her stopped when he was twelve, so he can't call her anything more adult.

'By the way,' he says over his shoulder as he goes downstairs, 'I'm the academic, in case you were wondering.'

I stand at the bottom of the ladder and try to get my breath. If this is true, why hasn't Adrian told me?

Because every time I've seen him recently, he has spent most of the time telling me off for being irresponsible.

But he could have told me this. It's important.

I consider chasing after Paul, but decide not to when I hear my father still mowing in the garden. There's a lot of lawn, but it won't go on for ever.

I go up the ladder, one step at a time, unsure if I feel safe enough. I climb in and hover nervously at the loft entrance, trying to calm my breathing. Then I reach down and pull the ladder up into the loft. I don't like the idea of someone creeping up behind me.

I switch on the torch and shine it round. The loft is enormous, although a section has been bricked up to make my father's studio. In all directions, the light shines on old furniture, boxes, pictures, bags of clothes. I am appalled by the sheer quantity of everything and realize that I'll need more than an hour up here. This depresses me and makes me unwilling to even start. I should have taken up Paul's offer.

Make an effort, I tell myself, and be methodical. One box

at a time. Anything about my mother is bound to be furthest away. So, shining my torch in front of me and lighting up each section with astonishing clarity, I pick my way across the joists. Everything is stored haphazardly. Whenever anyone wanted to put more stuff up here, they simply hauled it up through the entrance and pushed the previous rejects further back.

There must be amazing things to find. The story of our lives over and over again – not just in one box, but hundreds. Momentarily distracted, I swing the torch round rapidly, expecting a high chair, a cot, a pram, but see nothing significant. It was probably given away or, more likely, sold second hand.

I stop and examine a bag, wondering if it might contain my mother's clothes. I prop the torch against a box and sort through the contents. They are boys' clothes – short trousers, braces, a tiny green and purple bow-tie on elastic. I stop and examine this. Who wore it last? Which of my brothers looked cute and intellectual in it? Adrian, who has always been serious? Jake, when performing in a concert? Paul, when he won the next round of the Maths Olympiad? Not Martin. It's the wrong colour. It wouldn't suit him. I stroke it. Henry could have worn this.

Perhaps the clothes have all been waiting here for the first boy of the next generation. I slip it into my pocket and move on.

There are boxes and boxes of bills and letters. I make an attempt to sort through one box, but it's impossible. The letters go on for ever. Letters to my father, from Lucia, Angela, Helen, Sarah, Philippa, Jennifer – who are these women who knew him so well? The dates are from before I was born. There are none more recent than thirty years ago, and none are sent to or from Margaret.

I realize that I could spend hours sorting through these letters and getting nowhere, so I shove them back into their boxes with the bills. Why does he keep them? What's the point?

I look in another box and find more letters, bills, receipts, invoices, my father's records of all his early paintings and the people who bought them.

What I am looking for is photographs. I want to see my mother when she was older, when she had me. I'm desperate to see myself as a baby being held by my mother.

I finally find a box of photographs and sift through them quickly. All the school photographs are here, including some of Dinah, who I recognize from her clear, forthright gaze; and even some of me. There are countless pictures of babies, chuckling, sleeping, crying babies. There are babies in prams, in cots, in high chairs, babies on laps, on shoulders, where the one holding the baby is hidden and anonymous, so that only a fold of dress is showing or a hand hiding coyly behind the baby's shawl. It's impossible to know who is who.

I pick one out and study it. The baby is very young, sitting propped up by a cushion covered with a lacy shawl, but slipping sideways, so her head is at a slightly uncomfortable angle, and there is a beaming smile on her face, rather as if she knows she can't sit up much longer, but will go on being happy until the last possible moment. A hand is just visible on the edge of the picture, hovering, waiting to save her. It's the photograph of a baby who knows that her mother is close by, who smiles at her mother's voice, waiting to be picked up. She has dark curly hair springing carelessly from her head. I want this baby to be me.

I eventually look on the back and see what I had missed the first time. Printed in faded lilac ink: 'Adrian 1951'.

I put the photograph away quickly and leaf through the piles in another box. I soon realize that although these date from before my mother's death, I'm not there, and neither is my mother. I rush through piles and piles of them and they are all the same. Just the boys as children, and Dinah. Why is my mother not here? It's almost as if she's not real, as if she never existed. Why am *I* not here? I search ever more frantically and find nothing.

As time passes, the light of my torch becomes yellower and less certain. I turn it off for a few seconds and listen. I can't hear the mower any more, but I can't hear anything else either. The loft is as silent as the photographs. It has nothing to say.

In the dim light from the loft entrance, I start to return the photographs to their boxes, trying to make neat piles at first, but then not bothering because it takes too long. I shovel them all up and stuff them in wherever there is a space.

There are plenty more boxes up here, gathering dust on their inaccurate memories, but I am convinced that my mother isn't here. It's as if, when she died, she took everything of herself with her. As if she knew in advance and sorted through her personal life, destroying all the evidence of her existence. She seems to have disappeared, suddenly and completely, and there is not even a hole where she was because she's bricked up the entrance.

I stand up awkwardly and find I have pins and needles in my left foot. I shake it, hanging on to a beam, until it's ready to work again. I switch on my torch and the black cavernous space shrinks behind my immediate surroundings, where boxes and joists brighten into cartoon shapes, too bold and angular to be real.

Weighed down by a curious, heavy exhaustion, I pick my way back across the joists. I have no idea how long I have been up here. It feels as if I have been on a trip to Narnia, filled with snow and the adventures of thirty years, while the world outside has blinked for a few seconds and then carried on in a normal way, bright and light and real.

I listen at the loft entrance before lowering the ladder. I

can hear nothing, so I gently ease it down to the floor and climb down.

'Kitty!'

I nearly pass out with shock and then realize it's Paul again. 'Will you stop doing that?'

He helps me fold the ladder and store it behind the mattress in the spare room. 'Find anything?'

I shake my head. 'You'd think she never existed.'

'That's what I thought.'

'You might have said so.'

'Not really. You needed to find out for yourself.'

'How long have I been up there?'

He looks at his watch. 'A couple of hours, I would think.' He leads me down the stairs. 'Come and have a coffee.'

I follow him, confused by his friendliness. It's not normal. Maybe he's run out of girlfriends. Maybe I am being given a glimpse of the mysterious charm that attracts the girlfriends in the first place.

I watch him make coffee, putting the kettle on the old Aga, rooting around in the cupboard for clean mugs.

'You seem very cheerful,' I say.

He looks at me in surprise. 'Do I? Oh, sorry.'

He starts to pour coffee granules into the mugs because he can't find any spoons. 'I knew you wouldn't find anything in the attic. After Mummy died, Dad took all her clothes, photographs, letters into the garden and had a huge bonfire. It lasted all day. He rushed backwards and forwards with armfuls of stuff, shouting to himself, dancing round the bonfire for hours until it all died down. We stayed in the house watching bits of ash shooting off into the sky, settling all over the garden. I think he took the ashes a few days later and dug them into the soil round the rhododendrons.'

Feeding the plants with my mother's memories. I'll never

look at the rhododendrons in the same way again. 'Why didn't you tell me this before?'

He pours water from the kettle into the mugs, his face away from me. 'I wasn't sure you wanted to know.'

'Did you go to the funeral? Did he dig in Mother's ashes as well as her things?'

Paul hesitates, holding the kettle over the mugs, but no longer pouring. 'There wasn't a funeral,' he says. 'Or if there was, we didn't go. We weren't told.'

I look at his back and see in his rigidity a great sadness, an incomplete grief.

'Nobody ever told me that,' I say in amazement. They all knew there hadn't been a funeral and no one has thought to mention it.

My father comes bursting in through the kitchen door, smelling of freshly mown grass, his crimson bow-tie crooked, grass stains on his shirt.

'Kitty! Why didn't you tell me you were here?'

'Just in time for coffee,' I say, searching for another clean mug to give to Paul.

But when I turn around, Paul is gone and he has left the two mugs of coffee on the edge of the Aga, steam rising from them and circling in the dusty, empty air.

I wonder how someone as small as Dr Cross could help me. Surely, there won't be enough of her to go round. She has short hair, soft and feathered, and it makes her look somehow fragile. What if she doesn't survive, if she's too gentle for today's world, if she can't go on being there?

My appointment is for twenty minutes – she always tells me to book a double appointment. When I am sitting with her, my mind slows down and I start to think properly. Sometimes we say almost nothing, but when I get up to leave, everything seems slightly easier, less muddled. I wonder why I stopped going to see her before.

'Suzy's going to have a baby,' I say.

'I thought there was some doubt about this.'

'Oh no. She's definitely pregnant. I expect she'll tell everyone soon and they'll all start knitting.'

I'm not sure who will start knitting. There aren't enough women in our family to care for babies. I bend down to my bag and pull out a ball of wool. 'Look. I bought cream. Then it doesn't matter if it's a boy or girl.'

'Which would you prefer? A nephew or another niece?'

A niece, I think. 'A nephew,' I say. All the babies related to me should be girls.

'Do you do much knitting?'

'Occasionally,' I say. Actually, I can't knit. There was never anybody to teach me. I just saw the pattern in the window of a local shop and bought it. The wool is a baby colour – warm, creamy, rich. I'll teach myself to knit because of this wool. Sometimes I put my hand secretly into my bag and feel it, smoothing my fingers along the folded strands, touching the living, throbbing colour. When I'm on my own, I take the wool out and hold it to my face to smell its newness and feel its texture with my lips, the part of me that can pick up the baby softness with most accuracy.

'What does James think about Suzy's baby?'

'I don't know. He didn't believe me when I told him.'

'Do you tell him what we talk about?'

I look at her in surprise. 'No. I don't think he'd be interested.' I never offer him information – his refusal to ask is his way of being supportive.

She says nothing and we sit quietly.

'It's a bit peculiar, isn't it?' I say. 'I don't suppose you know many married couples who live next door to each other.' I've probably said this to her before, but I can't remember her response.

'Does it matter?' she says. 'Does it make your relation-ship any less valid?'

I let the wool drop into my lap. 'Don't you think it's a bit – unethical to have two homes?'

'People live temporarily apart from each other for all sorts of reasons – jobs, family obligations. Things still work if you want them to.'

I need to think about this. I've always assumed that married people shouldn't be next-door neighbours. Most couples I know blend and merge when they marry, take each other's colours and become stronger. Like Adrian and Lesley, who are always apparently in harmony. Or Jake and Suzy. James and I don't seem to have worked out how to do that permanently, so our colours only combine for short periods of time, then easily divide back into two halves which exist next door to each other.

I walk home quickly. We're expecting James' parents for supper and Adrian said he would bring round his latest book, the autobiographical one, that might tell me something about our mother. He always gives me a copy as soon as he gets them, because I'm his little sister. The others have to go and buy their copies from a bookshop so that he can earn royalties. I'm the only one who will definitely read it and give a considered opinion. Martin will try, but he finds reading laborious and probably won't finish it, although he'll never admit this. He carries each book round in his lorry for about six months and then it mysteriously disappears.

Paul might read it so that he can offer criticism, which is usually brutal and possibly a little spiteful. I think Adrian accepts his comments with good grace, but pays little attention to them. Jake and Suzy read the books because they feel they should, but they don't realize that they could read them on a deeper level. Suzy takes things too literally – she is, after all, committed to mortgages, investments and insurance policies – and can't see the point of fiction. Jake says he doesn't have time for reading, but he'll try to read his brother's books if nothing else. This means he has nothing to compare them with. They're just isolated periods of escapism in his largely aural world.

Lesley reads them, of course. But since Adrian dedicates every book to her – in different words each time – she doesn't really have an option.

My father never reads books, not even the cookery books he keeps buying. He doesn't pretend to. 'Waste of time making up stories while the world gets on with living,' he says. 'Much too time-consuming. If you like a work of art, you stop and look for – what? – ten minutes maximum. A symphony takes an hour, a piano sonata half an hour. Think how much you can see and hear in the time you give to a book.'

Adrian doesn't argue. He says it's not important. 'If Dad never reads any books, he's not singling out mine for special criticism, is he?'

He said this to me a long time ago and I thought he was happy about it, but he still offers each book to Dad. Not personally – he leaves it on the hall table, or on the stairs leading up to Dad's studio, or in the glove compartment in Dad's car. They remain untouched for weeks until Adrian removes them in such an unobtrusive way that it takes me some time to realize they are no longer there.

'Why bother?' I asked him once. 'You know he's not going to read it.'

He shrugged. 'He might change his mind. I like to give him the chance.'

Does he secretly long for his father's approval? I watch him and wonder if all this mature, eldest brother act, encased and sellotaped down by responsible, diplomatic manoeuvring, is hiding an uglier, more private bruising. The child who lost his mother without saying goodbye, and would like his father to be proud of him.

I let myself into James' flat and find Adrian's book waiting for me on the hall table. The picture on the front cover looks vaguely familiar – four boys and a girl looking solemnly outwards – and, after a few seconds, I recognize the grouping from the photograph in the living room. It's not the actual photograph, but it's very much like it. The girl stands behind independently, like Dinah, and there's a circle round the boy who's in exactly the same position as Adrian in the photograph. The title is written in big purple letters: *Lost Boys* by Adrian Wellington.

I open the book and the newness of the pages breathes out at me. I would always have books around me even if I were blind. I need the smell.

'Kitty!' calls James and comes into the hall. 'Oh yes, Adrian dropped it in.'

James will read it after me. Carefully and precisely – he'll have opinions that differ from mine. We'll argue about it.

'Don't forget my parents are here for supper,' he says quietly, and leads me into the lounge. Since the wedding he's bought a white leather sofa so that he can entertain more than one person, although he never does unless his parents come, which is rare. By his standards, the room looks cluttered with the four of us and the sofa.

His parents are sitting opposite each other in the single chairs, sipping sherry. They rise as we come in, holding their glasses, because James has inexplicably removed the table, and his mother, Alison, moves towards me in an attempt to kiss my cheek. Her lips just miss, gliding smoothly past me, as usual, but at least we make a pretence at being civilized. His father, Jeremy, hovers in the background and smiles benevolently. He is a good-looking man with the same physical ingredients as James, more aesthetically distributed. He's tall and symmetrical. 'Looking well, Kitty,' he says. He always says this. He doesn't cope easily with illness, unless it's one he can operate on. Then he can move in smoothly and profession-ally and take over. There was nothing he could do when Henry died, so he moved back a step and smiled. He couldn't sew my womb back in again, or mend the baby. He was no use at all.

We sit down and James goes back to the kitchen to see to the supper.

'So how are you, Kitty?' says Alison.

'Fine,' I say. 'Fine.'

She tries very hard. She has no daughters – only me, a daughter-in-law – and she wants us to be friends. 'I see Adrian has a new book out.'

'Yes,' I say and show her the book. I would prefer not to give it to her until I have leafed through it, because I like the sense of the book being fresh and untouched when I read it. But she has stretched out her hand and I have to pass it over. They're impressed by Adrian. He is my passport to acceptability, my only relative they're proud to know. They find the rest of my family bewildering, but are reassured by Adrian's sense of responsibility, his reliability, his success.

'I've read the review in the *Times*,' she says. 'They seem to think he's scaled new heights.'

'Good,' I say, annoyed that it's been read by a reviewer before me. Why has he been so slow in giving me my copy?

'I'll buy one tomorrow,' she says, handing mine back. 'If I drop it in, you will ask Adrian to sign it, won't you?'

'Of course.' They think of it as an investment, in case he dies young, or he becomes great instead of just good. A signed first edition might be quite valuable in twenty or thirty years' time.

'We're ready to eat if you are,' says James, coming into the lounge, his hair springy and defensive. He tries so hard to please them.

'How nicely you keep the flat,' says Alison, with an admiring glance round James' immaculate kitchen.

'Thank you,' I say. James has never told them that I live next door. They must think I just go there to work. They see James and me together in his flat and think we are perfectly suited. The same taste, the same high standard of hygiene.

James has cooked coq au vin. We sit in his shiny kitchen, waiting obediently while he pulls dishes out of the oven and places them in front of us. He used to ask me to pretend that I had cooked the meal, but I made such a mess of the pretending that we gave up. Now everyone knows that James cooks and cleans while I read.

We murmur politely as we help ourselves and James sorts out the wine. I watch him. What I want to know is, why did he learn to cook before he met me? Who was he feeding and trying to impress? He must have practised on someone to be as good as he is now. He denies it. 'I just follow recipes,' he says. 'Anyone could do it.' He's never yet admitted to a previous girlfriend, but I can't resist asking at odd moments.

'So how was New York?' says Alison once we are all served.

'Wonderful,' James and I say almost together, urgent and desperate to prove we were really there.

'Good,' says Alison, and we lapse into silence.

For some reason – and I don't know what that reason is – I find it difficult to make conversation with James' parents. Nothing seems to lead us into a discussion.

'Have you been watching the tennis?' James asks his father after a few seconds.

Jeremy nods and drops a slice of courgette off his fork as he raises it to his mouth. He puts the empty fork into his mouth and looks slightly bewildered when he can't find anything to chew. He brings the fork down to the plate and tries again. 'We've been playing a lot recently – in between the showers,' he says. There's a tennis court in their garden and they always dress in white to play, even when there's no one to see them.

'Jenny has come to visit Marjorie for a few days,' says Alison breezily. Marjorie lives next door to them and she's a close friend.

James pauses in his eating.

'Jenny used to be at school with James,' says Alison to me.

'Yes,' I say. 'You've mentioned them before.'

'She brought the grandchildren, Katie and Ben. Such sweet children – Katie's only nine months, of course, but crawling, and her eyes are so big and round, as if she knows everything.'

Why do they do this? It's as if they want to make believe it never happened. As if they can persuade me to do it all again, but win this time round. Maybe I should mention it, remind them of the reality: 'By the way, I lost the baby and I can't have any more' – just in case they've really forgotten.

'More wine?' says James, leaping up.

Alison and Jeremy give off this glow of respectability. Professional, affluent, middle-class people, wanting grand-children, so they can start putting money aside for their education. Perhaps they're thinking about surrogate mothers, perhaps they want to donate money to the cause. I used to think they put on this air of respectability to impress everyone, but I realize now they're really like that. Everything they show us is genuine. They never lighten or darken. They are like a smooth, beige carpet, completely neutral, calm and secure beneath our feet, able to blend easily with anyone round them, offering co-ordination, not contrast. I see beige as a non-colour.

'Have you tried jogging yet?' Jeremy asks James. He's concerned about our lack of exercise.

'No,' says James.

Jeremy jogs for an hour every morning from seven till eight, trotting round his village three times, jumping up and down on the spot while he waits for the pelican crossing. He has to do it, he says, because he sees so many clogged up arteries on his operating table, he knows the dangers.

'James finds it difficult to jog because of his leg,' I say.

They both look at me. 'He can run on it,' says Alison. 'He always took part in school sports days.'

I know about James' torture on the school's cross country runs. He was always last, except the day when he cheated with three other boys and hailed a taxi. They were dropped two hundred yards from the school gates, but the others told James to wait twenty minutes before going in, because he would give the game away. He waited, but still arrived in the first ten. The sportsmaster refused to believe he'd run all the way in the time. He didn't exactly accuse him of cheating, but James didn't get a certificate and was told to put the episode behind him.

'We're off to Australia next week,' says Alison. 'The Great Barrier Reef.'

They dive. They rise every morning at 6.45, never eat anything with sugar in it and take three holidays a year, which they use to go diving.

'You must think we all have very boring lives next to yours,' I say.

'Of course not,' says Jeremy. 'You've just been to New York. We've only ever been there for conferences.'

'Well – actually –' I say.

James interrupts. 'I thought you went to the Great Barrier Reef last year.'

'Yes,' says Alison. 'It was so wonderful we thought we'd go for longer. You really should come with us. You'd love it, both of you.'

How can she be so sure that we'd love it when she doesn't really know us at all? I look at their lightly tanned faces and their trim, fit bodies and I don't envy them. They live for their work, their flexibility, their success, but somewhere along the way they seem to have missed the point. They only had one son, and he was physically flawed. Better than me, I think angrily. I couldn't produce one live child, not even an imperfect one.

They always look the same, amiably satisfied, interested, well-intentioned. I think they genuinely care about James and me. I don't think they would favour an early divorce so that James could try again with another potential mother. But they're like shadows. There's not enough colour in their world.

I look at James and I am proud of his uniqueness, his refusal to conform. No more operations on his leg, no compromise on his choice of career. He's got colour below the surface. He's inherited genes that they didn't know they possessed, and he refuses to bleach out. I love him for this.

'What's for pudding?' I ask James.

He looks up and catches my eye, realizing that I'm annoyed. 'Treacle tart.' He knows I like puddings. He made it for me.

'None for me,' says Alison.

'A cup of black coffee for us,' says Jeremy.

They know we know they don't eat puddings, but they're always scrupulously polite.

I know I'm being unfair about them. They can't help their ordinariness. They were born with it. When they first went out together, they each must have seen the other's sameness rolling towards them, meeting and merging, until it was impossible to tell where they joined.

Perhaps they know this. Maybe that's why they go diving – so that they can visit a great underwater world that is saturated with colour. Then they come back on to dry land and can't recreate it. They can't take it away with them and that's why they keep going back. To see a world they can't contain.

They are good people who save lives all the time. James and I are nothing next to them, with our failed trip to New York and our treacle tart. They probably know the latest advance in artificial wombs. It's only a matter of time, they'd say.

James wants me to stay after his parents leave, but I don't want to. I kiss his right ear lobe and leave him happily washing up, pleased that we have impressed his parents with our efficiency.

I take Adrian's book and slip back to my own flat. I want to read this one as soon as possible: I want to know if my mother is in it.

I put the light on, draw the curtains and relax on my sofa with the book. I am still reading when the sun rises and the postman drops the daily brown envelopes through my door.

I forget about eating. I forget about everything. The telephone rings and people leave messages which I don't listen to. At eleven thirty in the morning I read the last page. I get up from the sofa and find that my legs have forgotten how to walk. I wander unsteadily into the kitchen and drink three glasses of water. I go back to the living room and dial Adrian's number.

'Adrian Wellington.'

'Adrian? It's Kitty.'

'Hello, Kitty.' He sounds cautious.

'It's all right. I'm not asking you to let me have the children.'

'Oh.' He pretends not to sound relieved. 'Have you started my book yet?'

'Yes, and I've finished it.'

'And?'

'Why aren't I in the book, Adrian? Don't I exist?'

5

Outer Circle

I want to be angry, but before the hot rush of indignation sweeps through me, I want to cry. Then I think it is ridiculous to be upset and I'd rather be angry instead, so I let the rage take over, raise my temperature, heighten my blood pressure, sharpen my mind.

The book is good. He knows how to describe people, how to give them an inner life. He has used his family as a starting point and I know that much of it is made up. But not all.

There are four boys and a girl in the book – Andrew, John, Michael, Peter and Daphne – and they are, of course, Adrian, Jake, Martin, Paul and Dinah. This is so obvious that it would be impossible for Adrian to argue otherwise. My father roars through the pages as he does through life. There's no need for embellishment. He's theatrical enough in the first place. But where am I? I know the book isn't autobiographical, I know it's fiction, but it was unfair of him to leave me out.

'It's only a novel, Kitty. It's not meant to be real.'

'But you managed to include everyone else.'

'You weren't there when I was growing up.'

'Yes, I was. I remember your hair down to your shoulders and the flared trousers.'

'I didn't wear flared trousers.'

'Yes you did. I remember them.'

I can hear him getting annoyed. 'I never wore flared trousers.'

'You did. You've just forgotten.'

'Anyway, if you can remember that, it was past the time of my book. I'm writing about the childhood of a boy in a big family. I didn't grow my hair until I was about eighteen.'

'You were only fourteen when I was born.'

I can hear him sigh. He's trying not to be annoyed and his voice drops in pitch as he makes the effort. 'I didn't include you, Kitty, because I thought it would confuse things.' He's like a car engine. If he becomes slightly overheated, the thermostat cuts in and he falls back down a few degrees. Not just with his voice. He can do it with his mood. He analyses his anger, decides if it is too heated and regulates himself.

'So I just confuse everything.'

'I didn't say that.'

'But you meant it.'

'Kitty, it's just a novel. It's a made-up story.'

'Dinah's in it.'

'She was there when I was growing up. She was my older sister. She affected everything I did.'

'But it's only a novel. You could have left her out altogether.'

He stops. I can hear him breathing carefully. I try to work out how upset I am. I feel hot and uncomfortable. My stomach is rolling around, almost as if I am afraid, but I'm not quite sure why. The conversation is civilized. My feelings are not.

I can hear his breathing calm down and I try to do the same with mine. Long slow breaths; in, two, three, four, five; out, two, three, four, five. Relax the neck muscles, the shoulders, the fingers. Unclench the teeth –

'Apart from your absence, Kitty, what did you think of the book?'

'Was Mother really like that?' She comes over as a shadowy background person. Someone who put meals on the table, washed up, knitted jumpers, sewed buttons back on shirts. I'm sure she was more than this. Adrian should have acknowledged her nearly-degree, her love for life.

'Well, the book wasn't about the mother. It was about a boy called Andrew –'

'Who is you.'

'No, not exactly.'

'You can't write a story about a boy growing up without including his mother. The mother is the most important person in his life.' I stop and think of Henry. I would have been the most important person in his life. For ever. When he finally died at ninety after a long, happy and fulfilled life, his last thought would have been about his mother. He would have remembered me. 'Mothers and sons have a special relationship.'

'I know that, but I thought she would come over best by just being there. Most children don't analyse the significance of their mothers. They simply accept their existence. So the impact of her death would have seemed especially harsh – from always being there to not being there.'

'But she didn't die by falling out of an aeroplane.'

'No, I made that up. I am writing a novel, not telling my life story.'

'Do you remember how she died? Were you there with her? Was anyone in the car?'

'Who are we talking about now?'

'Who do you think?'

'No, there was no one with her.'

'How did you hear about it? What were you doing at the time?'

'Kitty, I don't want to talk about it.'

'Did you go with Dad to identify the body?'

'No, Kitty. Stop it.'

I stop. I'm being unfair on him, but I'm angry. We wait in silence for a while.

'Kitty,' he says at last. 'Are you still there?'

'Yes,' I say. 'No. Remember your book. I wasn't there in the first place.' I can feel tears brimming over my eyes, dripping down my face, plopping as they fall on to the telephone.

'Are you taking your pills?' he says gently.

'That's none of your business,' I say and put the phone down.

I sit for a long time without moving. The phone rings several times, but I don't answer it. I sit and watch the light fade for a second time. The darkness creeps in and settles over me. I sit alone and in the dark all night. Eventually, the phone stops ringing. I imagine Adrian going to bed and apologizing to himself for deserting me. 'It'll be all right in the morning,' he'll say to himself – or to Lesley if she's awake and interested.

But it won't be all right in the morning. I'll be as silent then as I am now. I have no past. No mother, no significance in my brothers' lives and no baby memories, because they have all been destroyed by my father. No future. No children to depend on me, take a little bit of me, to remember me.

I go out when the sun begins to rise. I don't want anyone to come and find me, because I'm afraid they might not see me. I'm afraid that I don't really exist at all.

I walk a long way, right into the centre of the city and out again on the other side into an area where I've never been before. There are a few people around, even at this hour, but I look at the ground and pretend not to see them. I have too much silence in me to smile or say 'Good morning'. They are people going to work. Postmen, milkmen, shift workers waiting for the bus to take them to Longbridge,

Cadbury's, all-night Sainsburys. They seem so purposeful. They know they exist, they know where they are going.

I walk fast. I want to look as if I know where I'm going, as if I have a purpose like everyone else.

Then I stop. I look around me, and I have no idea where I am. What am I doing here? I've never seen this road before: this pavement, these houses. I stop so abruptly that a woman with a pushchair bumps into me.

'Sorry,' she mutters breathlessly. She has a toddler in the pushchair, and two other children, one on each side, holding on to the handles. I can feel her irritation. The child in the pushchair is wailing constantly, not very loudly, on a jarring pitch that sets my teeth on edge. The two older children have red noses and puffy eyes. She's allowed to have three children but she doesn't even look after them properly.

'It was my fault,' I say, pretending to smile, but not meeting her eye.

The boy sneezes and sniffs very loudly.

I move aside and let them pass. I walk behind them, but slowly at first, so that I can disappear into the background if they notice me. They must be going to school, I think, and with a jolt, I realize that I've lost hours of time. Why am I here? The pavements are crowded with people, the roads full of cars and lorries and bicycles. Everyone seems to be going somewhere except me.

The mother and the pushchair are moving rapidly out of sight, and I walk faster so that I can watch them going to school. I would like to see the mothers outside the school, watching the children go in, waving at them while they stand and talk. A sharp stab of nostalgia for my yellow time pierces me and I start to run in my anxiety to reach the school gates.

The children on each side of the pushchair are carrying lunchboxes. The girl's is pink with a cartoon image of

157

Pocahontas, while the boy has the *Lion King*. They don't want to walk as fast as their mother. The boy has thick ginger hair that sweeps disobediently over his head and ends in soft curls just above his ears, which stick out rather more than most children's. I worry about him being bullied because of those ears. He walks with his head down, holding on to the pushchair, expecting his mother to guide him round obstacles.

The girl is older and her hair is fairer, tied up in a ponytail with a big fluorescent green clip. You can buy enough hair clips nowadays to have a different one every day for a year. Sometimes, I go and buy them, collecting them for the daughter I will never have. It seems that if you have children and a bit of money, the world opens up like a huge Aladdin's cave, beckoning in the children, offering them wonders, excitement, food, clothes, videos, toys. The world is made for children, and without them you're no one.

The girl's fair – yellow – ponytail is swinging, and she's arguing with her mother. I walk faster, because I want to hear what she's saying.

'Mum – why can't I?'

The mother seems breathless, whining like the girl. 'No, Emma. I've told you once and I'm not telling you again. It's too late.'

'I won't come home on my own. Sarah will walk back with me.'

'And who'll walk back home with Sarah?'

Emma pauses to catch her breath. 'You could.'

'If I could take Sarah back, I could come and fetch you in the first place.'

'Why don't you, then?'

'Who's going to look after Darren?'

'It's not fair – everyone else is going.'

'Mum,' says the boy suddenly.

The mother ignores him.

'Mum –' his voice holds the word for longer, letting it drift, setting up a painful discord with the wail from the child in the pushchair.

'What?'

'My foot hurts.'

'So?'

I don't like the mother. She doesn't seem to care at all about the children. I fall back, feeling Emma's distress at not being allowed to go with her friends, feeling the boy's pain in his foot.

The mother stops unexpectedly, leans over and smacks the child in the pushchair. A shriek of fury rises up in the air. The mother starts to walk again, dragging the boy along. 'How many times have I told you?' she shouts at the pushchair. 'Don't wipe your nose on your sleeve.'

But has he got a handkerchief? I think. Does he have an alternative?

I stop trying to keep up with them. I can't bear to watch.

We're approaching the school gates and I can see the mothers and children outside, a haze of yellow above them – the morning, the sun, the blond heads of hair . . .

They are moving so fast that the boy trips and falls over. 'Mum!' he screams.

The mother keeps moving. 'Stop messing around, Henry,' she yells.

I run forward and pick him up, putting him back on his feet. 'Oh dear,' I say and smile at him. He's only little, and as he turns round I see that his face is covered with a mass of freckles that are running out of control, spreading and joining up so that they are almost one giant freckle. He looks up at me, but doesn't stop crying. His eyes are round and bewildered and he backs away nervously.

'It's all right,' I say. 'You must be careful to watch where you walk, otherwise you'll end up on the pavement again.'

159

He looks at me and makes no response. 'Mum!' he suddenly shrieks.

She stops, turns round and sees us. Immediately, she leaves the pushchair with Emma and races up to me. 'Keep your hands off him,' she yells.

'I was only –' I begin.

'Don't you go near him,' she shouts. 'What do you want?'

'Nothing,' I say. 'He just –' I realize belatedly that she's much bigger than me in all directions, and expects aggressive confrontation, not reasonable explanations.

The boy continues to wail noisily. People are watching us. I can smell the change of atmosphere, the burning, as another yellow flame dies into a charred ruin.

I turn away. Rush back the way I've come. Listen for her footsteps behind me, her hand on my shoulder. Nothing. Just screams somewhere in the distance. Her voice fades away.

When I finally stop walking, there's no sign of the school. No children rushing because they are late, no mothers with pushchairs coming away from school. Somehow, I've separated myself physically and mentally, crossed a line dividing the life of school and the life of the rest of the world.

I stand still for some time and try to look for something that will tell me where I am: a signpost, a shop, a road sign. I don't even know what direction to take to get back to the city centre.

Then I see the 11C bus stop and almost cry with relief. I know the number 11. It goes round Birmingham in a giant outer circle, so if you set off at one stop and stay on the bus for two hours or so, you arrive back where you first started. Clockwise or anti-clockwise. 11C or 11A. A bit like the young lady called Bright.

There was a young lady called Bright,
Who could travel faster than light.
She set off one day
In the usual way,
And arrived there the previous night.

Could you get back to the same bus stop earlier than when you left? It depends on your perception of time, which seems to move in straight lines or circles, a rotating spiral that goes up or down, forwards or backwards, fast or slow. I struggle to hold on to it, but lose the thread every now and again. Sometimes, whole days disappear. At other times, a few seconds feel like several hours.

At the 11C bus stop, I wait and try to calm down. Breathing in and out, I pretend to watch the passing traffic, wanting to be invisible. It feels awkward, having to think about breathing. Shouldn't it be automatic?

The bus comes. I climb on and show my bus pass to the driver, who grunts briefly and drives off before I sit down. I nearly fall over, but save myself by grabbing the shoulder of a white-haired lady. For a second I think she is Miss Newman.

'Sorry,' I say.

She doesn't answer or react in any way. I wonder if she is dead.

I find a seat at the back, in a corner, and watch the changing passengers. They are mostly elderly. A younger man gets on with identical twins who look about three. They each have a packet of tomato-ketchup-flavoured crisps and sit staring at me, mechanically taking out crisps and eating them with their mouths open. They have a dull, jaded look about them with their green eyes and orange-stained mouths. They get off with their father at the job centre.

I watch them until they are out of sight and wish I could

take them and wake them up, shake them, tickle them, show them how to laugh . . .

I sleep on the bus, because I've missed two whole nights – one reading Adrian's novel, the other feeling myself disappear. As soon as I'm comfortable, I close my eyes.

Voices drift in and out of my dreams.

'Only six months to live –'

'Mum! I want the green lolly. You know I don't like yellow –'

'Well. I told him he could get out, now –'

'20p each in the market.'

I make one complete circuit in a clockwise direction. Selly Oak, Harborne, Bearwood, Winson Green Prison, Handsworth, Aston . . . Sometimes the bus moves very slowly, as if it doesn't have the energy to go on. Sometimes it stops altogether for ten minutes, waiting for a change of drivers. One driver stops in the middle of the traffic and gets out. He crosses the road and goes into a newsagent's. Nobody on the bus speaks. I watch from my sleeping corner at the back and wonder how long they will all wait before they decide he's not coming back.

After five minutes, he returns, clutching a *Mirror*, two bags of crisps, three Mars bars and a can of Coke. He gets back into his cab and we can hear him opening a bag of crisps. Then the engine starts and we move off again very slowly. Perhaps he's reading the paper.

I sleep again and dream of the pink van that took Dinah away, with the slithering question marks.

Sometimes it's empty and sometimes – like today – it's on the road, the people inside singing. 'Blowin' in the Wind'. Bob Dylan. Martin has all his records. He tapes them and plays them on his long journeys. He says the music does something to his insides. I spent many days of my childhood in his cab, listening to Bob Dylan. I know all the words.

162

The mingling voices croon like a lullaby, but the sound of the singing wakes me up. I sit, half awake, half asleep, trying to focus on the singers. Is one of them my sister Dinah, who I never knew? Or my mother? The question marks slide round me teasingly, leading me on, escaping when I reach out to grasp them.

Why do I remember Dinah's van?

Looking out of the window, I recognize where we are: King's Norton, near Jake and Suzy's house. I think of Suzy when I last spoke to her, and I know in that instant that I should speak to her again. She will almost certainly be at home, because she'll still have morning sickness. It lasts at least three months. I decide to wait and do one more circuit. I don't want to see Jake. I need to see Suzy.

I'm wider awake on the second circuit, waiting now for my return to Jake's house. I look out of the window, noticing landmarks, and begin to check the time on my watch every now and again. I feel better.

After about an hour, I start to feel hungry, so I rummage in my bag. I find a stick of chewing gum, a packet of mints and half a KitKat stuck to my comb. I separate them and start to lick the chocolate off the silver paper.

'Kitty!'

I nearly drop the KitKat and the comb in surprise. I never expected to be recognized on the number 11 bus. I raise my eyes and find myself looking into the slightly shocked face of Hélène, the au pair from outside the school.

'Sorry?' I say, unable to think.

'Kitty, it is I, Hélène.'

'I'm sorry. You must have the wrong person.'

But she knows. She looks into my eyes and knows that I'm Kitty. 'You disappeared. You ran away, never came back.'

I can feel my face going very red and hot. I reach up with a shaky hand and try to wipe my forehead, but the sweat

163

keeps coming and I can feel it dripping off my eyebrows on to my cheeks.

I look at Hélène, who seems to be opening and shutting her mouth as if she's talking, but I can't hear the words. 'Got to go,' I mutter and stagger to the front of the bus.

The bus stops obligingly and I get off, suddenly terrified that Hélène has followed me. But the bus sets off again and I can see her in the back window, looking out at me, her face sad and confused.

I stand at the bus stop for some time, trying to stop shaking. As I begin to calm down, the next number 11 comes along and stops for me. I climb on and sit at the front. The young man next to me has a yellow and orange backpack sitting awkwardly on his lap, and his feet – in Reeboks – smell.

I didn't mean to abandon her. Twice. What else could I do?

I look into the porch of Jake's house, which is really Suzy's house, and see the dark glossy-leafed plants wilting slightly, and dried mud from someone's footstep lying where it fell. This tells me much about Suzy's condition. I wonder why she isn't in. She can't possibly be feeling better already. I have a moment of panic when it occurs to me that she might have taken something for the sickness. Does she realize how dangerous that is in the first three months? Has she been to her GP, had it confirmed, received an appointment at the hospital?

I remember that first appointment – the bumpy ride on the bus, jumping off to be sick, getting the next bus just as I started to feel sick again. I remember the feel of the hospital: sterile, alien, smelling of disinfectant; the doctors in white coats, some of whom must have been students; women at various stages of pregnancy being led round the system by competent nurses; flat stomachs, bulging stomachs, gigantic stomachs; people talking to you about 'your baby', when you've not quite identified this tiny being who lives inside you.

I remember something I'd almost forgotten. Henry was a mistake. He took us completely by surprise and we didn't know what to do, because we didn't think we were grown-up enough to be parents. I was twenty-nine, James thirty-four, but we didn't have any experience. James was as worried as I was. Then, one day, we were standing by the fountain in Victoria Square. It was very hot and several children had taken off shoes and socks and jumped in. Some of them tried to splash passers-by, others practised doggy paddle, their little heads determinedly upright, swallowing the water and spitting it out. The fountain was alive with vividly coloured T-shirts, red, green, pink, turquoise, and parents sitting at the edge, bowed by the heat, longing to jump in too. The children looked very happy.

'But the water's dirty,' I said.

James smiled and kissed my cheek. 'We won't let our children go in then,' he said.

His voice of acceptance went right through me, cleaned out the fear and replaced it with a surge of warmth that had been waiting for exactly that moment.

'It'll be all right, won't it?'

'Yes,' he said.

I'll go and find Jake. He'll be able to tell me when Suzy is due home.

I take another bus into the city centre and look for Jake in New Street. As soon as I catch sight of him playing his violin, I'm shocked, even though I knew perfectly well that I'd find him here. He should have gone to the hospital with Suzy. She must need his support if she is so sick, and he should be able to sympathize because of his vast experience of ill-health.

He is playing Vivaldi. I stand on the edge of the group who have stopped to listen and I watch him. As he ripples through the frantic, glittering demi-semiquavers, he tosses out a misty, carefree spray of music on everyone who listens. In these brief, entertaining moments, the drops fly though the air, light and frivolous, and Jake looks almost cheerful.

There is a group of workmen in the crowd. 'Play us an Irish jig,' one of them calls out when he finishes the Vivaldi.

So Jake plays an Irish jig and becomes lighter still, his left foot tapping as he plays. Most people have stayed and when the workmen start to clap along with Jake, everyone joins in. I clap too, carried away by the fun of it all, and we are laughing, clapping, dancing on the spot, while Jake plays faster and faster. I've no idea if he's playing a recognized tune or if he's making it up as he goes along.

He finishes with a flourish and puts his violin down. His

face is red and shiny with the exertion and he's out of breath.

The crowd, a big one by now, throw money into his open violin case and drift away. Some hang around and speak to him. He talks familiarly to them – he must have regulars, people who come especially for a cheap concert; free if they don't have any money. I'm sure Jake doesn't mind about the money. Suzy earns enough for both of them.

He knows I'm here. He talks to a small group for a few minutes and then comes over to me.

'Hello, Kitty. Shouldn't you be at home, working?'

I don't understand what he's talking about. Why should I be at home now? I can work all night if I need to. 'Jake,' I say, 'which hospital is Suzy going to?'

His face freezes and I can see shock creeping up into his eyes. 'What do you mean? Has something happened?'

'No, no.' I lay a hand on his arm, realizing that I've confused him. 'It's all right. Nothing's happened. Suzy's fine.'

His face clears and he turns away briefly to give a wave of thanks to someone who has put money in his case.

'I mean the baby.'

'What baby?' His face seems to close up.

'Suzy's baby. Which hospital has she been sent to?'

'What are you talking about?'

I swallow hard and try to relax my voice. 'The baby, Jake. Your baby, Suzy's baby, that you're expecting in seven or eight months.'

His voice is tighter and less familiar. 'Go home, Kitty, and talk to James. I can't deal with this. Adrian was right.'

He turns away from me, a stranger. What happened to the kind, sympathetic brother who gave me sanctuary not so long ago? Why does everyone have more than one face?

He lifts the violin under his chin and changes the tension on his bow.

'But where is Suzy? Which hospital?'

'Go home, Kitty. You're distracting me. Phone me later if you want to. I'm busy now.'

'But where is she?'

'At work, of course. Where would you expect her to be?'

He turns away from me and brings his bow down fiercely, but with absolute control. The music that comes out this time is deep and passionate. The violin almost speaks, the way the bow pulls at the strings and lingers on the low notes. A new crowd gathers almost immediately, drawn by the anguish of the sound, and I watch them for a while, wondering what they hear. Does he take them down his road, or does he open a different door for every individual?

Jake plays to me, to Suzy, to the baby, even though he won't acknowledge it. He refuses to turn in my direction, because he knows I'm still here. Now the music is so deep, so dark that it hurts me inside.

I walk away, but as I walk, I can still hear the music and I can feel a cold fear creeping through me. I have to stop and catch my breath as I begin to understand what the violin is telling me.

I step into Suzy's bank and immediately see her at the far end, standing amongst the desks and paperwork, shaking hands in a business-like way with a middle-aged man with greying hair and earnest glasses. She's wearing a green suit – just above the knee – and a white silk blouse covered with geometric patterns in a green that matches the suit exactly. Her hair is washed and flicked back in an immaculately carefree way. She looks very good.

She glances past the man and sees me. She waves, says a few more words to the man and comes over to me.

'Kitty! What are you doing here? Not arranging another mortgage, I hope?'

'Why are you back at work?' I say softly.

She looks confused, then smiles. 'Oh, you mean my stomach upset. That was ages ago. It was just a twenty-four-hour thing anyway.'

I examine her face. Now that I'm closer, I see that she looks paler, more tired than usual. As if she is not sleeping well.

'A guilty conscience,' I say.

She frowns. 'What are you talking about, Kitty?' But she gives herself away. I see from her eyes that I'm right, and there's only one possible explanation for her denial. Jake's music throbs inside me. I want to scream at her.

'The baby,' I say and watch her reaction. 'Where is it?'

She pauses for a few seconds. She has understood. 'What are you talking about?' she says again.

'You know.'

She looks irritably at her watch. 'Look, Kitty, I have an appointment in two minutes' time. Can we discuss this later – whatever it is?'

'No,' I say, and my voice is louder than before. 'I want to discuss it now.'

People are watching us. Young men with open, friendly faces, in pinstriped suits, young women cashiers behind bullet-proof glass, who smile a lot and know how to say 'Good morning' pleasantly to everyone.

Suzy turns to the next desk with a warm, genuine smile. Her voice is bright and professional. 'John, I'm expecting Mr Woodall in a couple of minutes – you know him, don't you?'

John nods.

'Could you ask him to wait five minutes for me. I am a little behind schedule.'

'Of course,' says John. 'No problem.'

'Come with me,' she says and leads me away from the working area.

We go through a red door ('Please keep shut') and up two flights of stairs. Two fire doors, another door and we arrive at a small office with a desk, a computer, two chairs and a filing cabinet. This must be the room they use when they call in the overdraft, refuse the loan. The room of bad news.

Once we're in the room, we sit down, Suzy behind the desk, me in the lower, comfortable chair.

'Now look, Kitty. This won't do. I'm in the middle of a working day. I'm very busy and I let people down if I can't keep to my time commitments. You can't just turn up and talk nonsense and expect me to be pleased to see you.'

'I don't expect you to be pleased to see me,' I say. 'I expect you to tell me the truth.'

'And what exactly is the truth? Why are you here?'

'The baby.'

'What baby?'

'You were pregnant, weren't you, when I saw you the other day?'

'Don't be ridiculous. I was ill.'

'No,' I say slowly. 'I can tell. I know how it feels to be pregnant, I know about the sickness.'

She picks up a pen and starts to doodle on an empty pad. 'This is nonsense, Kitty. I've told you, I was ill.'

'No,' I say. 'You were pregnant.'

'I am not pregnant.'

'No,' I say – Jake's music was unmistakable. 'But you were then.'

Her face loses all its colour, and the words that come out are tight and furious. 'You are completely wrong. But even if you were right, what business is it of yours? Who do you think you are, coming here in the middle of the day, accusing me, refusing to leave, making a scene in front of everyone?' She's pressing harder with the pen, moving it angrily, making vicious ridges in the paper.

170

She's admitting it. She's angry because I've discovered the truth. 'I can't believe –' I say, and my voice is shaking, 'I can't believe that you could have had –' I can't use the word. I don't want it in my mouth.

'Why is it such a terrible thing?' She spits the words out and uncrosses her legs with her frustration. She doesn't look entirely at ease sitting there and I realize she must still be sore. 'People have different opinions about that, don't they? Otherwise it wouldn't be legal. Who are you to say if it is right or wrong for me to have a baby? You live your life, I live mine. You like your job. I like mine. I'm good at it. I want to go on working. I already have a child at home. His name's Jake and he needs a lot of my time and care. How dare you come here and make accusations you can't back up and judgements about how I should live my life?'

I watch her. She's looking over my shoulder, as if there's someone standing behind me. I think she's holding back the tears.

She takes a breath. 'Look, Kitty,' she says more gently. 'I'm sorry about – everything. I wish it hadn't happened, but nothing I do is going to make any difference. I'd like to help you in some way, but I don't know how.'

I can't speak to her any more. There's a howling rage inside me which is unfamiliar and frightening. I want to leap up and grab her perfect hair, to pull at her professional suit and tear it apart, shake her and shake her for the terrible thing she's done. I can't look at her. My hands are trembling.

'I think you should go now,' she says, standing up and opening the door.

I follow her silently downstairs. At the bottom she opens the fire door and I go through. As I leave the bank, I see her going over to a man in a suit with a briefcase. 'Mr Woodall,' she says and holds her hand out to him. She looks utterly professional. Her smile is wide and welcoming, her voice warm. There are just two red spots on her cheeks to reveal that she might have been mildly unsettled by my appearance.

I watch her and I know that I'm right.

I ring James' doorbell. I have a key, but I want him to know I'm coming.

He opens the door as if he's been expecting me. 'We can't see Jake and Suzy any more,' I say. 'I've only got two brothers left.' I burst into tears. He leads me in and takes me to the bedroom. I lie down fully clothed. He takes off my shoes and puts the quilt over me, then he holds me for a long time. He doesn't ask. He never asks. He just holds me. He's a good man. If it wasn't for me, he would be a wonderful husband.

Nobody rings for the next two days. I stay in James' bed and cry and cry for the baby that never had a chance. The baby that I could have had if they didn't want it. It's not fair, I keep thinking. It's not fair. Sometimes James comes and sleeps with me. Sometimes he doesn't. He occasionally brings me warm drinks and I swallow them eagerly, trying to get some of the warmth inside me. But it's only temporary. I eat some of the food he brings me and leave the rest.

'You must have the flu,' he says. 'Should we go to the doctor's?'

'No. It'll go on its own.'

'OK,' he says. 'But if it goes on longer than a week, you have to see a doctor.'

'Yes,' I say.

Suzy doesn't phone and Jake doesn't phone to tell me off for upsetting her. So she hasn't told him. Or she has told him and he too has a guilty conscience. Either way, I know I'm right.

*

I stay with James for three days. On the fourth, I wake up in the early morning and my mind is clear, so I write a note. 'Feeling better. Back to work. See you later for supper.' Then I leave him asleep and go home.

I start work immediately, anxious to catch up with myself. A manuscript a day. My weekly newspaper review comes first – only just in time, as always. My thoughts leap ahead as I type out each report, so I have to keeping going back to make corrections. The future opens up with the prospect of reading, reading and reading. Adrian and Lesley, Jake and Suzy, they're behind me, drifting further away by the second. Maybe I'll never see any of them again. Maybe I don't want to. They don't need me – I certainly don't need them. If I want to make contact with my family, I can go and see Martin and Paul and my father. No problems there with sisters-in-law. We are the same as we always were – just a bit older.

The phone rings and I am surprised to hear Martin on the other end. He seldom uses the phone.

'I'm going to Exmouth tomorrow.' His voice is slightly too soft, as if it has slipped back down his throat, searching for security in his comfortable centre. I have to strain to hear him.

'Can you talk a bit louder?' I shout. 'I can hardly hear you.'

There is a pause. I wait for him to register my comment and to think about it. His telephone conversations are always like this.

'I thought you might want to come with me,' he says, without changing his volume.

'Would we have time to go to Lyme Regis to see Granny and Grandpa?'

A long silence. You can't rush him.

'So is that yes or no?' he says.

'Well, it depends. I'd like to go and see Granny and Grandpa, but . . .' I'm working well. If I keep going like this for two more days, I'll have cleared my backlog. Caroline is on the phone twice a week. I really shouldn't miss any more time.

'I was going to stay the night – maybe two. You could spend the day on the beach, or go to see Granny and Grandpa.' Is he answering my question about Lyme Regis, or does he think he's just thought of it?

'I'm tempted.'

'Have you been to Exmouth?'

'Yes,' I say. 'You've taken me there a few times.' Has he forgotten that Dad met Mother in Exmouth?

'Oh, have I?' He pauses again. 'So do you want to come?'

I think of James. I don't want to go off and leave him behind. I don't want to stop working. 'No, I don't think so. I have too much to do.'

'All right then.'

'It was nice of you to ask.'

'Yes,' he says. He always sounds exactly the same, never disappointed. He lets the world fall into place around him, and he doesn't seem to realize that he could change anything. When the genes were divided between Martin and Jake, they went in opposite directions and there was no overlapping of the central characteristics, no compromise in the middle. They've nothing in common but their birth date. Jake has told me they couldn't even play together as children, because they had no connection. He says he's never felt as if he were a twin. He would be more convinced if his other half hadn't survived.

'I'll come another time.'

'OK,' he says. 'Bye, Kitty.'

'Bye, Martin. Thanks for . . .' My voice trails off as he puts the phone down.

I go back to my reading. Evacuees today. Yesterday it

174

was occupied France. My mind is full of bombs and Nazis and scattered families. The children's library is going to do an exhibition on the Second World War. It's part of the national curriculum. They want me to compile a recommended reading list.

As I read, I think about my father and his mysterious medals. He's never told me about his life during the war. He spends so much of his time talking that he never really says anything. I sometimes think that what I see isn't real. He throbs with rich vibrant red, but red is only a colour and you need a surface to paint it on. Where is the surface?

I work solidly for two more days and then decide it's safe for me to go out. Martin will be in Exmouth by now. I think of him walking along the seafront, visiting Granny and Grandpa, and I'm jealous. I decide to visit my father.

I check with James on my way out. He's working hard. He doesn't want to talk to me because his thoughts are following clean, logical paths.

'Do you want me to get any shopping?' I suggest, because I can see he's only half listening.

He looks past me as if I am not there. 'I don't know – bread, I suppose. Maybe some apples . . .' But he's not interested.

'I'm going out,' I say. 'I may be some time.'

He smiles briefly and accepts a kiss on his nose. Today I'm in control and he's not quite awake. This makes me feel good. 'I'm going to see Dr Cross,' I say. 'Want to come?'

He looks vague. 'No, I don't think so. See you later.'

Before I leave the room, his thoughts are back with his programs. His fingers chase each other over the keys, rapid but accurate. He seldom needs to correct. His fingers and his brain move along parallel lines. His work is as immaculate as his flat.

I don't mind. I'm not threatened by his intimacy with a computer.

175

*

The house is silent when I arrive, but Dad's car is parked in the drive. The garden is empty, the kitchen abandoned, with dishes piled up precariously, waiting to be put into the dishwasher, so I know he must be painting. I make him some coffee and carry it up to his studio, creeping up the stairs. I want to surprise him. I always want to surprise him.

I find him painting an enormous picture of a beach. 'Buckets, spades, sand, deckchairs, sandcastles, shells, seaweed, sand, waves, rubber rings, ice-creams, flip-flops, blanket, sunglasses, sand, shingle –'

I discovered recently that you can buy books of lists. My father has missed a golden opportunity.

'Sand, beach balls, sandwiches, swimming costumes, sand – Kitty!'

I stop. He's done it again. 'How did you know I was here?'

He grins and looks pleased with himself. 'I can sense your presence, that's all.' He takes his mug of coffee and looks at me over the top of his glasses. 'Are you speaking to Adrian and Lesley again?'

'I never stopped talking to them.' I don't tell him about Jake and Suzy. He doesn't know about their baby. There are only three people in the whole world (except the anonymous doctors) who knew about the baby. And once memory starts to malfunction, the baby will cease to exist. A non-event.

'I want to know about the war, Dad.'

He sips his coffee and watches me through the steam. 'Everybody has an opinion about the war,' he says. 'It was a world event. There are thousands of books, thousands of writers making money out of it. Go and ask them.'

'I'm reading the books,' I say. 'That's what I've been doing in the past week. I just –' I sit down on the sofa. 'I would just like to hear your version.'

He picks up a thin paintbrush and moves it delicately, marking tiny blue shadows on a little boy's face. 'No, you wouldn't.'

'How do you know? You should pass on your memories, otherwise they'll all disappear when you die.'

'Mmm. Nice to know you have me dead and buried.'

'That's not what I said.' I try not to get irritated. 'But you can leave something of yourself behind if you want to – a way of continuing. You can't just disown the memories you don't like.' I think of Miss Newman. She should have told someone earlier, when she could get it right. Then the memories would have been sorted out properly, and won't disappear into a puff of smoke at the crematorium.

'I will leave something behind – my paintings.'

'Not the war,' I say. 'You don't paint the war.'

'I hate the sea,' he says, slapping red and purple into his apparently calm sea.

This takes me by surprise. He has such fond memories of meeting my mother in the sea. Almost every picture he has ever painted has been of the sea.

'Well,' he says, as if he has heard my thoughts. 'OK. I'll tell you about the war, or the sea, or both, I suppose. I've parachuted into the sea in the middle of the night, and I can tell you, it's a lonely place to be.' He looks past me, suddenly urgent. I turn round to see what he's looking at, but there is nothing there except the door. This is a dramatic device. He's pretending to look into himself, to relive his experience for my benefit. Why don't I believe in this?

'My crew went down with the *Lancaster*. They slipped through the waves and never came back up.' As the plane slips into the sea, his right hand dives smoothly downwards, fingers first. 'I was absolutely alone in those few dark silent minutes as I floated down. You see things differently after an experience like that.'

I have a suspicion that he's enjoying himself. In the few

dark silent minutes, he stops pacing and his voice drops. He leaves short gaps between each word for emphasis. I try to look impressed.

He studies his painting, but possibly only for show. He steps backwards, leans forwards and peers. The picture is enormous, with detail everywhere – a departure from his usual practice of concentrating on a small object or space. He waves his paintbrush vaguely, moves to add some colour, but finally doesn't. He's pretending to be emotional, I realize.

'Some memories are best forgotten. We all change. The man I was then is nothing like the man I am now.'

'No problem,' I say. 'You might have been nicer when you were younger.' He might have been the kind of man who would show respect to his future son-in-law.

He's looking out of the window at the treetops. You can see my flat from here. 'They called me Boots. Wing Commander Boots Wellington.'

I'm not sure if he is expecting me to laugh, so I half smile and watch his reaction. He ignores me.

'We dropped bombs on Germany.'

I'm surprised. I've always seen him as a fighter pilot, another Miss Newman's Jack.

'Everybody thought it was a pretty good idea at the time. Dresden, Berlin, Munich, they were just names to us – points on a map. We chucked the bombs down and got out as soon as possible.'

'Did you know you were killing people – women and children?'

'Well, of course we did. That's what bombs do. What did they expect us to do? Send a message that we were coming, so they could all get away?'

Does he feel guilty? Is that why he's never talked about it before?

'The life expectancy of a bomber crew was very short.

Some of them went out on their first operation and never came back. They either crashed or ditched into the sea.'

The Dambusters – Richard Todd leading his men on a suicide mission. *Twelve O'Clock High* – Gregory Peck counting the returning planes. My father is seeing his life through a black and white lens.

I notice a baby on the edge of his picture. He's crawling towards the side, as if he wants to escape. His family haven't noticed. They're all looking at the man selling ice-creams. It reminds me of Brueghel – Icarus splashing into the sea, while everyone else is getting on with their lives.

'We came down in the end, just like everyone else, hit by shrapnel on the way out. We dropped our bombs short of the target and turned round. Only four of us were left alive – two badly wounded.' His voice is speeding up with the action. 'There was petrol everywhere, washing round the floor – could have been blood too, I suppose. Anyway, something kept banging into my leg while I tried to control the plane. I put my hand down to see what it was, and it was wet and sticky and warm. I picked it up and it was a severed hand. The glove was still on it.' He holds his hand dramatically in front of his face and studies it gravely for several seconds, as if he is searching for the right words. 'I didn't even know who it belonged to.' He says this casually, like an afterthought, but I feel that none of this is spontaneous. It's been worked on.

'Well,' I say, 'can I assume it wasn't yours?'

He ignores me. 'We were obviously going down. I told everyone to get out, then I scrambled on to a wing and jumped. My parachute opened almost immediately, but it was too dark even to see the plane hit the water. Just a loud bang, a roaring of water, and then nothing. I couldn't see any other parachutes. I couldn't see anything. I was the only one to get out.'

'What about the moon?' I say.

He looks confused. 'What moon?'

'The moon in the sky. You can usually see something by the light of the moon.'

He stops as if he's examining a picture inside his mind, then shakes his head. 'I don't know,' he says eventually. 'Maybe there was a new moon – or it was cloudy.'

'Was the sea rough?'

He stops again. 'I don't know. I can't remember.'

'So how were you rescued?'

'The navy fished me out at first light. There were no other survivors.'

He stops for a long time, still with his back to me.

'So why didn't you tell me all this before?' I say. 'It's a good story.'

He turns and looks at me sharply. 'Don't mock, Kitty.'

Thousands of people died in the fire bombs of Berlin. An aeroplane crew fell into the sea, and my father couldn't save them. Nobody would have noticed the bomber going down. There were too many other deaths to worry about.

'The sea is a very lonely place in the middle of the night. Huge and threatening and without horizons. I hate it.'

'But you spend all your time painting it.'

'Yes.' He sighs, a long, slow, exhausted sigh. 'Well – I feel as if I lost something that night. I keep thinking, if I try again, paint the sea from a different angle, a different colour, a different mood, I'll find what I've lost.' He sighs again. 'It never works.'

He won't look at me, and I suddenly know that this is the truth. Somewhere in amongst all that drama, he has told me something private and true. 'Did you go straight back to dropping bombs on Germany with another crew?' I ask.

'No. I had a leg wound. By the time it was patched up and functional, the war was all over. They gave me some medals and I took them, but I never wore them.' He seems to be saying, it's not his fault. He wasn't responsible for any of it: the war, the bombing, the death of his crew. I feel a rush of understanding for him.

I look at the back of my father's head and see that he's an old man. He must be nearly the same age as Miss Newman. Why have I never seen that before? His hair has gone grey without my noticing. His shoulders are more bent than I remember. As he turns back to the painting, I see that his paintbrush is trembling very slightly.

'I don't paint hands,' he says.

I drink my coffee. He studies his picture carefully, as if looking for something to criticize.

'I like the crawling baby,' I say.

He doesn't hear me. 'That's all,' he says. 'Nothing really.'

He hasn't told me much, I realize. Just a story that must have been heard in thousands of homes, dramatized in hundreds of films. A story he's been telling for fifty years inside his head, over and over again, neatening it, tidying it up, making it concise.

'I must get back,' I say and wait to see if he'll turn round.

He starts to mix colours together on his palette, squeezing and stirring angrily.

I pause at the door, but he's painting again and acts as if I've already gone. He is hurling paint on to the canvas, swirling it around in the sea. I'm sure that the baby has crawled further out than before.

'Crabs,' he says. 'Sand, tides, currents, rocks, jelly fish . . .'

As I walk down the stairs, I see that there is crimson paint on my skirt. I should have checked before sitting down.

I tell Dr Cross about my conversation with my father.

'Does it worry you?' she says, knowing that it does.

'Perhaps I shouldn't have pressed him.'

'Does it matter?'

'Well, he may not want to look me in the eye again. That bit about the sea – I think he was being honest, which isn't normal for him. He paints pictures when he's talking – so you never really know what he thinks.'

'Ring him up in a few days' time,' she says, 'and have something casual ready to say.'

I nod. Maybe we can both pass it by.

'How do you feel about Jake and Suzy's baby?' she says.

'I don't know.' And this is the odd thing. I can't think about it properly any more. It's as if it never happened.

'Have you tried talking to them?'

I shake my head. I don't want to talk to them now.

My father tells me something true, possibly for the first time in his life, and Miss Newman tells me her memories. I think I should be more honest, so I tell Dr Cross about my yellow period. I hadn't intended to when I came into her room. If I'd thought about it in advance, I wouldn't have been able to put it into words.

She sits quietly and listens. 'Thank you for telling me, Kitty,' she says.

I stand up to go, feeling clumsy and awkward, like a small child.

'Don't forget to make an appointment for next week,' she says. She doesn't smile as I go. She looks thoughtful.

I run home. All the way. I feel as if things have shifted slightly, as if I'm not quite going down the same inevitable road. Something is different. I rush in because I want to go and talk to James, drag him away from his work.

The phone is ringing as I come into the flat. I pick it up.

'Kitty, this is Dad.'

That was quick, I think. I haven't had time to think of something casual to say.

'Martin's just phoned. Granny and Grandpa Harrison have died.'

6

Locks

I throw some clothes into a suitcase, and James carries it for me on the bus to New Street Station. He'd like to come with me, but I want to go on my own. The rest of the family will come later for the funeral. Granny and Grandpa knew me properly, whereas they were a bit muddled about my brothers.

Granny cooked proper meals, and we would all three sit round their dining-room table and eat lamb chops and mint sauce, roast beef and Yorkshire pudding, pork and apple sauce, in an agreeable silence. They liked me to come. Granny would air the bed for me, putting hot water bottles between the sheets; there was always a vase of fresh flowers from the garden on my bedside table. Primroses and grape hyacinths, roses, marigolds, winter jasmine – something for every season. They would leave the window open a crack – 'to blow away the cobwebs' – and put glossy magazines they'd bought for me on the window seat: *Cosmopolitan*, *Elle*, *She*. I hoped they didn't read them after I'd gone. I didn't want them to know about what was happening in the world.

I stopped going to see them after the baby. They didn't write or telephone. I knew they would just be waiting for me to come, happy to see me if I turned up unannounced. I imagined them airing the bed regularly, waiting, knowing I would come eventually.

Martin meets me at the station in a taxi. We climb in and I study his face, wanting to know how he was affected by finding them dead. He looks the same as always.

'I had to break the door down,' he says. 'I thought they were out, so I went for a walk along the Cob. I had fish and chips and watched the sea.'

'They're never out.' I say. 'They can't walk far enough.'

We drive along the narrow lanes and I strain to see the view over the hedgerows. When we meet a car coming the other way, it has to reverse to the nearest lay-by. Our taxi driver makes no concessions.

'I thought they might have gone shopping,' says Martin.

'They don't go shopping,' I say. 'A neighbour does it for them. Neither of them can walk properly.' That was three years ago. The neighbour might have moved away or died. A small hard knot of guilt settles in my stomach.

'I came back the next morning, and one of their neighbours turned up as I was ringing the bell. She said she hadn't seen them for over a week.'

'Was that Betty?' I say anxiously.

'I don't know,' he says. 'She was upset.'

She usually goes in every day. What had gone wrong?

'I've never broken a door down before,' says Martin. I look at his huge hands in his lap, one white, one brown, and I'm glad that he's a gentle man.

'Was it difficult?'

'Yes,' he says after a pause. 'Not like on the telly. I had to go round the back.'

I think of their locks. A Yale lock, a mortise lock, two large bolts and a chain on the front door. They were proud of their door chain, because a policeman had suggested it when he came round to advise them on security.

Grandpa had been delighted. 'We don't have to open the door to anyone now if we don't want to,' he said and laughed, slapping his leg. He showed me how the chain was fixed. 'Two-inch screws into the frame of the door. No one's going to break that in a hurry.'

I admired the efficiency.

'Try it, Kitty. Look, I'll go outside and you use the chain.'

So he went outside, leaning on the door frame to support his weakened legs, while I locked the door and put on the chain. He rang the doorbell. I opened the door and peered through the gap.

'Who is it?' I said in a doddery voice.

'Double glazing,' he said.

'No thank you,' I said and shut the door.

When I opened the door to let him in, he was almost bent double with laughing. I led him to his chair in the lounge.

'Mrs Harrison,' he shouted between his wheezes of laughter. 'We need a cup of tea.'

Granny brought in the tea and a plate of chocolate biscuits. She winked at me over Grandpa's bald head. 'Mr Harrison loves his locks,' she said. 'Always did.'

'That's right,' he says. 'I've always loved locks.'

So they had locks on their windows, the back door, the shed door and the back gate. Granny and Grandpa were frail and vulnerable, but they were never burgled. Even the burglars knew it wasn't worth trying. Grandpa used to go round and check all the locks once a month. I think he would have liked a burglar to try – so he could congratulate himself on his locks.

'They were dead in bed together,' says Martin.

I try to imagine them side by side, dying together.

'There's got to be a post-mortem before we can arrange the funeral. Suspicious circumstances.'

I can't see why it's suspicious. They should be allowed to die together if that's what they wanted.

We go in through the back door, which is secured with a padlock and chain because the original locks are too badly damaged. I'm impressed by Martin's strength.

Nothing has changed. The house smells nearly the same as it always did – shoe polish, roast potatoes, ironing. It feels old and creaky. I can feel the slow movements of old people around me. There is a new, sickly smell coming from the kitchen, so I go to have a look. The yellow tops are bare, as clean as ever. On the table two places are laid for breakfast. The blue and white striped cups and saucers sit waiting for coffee. The matching milk jug is there in the middle, a hard yellow crust formed where the milk should be. The knives and forks and spoons gleam warmly. Granny always polished them after washing up.

'I like a good shine on my cutlery,' she used to say. 'People don't bother nowadays. But I do. I like to see my face in it.'

I remember picking up a spoon and trying to see my face in it. I couldn't understand why it was upside down. 'That's a test to see if you're a good girl,' said Grandpa. I soon discovered that I was the right way up on the other side and wondered why they hadn't explained it in more detail. I worried if I was good or bad.

On top of the cooker there are two plates, with bacon, egg, beans, sausage and fried bread arranged carefully, in exactly the same way on each plate. The eggs' centres have sunk and congealed, grey mould has appeared on the fried bread and the shrivelled sausage, the beans sit solidly in their tomato sauce that has hardened and cracked.

Martin sees me looking. 'I didn't like to throw it away,' he says. 'I thought it might help us work out what happened. Evidence.'

I don't want to throw it away either, despite the smell. It seems so typical of their life together. Mrs Harrison in the kitchen, Mr Harrison watching the telly. A picture of a life that doesn't exist any more. A generation that saw the beginning of the century and survived two world wars.

I go to look in the bedroom where Martin found them.

The bedcovers have been pulled back and you can see the imprint of their two bodies lying side by side, two hollows that represent over seventy years on the same bed. You can see which side Grandpa slept in – he was heavier than Granny. I should have encouraged them to buy a new bed years ago.

Granny's hairbrush and comb lie neatly on the dressing table – wooden handles with inlaid mother-of-pearl. I used to play with them when I was little, tracing the patterns with my finger, stroking the smoothness of the wood. There's a lace cloth on the dressing table and a three-way mirror where you can see yourself watching yourself.

On Grandpa's bedside table there's a book about gardening, although he had to abandon the roses in his last few years. There is also a tea-maker, which they saw as a life-changing invention. When I stayed with them, I could hear it boiling up at six o'clock every morning.

'Have a good lie-in,' said Granny. 'Don't get up when we do. We're older than you. We need less sleep.'

But I woke anyway, when the tea-maker started to gurgle and hiss as the water came to the boil. Then I waited for Grandpa to get out of bed at 6.15. I heard the tea being poured out, comfortable and satisfying, and I heard the clink of china as he passed a cup and saucer to Granny. They would have whispered conversations and I could catch isolated words. ' – Margaret – dahlias – rain – Kitty –' After a while, I'd turn over and go back to sleep, soothed by their predictability.

Granny's bedside table has the clock, a reading lamp and her glasses.

For as long as I've known her, she's been trying to read *Jane Eyre*. I used to watch her as she read. Every now and again, she would turn a page, sometimes forwards, sometimes backwards, and I saw that her eyes weren't moving. She wasn't reading it. Perhaps she couldn't read at all, but gained some restful moments of peace without having to justify her inactivity.

I find *Jane Eyre* fallen to the floor, and the two cups and saucers on the window sill, still stained by the last drops of tea. They drank their tea before they died, but didn't make it to breakfast.

There's a wedding photograph of them both on the wall. Black and white, both of them rigidly upright, a crack across one corner of the glass. Two fresh young people – not like Granny and Grandpa at all. He's handsome and looks like Adrian in the picture, although I was never able to see the resemblance in real life. She's tall, black-haired and a bit like me now. Neither of them is much like Margaret, my mother. I examine the photograph and long to know what was in their heads when it was being taken. They seem so – young. Unmarked.

'They were dressed,' said Martin. 'It was very strange. Both in bed with their clothes on, but covered by the blankets.'

I try not to see their old bodies lying side by side on the bed that they bought when they were first married, dressed in clothes that had never changed in style for all my life. A knee-length skirt in mottled green Crimplene, polyester pinstripe trousers and an Aran jumper.

Martin and I sleep in the lorry. We neither of us feel able to sleep in the house, because we feel it doesn't belong to us.

During the day, I go through their lives. Piles and piles of old bills going back to the thirties: letters, cinema tickets, premium bonds, things they didn't want to throw away. A pile of cards from their golden wedding anniversary, wedding presents they had never used – a tablecloth of Irish linen, still in its original wrapping, a box of sherry glasses that has never been opened.

Each time I sort through a drawer, there are more things

to remind me of them. I have to cry a little before I probe into each new compartment of their life. I feel I owe it to them. I can't just throw things away without a struggle, but we fill black bag after black bag.

'What do we do about the furniture?' I ask Martin.

He shrugs. 'I suppose we see if anyone wants any of it and then sell it to one of these house-clearing firms.'

I want it all. How can I let any of it go to a stranger? Every item of dark, heavy, cumbersome furniture is precious. It bears the handprints of all those years, polished by Granny's busy hands, sat upon by Grandpa every day of his adult life, opened and shut daily throughout their quiet old age. If it's sold in an auction, it'll be stripped down, painted, varnished, years of familiarity rubbed away by harsh chemicals.

On the second day, the police arrive. I invite them in, a sergeant in uniform and a policewoman, and we stand awkwardly in Granny and Grandpa's sitting room.

'We have the results of the post-mortem,' says the sergeant. 'Could we sit down?'

'Of course,' says Martin, and we perch on the edge of the furniture, unable to make ourselves at home.

'It seems that she died first. She had a massive heart attack ten days ago. He died about eight hours later, also of a heart attack.'

'But why didn't he ring for an ambulance when Granny had the heart attack?'

The policeman clears his throat. 'Well – we think that they both got up in the morning and drank their morning tea. Then she dressed and went to make breakfast while he shaved. She felt ill and came back to the bedroom where she was hit by the heart attack. He got her into bed, and then . . . We think he lay down beside her and waited to die.'

I look at them. 'You mean he wanted to die with her?'

The policewoman nodded. 'They were very frail, weren't they? He must have been dependent on her.'

I remember two cats that a schoolfriend once had. One of them had to be put down by the vet and the next day the other one was found dead in her bed.

'It's not particularly unusual with the very elderly,' says the policeman. 'They lose the will to live without each other.'

I look out of the window at the distant sea. There are several sailing dinghies out in the morning sun, their different-coloured sails scattered gaily amongst the sparkling waves, forming a pattern in their randomness. I suddenly, desperately, long for James.

We arrange the funeral for five days later. Martin has to go home until then, to finish off his work contracts. I move into the house, taking over my old bed, where I always slept when I came to visit. The sheets and pillow-cases are in a linen-press in the hall. It's so neat – not neat like James' obsessive tidiness, but neat and cared for. I can see Granny's old, bent hands folding slowly and carefully, smoothing the fabric down with every fold, taking pleasure in her role as a housekeeper, a carer.

I phone James every evening, so that I'm not alone too often. We have long talks, better on the phone than in real life. I tell him about staying in Granny's house. 'They're here with me,' I say. 'I can't imagine anyone else living in the house.' New owners, who would breathe their air, walk over their dust that has drifted down into the floorboards. They would dig Grandpa's garden, plant their own plants in soil enriched by Grandpa's compost.

James finds our separation difficult. 'Shall I come down early, Kitty, before the funeral?' He's more lonely than me. He has days, even weeks on his own when we're both working hard, but he can't cope with the distance. He feels that the length of string that binds us together is stretched too tightly. He's afraid it might break.

'Don't come down yet, James,' I say. 'Come the day before the funeral.' I want him to come now, to be here with me, but I need time on my own to think. I need to remember Grandpa and Granny properly in case I forget later on.

James phones up over and over again. 'Where did you put my red tie, the one with Bugs Bunny on it?'

'How long should I leave the fish in the oven?' He rings me? He's the one with the cookery books.

'Should I cancel your doctor's appointment?'

'Yes, please. Unless you want to go instead.'

'No – I don't think so. I'll just cancel it, I think.'

Every evening before going to bed, I go for a walk and watch the sea. It's calm and smooth all week. The sea that my father says he hates. The waves roll in over the pebbles and out again, over and over, endlessly. My grandparents have died, I think.

We meet up at the crematorium. Everyone is here except Lesley, who has stayed at home with the girls. It's the first time we've all been together since our wedding. We sit in pairs: my father and Adrian, Jake and Suzy (who I avoid looking at), Martin and Paul, me and James. They are all wearing suits and ties. I love men in suits, especially the back of their necks and the sweep of their shoulders. Only Jake and Adrian have black suits – they have wives, who insist on doing things correctly. My father wears his usual herring-bone jacket but his bow-tie is maroon rather than red – his concession to the occasion. Martin and Paul wear brown suits. Suzy is in a black dress, which I look at instead of her face. James looks devastating in his grey suit, and I'm glad he's wearing the Bugs Bunny tie.

I wear a pink dress from a small, expensive shop in Lyme Regis. I chose it because it was intense and challenging, so that I wouldn't look like Suzy or Lesley in any way. It shimmers. When I move, it shivers through purple, blue, grey, reflecting my changing moods back to me. It's not a safe pink; there is no connection with the pink of Adrian's house. It is bold, daring, angry.

The funeral is at twelve thiry. James and I have spent the morning preparing food at the house. We make platefuls of egg and ham sandwiches and cover them with clingfilm. We cook sausages and put them on sticks and leave crisps and peanuts waiting to be poured out into dishes. We buy packets of chocolate biscuits, Cherry Bakewells, miniature Battenbergs, ginger cakes and leave them all in their wrappings because there aren't enough plates. We have no idea how many people will come.

At the crematorium, there are a few other people besides our family, but we make a small and unimpressive group in the bleak emptiness of the chapel. Somebody gives a short talk about Granny and Grandpa, but he talks in clichés and I know that he never knew them.

'This devoted couple,' he says, 'faithful to the end – deeply loved by children and grandchildren.'

What does he know? Their only child is dead, and only one grandchild really knew them and then not for the last three years – I stop listening to him. We're supposed to have our eyes shut in prayer as the coffins go down, one after the other, but I watch them go. I think of the flames waiting to eat them. I wonder what temperature is required. I see their old, tired bodies crumpling in the heat, folding up, abdicating. How many here really knew them, really cared about them? I did! I want to cry out. I loved them.

But I am silent. I don't want the ashes. How can ashes substitute for those old hands smoothing down the bed-linen? Or Grandpa's lovingly pruned roses?

We go back to the cars without saying much. Everyone is polite. The men stand back to let the women in first. My brothers are respectable, polite people. Grown men who know how to behave. I sometimes forget to see them as others see them.

We drive back to the house and James takes the clingfilm off the plates of sandwiches while I go and switch on the kettle for cups of tea. There are several people here I've never met. A few elderly couples who are neighbours, a friend of Granny's from Exeter, two old colleagues from the school where Grandpa used to teach – both retired years ago. The house is old, the people are old. I feel too young to be here.

Betty comes to talk to me in the kitchen, an old woman herself. She fusses over details, moving cups and saucers on to the table, putting more milk in the cups, an extra teabag in the teapot. 'I feel so bad, Kitty,' she says. 'We went on holiday. I asked my neighbour to call in and check, but she was ill and forgot.'

'It's not your fault.'

193

'To think of them dying together like that. What a thing.'

The kettle boils and I pour the water into the teapot, filling it up again immediately for the next round. Betty stirs the tea in the pot and starts pouring without giving it time to draw. She does everything very quickly, darting backwards and forwards, shaking with a strange high-pitched laugh at unexpected moments. She reminds me of a bird.

'It's a pity we didn't see you in the last few years,' she says. 'They missed you.'

I pick up the tray of cups of tea and take it into the sitting room.

There is a gentle murmur of conversation, an occasional suppressed laugh, an awkwardness as people run out of things to say.

The front door is open in case anyone comes late. I offer tea to Martin and try to avoid Suzy, who is talking to him.

A strange woman is standing in the doorway, watching us in a way that makes me uneasy. I don't remember seeing her at the crematorium. She is tiny, with long hair, pure white, that bushes out down her back in a curious, uncared-for way as if it is rebelling against her size and age. Her eyes, very bright and intense, project a kind of fury as she looks round at all of us in the room. They dart accusingly from person to person, and just as she's about to meet my gaze, I look down, awkward, somehow guilty for having watched her. When I raise my head again, she's looking past me. It isn't me she wants, I think with a sense of relief. She is wearing a faded pink corduroy pinafore over a purple blouse, which is made of a flimsy, chiffon material. Underneath the long skirt, you can see grey socks and flat sandals. On her head is a floppy cloth hat, with a blue paisley pattern. It is slightly grubby, giving her a neglected appearance. She looks like a bag-lady. A woman of seventy acting as if she's Alice in Wonderland.

194

I take my eyes off her and offer Adrian a cup of tea, but he ignores me.

'Adrian,' I say, 'have some tea.'

'Yes,' he says, but he still doesn't take it.

I look at the woman again, and think perhaps there is something vaguely familiar about her.

My father is debating with Paul about the value of living to a hundred. James thinks he's joining in the conversation, but my father ignores him.

'What's wrong with a telegram from the Queen?' says my father. 'It's an acknowledgement of your staying power.'

'Well let's hope you never get one, then,' says James.

'I've done three quarters of a century already. I see no reason why I shouldn't make the final quarter.'

'But when you get older,' says Paul, 'you can't do so much. Is it worth the effort?'

'Of course it is. Your brain still works, you know. I've got years ahead of me.'

'It's unfortunate,' says James, 'that we'll all have to pay for your medical expenses through our tax.'

'I'm not ready to go,' says my father. His voice slows. 'I only feel about – twenty –'

Surely James hasn't got to him. But he's not responding to James. He's studying the woman in the doorway. We all look. Everyone stops eating, tea-cups are replaced on their saucers in people's hands.

'What – ?' says my father, and stops. He frowns, shakes his head, confusion creeping into his face.

The woman laughs; shrill and slightly hysterical. 'Well,' she says. 'Guy. Hello.'

My father stares at her as if he can't believe his eyes. I wait for him to say Lucia, Helen, Angela, one of those names on his letters in the attic, but I somehow know what's coming.

'Marg –' he says, and stops. 'Margaret?' He puts his cup and saucer down and turns back to her. I can see his face turn red. 'How dare you?' he says slowly, then much louder: 'How dare you show *your* face here?'

Mothers. Babies. Joined biologically by a cord. When I was born, a passageway closed and in a pinprick of time, the blood was shifted from the heart to the lungs. Just like that. Once I was part of my mother, then I was not. Our separation should have been more gradual. Not sudden. It feels as if I was thrown away.

I hear the breathing of everyone in the room, but I can't hear my own. Is this woman Margaret, mother of Dinah, Adrian, Jake, Martin, Paul and me? A dead person resurrected into the body of a tiny, angry old woman? She doesn't look big enough to be the mother of six, not important enough to be my mother.

'Guy Wellington,' she says. Her voice is lower than before, but menacing all the same. 'You have the cheek to stand there and ask why I'm here? At my own parents' funeral? How dare you show *your* face here?' Her accent is unexpectedly educated and doesn't match her appearance.

Paul is looking at her with complete disbelief. 'Who are you?' he says.

Adrian edges towards her, his hand outstretched. 'I'm Adrian,' he says. 'I was expecting you earlier.' His voice has changed: higher in pitch and oddly unsteady.

'Expecting?' says my father.

She stands and looks at him, her eyes travelling from his feet to his head. She doesn't seem impressed. 'Adrian,' she says eventually. 'You don't look like I thought you would.'

'Neither do you,' he says.

'What do you mean, expecting?' says my father.

Margaret and Adrian shake hands awkwardly, both unwilling, as if the other one is contaminated, letting go as soon as possible.

Granny's friend from Exeter puts her cup and saucer down on the table next to me, the clink of china briefly distracting us. She hasn't finished drinking the tea. 'Well,' she says briskly. 'I think it's time I was going.' She looks round vaguely. 'What happened to my coat?'

Nobody replies, each hoping someone else will deal with her. James should do it, since he's not personally affected by the return of my mother. I would like to nudge him into action, but he is sitting on the other side of the room, looking at Margaret with the rest of us, and I can't catch his eye.

'My coat –' Granny's friend says again, nervously.

'Yes, of course,' I say. After all, I'm the one who knows the house.

I lead her into the hall and along to my bedroom where the coats have been left on the bed. I walk briskly in front of her, trying to get her to speed up. She seems frustratingly slow. I'm terrified that I will miss something important.

'Thank you, Kitty,' she says as she buttons her long mac. She's wearing brown walking shoes that match the woolly scarf she winds around her neck. I'd like to say, It's only June. You don't need a scarf in summer. But I don't, because it would take too long.

'They loved it when you came to see them,' she says. 'They were so proud when you passed that exam –' She stops and pulls out a handkerchief from the coat pocket and blows her nose loudly. Her eyes look red. What exam is she talking about? Is she confusing me with Margaret?

'I'm sorry,' she says again. 'I knew your grandparents for such a long time. They were always so good to me.'

She blows again. Then she kisses me awkwardly on the cheek and walks out down the hall. I've never met her before. I don't know how she knows my name.

When I return to the room, people who are not part of the family are leaving hurriedly. They know where to go to find their coats and don't need any help. Only Betty remains. She's interested in Margaret.

'We were at school together,' she says casually, as if she's continuing a conversation.

'What?' says Margaret. She looks round in confusion. 'What school are we talking about?' Her voice is now less certain.

'Betty Thompson I was then. In the class below you at the village school. I invited you to a party once, and you said yes, but you never came.'

'Oh yes, Betty Thompson,' says Margaret after a pause. 'How are you?'

I know that she doesn't remember her at all, and Betty realizes it too. 'Another time, maybe,' she says and walks out of the room somehow diminished. She no longer reminds me of a bird. Her small movements have become heavier, less fluid.

So now we are left alone with this woman who cannot possibly be our mother. All the family minus Dinah, Lesley, Emily and Rosie. We are miles from home, eating picnic food, trying to have a conversation with a mother we thought was dead.

My father has been waiting for the room to clear. As soon as the last unrelated person is gone, he attacks. 'You have no right to come here. When was the last time you did anything for your parents? I bet they'd be thrilled to know you came to their funeral. Bit late, don't you think? Bit late for everything.'

'How dare you judge me?' she says, her voice tight with anger. 'You who have no notion of loyalty or –'

'You talk to me about loyalty? What would you know about it?'

'A great deal more than you –'

'Oh yes, a woman who walks out on her family, she knows all about –'

'*Walked* out? Driven would be a better –'

Their voices are fighting for supremacy, more over-wrought by the second.

'Stop it!' shouts Adrian, and they pause and look at him.

'Well,' says Jake in the unexpected silence. 'You seem to have us all at a disadvantage. We said our goodbyes thirty years ago. We didn't really expect to have to say hello again later.' He blows his nose loudly and sneezes three times. He picks up a Cherry Bakewell.

Martin looks bewildered. He takes gulps of tea and starts eating the sandwiches on the table next to him, neat little triangles of tuna and brown bread, demolishing each one in a single mouthful. There are plenty on the plate. They should keep him occupied for some time.

'I don't understand what's going on,' says Paul, just in time to stop them shouting at the same time again. 'We thought you were dead.'

'You were misinformed,' says Margaret.

'But where have you come from?' says Jake. 'Why are you here?'

'Don't ask her why she's here now,' says Dad. 'Ask her why she hasn't been here for the last thirty years.'

'Don't ask me,' she says. 'Ask your father.'

They glare at each other.

'I invited her,' says Adrian.

Everybody turns to look at him in amazement.

'Ah,' says Dad loudly. 'You were expecting her.'

'What?' shouts Paul. 'We all believe our mother to be dead, but you invite her to a funeral. Could you explain the process in slightly more detail? How do you go about inviting a dead person to a funeral?' He stops for a second. 'Providing it's not their funeral,' he adds.

My father is glowering at Adrian. 'What did you know about it?' he says.

Adrian doesn't look right. Adrian, the calm man of letters, the confident analyst of human psychology, is struggling. 'I found out,' he says defensively. 'OK?'

'No,' says my father, 'it's not OK. If I'd wanted you to find her, I'd have told you myself. What's wrong with asking me?'

'Ask you?' Adrian's voice is rising. 'How could I ask the man who told me my mother was dead?'

My father turns on him furiously. 'She was dead, as far as you were concerned. As good as dead. Walked out on you –'

'Have you told them why?' says Margaret, savagely. 'Like what a wonderful husband you were? Like what you got up to, like how you destroyed me with your endless domineering demands and everything else?' She's pacing round the room, frustrated by its smallness, her strange white hair bouncing up and down with each step, her dress sweeping wildly behind her.

'She drank,' says my father to all of us. 'Whisky, all day and every day.'

'No, she didn't,' says Adrian. 'That's not true.'

Margaret stops pacing and turns to him. 'Thank you, Adrian,' she says, and she sounds almost normal.

Adrian nods, and for a brief, terrible moment, I think he is going to burst into tears. The thermostat cuts in at the last moment and he tries to smile instead.

'Except it is true,' says my father. 'Can't remember a single time when she wasn't drunk.'

'But where did you find her?' says Jake.

Adrian shrugs. 'You can find people if you want to. Hospital records, electoral rolls, the Salvation Army.'

'Ha!' says my father. 'She wasn't living a civilized life in a respectable neighbourhood then, was she?'

Silence. It's obvious that he's guessed right.

'Drunk,' he says in triumph.

'What do you know?' says Margaret scornfully. 'People change. Even when they've been treated so badly.'

How do you know if your mother is an alcoholic? When you are three, your mother is as she is; any behaviour would seem normal. But Adrian was sixteen. Surely he would have noticed. Was he really looking?

I hold on to the side of my chair and wish I was next to James. How do I know if she really is my mother? She's not as I expected. But I had no expectations. I've had no mental picture of her physical presence. She has only ever existed in my mind as a person with no body. She has never been real, but this elderly woman who looks half mad is real, and I find her far more alarming than reassuring.

'You're not welcome,' says my father. 'You've managed to upset everybody.' He starts to mutter. 'We come down here for a funeral, the food is prepared, we're all dressed up – it's a funeral, you know, not a wedding – maybe you should have come to a wedding – it might have been easier to take at a wedding –'

'No,' says Paul, picking up a handful of peanuts. 'My mother is dead.'

My father starts again. 'You deserted us, remember. You were the one who left. "Learn to cook," you said to me. No thought for the children – putting your own selfish needs first –'

'Perhaps you should have told them the truth,' she says,

and although her voice is softer, there is a dangerous edge to it. As if there are lots of things we don't know and she's about to tell us.

'Yes,' says Adrian. 'I think we should have the truth.'

He already knows the truth. He has spent the last few months trying to find her. He's been writing letters, telephoning, talking to people who might know her. Why didn't he tell us what was going on? Why didn't he tell me?

'It was the book, wasn't it?' says Jake suddenly.

Adrian looks defensive. 'No, not really –'

Paul stops crunching peanuts. 'What book?'

'Yes it was.' Jake's voice is sounding more confident. 'You wanted to write a book about our family, and when you did, you decided you were going to look for an exciting family secret, didn't you?'

'The book is fiction,' says Adrian.

'Oh,' says Paul, 'that book.'

'It's just that, when I really thought about it –' Adrian looks uncomfortable, moving his neck awkwardly, as if his shirt collar is too tight. He doesn't look a healthy colour at all. I worry about his blood pressure. 'It seemed odd that there hadn't been a funeral –'

'Nothing odd about that,' says Dad. 'Lots of people don't have funerals.'

'No, they don't,' says Paul.

'Yes, they do. Far too expensive. Waste of money.'

Paul bites a sausage off a stick and points the empty stick at Dad. 'Most people do something: have a memorial service, or scatter ashes somewhere. They don't start pretending the dead person never existed.'

'Anyway,' says Dad, 'you have the truth now. She left us to get on with it on our own. Does it make you feel any better?'

'But you didn't tell us that, did you?' says Adrian. 'You told us she was dead.'

202

'What about the car accident?' says Jake. 'None of that was true?'

'I was protecting you,' says Dad, pacing around the room. 'You were all young. You couldn't handle being deserted – better to lose a mother in death than desertion. How could you have coped with the idea that your mother didn't want – ?'

'Don't poison their minds like that,' says Margaret. 'Feeding them with your warped ideas –'

'You left us without a word of goodbye,' says Paul. 'I went to bed one night and you weren't there in the morning. You hadn't even washed my jeans. You promised they would be ready for the first day of the holidays. I found them screwed up on the floor by the washing machine, mixed in with everyone's socks. I was never able to get rid of the smell.' Paul's cheeks have gone very pale, almost blue, but a pink flush is creeping upwards from his neck. He is forty-two years old, and he's angry. I have never seen him angry before. Only ever indifferent.

The smell of Paul's jeans, the smell of babies, the smell of your mother. I've identified the emptiness inside me: I don't know the smell of my mother. I have no memory of smell.

'I don't know who is who,' Margaret says, and she sounds annoyed. She looks carefully at all of us, one at a time, as if she is trying to match us up with our childhood selves. I'm Kitty, I want to shout. Look at me, notice me, remember me as a baby. But I can't find the words.

'You lied to us,' says Adrian to Dad.

'I protected you,' Dad says again. 'Don't look at me like that. You do all sorts of things for your children. You'd have done the same for Rosie and Emily –'

'You've got children?' says Margaret. 'I've got grandchildren?'

She looks excited. Why? Are grandchildren more valuable than your own children?

Anyway, it's all in the biographical notes at the front of his books. Married with two daughters, lives in Birmingham. Does she even know he's a writer?

'And you went on lying to us all that time,' says Adrian. 'For thirty years, I believed she was dead. I am astonished by the scale of your deception.' He is calming down, as he finds words to substitute for his anger.

'But you weren't deceived, were you?' says my father. His hands are working compulsively in his lap, washing with imaginary soap, round and round, wringing out and starting again. 'You decided that you knew better.'

'And it turned out I was right. I just needed to make things easier in my mind.'

'Easier?' shouts my father. 'How can it be easier to be abandoned – like unwanted orphans, left to fend for ourselves? I didn't even know how to work the washing machine –'

Martin next to me is strangely still. I can hear him breathing very evenly. He's still devouring sandwiches, but it's an automatic process and I'm not sure that he is chewing them enough. I try to move closer to him, to reassure him a bit, but he moves away at the slightest contact.

I'm having difficulty with Margaret. The others all remember her, they have pictures in their minds. They can remember having breakfast with her, going to school with her, being read bedtime stories, calling her in the night when they felt sick. Did she tell them off, was she often angry? They've never told me bad things. Perhaps they've forgotten all that – the bad things slipping out of reach, the good things sharp and bright in their memories, cancelling out her anger, her frustrations. I can only produce a crinkled skirt, a lap, a low voice singing 'It's been a hard day's night'. Nothing more substantial than a vague memory of warmth, and the wedding photos, which are over fifty years old. There has never been any place in my imagination for how she might have been if she had stayed with us. That she would grow old, that her hair would go grey and her voice would be harsh and shrill. It has never occurred to me that she could be alive.

'Well,' says Margaret. 'Tell them the rest, Guy.'

Dad stops pacing and stares at her. 'There's nothing else to say,' he says. 'Only the fact of your desertion –'

'What about the women?' she says. 'You can't have forgotten Angela, Helen, Sarah and the rest. More than one on the go at the same time – popping in and out of my house in relays –'

'My house,' says Dad. 'It was never your house.'

Margaret looks at him triumphantly. 'Quite,' she says, and almost smiles, looking round at everybody for their reaction.

'I don't remember any women,' says Jake.

'You were too busy playing your violin,' says Adrian.

'There weren't any,' says my father.

'What?' shouts Margaret. 'What about Angela, Helen, Sarah, Philippa, Jennifer, Lucia? Dozens of them, one at a time, two at a time, one in the morning, another in the afternoon, two in the evening, another at night? Are you telling me I've got that wrong?' She looks as if she might spit at him.

'I remember Lucia,' says Paul. 'She used to bring me comics.'

'No,' says Adrian. 'That was Philippa. Lucia brought sweets.'

They knew about the women. They knew. Why didn't anyone tell me? Martin is still breathing heavily. Jake jumps up and takes a bowl of crisps from the table. 'Have a crisp,' he says and offers them round. We all obediently take a handful and crunch them together. Salt and vinegar, strong and sharp. Martin puts his crisp in with the next sandwich, but I still don't hear him chewing. I worry that the crisp will scratch his throat.

So what do most women do if their husbands are unfaithful? Not just with one woman: lots and lots? I look at James, but can't imagine it. I think I would have to leave. *But what about the children?*

'Anyway,' says my father. 'They never came again after you left.'

'No, of course not,' says Margaret.

'No, really. I gave them all up for you.'

'Don't be ridiculous. What was the point of that?'

'They became irrelevant.'

She looks at him, clearly amazed. 'Well, that's logical.'

My father doesn't reply. He looks out of the window. It's raining and the room has darkened so we can't see each other clearly.

'I thought you were dead,' says Paul suddenly. 'I can't believe you did that.'

'Did what?' she says. 'I didn't tell you I was dead.'

Martin gets clumsily to his feet. 'Stop it!' he shouts. 'Stop it, all of you. This isn't our mother. She's only come to upset everyone. She's not real, you know. My mother has been dead since I was fourteen. You're just encouraging her when you talk such rubbish. She's not my mother –'

He walks over to Margaret. She flinches as if he's going to hit her. But he just throws an arm out over her head. 'Go away!' he shouts. 'Leave us alone!' He stands motionless over her for a moment, tears pouring down his cheeks. Then he turns his back on her and marches out of the room. We hear the front door slam behind him.

*

'Well,' I say loudly, 'someone needs to go and see if Martin is all right.'

There's a heavy silence, as if everyone is talking frenetically, but without sound.

'Looks like it's me again, then, doesn't it?' I'm not sure if I have said this out loud, but I get up anyway.

I've always been the baby, the kitten, the Kitty. So if my brothers become children, I go further back into non-existence. There doesn't seem to be a part for me in this performance.

I find Martin on the seafront. It's been raining or drizzling for some time now and the sky is heavily overcast. It presses down, forcing our thoughts inwards. Martin is standing near the edge of the water, hurling stones into the sea, a fighting machine with no enemy. He's soaking. I want to take him home and find his brown slippers, make him a drink in his Pooh Bear mug. There are only a few other people on the beach, mostly with dogs, some serious walkers. A young man stands in the shelter of the sea wall practising juggling.

'Hello,' I say to Martin, but he can't hear me against the sound of the waves. They rush up and break noisily, then suck back, the pebbles shrieking an anguished protest as they're forced back under the sea.

I stand next to him, watching the power of his right arm as he flings the stones far out into the water. He must know I'm beside him, but he gives no sign.

A larger than average wave is gathering strength on its journey inwards; it's going to come much further up the beach. At the last minute, I turn and run back, just avoiding a soaking. Martin doesn't react, and when I look round again, he's standing in a few inches of water as the wave lazily creeps up the beach. He looks down for another stone to throw and doesn't notice that his shoes are full of water.

When the wave has retreated, I go back and shout at him. 'Move back, Martin, you're getting soaked!' I know he can't get much wetter, but I need to say something.

He ignores me, so I grab his hand and try to pull him back. He looks down, but doesn't seem to recognize me.

'Come on! Move further back!' I yell.

I can't shift him. It's like trying to move a concrete statue. But I don't give up. It must be possible to reach him somehow.

He stops resisting me and I nearly fall over.

'Kitty,' he says, 'what are you doing here?'

I'm tired of shouting. I crunch back over the pebbles, away from the sea, hoping he'll come too. Once I can hear his footsteps following me through the shingle, I stop and sit on the stones against the sea wall. I draw my knees up and Martin sits down heavily beside me. We are sheltered here from the wind and the rain, and a quietness settles over us. A man with a metal detector walks past us, head down, eyes on the stones just in front of him. Rain drips off his yellow waterproof jacket.

I begin to realize how wet I am. My hair is plastered to my cheeks, rain is sliding off the ends of the hair and on to my jacket. I can feel the damp reaching my pink dress.

'We ought to go back,' I say. Where's James? I came to find Martin, and James should come to find me.

'Do you want to?' says Martin.

I hesitate. It all seems so frightening. 'I don't know,' I say.

'She's an impostor.' Martin starts building a small tower with the pebbles beside him. His voice is hard and he's no longer crying.

'But why?' I say. 'Why would someone pretend to be her? What would be the point?'

He shrugs. 'Maybe she's after the money.'

'What money?'

'What she could inherit from Granny and Grandpa.'

'But there isn't any, is there?'

'She wouldn't know that, would she?'

This is surprisingly logical for Martin. I start to play with the wet pebbles. Their colours have risen to the surface. The reds and blacks glow, strong and vibrant, the browns and yellows gleam. They shimmer when moved, changing shades, as if the wetness wakes them and releases their rich textures from a dry, grey sleep.

'There must be a way to find out,' I say. 'Ask questions, things you remember. See if she remembers them.'

'But she might have forgotten them anyway,' he says. 'And I might remember them wrong.'

I think of the images in the wedding album and compare them with the woman with the long white hair. In the photographs, she seems tall, graceful, neat. There's a seriousness in her expression that I've always liked. The woman in Granny's house is sharp and angular and – furious. But anyone's appearance would change in such a long time.

I start to wonder if I can identify an independence, a self-will in both images, a tilt of the head, the line of her jaw. Am I really seeing this, or am I just embroidering the links?

'Dad obviously thinks she's real,' I say. 'He recognized her.'

Night-feeding. My mother and I were once alone together in the deep silence of the night. Shouldn't there be something inside me that remembers it subconsciously, that should recognize my mother if she returns?

Martin's tower falls over and he sits looking at it. A large black poodle runs up and stands in front of us, wagging its tail. His fur is strangely flattened by the rain. Martin picks up a stone and throws it along the beach. The poodle scampers off and then stops, perplexed, unable to work out what he's looking for.

'Kitty,' says Martin.

'What?'

He pauses. 'Nothing.'

We sit in silence for some time. I really want James to come and find me. The owner of the poodle appears along the edge of the sea and the dog dashes into the water to meet him.

'I was fourteen when she left.'

He is going to tell me something. Something he's not said before.

'She used to fight everyone –'

I look at him in surprise.

'I mean people who were nasty to me. She would go into the school and see my teachers, the headmaster, the children who were bullying me, their parents. She never gave in, she made them sort things out. I think she might have beaten up the children herself if they weren't punished properly.'

I look at him and he's crying again. 'I didn't know you were bullied,' I say.

'Well . . . They used to call me Simple Simon, didn't they? I couldn't do things as quickly as them.'

'Oh, Martin.' I want to give him a hug and tell him that he's a brilliant lorry driver, and the best brother in the world.

'So why did she do all that and then leave me behind when she went, as if she couldn't care less about us?'

'I don't know.'

'One day, she just wasn't there any more. I remember the date: July 21st, the first day of the school holidays. We got up for breakfast and there wasn't any. We looked everywhere for her. We thought she might be shopping, or gone for a walk, or out in the garden. Back in bed.'

I could see the boys searching for her, running out into the garden, opening cupboards, looking under the beds.

'We called her. We thought she was playing a game. "We give in," we shouted. "You can come out now." But she didn't come out. She never came out, ever again.'

Where was I in the middle of this search? Asleep in my cot, or running around on my little toddler legs, calling 'Mummy, Mummy'?

'Then Dad came back and told us about the car crash.'

I watch the water of the rain piercing the water of the sea. Gulls swoop down, balance on the surface and ride the waves. They rise and fall with nonchalant expertise, unthreatened by the hostile weather. The day, the sky, the sea are grey, but there is a vigour to the greyness here on the beach. It is not cold and lifeless, it's rich and multi-layered.

I imagine myself awake at night, listening for Henry's breathing, because I know that this is what mothers do. The love that children never hear. Did she do that for me? Do I know about it in some secret inner part, or did I lose it somewhere in the thousands of nights between then and now?

'Why did she do it?' says Martin, with a catch in his voice. 'How could she leave her own children?'

'I don't know.' To leave Henry would have been so inconceivable that I can't think myself into the role. Margaret left five children. Inconceivable five times over.

'If it is her,' he says, 'I hate her.'

'Kitty!'

And here comes James, finally, a bit later than acceptable. He stumbles awkwardly over the shingle, stopping to look and shout at regular intervals. 'Kitty! Where are you?'

'Over here,' I shout, but my voice gets caught up and lost in the wind.

He stops and turns round, looking in all directions. I stand up and wave to him, my clothes wet and cold against me, my hair sticky and salty round my face.

James sees me and immediately changes course. He moves determinedly towards me and I stay standing. I want him to hold me for a bit when we meet.

'You took your time,' I say.

James is obliging. He puts his arms round me and holds me tightly. 'Kitty,' he says gently and pats me rhythmically on the back.

Martin stands up next to us. He doesn't speak. He half smiles, then looks away at the sea.

A woman walks past us, fiercely pounding across the stones. She looks like Granny's friend from the funeral, but I'm not sure, so I watch her carefully. She won't meet my eyes. She strides on with her head down, so I don't find out if it's her or not.

The three of us climb the stone steps back up to the road. It is quieter now, further from the sea. My pink dress is dark enough to be red and sticks to me uncomfortably. I wonder if it's transparent.

'Have I missed anything?' I ask James. 'Has she explained anything?'

'There's a lot of arguing going on, but as far as I can make out she had some kind of breakdown. She says she didn't know what she was doing.'

'She would say that, though, wouldn't she?'

Martin stands beside us, looking awkward. 'I think I'll go and sit in my truck,' he says.

'What if she wants to speak to you?' I say.

'Tough.'

'We'll come and fetch you if she asks for you,' says James.

'I'll think about it.'

He walks away from us, head down against the wind, shoulders broad and somehow closed, locked on the inside.

We make our way slowly back to the bungalow. 'Apparently,' says James, 'it wasn't just your father. Something to do with Dinah. All the rows they were having, and then Dinah leaving. She disappeared, she said, and they had no idea where she'd gone. She says everything just fell apart after that. She thought she was no good for her children, that you would be better off without her.'

'So she had a breakdown. Why didn't she come back later, when she got over it?'

'I think she'd had enough of Angela and Philippa and Lucia and the rest.'

'But what about us?' I say. 'Why didn't she come back for us?'

'Maybe your father's right and she was an alcoholic. Maybe she couldn't cope.'

I picture my father burning everything connected with my mother's life, scattering the ashes on the rhododendrons, and I see that his anger then was greater and possibly more justified than I'd realized. I see him painting in the attic, slapping on the paint, crimson, full of energy. 'Kitty!' he says, as I creep up silently. Always welcoming, always pleased to see me – and all the time he's been telling me lies.

'Regardless of whether he was right or not,' says James, putting an arm round me and guiding me in the right direction, 'your father was trying to protect you. He stayed, she didn't.'

'But was he to blame for it all?'

James hesitates. 'If she really wanted you, she would

have found a way. She knew where you were. She could have made contact with you any time she wanted. She chose not to.'

He's right. She can't just appear thirty years later and say it was my father's fault. She is, after all, our mother. I feel a silence begin to take shape inside me, settling coldly, soft and unstoppable as snow.

'Do the others admit she drank?'

'No one's saying. They don't seem sure.'

I start to shiver. James stops, takes off his jacket, then puts it round me. He won't get too wet. It's only drizzling now. I slip my arms into the sleeves, which are too short, and smell his warm familiar smell of deodorant, computers, wooden floors, cleanness. I wrap it round me tightly, but I still shiver.

'Actually,' says James, 'you can't entirely blame her, can you? Who could live with your father and remain sane?'

I suspect he might be secretly pleased that my father's world has fallen apart. This is what happens if someone is perpetually ignored. It takes away their objectivity.

Dinah and Margaret and their rows. How do you get to that stage of non-communication with your child? Does it inch up on you, your voices rising a little more every day? Or does it jump out suddenly, and there you are, angry without any warning? Is it inevitable or avoidable?

How would I know?

The bungalow looks innocent from outside. It's too precise, too normal to contain all the emotions that are bubbling away inside, all that anger – just a tiny desolate house for two old people. Grandpa's roses in the front garden have become bushy and neglected and many of the petals have fallen in the heavy rain. It's a garden that needs attention. They had a gardener once a week for the last three years, but it wasn't the same. Weeds amongst the roses, moss and daisies in the lawn. There used to be clusters of yellow-orange stones edging the flower beds, lifted from Chesil beach when Granny and Grandpa were younger and had a car. Now they lie haphazardly over the path and rose beds.

I might never see the house again, I think with a jolt. It will all be divided up, sold and scattered.

We pause outside the front door and look at each other.

'Never mind,' says James. 'The worst is over. The next thirty years should be more predictable.'

No such complications for James and me.

As we come back into the room, I look at Margaret – my mother. I try this in my head. *Hello, Mother, I'm Kitty*. I turn towards her, ready to identify myself, ready to call her Mother. But as I look at her, I see a strange blankness in her. She doesn't glow, sparkle, reflect colour from anyone else. She has no colour. She's not a mixture, a combination of colours, a half-colour; not pastel, not bright, not dark, not light. Is this what happened to her thirty years ago? Did my father wipe her out? Perhaps she has to be angry to stop herself from disappearing.

'Don't be ridiculous,' my father is saying. 'Are you seriously suggesting that I got up early every day for the past thirty years, so I could sort through the post and remove anything written in your handwriting?'

'Yes,' she says, almost spitting at him.

I slip down on the sofa, anxious not to disturb anyone's thoughts. I keep James' jacket on, even though it's warm inside, because I feel comfortable in it. It might shield me from the next round of accusations that will, inevitably, start flying about the room again. James hovers over the table and comes to sit next to me with a plateful of ham sandwiches and slices of ginger cake.

'As if I'd bother –'

'Of course you would – you always wanted to come between me and the children.'

'Rubbish.'

'What about that time I said they couldn't climb the cliffs on holiday?'

My father looks bemused. 'What are you on about?'

'You know. You just wanted to undermine me, appear as the benevolent father –'

'I don't know what you're talking about –'

Jake and Suzy come out of the kitchen with a trayful of cups of tea. Jake is strangely calm. I know he's good in a crisis, but this is an exceptionally big crisis and he doesn't

216

even look flushed. Only a few coughs or sneezes. 'You'll probably be ill tomorrow,' I say to him.

'Did you find Martin?'

'Yes,' says James. 'But he doesn't want to come back for the time being. He's decided to retire to his truck.'

I would like a truck, I think. Somewhere to go when things get difficult.

Suzy is handing out the cups. James and I both take one and avoid looking at her directly. We seem to have come a long way since the pregnancy issue, but as far as I'm concerned, all the resurrected mothers in the world don't cancel out a dead baby.

Jake and Suzy sit down at the table. 'Have a cup of tea,' Suzy says to Margaret.

Margaret looks at her suspiciously. I can see her thinking, 'Who are you? Are you Kitty, or someone's wife?' I wish she'd say it out loud.

'Why turn up now, after all this time?' says Paul angrily. 'Wouldn't it have been better to have left us with the fictional version?'

If you don't know the truth, but you think you do, it's not so bad. Your truth will do. We believed she was dead. Was it fair of her to come back? Who does it benefit? Her or us?

Margaret reaches over and takes an egg sandwich from a nearby plate. She eats it greedily, as if she's ravenously hungry, and won't catch anyone's eye. 'I didn't realize you thought I was dead. I thought you'd all rejected me,' she says, and her voice is harsh and high-pitched again.

But she was an adult and we were children. We didn't know how to think.

'Adrian invited me,' says Margaret. 'They were my parents, after all. Why shouldn't I come to my parents' funeral?'

217

'But you let them believe you were dead,' says Paul.

'No, I didn't,' she says. 'I often talked to them on the telephone.'

I stare at her. This can't be true. Granny or Grandpa would have told me. They looked after me for years of holidays. Grandpa would have slipped it in with the locks. 'Can't lock your mother out, can we?' he'd have said, chuckling away. Granny would have told me as she fed me with home-made scones. 'I'd better put some away in case your mother turns up.'

'So you would have come to the funeral anyway?' says Adrian.

She hesitates. 'Maybe,' she says defiantly, but we know the answer is no.

She's lying. She must be. Granny and Grandpa couldn't have kept this from me for all these years. They were too transparent for secrets. My mind is racing, listening to her, but thinking about Granny and Grandpa. Did they drop me hints that I didn't notice? Didn't I listen to them properly?

Margaret puts her cup and saucer on the mantelpiece and sits down in an oddly calculated way. She places her feet exactly together and straightens her back. Maybe she's been taught relaxation. Take a breath, relax your shoulders, stop your hands from moving unnecessarily. It's something that she'd never have learned if she'd stayed with us. It's difficult to learn calmness when you have six children. The veins on her hands are raised, the skin pink and mottled.

'I'm a different person now,' she says. 'I live with my husband in Norfolk. By the sea. In a caravan.'

'Husband?' says Adrian into a shocked silence.

We think we're grown-up, but we're only pretending. I'm three years old again, with a cold gap deep inside me, an unfilled hole. My brothers are boys, the gap inside them only partially filled. They're trying to grab everything desperately, pour it in, press down the lid.

'Bigamist!' yells my father, leaping out of his chair. 'We're not divorced.'

'Don't be ridiculous,' shouts Margaret, equally loudly. 'People just think we're married. He looks after me.'

'Living in sin!' says my father, and he's so pleased with himself that he sits down again and folds his arms triumphantly. Philippa, Angela, Lucia, Helen, etc., are congregated round him, over his shoulder, but he doesn't see them.

'Did you bring him with you?' says Jake.

She looks at him sharply. 'Of course not. Why should I? You don't know him. Who are you?'

I can see Jake struggling with himself. He can't decide whether he should identify himself and thus legitimize her inquiry, or remain anonymous. His observations will be freer if she doesn't know who he is.

'Jake,' says Adrian.

Margaret nods. I think she's forgotten him but she adds, 'Do you still play the violin?' she says.

'Did you even think of us?' says Paul.

'Of course I did,' she says and looks directly at him. 'Every day, every hour, every minute.'

I don't believe this.

'Then why didn't you come back for us?' says Paul. 'You don't seem to have made much effort.'

'No effort?' Her voice rises hysterically. 'You think I made no effort? I wrote and wrote and wrote to you all. Nobody replied. It was as if you'd wiped me out of your life. I came back and stood on the corner of the street when you came home from school, waiting to talk to you.' She pauses. 'But you didn't recognize me. You walked past me, talking to your friends. It was as if I didn't exist.'

'We wouldn't have been looking,' says Jake. 'We thought you were dead.'

Could she be imagining this? Why didn't she rush up to us with open arms? I try to picture myself not talking to Henry at sixteen. I wonder if she has a cold dark space inside her which stopped her loving us enough.

If a mother has this emptiness inside her, can she pass it on to her children? So it spreads onwards and outwards. An inherited disease. The mother thinks she knows everything. She knows nothing.

'I came back and watched you at the school gates. I saw other children being met. You didn't seem to mind. You had friends, you talked to each other. You didn't look as if you missed me.'

I was three years old. I didn't know how to miss someone.

'Why didn't you speak to us?' says Jake.

'I don't know,' she says in a voice that is suddenly bleak. 'The longer I waited, the harder it became. Now I can't really understand it myself. I thought you didn't need me – and in the end I gave up.'

'But you were wrong,' I say.

'No, she's right, quite right,' says my father, sounding pleased. 'We didn't need you. We managed perfectly well on our own.'

'We should have been asked,' says Adrian angrily. 'You made our choices for us. We weren't given the option.'

But we would have spent the last thirty years wondering if she was going to turn up. Watching. Waiting.

'No,' says Margaret. 'You should have been given the option.'

'You could have told us where she was,' says Adrian to Dad. 'An address would have been helpful.'

'I didn't have an address,' he says.

'Yes you did. It was on every letter I sent.'

'I threw them away unopened.' He realizes that he has confessed to something he has only just denied, so he picks up a mini-Battenberg and stuffs it into his mouth in one piece.

'Where did you go?' says Paul.

'Lots of places. In and out of hospital. I found jobs here and there for a while. Waitressing, shop work, cleaning.'

So my mother was a cleaner. The mother who was clever and went to university, but never qualified because of my father. The meeting on the beach, the wedding, six children. A golden age to my father. Dark ages to my mother.

'A burden to society,' says my father. He eats a handful of crisps, loudly.

'I paid my way when I was well enough,' says Margaret. 'I worked in a maternity hospital for a bit. They let me look after the babies.'

It is difficult to reconcile a woman who helps others give birth with a woman who has abandoned her own children. We were all babies once – her babies. We were all delivered by her from her own womb. How many unknown babies must you look after to compensate for your own lost babies? Is there a specific number? Two unknown babies equal one lost baby? Three, four, ten? Do you get there if you keep it up long enough? Does the guilt subside more quickly once you've passed the hundred mark?

'Waste of a life then,' says Dad. He unfolds his arms and takes his tea off the table. We can hear him sipping it – unnecessarily noisily – and then its progress as he swallows it. I try my own tea, but it's still much too hot; he must be burning his tongue.

'Who do you think you're fooling?' says Margaret. 'Do

you seriously imagine I had a meaningful life living with you? You couldn't even be bothered to hold a conversation with me. At least I wasn't dancing artistically from one nonsense to another.'

'That's not fair,' Paul says angrily. 'Dad's painting is art, not nonsense.'

'I earn good money,' shouts my father.

Some of it is nonsense, I think, remembering the painting with a hole in it on my wall.

'There is some value in being artistic,' says Jake, still calm. 'We must have inherited some of this nonsense from Dad, I suppose.'

Margaret looks away from Jake and says nothing. She probably thinks he's a serious violinist, not someone who busks every other day and lives off his wife's earnings. How can we ever hope for a real truth? It will be different for everyone.

Dad unfolds his arms and smiles. I'm annoyed by his obvious delight in her discomfort, disappointed that he's so unforgiving. I want him to stop acting like a child and to demonstrate the generous and kind spirit that I know is there.

'So you gave up in the end,' says Adrian. 'You didn't come back to the house to try to talk to us?'

'I did come back, almost straight away, in the first week, when I thought you'd all be at home – it was the summer holidays – but you weren't there. I watched your father go out, then let myself in to talk to you and to collect some of my things. Just a few clothes, books, photographs. I thought you could all join me later, when I had a home. But you weren't there, and everything, all the evidence of my life was gone. Completely disappeared. As if I never existed. What do you think it's like to come back to somewhere you have lived for the last nineteen years, and discover that there isn't even a space where you were?'

'Dad burnt it,' says Adrian. 'We watched him do it.'

'Typical.'

'You didn't think I'd keep all your stuff and wait sweetly for you to come back –'

'Hardly. I knew how your mind worked –'

'You had no idea. You were incapable of understanding.'

Where was I? My father was out, the boys were presumably off with friends, so where was I? Who looked after me?

'Why didn't you leave us a note?' says Adrian. 'You could have left it in my bedroom. Dad would never have known.'

'I thought –' Her voice rises. 'I thought you'd all wiped me away. You obviously don't need me, I thought. So I left and I've never gone back.' She is crying, great tears oozing out of her pinched, tiny eyes and rolling down her cheeks, black with smudged mascara. I can't look at her. 'Now I see your father again and realize I was wrong. I shouldn't have left you in his care.'

'You wouldn't have got in a second time,' says Dad. 'I changed all the locks.'

'Surprise, surprise. I couldn't work out why you hadn't done it already.'

'I wanted you to come back and find you'd left no mark on our lives.'

She wipes her eyes and looks round at us all. 'See,' she says. 'This is the man I lived with. He couldn't wait to get rid of your mother.'

Why is my father so cruel? I haven't seen this in him before. What is this nastiness that makes him enjoy her misery? Where does he keep it hidden? Does he practise it when he's on his own, so he can bring it out when it's needed, all perfect and fully formed?

He is muttering to himself. 'All that time when I could have been painting – wasted on cooking, ironing, washing-up . . .'

223

I wish he would stop. He mutters away, gradually subsiding into a semi-silence punctuated by the occasional inarticulate word. I wish I could reassure him. He brought us up on his own – no help from Angela, Philippa, Mary, etc. He loved and cared for us all. He was my mother and my father. I have a sudden clear picture of me in his studio, playing with paper and felt-tip pens, trying to imitate his picture on the easel. 'Be bold, Kitty,' he said. 'Put in all the colours, mix them up, don't be afraid of them. Colour is life.'

'You haven't changed, have you? As pretentious as ever. "I'm an artist," you told me and my parents, and I believed you for years. If you hadn't wasted so much time painting –'

'Wasting my time painting? I'm highly successful, I'll have you know. I've sold pictures in America, Brazil, Ceylon –'

'It's not Ceylon any more,' says Adrian. 'It's Sri Lanka.'

'Whatever,' says Dad. 'Sri Lanka, Cambodia, Outer Mongolia, Peking –'

'You're exaggerating,' says James irritably. 'Why would anyone in China want your pictures of European beaches?'

'Actually,' says Dad, 'I sell a lot of pictures in China.' He picks up a pack of cards and starts flicking them one by one at James. Some miss, some don't. They make contact and slide miserably to the floor. There's a picture of *The French Lieutenant's Woman* on the back, from the film, on the end of the Cob. Jeremy Irons and Meryl Streep.

'Reverting to childhood?' says James, and smiles charmingly. He loves to see Dad cornered. He picks up the cards carefully and starts to neaten them into a pack again.

I look at my father. I know he would like to throw books, plates, furniture, but he restricts himself to cards. He's more in control than he would like us to believe, I think. But I can see real anger too. He resents being found out.

This happened such a long time ago, and we have all survived, after all. I'm not sure we are giving him enough loyalty.

'Anyone for bridge?' says James, once he has collected all the cards together.

Margaret laughs – too enthusiastically. 'So who are you?' she says. 'Not one of my children, of course.'

James smiles back. He seems to be enjoying himself more now that he can argue with my father. 'I'm James,' he says. 'I'm married to Kitty.'

'I'm Kitty,' I say at last, and I seem to be leaning towards her, pulled by an invisible thread that was once physical and is now emotional.

But she looks puzzled. 'Kitty?' she says. 'I thought Kitty was the cat.'

There's a silence. Then I realize that she wouldn't know my nickname. 'No,' I say quickly. 'I'm Katie. They only called me Kitty when the cat died.'

There is another silence. My father starts to mutter.

'What?' I say loudly. 'What are you saying? I can't hear you.'

More silence. I can hear everyone breathing. I can hear everyone thinking. There is no movement.

'Dinah's daughter,' says Dad. 'They brought her back after Dinah died.'

An shaft of sunshine pierces the window and lights up the room.

The silence is not in the room. It's inside me.

It is cold and empty and vast.

7

A Seriously Happy World

James and I are travelling back to Birmingham on the train. He sits opposite me and doesn't speak, but even if he does I won't hear him. I'm far away from here, lost in this silence inside me.

Strangely, my first reaction after the initial shock of Dad's announcement was relief. It's all right, I thought. I don't have to make her my mother. I don't have to try any more. My legs went weak and I was pleased that I wasn't standing. Then I had to get up anyway, because I was going to be sick. I dashed outside just in time and threw up all over Grandpa's dying roses. The egg sandwiches, the salt and vinegar crisps, the Cherry Bakewells – they were all there, part-digested, vomited painfully over the stones from Chesil beach.

I leant against the side of the bungalow and tried not to think of being pregnant. I could feel sweat dripping off me, but I was bitterly cold. I looked at the distant sea, which blurred into the sky so you couldn't see where one ended and the other started. The greyness was more desolate than before, with none of its earlier vitality. A dead, dry greyness, which fell round me, seeping in, merging with my own bleakness. I couldn't stop shaking.

Eventually, I realized that James was standing beside me. I ignored him for a bit, but he wouldn't go away, so I let him stay there while I tried to stop my teeth chattering.

Maybe the others came out to see if I was all right. Maybe Dad came out. 'Kitty!' he would have said, but I didn't hear him.

I thought he was my only parent, a father and a mother to me. I accepted his faults, his eccentricity, his unreasonable short-lived anger because he was my father, but all my life he's been pretending. I thought we had a special relationship because I was the youngest. I pretended to myself that I reminded him of Margaret.

I think of how clever my brothers have all been, how they've never even hinted that they're really my uncles. Uncles are not the same as brothers. I try to look at them again: Adrian, bringing me back jugs from all over the world; Jake offering me sanctuary; Martin taking me for trips in the truck; Paul putting up the ladder to the loft. The brothers who met me from school. The brothers who are not my brothers.

'I want to go home,' I said to James.

And then, somehow, I found myself in a taxi, with my coat, my case and James.

'Did you know about my mother?' I said to James as we sat rigidly next to each other.

He looked unusually angry. 'Of course not. Do you think I'd have lied to you for all this time?'

It hadn't bothered my father or my brothers. How stupid I must have seemed to them when I asked about my mother – who I thought was Margaret. Perhaps they'd described Dinah anyway. I don't even know who the mother is in my mind – Margaret or Dinah.

The station platform was crowded with students and their clusters of rucksacks, suitcases and backpacks. I wanted to sit down, but there was no room, so we leaned against a large pipe that ran along the rear of the platform, the wind whistling round us. The greyness had come with me and found its way into the station. The train was late and everyone was hovering nervously, checking their watches, keeping an eye on the hanging monitors that said our train was ten minutes late, then twenty, then thirty. I watched the people round me, afraid that I would see my brothers or father among them. Every time I thought of them, I felt sick. All those years, they'd been pretending, and I didn't know. None of it was real. Everyone was acting. Everyone was lying.

The train pulled in and we found some seats. There may have been conversations as people took out their books, their newspapers, their sandwiches, but I haven't noticed. I don't want to look into anyone's eyes or acknowledge anyone else's existence. James will have been looking out of the window, his eyes darting from side to side as he spots distant road lights and the glow of towns and estimates the train's average speed per hour, as he always does. He carries a map inside his head; he knows distances and times.

A trolley comes down the aisle between the seats, and from a distance I can hear James asking for two coffees.

'Anything else?' he asks me, but it's too much effort to shake my head.

He takes a sandwich and a Danish pastry. He gives the man the pound coins first, neatly on top of each other, then the ten-pence pieces, then the pennies. How does he always manage to have the right change? I don't know how he survives in a world that is seldom neatened up, where you can't always tie up the ends.

I sip my coffee. James smiles at me and opens the sandwiches. He tackles the complexities of the packaging with meticulous care. He is like a magnet. Stray crumbs are drawn towards him so that he can keep them under strict control, liquids never spill because they recognize a force more powerful than their own. He offers me a sandwich, but I look past him.

228

Emily and Rosie aren't my nieces, I think in a sudden panic. We're only cousins. I'll never be allowed to look after them again. I can't be their favourite aunt any more.

The train is warm and glowing, protecting us from the outside darkness. We stop at stations, we move on. We could have gone through the Channel Tunnel and been in France by now, for all I know. I don't read the names of the stations. We are a small yellow entity moving through the uncertainty of a black world. And yellow is deceptive. It is hard and bright and brittle and can disintegrate at any time. The darkness is constantly threatening to break through. I always thought I could easily separate colour from absence of colour, but how simple it is to step from one to the other without even realizing.

'Why didn't anyone tell me?' I say out loud.

'I don't know,' James says.

'What difference would it have made? What was the point of the secret?'

That's what bothers me most. Not losing a mother – who I thought was dead anyway – not being a grand-daughter when I thought I was a daughter, not being a niece when I thought I was a sister. It's the pointlessness of it all. The realization that everyone else was in on a secret that I knew nothing about. They were all together, conspirators huddling over their makeshift fire, while I was out in the cold, in the dark, because nobody thought fit to invite me in.

'Perhaps they thought it would be better for you at first,' says James. 'And then no one knew how to tell you the truth as you got older.'

I sip my coffee, which has gone cold.

'I'm probably not even called Kitty Wellington.' I stop and think about this. There is no such person as Kitty Wellington. I feel the blackness surround me, and I try to look inside for solace, but there's nothing there. James is saying something and I can't hear him.

The lights start to flicker, but it's so brief that I might be imagining it. I shut my eyes and open them again. There. Is it real or imaginary? I watch the other passengers for signs that it's real, but they're reading, sleeping, looking out of the window with glazed eyes.

'Strange,' says James. 'Something wrong with the power, I suppose.'

The lights go out, suddenly and completely, and I hear a howl of fear. It takes me a few seconds to realize that the sound came from me. I shouldn't have done that, I think. I knew it was going to happen. Yellow never lasts.

I can hear James' voice, repeating something over and over, but I can't hear the words because the blackness is pushing its way inside me, pressing so hard that I need all my energy to resist it.

I feel his hand on mine as it rests on the table. 'It's all right,' he says. 'It's all right.'

'Ladies and gentlemen.' The metal voice makes me jump. 'This is the guard speaking. We appear to have a fault with the lighting, but rest assured we are doing our best to put it right and normal service will be resumed as soon as possible.' He over-accentuates the end of some words and it takes time to make sense of the extra syllable.

I look out and discover that the blackness outside is not as black as I thought. I can see windows in houses, cars on distant roads, even light from the moon. The pressure in my head eases a bit. James' hand is rubbing mine gently, soothingly.

The lights flicker on briefly, go off again, and then come back and stay on.

I look at James looking at me.

'Oh, James,' I say, and start to cry.

The receptionist looks at me across the desk. Her short black fringe makes her look like Cleopatra, but her label says Antonia. Her lipstick is perfect, immaculately drawn and coloured in, so her lips look artificial, painted on to disguise the fact that her mouth is small and tight. 'You missed an appointment,' she says sternly.

'I'm sorry,' I say. 'My grandparents died suddenly.'

She still looks too authoritative, but her voice softens a little. 'Oh dear.' She pauses to think what to say. I can see it's not easy. 'It's hard to lose grandparents, isn't it?' she says.

It's hard to lose a mother too, I think, and to gain a new grandmother.

She looks at the screen in front of her. 'We have a cancellation this morning – ten thirty. Do you want to wait?'

'Yes,' I say.

The waiting room is crowded, and a woman with a baby and an older girl sits down next to me. The girl has to stand, while the mother puts the baby on her lap.

'Mum,' says the girl, 'I want to sit down.' She has wispy light brown hair tied into two long plaits. The plaits are too thin and end in a tiny feathery curl. I remember girls at school like this, who'd never had their hair cut. It doesn't get a chance to thicken and flourish. The girl looks about eight, and is picking at patches of leftover purple varnish on her nails. She stands defiantly close to her mother. 'I want to sit down,' she says again, quietly, but firmly. Her face is very pale and the skin below her eyes has a purple tinge, as if she hasn't slept all night. She has enormous eyes – blue and very bright. She might be older than I first thought. She stands close to her mother and stares at her fiercely.

'Sit on the floor,' says the mother, and pushes her down. The girl reluctantly bends her knees and crouches on the floor, holding herself tightly in a neat bundle.

Then she looks up at me, her eyes steady and intense, as

if she believes she can hypnotize me into moving. I try a nervous smile, but she doesn't respond, so I look away.

'Ma-ma-ma–' says the baby.

'Henry!' says the mother delightedly and holds his hands while she shakes him up and down on her lap.

He chortles. His laugh is long and infectious, a perfectly tuned, rhythmical giggle. ''Gain,' he keeps saying, ''gain.'

I watch him. I want to put out my hand and touch his chubby arms, kiss his padded cheek, make him look at me as he giggles. I smile at him.

The girl is interested in his fun. She puts a hand up to him. 'Henry,' she calls gently, tickling his elbow.

Henry tries to turn and see her, so his bouncing rhythm is lost. 'Leave him alone, Megan,' says her mother sharply.

Megan's hand falls back and she turns away from them.

I catch her eye again and smile sympathetically. This time, I see a flicker of response in her eyes and a quick grin flash across her face.

The mother tries to jiggle Henry on her lap again, but he has lost interest. He puts a finger into his mouth and sucks urgently. Then the finger slips out and he starts to wail. I want to take him, put him on my lap, cuddle him tightly.

'Mrs Maitland.' The receptionist is calling my name. 'You know which room?'

I nod and walk quickly down the corridor to Dr Cross's room.

She's expecting me. The receptionist must have rung through.

'Hello, Kitty. Come and sit down.' She always looks pleased to see me. I enjoy the sensation of being welcomed, until I remember that she must say the same to everyone. It's just a professional skill.

I sit. I look at the ceiling, out of the window past the venetian blinds, without seeing. They ought to have mirror windows, so that people inside can see out, while people outside only see their reflections. They could know how ill they look before they meet the doctor.

I tell Dr Cross about my grandparents dying. I tell her about the funeral. Then I stop. She knows there's more and she waits. She doesn't push or prompt me. I experiment with various phrases in my head, then I give up and let the words come out in the way they choose.

'My mother came back from the dead,' I say. 'The prodigal mother. And it turns out that she's not my mother at all.'

I tell her the story, about Margaret and about Dinah, about the terrible betrayal I feel from my father who is not my father, and the brothers who are not my brothers.

She listens and doesn't say anything immediately. She appears to be thinking. So I sit in her silence, which wraps itself round me like a blanket, a protective layer of comfort. All the confusion, anger and loneliness that have been racing around in my mind seem suspended for a time. I would like to stay like this all day.

'Did James know?' she says.

I hesitate. 'He says not.'

'Then we must believe him, mustn't we?'

I like the way she has identified the most alarming part.

'What do you want to call your father now?'

This takes me by surprise. I've been so tied up by the difficulty of knowing what to call my mother, or even myself, that I haven't realized I can no longer call him Dad. I couldn't call him Guy, and I can't think of an alternative.

Dr Cross somehow knows this. 'Perhaps we should go on calling him your father for the time being.'

I feel absurdly relieved.

'Have you talked to him since all this happened?'

'No,' I say.

He's been to my flat. I heard him ringing the bell, banging the knocker, calling through the letterbox. 'Kitty!'

he called. 'Kitty, I need to talk to you.' And then, more quietly, 'Please let me in, Kitty. Please.'

I've never heard him sound like this before. He demands, he shouts, he expects; he never asks. Eventually he went away. I wonder if he's tried James' flat, but I'm not sure if he realizes that James and I live next door to each other. He hasn't been back to my flat since the day I moved in. I always go and see him.

He tried phoning, but I didn't pick up the phone. I heard him on the answer machine. 'Kitty. It's Dad. Talk to me.'

After five attempts, he decided to offer an explanation. 'I was going to tell you, Kitty. I always said I would tell you the truth when you were eighteen, but you grew up before I realized. Why does it change everything? Have I ever let you down?'

That's not the point. You lied to me.

'I like being your father,' he said again. 'I want you to stay being my daughter.'

Fine. Whatever you want.

I still didn't answer the phone.

Dr Cross listens to this in silence. I am sorry to be burdening her with this, but who else can I tell? She seems to absorb it all. Nothing surprises or shocks her.

Eventually I realize that I've stayed for longer than usual. Her appointment system will be disrupted.

'Come tomorrow,' she says. 'Ask the receptionist to put you at the end of the day if there are no available gaps.'

I feel a huge surge of affection for her. How does she manage to absorb all this complexity and remain calm?

'Thank you,' I say and leave.

Outside, I wait to make another appointment. Henry, Megan and their mother are still waiting. Megan is sitting on my chair, swinging her legs. She smiles quite openly when she sees me. Her mum looks up, makes a connection and notices Megan next to her. 'Keep still,' she says sharply, but Megan's legs don't stop moving. Her lips move slightly as she chants a song to herself in time with the rhythm of her legs.

Her mother gives up and turns her attention back to Henry. 'Half a pound of tuppenny rice, half a pound of treacle,' she sings softly. He stops moving and watches her, waiting for the 'Pop goes the weasel', when she parts her knees and he nearly falls through. Then he chuckles and she enfolds him in her arms and kisses his head.

I have to look away.

The receptionist gives some leaflets to the woman in front of me. 'An appointment will be made for you at the maternity hospital,' she says, 'and they'll write directly to you.'

You can't tell the woman is pregnant. She looks healthy and cheerful and fit – not at all like Suzy or me.

I look at Henry on his mum's lap. He could have been killed like Suzy's baby, he might never have existed. He is looked after by his mother who feeds him and changes his nappy and loves him.

I leave the queue without making an appointment.

I nearly fall over a mother with a baby boy in a pushchair. He is wailing.

'Sorry,' I say.

'Please don't start all that again, Henry,' I hear from the mother, who has a tired desperation in her voice.

'Harvey Patterson.'

'Oh, yes,' says the woman with the pushchair. 'We're here.' She picks up her baby. 'Shh, Henry,' she says.

I go out, walk through the park, back to my flat.

The world is full of baby equipment and I want my share of it. I stand outside Mothercare for a while, looking round before going in, to see if there's anyone who might recognize me. I stand in front of a display of little dresses for baby girls of 3–6 months, and gradually relax slightly. They're so pretty – a maroon velour dress with matching knickers, a pink check smock over a frilly blouse, tiny pink socks that look like kittens. I want to buy all of them, but I don't. I haven't got a baby girl.

Buy me, the pram covered in vivid red, green and yellow squares shouts at me from the far end of the shop. Me, me, says a cot with Winnie the Pooh bedding. He's watering the garden and picking flowers. There are riotously coloured mobiles above me – Pooh Bear again, teddies going to bed, Hey Diddle Diddle, with a cat with a fiddle and a cow jumping over the moon.

Babies are fun, they all say to me. Without babies, you are excluded from a seriously happy world.

I want something cream. The same cream as the wool I bought for Suzy's baby. It smells warm and comfortable, the only colour that will do. I look at the clothes for newborn babies. I hesitate over the white perfection of the packs of nappies, but I know everybody uses disposable ones.

I pick up a packet and hesitate. No, I think. It's easier to buy them in Sainsburys or Safeway's. I already have several dozen at home, piled into my wardrobe, pushed up against the back wall, hidden behind some old blouses.

My eyes finally find the packets of sleepsuits. They skim past the white ones, until they see the cream I am looking for. I pick up a packet and study it. The suits are so tiny, for a new baby, maybe a premature baby, and the cream is subdued and gentle. More human and loving than white.

I run my hand over the packaging, longing to take them out immediately. I almost have the baby in my arms, alive and warm, in a disposable nappy, its skin pink and wrinkled, its miniature heart beating on its own, pumping the blood round its tiny, perfect body.

A woman stares at me as she sorts through the boys' clothes. She picks up a jumper, examines it, glances over at me, and then puts it back. What does she want? Why is she looking at me? Does she know something that I don't? I want to buy the mobile with the teddies in pyjamas – they're clutching a clock, a hot water bottle, a pillow. But the woman makes me uncomfortable, so I go straight to the checkout with only the sleepsuits. I can always come back another day.

I come out into the Pallasades shopping centre, proud of the Mothercare carrier bag. I'm a normal expectant mother, just like everyone else. I know about babies, about children and prams and cots.

I need to find another exit out of the Pallasades, in case Jake is playing the violin in his usual place. I hover in the entrance of a shop selling accessories and look through the windows. Hairbands covered in sunflowers, gold and silver tiaras, key rings with dangling pink pigs, earrings of treble clefs, slides with sparkly green frogs on them that change colour when they move. I step into the doorway. What's the point of buying these things? I come out. Maybe I will never see Emily and Rosie again. I go in. I could always buy some frivolous odds and ends and send them in a parcel as a surprise present. Providing Lesley doesn't censor all the incoming mail. She could be a disciple of my father. Throwing away anything sent by me. I'd have to disguise my handwriting.

I go in and pick up a few slides and earrings without examining them too carefully. I take them to the checkout. The girl smiles at me. I don't smile back. I don't want to look at her in case she can tell I don't have daughters of the right age.

'Those frogs are lovely, aren't they?' she says. 'I'm going to buy some for the weekend when I go clubbing with my boyfriend.'

She looks about fourteen. Her hair is an unnatural red and it hangs loosely and unevenly to her shoulders. Her face is hidden under a mask of meticulously applied make-up. There is a gap between her top and her trousers and I can see her tummy button, pierced and adorned with a silver ring.

'That's £24.92,' she says.

I can't believe they cost so much. It's only a few slides and earrings. 'Fine,' I say, determined not to reveal my alarm.

I have to write out a cheque. Partway through, I realize that I have bought several pairs of earrings for pierced ears, and I don't think Rosie and Emily have pierced ears. Lesley wouldn't approve.

I sign the cheque and give it to the girl. She looks at me and I look at her. Does she know that my nieces who are now my cousins don't have pierced ears?

'Do you have your cheque guarantee card?' she says sweetly.

She knows I don't really want these things. She knows I am a fraud.

I give her the cheque guarantee card from my purse and watch her writing my number on the back of the cheque. Then I stuff the bag into my Mothercare bag with the sleepsuits and leave the shop hastily, wondering what I'm going to do with them.

I take an escalator down to New Street Station. Huddles of people are watching the times of trains clicking up on the display board. I stand and look too, in case anybody wonders why I'm here. Then I walk to the back doors that take me out past the taxi ranks and to the bus stop where I can wait for a bus home.

*

The post is lying on the hall floor, so I know James hasn't been in. I wish he would just come, uninvited. But he won't. He's too careful, too considerate. I recognize most of the letters from the writing and their postmarks so I put them aside to open later. Just one looks interesting – hand-written and quite heavy. I look at it, balance it in my hand. A Birmingham postmark, posted yesterday. I have no idea who it's from, although the handwriting is vaguely familiar, strangely ominous. The telephone rings and I go to answer it, putting the letter in my bag. My hand hovers over the receiver, not sure if I want to pick it up, and the answer machine cuts in.

'Kitty, it's me. Are you OK?'

Yes, James, I'm fine.

I intended to read today – my mind is moving very fast – but once I sit down, I don't want to move. I can reach the answer machine though, so I rewind it and listen to the messages.

'Kitty – it's Caroline. I need your reports back by the end of the week.'

'Hi – it's Ruth. I can't seem to find this week's review from you. Have I lost it?'

'This is Peter Smith from Smith, Horrocks and Smith. Could you phone me, please.'

Who are Smith, Horrocks and Smith? Why is Peter Smith so arrogant that he would expect me to know his name? People should identify themselves if they want me to phone them.

'Kitty – it's Caroline again. Did you get my message – about your reports?'

'It's Adrian. I need to talk to you, Kitty. Ring me back.'

'Ruth again. Are you all right, Kitty?'

'Peter Smith here again. Could you ring me urgently?' If it's that urgent, you can write me a letter.

'Kitty, what's going on? It's Ruth. Please send my books back. I have a deadline to meet.'

'Kitty. Are you all right? Come round.' Only James does not need to identify himself.

'Caroline again. Where are you? What's going on? I need the manuscripts – just send them back if you don't have time for the reports.'

'Adrian again. Ring me.'

'It's Caroline. Ring me.'

'Peter Smith. Ring me.'

'Ring me, Kitty – it's Ruth.'

'Kitty, wake up and come round for a Chinese takeaway. I want some company.'

Oh James. I wish I could. I'm walking down a path that I can't leave. Even if I turn my head to look at the scenery, I know that my feet will keep on walking firmly in the same direction.

I wake up into complete darkness with an ache in my neck. I sit up and search the darkness urgently, trying to locate the clock. Then I remember that I'm not in bed, but on the sofa. I've been dreaming about grandmothers and great-grandmothers.

I stand up and stumble into the bedroom, where I collapse on to the bed. When I close my eyes again, I see the pink van with its wandering question marks.

I can hear Suzy disowning it. 'It's nothing to do with me.' I know that she's talking about babies, not the pink van.

'It's your baby,' I say to her, but she doesn't hear me. 'Look!' I scream at her. 'Look at the baby. It's yours!'

My scream wakes me up and I lie there sweating, though the air around me is cold. I start to shiver. I climb under the duvet and try to pull it round me, but the cold penetrates through invisible channels. I sit up and put on the lamp.

The light swirls round and engulfs me. Babies fill the flat, screaming. I'm coming, I say, getting out of bed. I can smell their rich, creamy smell, the talcum powder, their little bits of sick, the milky, baby smell.

I walk through the flat, putting on my dressing gown, and go out of the front door, leaving the babies behind. At the last minute, I pick up James' key. I leave my door open and wedge it with a package that the postman delivered yesterday, so the babies can escape while I'm gone. I let myself into James' flat and creep across his bare, cold, wooden floor, listening to my booming footsteps. There are no babies here – it's too clean. I push open the door to James' bedroom. He's lying on his back with his mouth open, snoring gently.

I roll him on to his side away from me and crawl in beside him, stretching my legs out to mirror his shape, wrapping my body along his contours, moulding myself until I feel that I'm his second skin. He stops snoring. I lie very still, hoping he won't wake. I want the warmth to flow from his body into mine so that I don't have to be cold any more. I want to steal his heat.

When I wake again it is six a.m. I can see the numbers on the clock glowing redly. They play games while the world sleeps, flowing out of their shapes and winding each other into knots, writhing like snakes, challenging like question marks, intertwining on a pink van –

Now I know why I see the van in my dreams. Perhaps I was born in it, lived there with Dinah until something happened to her and I was brought back to Birmingham.

I sit up. Who brought me back to Birmingham? I must have a father somewhere. There must be someone in the world that I can belong to.

James groans and rolls over, pulling the quilt over his head. 'It's cold,' he mutters. I don't think he knows I'm here.

I tuck the quilt round him and kiss the nape of his neck. Then I wrap myself in my dressing gown again and tiptoe back to my flat, where the door is open and waiting for me.

I dress in jeans and a thick maroon jumper, dithering as I pull on socks and trainers. I don't know where I'm going exactly, but I know how important it is to go out. I can't stay here any more. My flat holds me in a half-world where I lose my sense of time. I need to go where I can see the sun rise, where there are people talking and walking and doing things, where the world is more real.

I check the baby clothes in my wardrobe. Two dozen nappies, three cream sleepsuits, soft and tiny. I rub my cheek against them and breathe in their baby smell. I have talcum powder, cream for nappy rash, sterilizing equipment, bottles, blankets, rompers in pastel blue with teddies embroidered on them, tiny blue socks that look like sheep, little enough to fit on my thumb. I ache at their smallness. I stand and touch everything and feel their textures. Nearly there. Only a pram and a cot now. Best to leave the big items to last, just in case –

I hesitate at the front door when I see a pile of unopened packages on the hall table. These must be the books they are all getting so excited about on the answer machine. I'm surprised at how many there are. I can't understand why I haven't seen them before. Did James put them on the table? But it must have been me because James doesn't come uninvited. I can't remember doing it. I pick them all up and carry them back into my lounge.

I sit down with a pen and cross out all the addresses. Underneath, I write with a flourish: 'Not known at this address.' I pause for a few seconds to admire my ingenuity. Then I find some carrier bags and carry them all out with me. They're very heavy. I decide not to close the front door because I feel a sudden desolation at leaving the warmth and familiarity of my flat. I don't want to shut it away. I want some of it to escape and follow me.

As soon as I see a postbox, I stop to post the manuscripts. It's not easy because they are so large, but I discover that if you bend each one at a particular moment, it will squeeze past the opening and slide down inside.

'There,' I say with some satisfaction. 'That'll give the postman something to do.'

A girl whizzes past on rollerblades and makes me jump. She glances over her shoulder at me for a second, then looks quickly back to where she's going. She's carrying an orange bag over her shoulder, full of newspapers. It's early for her to be out on her own, I think. I won't let my child deliver newspapers.

I feel strangely light as I walk away from the postbox, breathing freely now that I've disposed of all my burdensome responsibilities.

I run, watching my feet slap down on the pavement, getting pleasure from the sudden burst of energy. I slow down after a while, knowing that I'm much too early for where I want to go, and find a number 11 bus stop. My usual two circuits should fill a few hours. The driver recognizes me. 'Another fun-packed day, then?' he says.

I pretend to smile without looking at him directly. There's something about these totally casual acquaintances that I like. The idea that you know people when you don't know them at all. The feeling that you can trust someone because he smiles at you. He could be an axe-murderer. Or I could be. One day he'll see my picture in a newspaper, recognize me and point me out to his wife. 'I know her,' he will say. 'She used to do the outer circle every now and again. Quite pleasant she was. Didn't talk much.'

'Well I never,' his wife will say. 'Fancy that.'

Harborne, Selly Oak, Bournville, King's Norton, King's Heath, Hall Green, Yardley, Erdington, Aston, Perry Barr, Handsworth, Winson Green, Bearwood, Harborne, Selly Oak . . . I say the names to myself as we go round, like a nursery rhyme, old and loved. Words that have no meaning, yet are reassuringly familiar. We pass the road leading to the Maternity Hospital – between Harborne and Selly Oak – twice, but I don't get off. I'm waiting for visiting hours. Two till eight. When I was there, they put the mothers of dead babies on the same floor as mothers of live babies. How could they do that?

I change buses and go into the city centre for some lunch in the restaurant at the top of Rackhams. I choose salmon salad and a slice of lemon meringue pie with a cup of tea. I sit for a long time, eating slowly, watching everyone else. Most people come in pairs, mainly female and elderly. Respectable people with perms and lipstick and handbags. They seem to have so much to say to each other.

I look at my watch. The minute hand moves so slowly. Everything I do stretches out into slow motion. I pick the fork up, put it down again, bring it up again, put the fork into my mouth and eat. Inside, my stomach has become a furiously active washing machine, rotating and pounding, rocking and mangling. I move even more slowly.

I set my mind to leave at 12.50. Mustn't be late. Then I can slip in with everyone else.

The minute hand reaches ten. I eat the final mouthful of lemon meringue and gulp down the last of the tea while I stand, pushing my chair away.

Now that it's time to go, I can't wait. I pull on my denim jacket as I walk out through the tables, flinging my bag over my shoulder.

'Excuse me.'

I hear the voice behind me and nearly start to run. They know, I think, they know. I walk deliberately, moving every muscle with enormous care, forcing myself to look normal –

Someone in front of me puts out an arm to stop me and I try to push past him. 'I'm late,' I say. 'I can't stop.'

But he holds my arm firmly. A big, plump man with a red face and dark hair which is too bushy and black for his age. 'I'm sorry,' he says. 'I think perhaps –'

The person behind me reaches us. I don't want to turn and look at her. 'Sorry,' she says.

I turn. She's a waitress. She thrusts out a hand, holding a purse which looks like my purse.

'You forgot this,' she says.

I stare at her in astonishment. 'No,' I say. 'Mine's in my bag.'

The man has let go of my arm. I could just make a run for it.

'But it must be yours,' says the waitress. 'You left it on your table.'

'No,' I say, shaking my head. 'Look. It's here in my bag.'

But it isn't. There is no purse in my bag. 'I'm sorry,' I say. 'You're right.'

The waitress smiles and hands it over. The man goes back to selecting his tray of food.

'Thank you,' I say. 'Thank you.'

I turn away and walk quickly to the escalator. I've lost valuable time. It is already one o'clock and I haven't even got to the right bus stop.

Hurry, I think. Hurry.

The Maternity Hospital smells new and modern and comfortable. The atmosphere is restful, with a gentle pink carpet and pale wood fittings. It's amalgamated with the Women's Hospital now, combining babies and women, so the doctors don't have to travel from one hospital to the other any more. I don't know how they find room for both, when there was once only room for babies, but everything looks organized and controlled.

I'm early after all, so I stand outside the glass doors for a while before going in. I check my watch occasionally and study the various approaches as if I'm waiting to meet someone. Just in case anyone is watching me.

People walk in through the automatic glass doors easily, talking, carrying flowers and boxes of chocolates, preoccupied with their own lives. Other people come out and walk briskly to the car park. Some medical students pass me, shivering in their white coats and chattering enthusiastically.

'Caesarean', I hear them say, 'balti', 'stethoscope upside down'. I watch them enviously, admiring their enthusiasm, but they make me feel old. They're like children. They know instinctively how to enjoy themselves.

The automatic doors open, and a small group of people emerges. Among them, there's a young woman who looks tired and slightly unsteady, with unnaturally bright eyes. Another, older woman beside her, is almost her twin. They have the same tidy hair, but the younger woman is blonde, while the older one has streaks of grey. They're the same height. The younger one looks pale and unwell, the other tanned and at ease. With them is a nurse who's holding something in her arms, wrapped in an exquisitely knitted cream shawl. It takes me some time to realize that she's carrying the new baby – a tiny, perfect baby who must only have been breathing independently for about twenty-four hours.

'Where is he?' says the young woman, stamping her feet up and down. 'The baby will get cold.'

'He'll be here in a few minutes,' says the older woman. 'Don't forget he's had to walk all the way to the car park.'

The nurse looks down at the baby in her arms. 'Look at him,' she says. 'Not a care in the world.'

The young woman leans over to the baby and her face softens. She puts out a finger and strokes the baby's face gently. I can't see the baby from where I am standing but I can see the calming effect he has on his mother.

'Here he is,' says the older woman and waves to a silver-blue BMW which is rolling gently towards the entrance. The driver parks the car and jumps out immediately to open the door for the women. He's older than I expected, old enough to be the younger woman's father.

They fuss over the baby and who is going to hold it. The man opens the door and the young woman slides into the back seat. The nurse hands the baby to her.

'Steady,' the man keeps saying. 'Be careful now.'

'Stop fussing, Dad,' she says as she pulls her feet in neatly behind her.

'Stop fussing, Ronald,' says the older woman, and walks round to the passenger side.

Ronald grins cheerfully at the nurse before he gets back in. 'I'm a grandfather,' he says. 'I don't look it, do I?'

'Not a day over twenty,' says the nurse. She waves as they drive off, and then goes back in to deliver another baby.

I try to imagine Margaret doing the same thing, but I can't make her fit.

This is a place full of babies.

Babies calm people –

Babies make people normal –

Babies are real –

I find I am sitting on a pink seat in the Maternity Hospital, gazing into space, thinking of mothers. I look at my watch. Two o'clock. I can't believe it. I don't remember coming in. Where has all the time gone? I jump up and bump into a nurse who has just come out of the lift with a woman in a wheelchair.

'Sorry,' I say and dodge round her to catch the lift while the doors are still open.

The nurse expects people to respond to her authority and make room for her. You can see it in the way she moves, the way she looks at me.

'Please walk more carefully,' she says.

A flush creeps up my face. 'Sorry,' I say again and look past her at the reception desk. Nobody is watching us. Just as I reach the lift doors, they close. I press the button and wait.

The lift comes down again and three people step out chatting animatedly. They don't see me as I slip in behind them.

I study the buttons for the different floors. What am I doing here?

Looking for a baby.

There are plenty of babies here. Which one do you want?

Any one. It doesn't matter.

There are sleeping babies, screaming babies, fat babies, skinny babies, blue eyes – don't they all have blue eyes? – blond hair, black hair, no hair.

It doesn't matter. Just a baby.

I reach out and press a number at random. The lift glides up and I step out on to a floor that is immediately familiar. The smell jumps up at me and I stop. I've been here before.

I came in on a trolley. It was an emergency. People were talking around me. I was looking at the ceiling, knowing that something was horribly wrong, wondering if I was going to die. It's a shame for James, I thought.

Then the trolley stopped moving.

'When did you last eat?' said a voice.

'I don't know.' I was annoyed that they should be interested in my diet, but his voice sounded so urgent. I tried to remember where we were in the day. 'Breakfast, I suppose.'

'Good. You're going to feel a small prick on your hand. Can you count backwards from twenty?'

Everything hurts. How can I count while it all hurts so much? But I did it anyway, too tired to argue. 'Twenty, nineteen, eighteen, sev-en-teen, six . . .'

When I woke up, I could smell the hospital around me, and I still hurt, but not so much. I was lying in a bed in a clean, organized place that smelled of disinfectant. I wanted to know about the baby, but I didn't want to ask. I knew, really. Nobody had to tell me.

They did tell me eventually. 'I'm sorry, Katherine –'

Who's Katherine? Who are they talking to? Do I know her?

'Your baby didn't survive.'

I know. It's not necessary to tell me.

And later they explained that they had to take away my womb as well. Cut me open, take away the whole thing, the baby in its little sac, the miracle creature who lived off me for six months, lift it out, tie up the blood vessels, sew me back up again. Chuck the waste down the sluice. A nice neat job. The mother survived. Mission accomplished.

'You had a ruptured womb,' a doctor told me. 'There was nothing else we could do – you are lucky to have survived at all. We weren't sure you were going to make it.'

But what was the point? Why not let us die together? That would have been much more reasonable.

'Why?' I said. 'What did I do?'

'Nothing,' he said. 'These things happen. Nobody knows why.'

If I hadn't painted the spare room in James' flat, if I

hadn't run for the bus, if I hadn't climbed the stairs to my flat so often in the last few days – if I hadn't done any of those things, or all of those things . . . They said it wasn't my fault. But it doesn't happen to everyone. Only me. So it must have been my fault.

'Can I help you?' A nurse is standing beside me – a girl, a child.

'I'm looking for my sister-in-law. Wellington. Suzy Wellington.'

The girl looks puzzled. 'I don't think she's on this ward,' she says. 'What's she in for?'

'A baby. She's just had a baby.'

Her face clears. 'You're on the wrong floor. We only deliver babies here. Then they go up to the wards. But I can go and check for you.'

I shake my head. 'What floor am I on?'

'Third.'

'Oh, sorry,' I say quickly. 'I must have pressed the wrong button. I thought I was on the fourth floor.'

I turn back to the lift, which is still open. I go in and press for the fourth floor. As the doors glide shut, I smile at the nurse.

There's no one outside the lift on the next floor. I step out and look round. The place seems deserted, although I can hear the gentle murmur of people talking in the distance. I wait for a while and nothing happens. It feels quiet, sleeping, unoccupied.

I walk down the corridor. Softly, then more boldly. No one is going to challenge me. I look into the first room of four beds. This is OK. All visitors look round the rooms like this. Looking for the right person. Three women lie there, talking to each other. Babies in cots at the foot of their beds. Their miniature, breathing forms, wrapped cosily in cream hospital blankets.

The next room. Full. Two women asleep, the others with husbands, mothers, aunties politely round the beds. Talking in low voices about the weather. Television, the price of nappies.

The next room is empty. I step in. A sudden snore. There's a woman in the far corner. Fast asleep with her mouth open, breathing fiercely.

A baby is sleeping in the cot at the end of her bed. A baby. I stand above his cot and look at him. He's the baby I have come for. My baby. His face is pink and smooth, the tiny line of eyelashes resting moistly on his cheeks, a little tuft of black hair coming to a point just above his eyes.

I lean over to pick him up. Just as I get my hands underneath him, a loud snore erupts from the bed. I freeze as the woman rolls over to face me. But she is still asleep, her eyes shut, her face loose and crumpled.

I pick up the baby, who murmurs. I hold him in my arms and look at him. This is the baby I've been waiting for. It's difficult to breathe properly, the pain of love is so hard to bear. I take him into the nearest toilets, marked 'For patients only'. There's no sign of anyone, so I slip into one of the cubicles.

Once inside, I put Henry gently down on the floor, and open up the large Marks & Spencer carrier bag I've brought with me. I lay him inside, on his back, so he won't die of cot death. I wrap him all around with my own blanket, tucking it firmly round the little tag on his ankle. If it goes off, we'll just have to run. He sleeps through all of this, with only a snuffle.

Then I step out confidently and go straight to the lift. I decide to take the stairs instead of the lift. I'll be less conspicuous. Anyone I meet will be doing the same as me, visiting or leaving after a visit.

I walk through the entrance hall carefully, waiting for an alarm to go off, or someone to stop me, but nothing happens. Pink carpet, automatic doors. Out into the fresh air.

I walk away from the hospital briskly, feeling the weight of Henry in his Marks & Spencer bag. He's slightly restless now and makes sudden jerky movements with his arms. The bag crackles.

I should get to a number 11 bus stop, so that I can take him home as quickly as possible in case he wants a feed. It'll be difficult if he cries. People don't expect Marks & Spencer bags to contain a baby. I don't see why not. He fits easily enough.

But instead of waiting for a bus, I decide to walk. I'm afraid of going home. I can't associate my home with a baby. It's my home, my colours, my books. There's no room for a baby there. So I go on walking, towards Harborne. Several police cars pass me on the way to an emergency with their sirens blaring. I wonder what could be so urgent.

It's getting chilly and I'm glad I remembered to bring the extra blanket. Fresh air is good for babies. Every so often, I stop and look in at his little pink face, see a tiny smile stretch out his mouth, see the miracle of his nose, an exact miniature replica of an adult nose.

I move him from one hand to the other, but my arms are beginning to ache, so I look for somewhere to sit down. I need to work out what to do next. It hadn't occurred to me that it would be so easy. I haven't sorted things out carefully enough. The fact that nothing went wrong has confused me.

I've reached Harborne now, the park next to the doctor's surgery. I find a bench and sit down, arranging Henry gently in his bag. I long to pick him up and hold him, but I'm too conspicuous here. I just put a finger in the bag and stroke his tiny cheek. His eyelids flicker slightly, but remain closed, alive and pulsing with warmth. He gurgles, and I know he's recognized his mother's touch.

I don't know what to do, where to go or who to talk to. He'll wake up soon and need feeding. He'll probably cry. What will I do then? My stomach churns like a cement-mixer. What if I'm no good with babies? What if he doesn't stop crying?

But I'm all right here now, sitting in a park in the late afternoon with my baby beside me. I don't want to move. I'm not sure if I can.

'Hello.'

I jump. A girl is standing in front of me, a girl with long plaits and very big blue eyes. She looks familiar.

'Hello,' I say.

'I know you. You were at the doctor's.'

I look at her more closely and recognize her as Megan, the sister of the baby Henry, who I sat next to on my last visit.

'Yes,' I say. 'At the doctor's.'

She sits down on the bench beside the Marks & Spencer bag. I move the baby closer to me.

'What's in the bag?' she says.

I shrug. 'Nothing much. Odds and ends.'

'Can I look?'

'No.'

Henry is becoming restless and lets out a little cry. Megan looks at me and I look at her. 'You shouldn't talk to strangers,' I say, remembering Emily and Rosie and Captain Hook. It feels like a million years ago.

'It's a baby,' she says.

'Yes.'

'Why is it in a bag?'

'I don't know.' I try to think. 'I haven't got a pram.'

'You can buy them.'

'Yes. But they're expensive.'

'I know.' She starts to swing her legs under the bench and

253

half smiles at me. She seems suddenly clever. 'Can I come with you and the baby?'

'No, of course not.' I can feel my insides starting to panic. 'Where's your mum?'

She gazes into the distance and swings her legs, humming under her breath. Henry settles down again.

'I've run away from home,' she says after a while, and then hums again.

'That doesn't seem a very good idea. Won't your mum worry?'

'You don't know my mum.'

'Yes, I do. I saw her at the doctor's. You have a baby brother called Henry.'

She stops swinging her legs and looks into the bag again. 'What's it called?'

'Henry,' I say proudly.

She screws up her nose. 'Couldn't you find a better name than that?' She looks at him more closely. 'Anyway, it's a girl,' she says.

I look at her in astonishment. It has never occurred to me that Henry is a girl. 'No he's not. He's obviously a boy.'

'Then why's he wearing a pink sleepsuit?' she says. 'Pink is for girls.'

'No,' I say. 'I don't want a girl.'

'It's easy enough to find out,' she says.

We spotted the empty pram outside the butcher's. We watched the mother pick up her own baby to carry him into the shop.

'Come on,' says Megan. 'We haven't got much time. There's only a short queue.'

We leave the park and walk over the zebra crossing. Just before we reach the butcher's, I stop and take the baby out of the bag. I feel her in my arms. I look down at her – that perfectly formed face – and there is a great pain inside me.

'Hurry up,' says Megan.

I put the baby into the pram, covering her with the blanket. She waves her arms wildly and starts to whine. I stand over her.

Megan pulls my arm, so I turn away with her, leaving the baby in the pram. The baby who was never really Henry after all. I wonder what the mother will do when she finds she has two babies. I wonder if she will keep them both.

8

Neverland

I'm on a train again, but now I'm the protector, not the protected. I wonder if James understands. I turn away from his image; I can't think of him now. Instead, I think of baby Henry who was probably Henrietta. I should have realized it wouldn't work. Nothing changes. The mother that I haven't got is different from the one I thought I hadn't got, but I still end up with no mother. So no past, and no future.

I look at Megan beside me. She's holding a comic on her lap and pretending to read it, but hasn't turned a page for some time. She must be tired. I didn't make her come with me. She insisted that she wasn't going home and I thought it would be better if she stayed with me rather than go off on her own. At least I can look after her for a while. Perhaps we'll just borrow each other for a few days and then go back home afterwards.

'Mum won't mind,' says Megan. 'She spends all her time with Henry. She doesn't look after me properly.'

I'm sure she's right, because I saw them at the doctor's. I can understand why her mother would be diverted by such an enchanting baby, but she should give Megan some of her time.

'What about your dad?' I say.

She looks up at me with a slightly confused expression on her face. 'Haven't got a dad.'

Just like me, except that I had someone who pretended to be my father. 'Does he live somewhere else?'

'No,' she says. 'I haven't got a dad. I told you.'

'Has he died?' I say gently.

She thinks for a while. 'You can't die if you never existed.'

I'm beginning to think that she's older than she looks.

We've had fun together. We went shopping, and bought lots of clothes for her. She tried on so many things. We dressed her in jeans from Tammy Girl, a top with a heart on it from Miss Selfridge and a warm coat from Marks & Spencer. And we found some trainers with a red light that flashes off and on as she walks. Not the sort of thing that Lesley would buy for Emily or Rosie.

We went into Rackhams and bought a hold-all to put all the old clothes in. Then I did what I had wanted to do since I first saw her. I walked into the hairdresser's and asked them to cut off her plaits.

She came out to show me, swinging her hair round her face, grinning in a way I had not seen before. 'Cool,' she said.

'You look so much older.'

'Do I look as if I'm thirteen?'

'Easily. You must be at least fifteen.'

But she wasn't that old, because she slipped her hand into mine and it felt as if she belonged to me.

'Do you want to go home now?' I said.

'I told you,' she said. 'I'm not going home. I'm running away.'

'Let's go and have some tea,' I said.

In the last half-hour before Rackhams closed, we went up to the restaurant on the sixth floor to see what they had left. Megan had chocolate cake and a cream bun and fizzy orange. I had a scone and a cup of tea.

I sat for a while and watched her eat. She looked like a different child in her new hairstyle, certainly older, but she was still very pale. She didn't look very well. Her huge eyes were strangely dark and translucent, with purple shadows underneath.

'Why were you at the doctor's?' I said.

She met my eyes for a few seconds, then looked down again without speaking. I saw that she hadn't eaten very much. Most of the food was broken into crumbs and scattered over the plate. 'Nothing much,' she said.

'Who was ill?' I asked. 'Mum, Henry or you?'

'Don't know,' she said.

'Was it you?'

Her eyes slid away from me. 'I've got – asthma,' she said.

I relaxed. Thousands of children have asthma. Emily has it, although not badly. 'Do you have an inhaler?'

She nodded.

'Do you have it with you?' I knew she didn't. I'd helped her take her clothes on and off when she tried on the new ones.

'No,' she said. 'I forgot it.'

She looked older, but was acting as if she were younger. 'How often do you use it?' I asked.

She shrugged. 'Not much.'

It couldn't be too bad. She was breathing all right now, and she had been all afternoon. It's nothing, I thought, just an inconvenience. But when I looked at her closely, I could see something not quite right – a fragile, vulnerable look. Her face seemed too clearly defined, as if the skin were shrinking and needed to be stretched very tightly over the bones.

'Shall I take you home now?' I said.

'No,' she said, and a warmth crept through me, a secret pleasure at the discovery that she really wanted to be with me. 'What are we going to do now?' she said.

I thought of Emily and Rosie and what we used to do together. We went for walks, read books, played hopscotch.

Megan is older than both of them, more capable of acting independently. There must be far more things to do.

'Have you ever been to the theatre?' I asked.

She screwed up her nose. 'I went with our school. It was a stupid play about people who fly and pirates.'

So she's already seen *Peter Pan*. 'Didn't you enjoy it?'

She rolled her eyes and didn't bother to reply. I was amazed. How could she, a lost child, be unable to identify with the lost boys?

'Couldn't hear it. The boys next to me were talking all the time. Sir took them out in the end, but then I couldn't see properly because Sarah Middleton was in front of me and she's so big and fat nobody could see round her. I kicked her a bit, but she wouldn't move.'

I didn't know what to say. I tried to imagine Rosie and Emily kicking the people in front of them and calling them fat, but I knew they'd never do that. Lesley wouldn't allow it.

'Can't we go to your house?'

'My house?' Did she mean Dad's house, with Paul and Martin and my father? Or my flat? Where a baby wouldn't fit. I couldn't take her there because – well, what about James? If I couldn't see a baby in my space, I certainly couldn't see an older child of indeterminate age. Even if she had no father.

'No,' I said. 'That's not possible.'

We were still in the restaurant on the top floor of Rackhams. You ought to be able to sit and look down on Birmingham, but you can't because there are barriers outside the windows. You have no good way of knowing that you're high up.

An idea shot into my mind. I *am* high up, I thought. I could leap out of the window and fly. We could do anything, go anywhere. Maybe if I let go of the table, I would float upwards – to a distant Neverland.

'When did you last go to the seaside?' I asked.

'I don't know.'

'What do you mean, you don't know?'

She frowned and looked confused. 'It's not my fault if I've never been.'

I was appalled. 'Never?'

'I don't know. I can't remember.'

I leaned forward and grasped the table tightly in case I floated off. 'Would you like to go to the seaside?'

She shrugged. 'How should I know?'

'It's wonderful. Playing in the sand with buckets and spades . . .' I thought of my father's picture of the baby crawling off to the side. He was right about one thing. Babies are not for keeping.

'You can make sandcastles – Seaweed, shells – Real sandwiches with sand – Kites. You can watch boats – or swim.' I nearly tip over the teapot with my hand, but save it just in time.

'I can't swim.'

'You don't have to. You can paddle.'

She looked uncertain.

'We can go together. It'll be your first time on the beach and we can do all the things you've missed.'

'Now?' she said.

'We could go down on the train tonight, find somewhere to stay in Exmouth. Have all day on the beach tomorrow.'

She drank up the last of the fizzy orange. 'OK,' she said.

So here we are on the train. We bought some books at the station, although Megan didn't show much enthusiasm – she was more interested in *Just Seventeen* and *Mizz*. I bought her one of each reluctantly, but I'm sure they're too old for her. I'd like to encourage her to read something more challenging, and I'm just about to ask if she would like me to read to her when I notice she has fallen asleep, leaning against my arm. Very gently, I ease her round so that her head rests on my lap and her feet are up on the seat. She moves restlessly, muttering in her sleep, but then she calms down and becomes still.

I listen anxiously to her breathing, worrying about the asthma, but I can't hear anything unusual. I look at the side of her face on my lap and try to work out her age again. She looks very young in her sleep, almost a baby. I smooth the light wispy hair off her cheek, and notice again the thinness of her face, the sharp definition of her nose and cheekbones. I feel the warmth of her body on mine, the rise and fall of her chest as she breathes and I am filled with love for her.

I'd like to sleep myself, but I'm afraid I won't wake up at the right moment and we'd miss Exeter. I rummage carefully through my bag, hoping to find some leftover chocolate, a few Rolos, a square of Dairy Milk. But there's nothing to eat.

I come across the letter that I picked up this morning in my flat – so long ago in another life, when I had no children or responsibilities. I take it out and examine it, trying to guess who wrote it. Someone has given up a sizeable portion of their time to think of me and record their thoughts. I stop guessing and open it. The letter is from my father.

But my father doesn't write letters. He telephones and shouts, or waits until the person turns up at the house. I've never seen him sit down and write a letter. I can't even imagine it. Hardly anyone writes to him because they know they won't get a reply. Even Dennis the agent comes up from London to ask him a question or to sign a form. It's the only way he can get a reaction.

My father has written me a letter. I think of all the letters in the attic from Janet, Louise, Philippa, etc. He never wrote to them, but he's written to me.

I'm not sure about this. What does he want to tell me? About Dinah, my mother? But I wish he would take time to think. To sort out real memory from pretend memory. I don't know if he can do this, but I think he ought to try.

Dear Kitty,
Don't tear this letter up and destroy it before you read it. *(That's good coming from someone who spent over thirty years tearing up letters from his children's mother.)* I want to explain, and it seems easier to write it down. *(He wouldn't even write a letter to school when I was ill. Paul had to forge his signature.)* I have nothing to say about Margaret, and I still believe I did the right thing. She can appear or disappear for all I care.

I imagine you want to know about Dinah. I can't tell you much, because I didn't have much to do with her, but I do remember that she was a very difficult child. She cried as a baby, screamed as a toddler and argued as soon as she could talk. There were endless rows as she grew older, especially with Margaret, who insisted on confronting her over every issue – mistakenly in my opinion. In the end, Dinah stopped talking to us altogether.

Then one day, when she was fifteen, she went out and never came back. We thought she would eventually turn up when she was hungry, but she didn't. We tried to find her. We went to the police, drove round to her friends' houses, but they had no idea where she was. There had been a group of hippies in the area for a while, who disappeared at the same time, and we finally decided she had gone with them.

That was it. We never found her and in the end we stopped looking.

Margaret will no doubt claim that she was depressed by Dinah's departure, and that's why she abandoned us.

What does my father know about depression? Anyway, I don't want to know about Margaret, I want to know about Dinah. Megan stirs on my lap and I shift slightly, trying to stretch my legs without waking her. She murmurs incoherent words, then quietens again and breathes more deeply. In and out. In and out.

Three years later, a man appeared on our doorstep with you, saying that Dinah was dead. She fell off a mountain in Austria. Messing around as usual, dancing without being careful, and she slipped and fell 800 feet. Once they realized she was dead, they left her there, where someone else would find her. Nobody seemed to have any idea of responsibility. I gather they just drove over the next border into another country. *(So my mother died in an unfamiliar land, buried in an unmarked grave. The end of her past, the end of her future.)*

That's all he said. He didn't give me any choice about taking you. He might have been your father, but I wouldn't recognize him again – he had a long beard and hair down his back. He was very vague – probably on drugs – but he kissed you and gave me a Tesco bag containing your possessions. There wasn't much – a dirty blanket, a dummy and a threadbare pink fluffy duck.

Dinah must have been pregnant when she left here. Fifteen. What a way to mess up her life and yours. But you were all right once you were cleaned up. The boys liked you. They were pleased to have a baby sister.

I know your birth certificate says Margaret and I

are your parents. I lied. I paid a lot of money to get that sorted – it took months after you came back, but you don't want to know the details. I'm afraid your date of birth isn't accurate. It was a rough guess.

That's it really. I know it's not much. I might have the Tesco bag somewhere with all its filthy contents and I'll look for it if you want me to.

Sorry.

Dad.

I'm crying, the tears rolling down my cheeks and falling on to the letter. I imagine Dinah falling off into a ravine, her long hippy skirt billowing out round her like a failed parachute. I wonder if she thought she was flying at first, free from the natural laws of the universe. Were the last few seconds of her life deliriously happy, free, untamed? Was I in her thoughts in those last moments before landing? I don't believe she was bad, just different. I remember warmth, a comfortable lap, singing, the pretty tasselled dress.

Perhaps my memories aren't of Dinah. Perhaps I was handed from person to person, although Dinah must have felt some responsibility for me. Otherwise they wouldn't have brought me back after she died. I want her to be the mother in my mind.

I look down at Megan, asleep on my lap, and I stroke her arm. Mothers can't reject their children, however hard they try. I think about the kiss given me by the bearded man. Was he my father? I am grateful for his kiss.

I want James. I want him so much. I need to tell him about this, to explain to him that Dinah wasn't bad.

But I'm sitting in a train in the dark, going in the opposite direction, away from James, going to the seaside with an unpredictable child whose age changes every time I look at her.

*

We don't arrive in Exeter until eleven o'clock, far too late to go to Exmouth. We come out of the station bleary-eyed, and I don't know what to do. Megan stands miserably next to me, sucking her thumb. She looks even paler than before and very miserable.

'Come on,' I say. 'We need to find somewhere to stay.'

We walk up a hill without speaking. Judging by the road signs, we're near the university, so there must be places to stay nearby. Margaret came here once, I say to myself. My grandmother. We have a connection. We walk past a row of houses, until, with a rush of relief, I see several bed and breakfast signs. I keep walking until I can see a light still on downstairs.

I ring the doorbell twice before anything happens. An elderly lady with ragged grey hair peers round the door.

'Hello,' I say. 'I'm sorry to be so late, but do you have a room for me and my daughter?'

The door opens a bit wider as she studies us. She's wearing a pink nylon overall over a knee-length orange flowery dress and enormous hedgehog slippers, and she's holding a kettle. 'It's a bit late,' she said.

'Yes,' I say, nodding vigorously. I struggle to find an explanation as the silence grow longer. 'We meant to get here earlier, but the car broke down and we had to take the train.'

She looks vaguely puzzled. 'Was I expecting you?'

'No, no. We're on our way to Exmouth.'

Her eyes fall on Megan and her lined, scrubbed face becomes more tender. 'Well,' she says, 'you can catch an early train tomorrow. The station's only five minutes away.'

'Yes, I know. It would be so helpful if we could stay here.'

'You'll have to make your own beds.' She opens the door wider and we go in.

265

*

I am woken by a sudden sharp sound. My eyes fly open, and there are a few seconds of confusion while I struggle with the unfamiliarity of the darkness. Then I remember. We're in Exeter, in the bed and breakfast. I'm in a creaky double bed which has a headboard made from yellow and black tiger-striped acrylic fur. Megan is in a little camp bed at the foot of mine. As my eyes become gradually accustomed to the dark, I can pick out the forest of plastic plants in one corner of the room and a pile of fluffy toys in another. The orange and blue teddy bear that was on my bed went straight into the corner to join the others, but Megan kept her orange fluffy cat and went to sleep with it in her arms.

The same sharp sound that woke me comes again. A flickering light briefly illuminates the room, and there's a strong smell of matches. I sit up.

'Megan?' I whisper. 'What are you doing?'

Complete silence.

I wonder if I'm dreaming, but I'm sure I recognize the smell. I lean over and fumble for the switch on the bedside lamp. It clicks on and I spend a few more seconds adjusting, focusing my eyes on the lamp, which I'd hardly noticed when we came to bed. It is made out of brass and shaped like a swan, its long neck arching upwards to the head.

Then I lean over and look at Megan. She is lying with her back to me, the quilt pulled up tightly round her neck.

'Megan,' I whisper.

There's no reply and her breathing sounds calm and even. I lean over to pull the duvet back, but it won't come. She's resisting me.

'Megan,' I whisper more urgently. 'What are you doing?'

I relax my hold on the duvet, then try to yank it off, but she's still pulling hard in the opposite direction. I give up, get out of bed and walk round to her other side. I am still in my underwear because we didn't think about nighties when we decided to go to the beach.

I grab the duvet from the bottom and pull it off very quickly. Megan is hunched up tightly, hiding something with her hands.

'Come on, Megan,' I say. 'Give me the matches.'

She screws up her eyes and doesn't move.

'It's all right,' I say more gently. 'I won't be cross.' I stroke her arms, hoping she'll relax. She refuses to acknowledge me.

'Give me what you have in your hands,' I say, willing her to obey me, but still nothing happens.

I start to get annoyed by this ridiculous situation. It's the middle of the night. I want some sleep and I don't want to wake up in a burning bedroom. 'I'm going to ask you one more time. Give it to me.' As soon as I've said this, I realize it's a mistake. She doesn't respond to the authority in my voice and I have no way to make her obey.

I reach out and start to pull her hands apart. She doesn't say anything, but she resists me with all her strength. I have to pull really hard, prising every finger apart and holding them back until I can grab the box of matches. Just as I free them she bends her head down to my hand and I snatch the matches away before she bites me.

'Go away,' she says angrily. 'Leave me alone.'

'Shh.' I lower my voice and speak slowly, hoping that she'll copy me. 'You mustn't play with matches, Megan.'

'Go away,' she says again. 'You're stupid.'

'Shh. You'll wake up Mrs Benedict.'

'I don't care. It's horrible here anyway. I hate it.'

'Matches are dangerous.'

Megan doesn't reply.

'We can buy a torch tomorrow if you want one.'

'You're stupid and horrible.'

I stare at her in bewilderment. I don't understand why

she was playing with matches or why she's turned against me. The bubble of pleasure that we constructed together has inexplicably collapsed and I don't know how to reconstruct it.

There is a knock on the door. 'Are you all right, Mrs Wellington?'

I close my eyes and try to breathe evenly. 'Yes – yes. I'm sorry. Megan hasn't been feeling well.'

'Is there anything I can do?'

'No, really. We're fine. I'm sorry we disturbed you.'

'Well – as long as you don't need anything . . .'

If Megan starts shouting now, I shall gag her. 'No, thank you. I think we're all right now.'

She goes back down the landing. The light switch clicks off and her door opens and shuts.

I turn back to Megan. 'We have to be very quiet,' I say. 'Mrs Benedict might be really annoyed if we disturb her again.'

'So?'

'Well – we should consider other people when we do things.'

'You're stupid.'

She might be right. 'Why were you playing with the matches?' I say.

She doesn't reply.

'Where did you get them?'

'I don't know.'

'But you must know.'

'Oh, shut up.'

I give up. At least I have the box of matches and we'll all wake up alive in the morning. Then we can talk about it properly. 'We'll feel better when we've had a good night's sleep,' I say, with no real faith in the truth of this.

'I hate you,' she says as I climb back into bed. The pain of her rejection hits me like a fist coming out of nowhere.

268

'No, you don't.'

'Yes, I do. I want my mum.'

I turn the light out with a trembling hand and lie sleepless in the dark. I can't understand the change in her. We seemed to be getting on so well. I thought she wanted to run away from her mother. A sick and panicky feeling is creeping up from my stomach. I try to push it back. I need to think of something else. James. Where is he? I want him to come and find me. If I rang up tomorrow, would he come for me on the train? Would he walk in here, assess the situation, tell Megan to get dressed immediately and take us straight back to Birmingham? I think of him doing this, although I have no idea if he's any good with children. He always leaves Emily and Rosie to me. I think of the emptiness of his flat, the calmness, the light and the space, and I begin to relax . His flat has become good for me. I can shut the door on my cluttered, muddled life and find an easy, untroubled world with James.

I listen and realize that Megan must have gone to sleep. I can hear her slow regular breathing. She may be pretending, but if she keeps it up long enough, she'll fall asleep anyway.

I wake into the sunlit room and see from my watch that it's 8.30. I sit up. The night seems to have taken a long time. I look at Megan, but she's still asleep, so I get up and go to the bathroom.

When I return, Megan is sitting up, looking confused.

'Hello,' I say cheerfully. 'Have you forgotten where we are?'

She stares round her. 'I like that,' she says, pointing to the plastic plants in the corner. They are arranged according to height, with several spectacular flowers that are not arranged according to colour.

We go down to breakfast. Mrs Benedict is cooking an

enormous meal of sausages, bacon and tomatoes, mushrooms, eggs and fried bread.

'Come and sit down,' she says and leads us into a back room opening out from the kitchen where she has set up a table for breakfast. A television is on in the corner. Two of the walls are decorated with bright yellow wallpaper, a profusion of sunflowers. The wallpaper on the other two walls is covered with half-metre images of the top part of a naked woman, barely covered with an elegantly draped, inadequate piece of material. She is repeated over and over again, like a series of negatives.

Mrs Benedict sees me looking and giggles. 'Aren't they lovely, my young ladies?' she says. 'You can't buy them any more, so I am looking after them very carefully.' She's wearing black trousers, held down with foot straps, and she looks different in daylight. Her hair is fluffed into a challenging white bush round her face and she's wearing make-up. Very blue eyeshadow and very red lipstick.

She brings our plates to the table. 'I have to leave early – my son's picking me up. We're taking part in a car rally. So if I leave you a key, could you lock up when you leave and pop the key through the door?'

'Of course.' I start eating. The television is telling us about a bomb in Jerusalem. Mrs Benedict hovers, but I don't know why, so I wait for her to say something else. Megan is looking at her plate with an expression of disgust.

'I'll be going shortly,' Mrs Benedict says.

I nod.

'Only, I didn't tell you how much –'

I put a hand to my mouth in embarrassment. 'Yes, yes, of course. I'll go and fetch my bag.'

I rush upstairs. I've never done this sort of thing before. James has always taken charge. I'm missing him and we've only been gone for a day and a night. I find her at the bottom of the stairs and count out the money in cash. 'Thank you for taking us so late,' I say. 'I'm very grateful.'

She beams, a wide, cracked, lipsticked smile. 'It's a pleasure.' She lowers her voice. 'Is the little one all right?'

I am confused for a minute. 'Oh, yes, of course. She's fine now.'

'Only I couldn't help noticing –'

I look at her, not at all sure what she is going to say. Does she know Megan doesn't belong to me?

'She doesn't look well. Shouldn't she be in school?'

I nearly panic. I hadn't thought about school. I grope for some explanation, any explanation. 'She's ill, you see – leukaemia. I wanted one last holiday with her.'

Mrs Benedict covers her face with her hands in a truly dramatic gesture. I wonder if this is spontaneous or if she's seen it so many times on the television that she knows the appropriate response. 'Poor little thing. No wonder she looks so thin and pale.'

She's right, I think, suddenly shocked. Perhaps Megan really does have leukaemia.

Mrs Benedict picks up the money and hands it back. 'I don't need this. Go and spend it on something nice for the little one. Give her whatever she wants while she has the chance.'

I'm embarrassed. I try to give it back to her, but she's insistent and it's clear that she's gaining considerable pleasure from her sacrifice. I don't know how to refuse her, so I take it and decide to leave it on the table when we go. I return to Megan, hot and uncomfortable.

Megan isn't eating. She's wandered into the kitchen and is standing looking at the cooker. I think again of her matches in the night and have a cold sense that everything is slipping away from me. She hasn't touched her breakfast.

'Come and eat something,' I say.

She looks up at me and her eyes are a darker blue and even bigger than I remember. 'I'm not hungry,' she says.

'You'll have to eat something if we go to the beach.'

'I don't have to eat if I don't want to.'

I decide not to press it. If I sit and eat something myself, she might join me. But the food has cooled down. It looks like Granny and Grandpa's congealed breakfast and I have to force myself to cut up a piece of sausage and put it in my mouth. I feel very sick and want to spit it back out again, but continue chewing to set Megan an example.

'Disgusting,' says Megan as she watches me. 'Why aren't there any Coco Pops?'

'She might have some.'

'No, there aren't. I've looked.'

I swallow the sausage with difficulty. 'How old are you, Megan?'

She stands still, but turns her head away from me. 'Guess,' she says.

'I don't know.' If I guess too low, she will be offended, and if I guess too high, she might be tempted to exaggerate. 'Eleven,' I say eventually, hoping this will flatter her.

'Don't be stupid.'

'Well, I can't guess then. You tell me.'

She hesitates. 'Thirteen,' she says.

I decide not to respond. I wonder if this could possibly be true and the more I think of it, the more uncertain I become. She could be absolutely any age. I attempt a piece of bacon. On the television, a man in a windswept Washington is analysing the implications of a law limiting handguns.

There's an old-fashioned sideboard on the other side of the room. It has an enormous gilt-edged mirror with carvings of cherubs down the side. I can't decide if it's hideous or magnificent. Megan starts opening the drawers and inspecting the contents.

272

'Megan,' I say, shocked. 'You mustn't do that. It's private.'

She ignores me and pokes around in each drawer, but doesn't find anything of interest. 'I'm going upstairs,' she says, and I nod with relief. I give up on the breakfast and sip the cup of coffee, which feels warm and comforting, while I watch the television. There's been a meeting of the heads of Europe, a scandal in the cabinet and a missing child. I switch it off. It's too depressing.

I look at our two plates on the table. Between us, we have eaten almost nothing. I can't leave them like this. Mrs Benedict will be so offended. I look around the room for inspiration and spot a pile of empty carrier bags stuffed between the sideboard and the wall. I grab one and scrape the contents of both plates into the bag. Then I pile the plates together and carry them into the kitchen.

'Bye,' Mrs Benedict calls from the hall and I jump, nearly dropping the plates.

'Bye,' I call out as casually as I can, and remain motionless until the front door bangs. Then I put the plates down and go upstairs with the bag of food.

Megan is sitting with the soft toys and arranging them in rows, talking as she moves them around, giving them names. I sigh with relief. At least she is doing something normal for a girl of somewhere between eight and thirteen. She can't possibly be thirteen. She wouldn't be playing like this if she were, although I don't exactly know what thirteen-year-old girls do. I only know Rosie and Emily and they play with fluffy toys in exactly the same way as Megan is playing now. Is she ill? I try to see her objectively. Lots of children are pale and thin. I see them all the time, neglected by the mothers who are supposed to care for them.

A sudden hoot from outside makes me go and look out of the window. A gleaming old car has pulled into the drive. It's cream and silver, with highly polished chrome edges and a long running-board along each side, like a car from the old films. It makes me think of Cary Grant, James Stewart, Al Capone. I know nothing about cars, but I can see that this is something special, cared for and loved.

A man, presumably Mrs Benedict's son, is sitting at the wheel, with a pair of goggles pushed up on to his forehead. Mrs Benedict is climbing in, over the top, without opening the door. It's a good thing she's wearing trousers.

'Look, Megan,' I say, but she won't come to the window.

Mrs Benedict ties a bright yellow and red headscarf over her head and under her chin, then puts on her own goggles. She looks up, sees me in the window and waves her arm vigorously. Then they roar up the road and disappear.

I turn back to the room and see that the bag containing our breakfast is leaking. A small damp patch of fat is seeping into the carpet.

The train to Exmouth is a toy-like, two-carriage train which chugs along very slowly, squealing as it brakes, creaking as it starts again, unwilling to admit that it can get us to where we are going. Megan and I sit in a cramped double seat and look out of the window. The sky is sapphire blue, but there's a savage wind and banks of heavy clouds are building up on the horizon. In the protected warmth of the train, I try to tell myself it's a perfect day for the beach. But then I see the tops of trees swaying wildly. At each stop, a handful of people leave the train, stepping into a whirlwind, struggling to keep their balance. A tiny black poodle is caught by a sudden gust and swept off its feet, but a man in a pinstriped suit grabs it just in time. The poodle is wearing a tartan jacket edged with white fur and it looks too small to be real. A middle-aged woman struggles to hold down her skirt, Marilyn Monroe style, but she doesn't look like Marilyn Monroe: she has greying hair and is wearing black, knee-length socks under her skirt.

Megan is interested in what she can see out of the window. Because we are travelling so slowly, the surrounding world is closer than yesterday, as if we're somehow involved in the passing dramas of people's lives. There's a smallness about it all that leads to a superficial intimacy. It's like watching television, seeing people's lives without making any impression on them.

'It's better on this train, isn't it?' she says.

I smile, relieved by her ordinariness. 'That's because it's daylight and we can see properly.'

'I know that.'

Halfway through the journey, just after Topsham, the train line takes us along the side of the Exe estuary. The tide is coming in and the water's brown and angry as it advances towards the patches of stony beach alongside the railway track. Water swallows up the mud flats and brings to life the little boats which are anchored into the mud. The sky is full of seagulls and my mood lightens at the sight of them.

'Is this the seaside?' says Megan.

'Not really. There's sand where we're going.'

'Is that good?'

'Wait and see.'

I've always wanted to take children to the seaside. It's like waiting for them outside school. I'm aware of a latent excitement swirling around inside me. My blood is travelling faster than usual, coursing through my body, whizzing up the arteries, racing along the brain cells.

When we step on to the platform in Exmouth, I can already smell the salt in the air. 'Shall we get something to eat?' I say, worried by our lack of breakfast. The eggs, bacon and fried bread are now sitting in an Exeter rubbish bin, waiting to give a homeless person a lucky day. I wonder if they have homeless people in Exeter.

Megan hesitates. 'What?'

'You mean, what shall we eat?'

She nods.

'What would you like?'

'Chocolate.'

'Just chocolate? No fish and chips, or a McDonald's, or – ?' I stop. What might she like to eat? Rosie and Emily eat all sorts of healthy things, but that is probably because their mother is Lesley, who doesn't stand for any nonsense. I don't want to be like Lesley.

'Yes. Chocolate.'

'Right. Let's go and find some.'

We wander round the shops until we find a Woolworths, which is full of chocolate. We buy a very large slab and find some seats in the middle of a small shopping centre where we're sheltered from the wind. I break chunks off and we eat our way through it, slowly at first, savouring the taste, then more greedily, chewing faster, swallowing it quickly, ready for the next chunk while there's still some left.

'I'm thirsty,' says Megan, so we go to find a café.

We sit at a table and I order a cup of coffee for me and Coca-Cola for Megan.

Megan seems to have woken up properly and is showing more curiosity. She was like this yesterday, when we were shopping in Birmingham.

'Where do you live?' she says.

I smile. 'Birmingham, of course.'

'Why have you come here then?'

'I thought you'd like to come to the seaside.'

She blows down her straw and watches the bubbles rise in the glass.

'Megan!' I say, but I'm too late and some of the liquid fizzes over the top and spills on to the table cloth.

She grins. 'My mum won't let me do that.'

'I'm not surprised,' I say, finding a tissue and trying to mop it up. I look nervously around me, but the girls who are serving behind the counter in their red and white gingham overalls are busy selling bread and putting doughnuts into bags.

I know the two elderly ladies on the table next to us saw the drink spilling. I noticed them when we came in, sitting in front of giant cream cakes, eating polite bite-size pieces from silver forks, apparently too familiar with each other to have anything to say. They eat and drink their coffee in silence, watching the people around them as if we're on a stage and they're the audience. I can feel their eyes on us and I know they're thinking, Shouldn't the child be in school? I want to turn to them and say, Look, she's ill. Can't you see? She doesn't have long to live.

'Where did the baby come from?' says Megan.

I'm appalled. Surely every child knows about babies

nowadays. She reads *Just Seventeen*. She must know. 'Well . . .' I say. 'You need a mummy and daddy –' I stop, afraid that she doesn't know this. She thinks she doesn't have a daddy.

She looks at me scornfully. 'I meant, where did yesterday's baby come from?'

I don't know what to say. I've had all this time to think up an explanation and I haven't even thought about it. 'I found her,' I say. 'She wasn't my baby.'

'Where did you find her?'

I take a sip of coffee, but still can't think of anything. 'In a cot.'

Megan nods and seems to accept this. 'Most babies are in cots or prams.'

I change the subject. 'Does your mum work?'

'What do you mean?' she says, looking confused.

'Does she go out to work – you know, to earn money?'

Her face clears. 'She's got money. She gets it from the post office.'

'And what about your dad?'

Her face closes. 'Haven't got a dad.'

I wonder why she is so resistant to having a father. 'Do you have a different daddy? A stepfather?'

She looks away, and I know I've guessed correctly. 'Don't be stupid,' she says. 'He doesn't count.'

'You need to expand your vocabulary,' I say. 'Stupid is becoming boring.'

'I thought we were going to the seaside,' she says.

When we go outside, the bright morning sunshine has clouded over and it's still windy. The dark clouds which seemed so distant when we were in the train are nearly overhead. I shiver in the sharp gust of wind that catches us as we step out of the café. I look at Megan anxiously, but she doesn't seem to feel it in her new jacket. She has a hood, so if it rains, she'll be protected. I look at my own

278

lightweight coat. I am wearing a skirt, tights, everything unsuitable for a walk on the beach.

'Which way?' says Megan.

'I don't know.'

'How are we going to get there, then?'

I look around uncertainly. 'Let's go and ask,' I say and go back into the café.

As we walk to the seafront together, Megan slips her hand into mine and I feel a sudden stab of happiness. This is enough for me. I could stay like this for ever. A thought jumps fully formed into my mind. Maybe Margaret was never a good mother. All this time, I've had an image in my mind of my mother, warm and caring, but I assumed this mother was Margaret and I was wrong. I know nothing about Margaret. I never met her.

A new pattern asserts itself in my mind. Perhaps Dinah was rebellious because her mother didn't understand her. Perhaps my father was right and we were all better off without her.

'Are we nearly there?' says Megan.

The sea is visible just beyond a low wall at the end of the road. 'Yes,' I say.

We cross the road, and the seaside is in front of us. A few people are sitting on the beach, behind carefully positioned screens, but it's too chilly for swimming. Seagulls hover in the wind, swoop down and up again. I stop for a second and watch them. Something in their piercing cries reaches inside me, penetrating the hole that has expanded inside me ever since Henry died. I am empty. I have nothing left to create a baby, just a hollow place where there should be new life.

Megan looks around. 'Is this it?' she says, sounding disappointed.

I look at the sea. 'Come on,' I shout. I pull her down the steps to the beach. She resists me slightly, but comes anyway and we leap into the soft sand at the bottom.

'Race you to the sea,' I shout, and launch myself forwards, floundering in the loose unmanageable sand, my feet sliding backwards with every step. I look round to see where Megan is, and she's right behind me. Once we reach the firm sand she runs ahead and we race to the water's edge.

'Look out!' I shriek as a large wave breaks. I grab Megan and lift her out of the way of the incoming water.

'Put me down!' she yells, so I put her down further back.

She runs straight back into the sea. 'Megan!' I shout. 'Your shoes.'

But I'm too late. She's paddling through the foam and seaweed, giggling wildly, jumping through the waves, bending down to pick up a strand of seaweed. 'Look,' she says. 'What is it?'

'Seaweed,' I say, laughing.

'What's it for?'

I shake my head. 'It's not for anything, it just is.'

She comes out of the water, trailing the seaweed, her trainers and the bottom of her jeans soaked. 'I'm a bit wet,' she says.

'Yes,' I say. 'Not to worry. We can always buy some more clothes.'

She looks at me in amazement and I'm taken aback by such a daringly extravagant thought. I don't normally behave like this; I'm always careful with my money.

I change the subject, bending down to pick up a shell. 'Look.' We examine it together – a small, beautifully shaped curl, perfect in its tiny meticulous pattern, glistening richly after its journey through the sea.

Megan is fascinated, and starts to search for some of her own. Our hands are soon full.

'We need a bucket,' I say.

'What for?'

280

'To put the shells in. Let's go back up to the road and see if there are any shops along the seafront.'

We leave our shells in a neat pile and struggle back through the sand. It penetrates my shoes and is surprisingly cold. We find a shop and buy two buckets and two spades, a special offer at £1.99 a set. As we leave the shop, I point out the ice-creams.

'We'll have an ice-cream later,' I say.

'Why?'

'Because you always have ice-creams at the seaside.' The wind whips round us as we stand on the seafront.

We walk back to the sea, stopping on the way to examine the layers of dried seaweed left stranded by previous high tides, and picking up more shells as we go. The wind is swirling the soft sand into the air in a hazy whirlwind dance around us. It dies down briefly, then starts again, sharp and burning against our legs.

We stay by the water's edge for a long time, building a castle with a moat, adorning it with shells, a feather for a flag, seaweed for grass, razor-shells for a drawbridge. Megan is completely absorbed in the task, but when the rising tide attacks our creation, breaching the castle's defences, she becomes hysterical.

'No,' she shouts, digging furiously to divert the water. But the sea wins, smoothing out the mounds of sand and the channels between them. In the end, she stands up to watch the destruction. She has been sparkling with enjoyment, but her vivacity drains away very quickly and she looks tired and pale again. She turns her back on the sea.

'Stupid sea,' she says, and starts walking back to the road.

I see the sand dunes further along the beach, so I take her hand, which is cold and damp. I've been shivering for some time, but she's looked warm enough until now. 'Look,' I say, pointing to the dunes. 'If we go up there, we can shelter from the wind.'

She doesn't seem interested, but lets me lead her. 'Why is there grass on the seaside?'

'Those are sand dunes. They always have grass growing. I think it makes them stay there.'

Just as we reach the dunes, a shaft of brilliant sunshine pierces the clouds. The dunes are unexpectedly pleasant and inviting. We find a hollow in the middle, and feel warmer and safer.

'Can we build another sandcastle?' says Megan.

I shake my head. 'The sand's too soft.'

'No, it isn't.'

'Try it then,' I say.

She digs slowly for a bit, putting sand into the bucket. She turns it upside down, pats the bucket with her spade and lifts it up. The sand streams out.

'Stupid sand,' she says, and kicks the bucket out of the way.

'We can dig a hole,' I say.

'Who wants to dig a stupid hole?'

If she says stupid once more, I will have to walk away. I take a breath, swallow and pick up a spade. 'Come on. I'll show you.'

I start digging, and when she realizes that the hole can be really big and easy to dig, she joins me.

We dig for some time, pulling out bits of wood, Coca-Cola cans, shells, dried seaweed, and sorting them into separate piles.

'Why is there wood?'

'Maybe it's from ships that have sunk and broken apart, or maybe people have brought it from their homes and had a barbecue.'

'What's a barbecue?'

Does she really not know, or is she pretending? 'You

know, when you cook meat and sausages and things outside.'

She nods, and keeps digging. After a time, she takes off her coat and then her shoes and socks. I lay them out in the brief patches of sunshine, in the hope that they will dry out. After a while, she flops down, exhausted. 'I'm too hot,' she says.

'You must put your coat back on when you stop digging,' I say. 'Otherwise you'll get cold again.'

She looks at me sideways, and I wonder again how much she really doesn't know and how much she thinks she's fooling me. 'I'm hot,' she says again. 'I thought we were going to have an ice-cream.'

'Good idea. Put your shoes and socks on and we'll go and fetch them.'

'I don't want to go. I like it here. You get them.'

'You'll have to come with me.'

'No,' she says.

Her determination confuses me. It's as if she can disconnect parts of my brain and divide up my thoughts, so I can't think clearly. How do you get children to do something if they don't want to? 'Please?' I say.

'No.'

It's quite warm here, with the shelter from the wind; she can't go far in the time it takes to fetch the ice-creams and I would see her if she came up to the road. 'All right,' I say. 'I'll be very quick.'

I pick up my purse and climb out of the hollow. The wind is cold and tugs against my coat. There are drops of rain in it which join the sand blowing harshly against my legs.

As I cross the road holding our ice-creams, I'm reminded of holidays with my brothers. My father wouldn't come to the seaside, so for a few years we went without him. I remember Adrian taking charge; sleeping in a caravan;

learning to swim with Martin who was much more patient than the others; Jake and Paul fetching the fish and chips, arguing over who had most chips.

I can't find the hollow. I struggle up and down the sand dunes, trying not to panic, furious with myself for not making a detailed map in my head before leaving.

'Megan!' I call.

There's no answer. I circle from above and below, looking for a familiar landmark – a pile of feathers, a dune that is higher than the other, another with more grass. I call again. Still no reply.

Then, suddenly, I'm there, stumbling over the bag with all our belongings in it. 'Megan!' I shout, but she's not where she should be.

I stand still to get my breath back. 'Megan!' My voice is torn to rags by the ever-increasing wind, which is now blowing into the hollow.

I look at our hole and see a small movement. I step forward and take a deep sigh of relief. She's in the hole: that's why I couldn't see her. 'Megan,' I say, fighting to stay calm. 'Why didn't you answer when I called?'

She doesn't acknowledge me, doesn't turn round. I lean over and smoke spirals up towards me. She's collected all the bits of wood, piled them into a wigwam structure and lit a bonfire. She is oblivious to everything else around her. Her face is rapt and attentive as she gives the fire her full attention. She's lost in a different world, a fantasy landscape within the flames, where only she exists, where I am irrelevant.

Great drops of rain start to fall and make strange flat patterns on the sand.

9

On Top of the World

I'm partway through a cheese and pickle sandwich when I realize it's no good. We have to go home. I take a bite and it stays in my mouth, so hard and dry that I can't swallow. I try to chew it, but there's no saliva to help me break it down. I want to spit it out, but I can't do that in front of Megan, so I force myself to keep chewing. Nothing has worked, except those short cold hours on the beach, and there's nothing else to do. I struggle not to cry as I face the reality of our situation and recognize the sinking, humiliating sense of surrender.

Megan is tearing her egg sandwich apart, her tight little face screwed up with disgust. 'This is a stupid sandwich. Why can't we have something nice?'

I don't reply. I look out of the window to see if there's still a normal life going on outside, but the scene is blurred. I'm never going to penetrate this normal life. Whatever gave me the idea that it was possible? This sense of failure is familiar – an old friend who left me briefly, but has just been hovering round the corner, waiting for a good moment to return.

'This is a stupid café,' says Megan.

I force myself to concentrate. I can't make up my mind whether I should comment on the café – which is perfectly all right – or the stupid, which pounds away in my brain every time she says it, hammering in another nail, and another, and another. Piles of stupids, mountains of stupids, falling over each other in their anxiety to be heard. 'Have another bite,' I say.

She looks at me with contempt and pushes the plate away. 'You're stupid,' she says. 'I hate you.'

She's right, of course. I am stupid. I've done crazy things, and I don't know where they came from. Did I really steal a baby? Did I really take Megan and believe that I could disappear with her? What about James? What about my family? Where did they fit into my mad dreams?

When I finally located Megan on the beach and found her playing with the fire, the sense of unreality that had been hovering round us for some time seemed to have taken over. The world in front of me was splintering into thousands of unconnected pieces.

'Megan,' I said. 'Ice-creams.'

I might as well have not been there. I knew I had to assert myself somehow, regain some control, so I stood on the edge of the hole and started to kick sand into the fire.

'No!' Megan shrieked. She tried to stop me with her hands, shovelling the sand out of the way as quickly as I pushed it in.

When I saw her hands so close to the fire, I panicked, dropped both ice-creams and reached across the small fire to grab her arms. She was incredibly strong, and kicked out at me, but I managed to hold on until I could throw her down on the sand away from the fire. I held her there for a few seconds and then she started screaming.

'Help! Help me, I'm being attacked!'

I didn't know what to do. 'Megan!' I shouted. 'Stop it!'

What if someone heard her? Would the police turn up? Would some stranger leap into our hollow and save her from me? I let her go and she crawled straight back to the fire.

The sand and the ice-creams had succeeded in stifling it. All that remained were some charred pieces of wood, a pile of sand and the white slithery mess of two upside-down ice-creams. Megan and I stared at it, breathing heavily. The rain was pouring down by then, and there was no chance of the fire surviving anyway.

'Come on, Megan,' I said tiredly. 'It's raining.'

She went rigid and her eyes seemed darker than usual, glaring at me without blinking. 'I hate you,' she said.

We ran all the way back into the town centre, away from the beach, and tumbled into the nearest café, soaked, breathless and disoriented. I only bought the sandwiches for something to do, while I tried to think where to go next.

But I can't think.

'When are we going to get dry?' says Megan.

'I don't know.'

'You said you'd buy me some new shoes.'

'Yes, I did, didn't I?' It now sounds preposterous.

'Well?'

'Well – I don't know.'

'I've got wet feet.' She must be used to addressing her mother like this, imperiously, expecting attention, demanding, but maybe not getting it.

'I don't really think it's a good idea to get more shoes –'

'You said –'

'Yes.' I give up. I get to my feet. 'Come on then, let's find a shop.' I can't stand up to her. I am weak and she is powerful. I have the strangest feeling that she's responsible for everything that has happened, somehow controlling me and bringing me to this café at the seaside in the pouring rain.

We go into a shoe shop and come out with an absurd pair of slip-on shoes with bows on the front. Megan is delighted with them and keeps looking down to check

287

they're still there. We carry the wet trainers in a carrier bag. My feet are very cold now, but I am too tired to think about them.

'I want to go home,' says Megan.

I am filled with a huge, overwhelming feeling of relief. I want to go home too, back to James. I want to speak to him now, urgently.

'Look,' I say, 'we'll go home as soon as possible. I need to make a phone call.'

She looks suspicious. 'Who to?'

'Just someone I know.'

'I thought you didn't know anyone at the seaside.'

'Well, I do. Let's go back to the café. I'll buy you some chocolate cake and you can sit there for five minutes while I make the call.'

She doesn't reply, so we retrace our steps and order the cake. 'Excuse me,' I say to the girl who serves us. 'Could you just keep an eye on my little girl for a few minutes? I need to make an important phone call.'

The phone box is only a few yards away. I can watch the café as I talk.

The girl smiles. She's wearing orange lipstick and green eyeshadow, and she has dimple in each cheek. 'Of course. I like children.'

So do I, I think, but Megan isn't a real child. She's a clever illusion. I hesitate at the door and look back. She's pulling the cake into pieces, taking a few crumbs at a time and compressing them into solid balls. She lines up the little balls on the table in front of her in a neat, ordered pattern. She looks misty, unreal.

I leave the café and run through the rain to the telephone box. It's red and shiny, and my insides jump with excitement at its redness. I think of my father – who is not my father.

I haven't used a phone box for years, but I know I'll need

lots of money for a long-distance call. I step in and sort through my purse. I only have about a pound in change – it may not be enough. Then I discover that I can use my credit card. Well, I think. Another thing I didn't know. Is there no end to it?

I dial James' number and he answers before I can hear a ring. Was he sitting by the phone waiting for me? I try to speak into the receiver, but no sound comes out.

'Kitty, is that you?'

How does he know? Can he read my silences as well as my facial expressions, the small inflections of my speech? Can he reach down inside me and see things that I can't?

'James,' I say at last, and hot tears brim out of my eyes, pouring down my cheeks. I can taste the salt as I open my mouth. 'James,' I say again.

'Where are you, Kitty?'

'At the seaside,' I say and try to laugh – the effect is unconvincing.

'But what are you doing?'

'Standing in a call box talking to you.'

There is a pause. I wish he were here now. With me, his arms round me, his uneven legs balanced on the concrete floor, his curly hair wild and bouncy.

'Kitty –' His voice seems lower – it's dropped a perfect fifth, I would say. 'A baby was taken from the Maternity Hospital. It wasn't you, was it?'

'I gave it back,' I say.

He doesn't speak for a few seconds. 'Are you alone?'

I look round the phone box. There is no one else here. 'Yes,' I say. My voice is stronger. I wipe the tears from my cheeks with a wet, rain-soaked sleeve.

'Thank goodness for that.'

'Why?'

'There's a girl missing. The police have been around, asking questions.'

'They came to see you?'

'Yes.'

'Why did they come and see you?'

'You disappeared. I didn't know where you were, so I rang them to report your disappearance. They can help, you know.'

'But –' He often doesn't know where I am. It's never bothered him before.

'I was worried. We haven't spoken properly since we came back from Lyme Regis, and you'd left your front door wide open –'

I've stopped listening to the words. I'm hearing his deep voice, the rise and fall of the intonation, this voice that represents safety and sanity.

I interrupt him without knowing what I am interrupting. 'I want to come home,' I say.

'Right.' His voice becomes business-like and reassuring. 'Where are you exactly?'

Why do I hesitate, why don't I want to tell him? I haven't got the energy to work it out. 'Exmouth. Where Guy met Margaret.' I struggle over the names. I want to say, Where my father met my mother, but that would be untrue.

'Catch the next train to Exeter St David's. There's a train to Birmingham coming up from Penzance at about four fifteen. You should get that one easily.'

I'm filled with pride and admiration. I knew his timetable memory would come in handy one day. 'You've always wanted to find a practical use for it, haven't you?' I say.

'I'll meet you at the station.'

'No,' I say. He mustn't find out about Megan. 'I'll catch a bus home.'

'Well . . .' He sounds worried.

'I want to come home on my own. I don't want you to meet me.'

Accept this, I think. Do it for me.

He pauses. 'All right,' he says, and I think he realizes that I might change my mind if he doesn't agree. 'Are you sure?'

'Yes,' I say.

'Why don't you get a taxi?'

'Maybe.'

'Kitty?'

'Yes?'

'Go to your father's house first. I'll meet you there.'

I don't understand. 'Why? I want to go home.'

'It would be better if you went to your father's house.' He doesn't want to explain. Something in his voice, the firmness of the tone, tells me this is important.

'All right,' I say after a pause.

I can hear his relief. 'Great. I'll meet you there.'

'Why?' I say again.

'Your father's worried, and your brothers. They'll want to see you.'

'Except they're not.'

'Not what?'

'Not my father or my brothers.'

There is a pause. 'No. But they are your family.'

We say goodbye and I put the phone down. We haven't told each other the complete truth. I don't know why I can't go home. He's not telling me. Are the police there – or outside perhaps – waiting for me to bring Megan home? But I didn't tell him about Megan. I'm the one breaking the thread of truth, the one who was not entirely honest with him. I've never done that before. We've always been open with each other – or at least as open as you can be with another human being. It's all relative. Did he believe me about Megan? Was there something in my voice that told him? Was that why he didn't explain properly why I shouldn't go home?

I stand in the phone box with the rain pounding down on the roof and dripping on me through the gaps in the door. I feel very alone and very cold. My feet are numb and I start to shiver, my teeth chattering uncontrollably. I consider leaving Megan and going home on my own.

It wouldn't be such a terrible thing. The police are looking for her and she'd easily be found in the café, playing marbles with her chocolate cake, waiting for me to come back. I could phone the police, tell them where she is, and then they'd come and fetch her.

I can't do it. I brought her here and I should take her home. She's only eight, or nine, or ten, or eleven. She needs me. I take a slow careful breath of calming air and step out into the rain.

When I get back, the waitress is sitting with Megan and they're having an animated discussion. I watch them for a while, wanting to walk away again, but I make myself go over to them. The girl with the orange lipstick – which matches her overall and looks silly – is flushed and smiling. She stands up as soon as she sees me. 'I've been playing I-Spy with Beth. She's very good at it.'

Who is she talking about? I look round to see if I can see someone called Beth, but there is no one else in the room.

Megan looks up at me from under lowered eyelids, a knowing look that seems to pierce me with accusations of neglect and disloyalty. Can she read my thoughts? Does she know that I considered abandoning her? 'Hello, Mum,' she says.

I'm finding increasingly that I can't hold things together. There's such an air of artifice surrounding our whole situation that it's difficult to remember how everything fits with everything else. We're living in a soap opera. Nothing is real. We've somehow built up this extraordinary fantasy edifice, and I don't know how to stop it. I want to clap my hands and say, That's enough for one day. Well done, we've all performed brilliantly. Act Two tomorrow.

Megan gets up and comes over to me. She takes my

292

hand. 'Come on, Mummy,' she says. 'Let's go and find Daddy.'

I look at the girl who is still sitting at the table, smiling fondly. Surely she doesn't believe all this? But she waves prettily with her fingers. 'Goodbye, Beth,' she says. 'See you again some time?'

Megan nods vigorously. 'You were really good at I-Spy.'

'Come along, darling,' I say, and take Megan's hand. 'We mustn't keep Daddy waiting.'

We walk out of the café. I can feel my legs trembling. I don't look back. Waves of uncontrollable laughter are building up inside me. Megan turns back once and waves childishly at the café window.

I walk faster, pulling her along with me. Once the café is out of sight, I let my laughter rise to the surface. We both start howling, staggering around, clutching a lamp post to keep ourselves upright.

'How old did you say you were?' I gasp out between the giggles.

She is jumping up and down with excitement. 'Six,' she says and dissolves into giggles.

The laughter takes over again, although I don't really know why. Why is it funny that she said she was six? Am I delighted that I'm not the only one who gets it wrong? Maybe Megan doesn't know her own age. The more I know her, the less relevant it becomes.

We calm down a bit and stand still, breathing deeply. I try not to look at Megan until I gain reasonable control of myself.

'Can we do it again?' she says.

There's a sharp, whining tone in her voice and she's not laughing any more. Her face is set and, although her eyes are looking at me, she sees past me, even through me, as if I don't really exist. 'No, of course not,' I say. 'I've made my phone call.'

'What are we going to do now?'

'We're going home.'

She stands rigidly in front of me. 'I don't want to go home.'

'But you said you did.'

She's silent for a while, and seems to shut herself off from me. 'Have we got to go back on the stupid train?'

I nod.

She looks into space. The same look that she had on the beach with the fire. Total absorption. Lost in a parallel but different world. Thinking about the fire reminds me that she must still have some matches. She must have taken them from Mrs Benedict's kitchen. I daren't ask her, because I know she'll deny it and she could easily become uncontrollable again. I can't cope with her screaming at me in front of a crowd of people.

We take the little train to Exeter and the big train to Edinburgh which stops at Birmingham New Street. Megan falls asleep almost immediately, curled up on her seat, her head on my lap. I study her sleeping face, searching for some evidence of the monster inside her. She sucks her right thumb, while her fingers flutter and grasp a strand of her hair. She glows with a childish innocence and it's hard to remain unconvinced by it. I long to stroke her cheek or kiss her forehead, but I resist the instinct, because I know she is not as she seems.

Finally, I sleep too, my head slumped sideways against the window. Every time there's an announcement, I wake with a jump and can only still my pounding heart by checking my watch and reassuring myself that we haven't missed Birmingham. I wake for longer when refreshments are brought round and buy a cup of coffee, my neck aching from my awkward position. Megan stirs, moves around, muttering, and then goes back to sleep. I place the coffee in front of me and doze off again without drinking it.

I have to wake Megan as we approach New Street Station and she sits up, flushed and irritable, her short wispy fringe bent at an awkward angle. We leave the train, go up the escalators and out into the main concourse. I look around anxiously to see if there are any police there, or James not keeping his side of the bargain. There's no sign of him and I start to relax. I take Megan's hand and pull her to the nearest bus stop.

'Where are we going?'

'Home.'

'Your home?'

'No, yours. You'll have to show me the way.'

The bus to Harborne comes and we climb on wearily. We walk to the back and I put our new hold-all on the seat next to me.

Halfway there, Megan says, 'I don't want to go home.'

'Well, you have to.'

'I want to go with you.'

'No, you don't. You think I'm stupid.'

'Everybody's stupid.'

'You might be right.' I say. 'I'd just prefer it if you didn't keep reminding me.'

We get off the bus in Harborne High Street and stand together. I know that Megan must live near here. 'How do we get to your house?'

She doesn't answer, so I start walking up a side street, assuming that she'll tell me if it's the wrong way.

She walks sullenly beside me, refusing to speak.

'Come on, Megan. It's late. I'm tired, you're tired, your mummy will be worried.'

'No, she won't. She'll be looking after stupid Henry.'

For a few seconds, I hesitate, seeing a real reluctance in her, frightened that I'm sending her back to an unhappy home. 'You have to go home.'

'No, I don't,' she says.

She turns and kicks the back of my knee very hard. I let go of her hand with shock, and she kicks me again, harder. I lose my balance this time and fall awkwardly on to the hold-all.

'Megan –'

'You're stupid,' she says, kicks me again and runs away.

We are in a residential area, completely alone in the dark. 'Megan!' I call, and then louder: 'Megan!'

But she's gone. A group of teenagers wanders down the road, puzzled by the sight of me struggling to get up. They stop to look. They're paired up, two sets of girls and boys, arms round each other, and not very old – out in the evening, allowed to wander aimlessly.

'What happened to you?' says a girl, retrieving her arm from her boyfriend so that she can stand upright.

'I tripped,' I say. 'The pavement must be uneven.'

'No,' says a boy. 'The pavement is very even.'

I look down and he's right. They roll their eyes at each other, then wrap up again in pairs and walk away.

'Thank you for asking,' I say to their backs.

I limp in the direction of my father's house.

I hesitate outside the front door. I usually walk straight in, but now – now everything has changed. I'm nervous, uncertain of my position. Perhaps I should ring the bell. I raise my hand, but then I feel foolish. Maybe I'll offend everyone if I'm too formal. I did live here once, I remind myself. This is my childhood home.

I lean against the door, groping for the key in my bag, and it swings open. It has been left on the latch. James believes in me. I'm expected.

I creep into the hall, over the old worn quarry tiles and towards the kitchen where I know I will find them. I can hear their voices.

My father gives a sudden cackle of laughter. 'Ha! Old Kent Road with a hotel. Gets them every time. Collect £200 as you pass Go and pass it straight on to me.'

'Hold on.' James' voice is quiet, careful. 'I threw a ten, not nine.'

'Rubbish. It was nine, clear as daylight.'

'Where's the dice?'

'Here in my hand. It was nine – we all saw it.'

'I didn't. I demand a rethrow.'

'Over my dead body.'

'Don't think I'm not tempted –'

Wonderful. I've been desperate to come home to them and they sit playing Monopoly, each playing to win, as always, channelling their antagonism into the game, fighting it out in a literal context.

I push the door open gently.

My father and James are sitting opposite each other, perched on the edge of their chairs, tight and angry as they always are together. Martin sits between them at the end of the table, gloomily contemplating the board, his arms folded, avoiding the appeals of the players. Apparently, he is not playing.

'Are you accusing me of cheating?' says my father.

'Of course,' says James. 'I don't remember any occasion when you haven't cheated.'

'Come on, Martin,' says my father. 'Tell him what he threw.'

Martin unfolds his arms. 'Well –' he says and stops.

'Hello,' I say into the silence.

They all turn round. My father and James jump to their feet, spilling Monopoly pieces on to the floor.

'Kitty!' says my father, and I'm five again, wrapped around by his words of welcome, made secure by his pleasure in seeing me.

I stand, quite still, and James comes over to me. He doesn't say anything. He circles me with his arms and I lower my head on to his shoulder. I know now that the love I have for him is as strong as the love he has for me. We stand together for some time. The silence is made extraordinary by the presence of my father.

'Come and sit down,' says James after a while, and I take a seat at the table, in front of the abandoned Monopoly.

'We don't need all this now,' says my father, and he sweeps the pieces into the box. The little dog and a hotel have fallen to the floor, but he doesn't notice. 'Just filling in time,' he says. 'Waiting for you. Do you remember the games we used to have with the boys? They all cheated.' He looks at James.

I look at him with amazement. 'You were the one who cheated – all the time.'

'False memories, Kitty,' says my father. 'You were only little. You wouldn't remember.'

James says nothing. He sits down next to me and fingers some crumbs on the table, crumbs that have probably been there for weeks, unnoticed by anyone except James. He sweeps them up, running his fingers along the grooves of the table, drawing them into a neat little pile.

'Let's have some coffee,' says Martin, and switches on the

kettle. He takes four unwashed mugs out of the dishwasher and rinses them sketchily under the tap. When he's finished, James gets up and runs the tap for a while. Then he fills the bowl with hot water and Fairy liquid and washes the mugs properly. He starts to work his way through the dirty crockery piled next to the sink. He rinses everything meticulously under a running tap.

'We do have a dishwasher,' says my father.

Martin watches for a bit, and eventually takes a tea towel and dries them.

James ignores him.

I sit watching them and feel suddenly secure. I can't think why I went away, why I thought I couldn't manage all this. The warmth of the kitchen spreads through me, finally reaching my poor cold feet.

'I thought it would be better to come here,' says James, turning round, 'because the police are waiting for you at home. I sneaked out by the back door. They think you might have taken this child – she's been missing for two days now. We'd better ring them and let them know they're wrong.'

'James,' I say.

He looks at me, but I can't go on. I'm too tired. I need to tell him, I want to tell him, but it's too difficult to find the right words.

The kettle is boiling, the warmth of the kitchen creeping into me, and I feel light-headed. It must be all that chocolate, I think. I don't want anybody to move, anybody to speak. I would just like to hold it all together, here in this old neglected kitchen where I grew up, where nothing is ever washed properly. I like the piles of empty jam jars and wine bottles in the corner which no one remembers to take to the bottle bank, the mounds of bills and documents waiting to be noticed, the chairs with unsteady legs. This is where I grew up, the centre of my childhood, when mothers didn't seem to matter so much because I had so many willing brothers.

I give up and let myself by swamped by this enormous feeling of relief. I watch Martin make the coffee, his huge fingers somehow neat and precise with the granules, knowing exactly how much he shouldn't waste.

We hear the front door creak open and shut.

James looks up. 'Paul,' says my father. 'He said he'd be back about now.'

'Should we ring Adrian and Jake?' says Martin.

'No,' says my father. 'They can wait. As long as Kitty's safe – that's the important thing.'

James still says nothing. He sits down beside me again. He doesn't smile, but he looks at me, and I think he is gathering every ounce of energy he has available and pouring it into me. How could I ever have forgotten to include him in my plans?

My father walks to the door. 'Paul,' he calls, but there is no answer. 'Funny,' he says. 'You'd think he would come in and say hello.'

'I'm sure he will when he wants to,' says James.

My father opens his mouth to contradict James, then stops, surprisingly. 'Food,' he says. 'What can we have? Chinese takeaway, fish and chips, balti, eggs, bacon, sausage, cheese on toast . . .'

There are footsteps in the hall and Paul comes in. 'Hello, Kitty,' he says nonchalantly. 'Nice to see you're all right.'

I don't reply. I can't think of anything to say.

'Anything to eat?' he says, looking inside the bread bin. 'Where's all the bread gone?'

'In the freezer,' says my father.

'Not much good there, is it? Shall I go for a takeaway?'

'Yes,' says my father.

'By the way, you left the door on the latch. Anyone could have come in. You shouldn't leave it like that.'

'Are you going to fetch some food then?' says my father. 'We're all starving, aren't we, Kitty?'

I try to nod, but I'm not sure if my head is moving properly.

'Right, I'll go for a Chinese, shall I?'

'Great,' says Martin.

'Cough up,' says Paul to my father. As I sit here watching, it's difficult to believe that we're all grown-up, middle-aged even. Paul's hair is starting to recede as well as going thin on top, Martin is growing a noticeable paunch, my father has to put his glasses on to check the money in his pocket. But the hierarchy is the same. My father is in charge, my brothers still boys.

'Cheers,' says Paul, taking the money.

'Get a selection,' says my father. 'Be extravagant. Get a couple of bottles of wine.'

'I don't think you've given me enough money for wine.'

'Hurry up, Paul. We're starving. We'll sort out the money later.'

Paul goes to the door. 'Back in thirty minutes,' he says and leaves, jangling his car keys in his hand.

He comes back in again almost immediately. 'Can anyone smell burning?' he says.

The smell comes strongly through the door. We get up and go into the hall, just as a violent, nerve-jangling shriek comes from our only smoke alarm on the first-floor landing.

Megan, I think. Megan and her matches. She must have followed me here, come through the open front door, crept up the stairs on her own, found a neglected bedroom, made a pile of chairs, beds, sheets, towels, anything, and used her matches –

'Megan!' I shout, and run to the stairs.

James is with me, behind me, somehow keeping up on his uneven legs. He knows, I think.

I don't know where anyone else is. 'Megan!' I shout again as we race up the stairs, opening doors on the first floor, checking the bedrooms, the bathrooms, along the creaky landing and up the spiral staircase to my father's studio. I can hear the fire now, crackling, almost comfortable, and I know that Megan is here, sitting on top of the world, lighting matches in my father's studio. She's creating her own secret, fascinating world.

I stop at the open door. A pile of objects in the middle of the room – Megan's wigwam – everything alight: Dad's easel; canvases; the red and black throw from the sofa; books and magazines. But it's still only a bonfire, still controllable. Megan's on the far side, perched on the window sill, gazing calmly into the fire, with no awareness of the danger. The smoke alarm is shrieking downstairs, hammering its way inside my head, pushing out all coherent thought.

'Megan!' I shout. My voice is swallowed instantly, and then I realize that the fire is much bigger than I first thought.

Megan looks across at me quite suddenly, as if she is waking from a dream, and her expression changes. She looks lost, bewildered, her fascination turning to fear. The noise from the smoke alarm and the fire itself overwhelms all other sounds. I need to reach her, before it's too late. She's staring straight at me, her mouth opening and shutting, and I know she's calling me. She needs me now. I am here.

James and Martin are shouting behind me. 'Water –' I hear '– blankets –' There isn't time for all that now.

I pick up one of the large blank canvases by the door, and use it as a shield. I have to get round to Megan before the fire gets too powerful. Someone is trying to grab me from behind, catching hold of my cardigan. I can hear voices, but I don't know what they're saying. I struggle out of my cardigan, leaving it behind with the pulling hands. Then I'm free, inching round the edge of the room, holding the canvas in front of me to protect me from the heat.

'I'm coming!' I shout to Megan. 'I'm coming!' I can't hear myself. My voice doesn't exist – I can only shout silence.

Time seems to have grown and stretched, like Dali's clocks, so a second is an hour, a minute a thousand hours, and I feel as if I've been crossing the room for ever. Behind my canvas I can see the flames: they've grown into something unreal. They're in front of me, on either side of me, but their roaring, flickering strength seems more exhilarating than dangerous. Every colour that ever existed is here in this room: the reds, the blues, the yellows, oranges, purples, green, brown, black, white, leapfrogging over each other, fighting for dominance, their dangerous fascination weaving beautiful and complex patterns around me.

I've lived all my life, come all this way to be here. This is my own, my only unselfish act, my chance to give a child life. This is it.

I get round the edges of the flames in the middle of the room, and reach the other side with Megan, watching myself from above. Kitty – incompetent in every trivial detail of her life, incapable of having children or even looking after them – is suddenly fearless. Kitty, the heroine, who leads a child to safety. I watch myself stamping at the fire with my feet, grabbing another painting from the corner, trying to smother some of the flames before they spread. But I'm mad. This fire is big. I arrived too late. The easel at the centre of the room is no longer recognizable, swallowed by the insatiable monster in the flames, which are spreading outwards now, towards Megan and me and towards Martin and James on the other side of the room.

Megan is huddled into a tight ball on the window sill.

'Kitty,' I think she says. I can't really hear her. She puts her arms out to me, and I hold her tightly. She's trembling with fear.

'It wasn't my fault,' she shouts into my ear.

'I think it was mine,' I splutter. But I don't think she can hear me. We're both coughing now, choking in the fumes. The sound of burning dominates everything – a rushing, cracking, angry roar that batters my mind.

I look back to the doorway and see James shouting. He tries to dive into the room towards me, but Martin grabs him from behind, holding him back. Good, I think. No point in both of us risking our lives for Megan. I'm the one who has to do this. I'm the one who brought her here. No one else should have to make sacrifices.

I climb on the window sill with Megan and we squeeze together in a corner. There's no chance of getting back. Martin and James have had to retreat from the heat. I keep hearing James' voice – 'Kitty, Kitty!' but I realize that the voice is in my head, because nobody could shout louder than the fire. I try to shut him out. I can't concentrate if I think of him.

I look to see if we could climb out of the window. But we are two storeys up with a sheer drop below. There are rhododendrons beneath us. Would they break our fall? If I open the window the air will feed the fire.

You have to lie on the floor. Why do you have to do that? Something about the fumes. They kill you before the fire gets to you. That sounds less alarming. I don't want to be burnt alive – I would rather be dead before it gets to me. But we are both coughing.

'Get down!' I shout at Megan. 'We have to lie on the floor.'

She looks at me without understanding. I try to edge her from the window sill, but she's rigid with fear, mesmerized by the fire.

Another of my father's paintings has fallen into the flames. The sea, of course, the pebbles on the beach, a fishing boat coming in. It looks like my mental image of the seaside, not the real one where I went with Megan. The fire is eating its way through the picture, devouring my father's red, rippling through the sea, swallowing it whole.

I can see anything I want in the fire. All the colours of the universe, swirling round each other, and merging, so they become one colour, shades and variations of a perfect whole. I can see the pink van with the circling question marks. It's real, fully formed, inviting me in. And I see Dinah, my mother, falling through the air, her multi-coloured dress billowing out round her, all the colours I have ever encountered, swallowing each other up and becoming one smudged, confused brown. I can hear her cry. I know it's her. I know that she's crying my name, realizing that she's going to die. And I know that I was there, that I saw her fall.

A bookcase from the side of the room crashes down, the books queuing up to be the next victims of the fire. The crash jerks me awake. I must do something. Someone's at the doorway, covered in a blanket, holding a coffee table as a shield, moving forward slowly into the flames. I can't look, the heat is so intense. I put my hand up and try to see through my fingers. Is it Martin or Paul, my father, or James? It could be any one of them. They would all rescue me if they could.

He's pushing burning objects out of the way with the table, clearing a passage to us. He shoves everything aside, stamping out flames under his feet. The blanket is on fire, but still he keeps coming. He's going to make it. He's going to save us.

A second bookcase topples directly on to him. He falls, tries to save himself, but loses his balance. I can see him trying again, but then he gives up, and lies there, surrounded by burning books. I hold my breath for him, willing him to get up. The floor collapses underneath him, and he and the blackened books disappear into a raging furnace.

'No!' I scream without sound. 'No!' And I don't know who it is that I'm crying for.

Megan moves beside me and I force myself to concentrate. The flames are reaching upwards to the roof. We have to get down. I climb off the window sill. The fire has not quite reached our side of the room. There's a hard-backed chair by the window and I grab it, hoping to use it to hold back the flames. There's still room for us to crouch down on this bit of floor.

I lift Megan off. She comes surprisingly easily. She thinks I'll save her. She believes I can do this miraculous thing, and I don't know how to tell her that I can't. She trusts me, but she really shouldn't. She clings to me, putting her arms around my neck.

'It's all right,' I mutter into her ear. 'It's all right.' She can't possibly hear me. I can't hear myself. But I feel calm. How is this possible when I could live or die? It doesn't matter which. But now, only now, I know instantly that it does matter.

I lower Megan to the floor and wrap my body round her. I want her to live. I will save her, even if I sacrifice myself. She needs to live. She's only a child and she has so much further to go than me.

The heat is like a solid wall, and I know we can never escape by going back through it. I think of us cooking, like sausages in an oven, turning brown, rolling over, splitting open. The flames are nearly upon us, and we can't last much longer. They have swallowed up my father's entire creative output for the last three months. They won't hold back when they reach us.

I hear a violent explosion. It takes a few seconds for me

to realize that the window has broken, shattered glass sprinkling down on us. Why don't they use oven-proof glass for windows? I wrap Megan more tightly, close my eyes and wait. I'm curiously unafraid.

There are new noises, bangs, crashes. I open my eyes. Two black legs have appeared. They move, they walk around and I am being picked up.

'Megan!' I scream, afraid that she'll be left unprotected. But there are two more legs, and she's being picked up too. We're carried back to the window. I wonder if this is death, come to fetch us personally, to check we don't escape through some unexpected loophole.

I'm wet. There is a another roaring sound, and water streams past me as I'm lifted through the window. The fire brigade. I forgot about the fire brigade. Someone must have phoned them. I'm carried down the ladder by a fireman, and it's difficult not to see him as superhuman. He seems enormous, at least ten feet tall, strong as an ox, safe as houses.

'Wait!' I scream. 'There's somebody else in there. Go back!'

'Don't worry,' says a deep voice. 'We'll find him.'

I'm astonished by the calmness of his voice, the voice of someone who's in complete control.

Outside, they make me lie down. 'I'm all right,' I say to everyone. 'There's nothing wrong with me.'

James' face is above me. So who was it who tried to save us and got swallowed up himself? I think James is saying, 'Kitty, Kitty,' but I'm only guessing. He has blood dripping down the side of his face. He's hurt, I think, and I try to touch him, but my hands are not where I think they are. He doesn't seem worried by the blood, but he's crying. Tears are pouring down his cheeks, and I feel his hand gently touch my cheek. I've never seen James cry before. I didn't know he could.

10

That Pinprick of Time

The nurses bring cups of tea at 6.30 in the morning, walking in cheerfully and loudly, pulling back the poppy-strewn curtains. They talk to us to wake us up: 'Morning, Helen. Did you sleep better, George? Why are half your pillows on the floor, Katherine?' They don't call me Kitty. I like that. I can believe that Kitty is the inward, secret part of me that I don't have to share with strangers. I hear everything coming to life before 6.30, when they start making the tea. A clink of cups and saucers, a murmur of voices, sometimes a stray giggle, followed by someone saying 'Shh'. I'm glad they're happy.

I can't use my hands because of the bandages, so they give me a cup with a straw, carefully positioned on the locker beside me. I lean over and sip slowly, waiting for the tea to cool. I feel like a child again, drinking Coca-Cola through a straw – except it's hot and not sweet.

I'm usually awake long before the tea comes. I think sometimes that I never sleep, but maybe I just can't tell the difference between dreams and reality. I've stopped taking their sleeping pills because they keep me awake. There are far too many other pills to take, anyway.

I lie painfully in the dim half-light and watch the other patients moving restlessly, creaking on their plastic mattresses. I hear the rasping of their breath, the snores and snorts, the sudden gasps for air. I listen to the nurses talking, watch them wheel beds around when a new patient is brought in, a motionless, sleeping body tucked up kindly in a blanket.

Then I remember and cry again. Tears that want never to stop.

James comes and helps me eat my meals. He cuts everything up, chasing the food around with a knife and fork, until he has a reasonable mouth-sized portion. I open my mouth and he pops in the fork. We tried a spoon at first, but it wasn't very successful. Spoons are not cleverly designed, we discovered, and it's almost impossible to get the food out of the hollow. We use a fork now. I chew, swallow and wait for the next mouthful like a child, three years old. I wonder sometimes if that's why James stays, puts up with me. He sees me as a child; it makes him feel wanted. Or maybe he's just feeding the child we'll never have.

'How would you feel about adopting a child?' he says one day – earnestly, afraid he might upset me. He's spent the last thirty minutes getting to the point.

I'm surprised that he hasn't thought it through. 'They're not going to let us, are they?' I say. 'Not after all this.'

He doesn't reply.

It was Martin, of course. I think I always knew it was Martin, wanting to be like Samson, or Porthos in *The Man in the Iron Mask*, powerful as a mountain, holding up the doomed building so that everyone could escape, dying in the process. And he didn't manage to save us. He didn't even need to try, because the fire brigade was just around the corner. James had made the first rescue attempt, but Martin had pushed him downstairs and taken over.

I like the quiet, dull routine of the hospital. The boredom of it all pleases me: I'd be happy to lie in bed and think of

309

nothing all day. Pain needs a lot of concentration. But they won't let me. I have to walk around the ward once every two hours. It's not very far, but it feels like twenty miles – I have to stop after every four steps because I can't breathe. They tell me there's nothing wrong with my lungs, that I'm holding my breath because of the pain. Am I holding my breath? I can't catch myself doing it. They bring breakfast, morning coffee, lunch, tea, supper, a soothing night drink. The price of a drink is conversation. They want to talk to me and I have to answer.

James comes in for all the meals except breakfast, feeding me, reading to me. He uses taxis, so he can keep his work going at home. We're reading the Narnia chronicles. We have reached *Prince Caspian*, and I love the ruins, the sense of nostalgia and loss, the children's return to a world which has gone on without them. I could be there, I think. Everyone has moved on while I've been standing still. I might even have been slipping backwards.

Sometimes, James just sits with me while I cry for Martin. He doesn't say anything, but I think he cries for him too, in his quiet, private way.

Dr Cross came to see me shortly after the fire. I opened my eyes one day and found her sitting next to me, calm, patient as always.

'Hello,' she said when she saw me looking at her. 'You're awake.'

I smiled. I can still do that – the burns are not too close to my mouth.

'How do you feel?'

'All right. I don't know. It hurts.'

I won't be too disfigured, apparently. My hands are the greatest problem, but the doctors think they'll be functional after a few operations to graft on skin from the top of my legs. I'll still be able to use a word processor, I've been told by one of the many doctors who appear and disappear mysteriously. My back will heal without interference, but they may need to do more work on the side of my neck, just below the hairline. Not too bad really. It could have been a lot worse.

Dr Cross and I didn't talk much. I couldn't think of anything to say. But we sat together and I felt her calm soak into me. Before she left, she told me that someone from the hospital would come and see me regularly.

'You'll like her, I think,' she said.

'I like you,' I said.

'She'll have more time.'

I wish she would stay, but I know she's very busy. 'Come and see me when you're home,' she said.

I will have to go on liking her, because it is impossible not to.

Martin's willingness to save us makes me feel inadequate. Like a terrible mistake, that I am not worth saving.

I think of all the people who will now never meet Martin. Never know what a likeable person he was, never see the simple goodness that made him special.

I cry again.

My father comes to see me every afternoon for thirty minutes. He usually arrives just after James leaves, so presumably he hovers around downstairs until he knows I'm on my own. I know he's not my father, but names are habits, and it's too difficult to change things yet.

He sits by my bed and talks. 'The insurance is paying up – no problem. But I don't know if I'll have the house repaired. It might be cheaper to sell the whole thing. They can knock it down and start again.'

I'm amazed that the house is still standing. The fire spread to two bedrooms and a bathroom on the floor below, but no further.

'There's a lot of smoke and water damage. It seems a good moment to give up the old place.'

I don't want the house to go. I want it to stay the same, the house where I was brought up by my father and my brothers. But it isn't the same any more – part of it has already been destroyed. I see the fire as the symptom of a disease, a cancer that spread through the house, growing stronger the further it advanced. It didn't reach every corner, every dust-laden mantelpiece, but it will get there in the end. The treatment worked on the surface, but the rot continues, eating its way through the house quietly, destroying.

'Pity I lost all that work. But I'm not too worried – I can remember most of it. I've been looking at new houses. I don't need anything so big, as long as I have a studio . . .'

I watch his mouth moving up and down and wonder what he's really saying. Is he just thinking about houses, or is there more that he can't speak about? It's impossible to know his real feelings – he's so good at being dramatic that nothing seems genuine any more. How do I know what is real and what is fake? Is he capable of responding instinctively to Martin's death?

I've tried to remember how it all happened, how everything got out of control so quickly, but my memory isn't clear. I can't even work out what happened when. Looking back now, it seems that I always knew it was Martin who tried to save us. I see his shape under the blanket. I see the bookcase fall on him, and it's Martin I see, not some anonymous hero.

I can't quite believe he's not coming home again. Every day, I open my eyes expecting to find him sitting next to me. The space left by his absence is enormous. I keep looking at the chair beside me, worried that it wouldn't be big enough for him, then I cry again, because the size of the chair is not important.

My father goes on talking, without saying anything. Does he lie awake and cry for his lost son, or does he hide it from himself?

'The funeral's on Thursday,' he says on Tuesday.

'I want to go,' I say.

'I don't think so,' he says, frowning.

'I'll ask a doctor.'

He doesn't reply. He's silent for the first time in days.

'You don't want me to come.'

'Kitty,' he says sadly and shakes his head. 'It will be hard to –'

'I want to go,' I say.

'I won't allow it,' he says as if I am still a child and he has the authority to make decisions for me. He picks up a chocolate before he goes, looking at it critically. 'Coffee cream,' he says. 'I'll leave it for Jake – he likes them.' He puts it back and takes three caramel cups.

When I try to look back at everything, I seem to have been caught up by a whirlwind and thrown around: dropped for a while in one strange place, then picked up again before I had recovered my breath and tossed somewhere else. I can't understand how all those things happened: my yellow period outside the school; Emily and Rosie; the baby equipment; taking the baby from the hospital; Megan. Was that person really me? Kitty Wellington? Something was twisting the world into unnatural shapes around me and however much I tried to stop it all I was set on auto. My feet kept on walking without my permission. There should have been a way to stop it, but I couldn't work out the formula.

In the end, I go to the funeral. Adrian comes for me in his car and the hospital lends us a wheelchair. James sits by me in the back of the car, hovers over me, fusses. He's so attentive that I want to give him things to do, but I can't think of anything.

The crematorium is almost identical to the one we went to for Granny and Grandpa's funeral: dark and cool, with wooden pews, men in black who glide effortlessly backwards and forwards, talking in hushed voices. It's all wrong, I want to shout. You've made a mistake! Martin wasn't ninety – there were lots of things he wanted to do, lots of places he will never go to.

Adrian arranged everything. He reads out a tribute he's written about Martin, and it makes us all cry, because he knows how to use the right words. He remembers him as a child and highlights his qualities of loyalty, stubbornness and reliability.

Martin has become a lost boy. No mother, like Peter Pan, no future, like Henry.

Several people have come from the firms Martin worked with. They wear black suits and ties and sit awkwardly together in the pews, strangers to our family and to each other. But I watch them and see that they are genuinely upset. I see one big middle-aged man with a beard, wiping away tears. I would like to go and talk to them. If they loved Martin, then they're my friends too.

Jake plays the violin while the coffin goes down. He and Adrian are in black, but Paul is wearing a powder-blue suit and looks as if he is going to a summer wedding. He just needs a white carnation in his buttonhole. My father is soberly dressed, not wearing a bow-tie, as if he knows nothing will ever be the same again. I watch his profile while we listen to Jake's violin and I finally see how he feels. There is a look of defeat about him, a downward-pulling force, an oldness. His cheeks sag, his mouth droops, his shoulders hang slackly. He seems to have shrunk, dragged down to the earth with Martin.

I sit at the back in my wheelchair, wiping away torrents

of tears, and then we go out and huddle together in a chilled family group. Margaret doesn't appear this time. Does she even know? A gusty summer wind whips round our heads, blowing Suzy's hat off, ruffling James' hair. Prematurely dry leaves scurry in miniature whirlwinds at our feet, magpies clatter in the beeches edging the cemetery and scattered drops of rain hide in the blustering wind. James wants to take me back to the car, but I make him stay for a bit. We're all there, except Emily and Rosie.

'They're too young for funerals,' says Lesley when asked. I try to make sense of this. She's very keen on life experiences – and I'm sure that includes death. I think children should know about death and funerals, so they won't spend the best part of their lives wondering why people disappear. Parents should explain things properly to children.

'Surely,' I say, 'if you explained –'

Lesley looks at me sharply and I realize that the girls are not absent because of the difficulty of explaining death. They are absent because of me. She will never let them near me again.

We hover awkwardly, but it's cold and nobody knows what to say. This is all my fault. If I hadn't gone off with Megan, it would never have happened. We would be like we were before Granny and Grandpa's funeral – like we were at my wedding.

But we didn't talk to each other then. Not properly. We missed the opportunity. Now, too late, we come together again, without the habit of speaking our real thoughts. The pain of losing Martin hurts us all, but we struggle to comfort each other.

'It's not a question of blame,' says Jane Harrow.

Dr Cross was right: I do like her. 'Call me Jane,' she says, so I do. She's much older than me, with grey wavy hair and a weathered, wrinkled face. She looks like a gardener. I can see her pruning the buddleia, down on her knees digging out bindweed, dandelions and ground elder. She's tall, with long, thin arms and legs. She's someone you feel safe with, like a mother. And she seems to know everything, but she waits for me to say it anyway.

'We all make mistakes and wish we could go back and undo them. It's worth working out why they happened, but we can't change things. We need to put them behind us and move forwards.'

I tell her about my life – no forwards, no backwards – but she won't accept this. 'There's always a forwards,' she says, 'and we need to go backwards occasionally to help us move forwards.'

'I can't do either. I have to live in that pinprick of time that is now.'

She smiles at this. 'I'm here to help you move forwards.'

It has never occurred to me that anyone could help me, and I'm still thinking about it. I'm not sure if I'm ready to step out of my pinprick of time.

Jane has told me what she can about Megan. No one else would answer my questions. Two policewomen came to talk to me as soon as I was able and I told them everything. It seemed best to tell the truth. I knew I was guilty. They were kind to me, but they wouldn't tell me about Megan. Detective Sergeant Pauline Ryan was very pretty, with long blond hair tied into a tight bun. It's difficult to imagine her seeing and dealing with the dark world of muggings and murders and abductions, but she appeared very capable and her questions were all precise and logical, unbiased. The other policewoman was called Beth Locke. She wore a uniform and acted like a trainee. They turned on their tape-recorder while we talked. Our conversation was very ordinary, like talking to a doctor, or someone next to you on the bus. But we went over it several times and they wanted proper details: times of trains, the address of the bed and breakfast. I hoped they wouldn't go and find Mrs Benedict. I wouldn't like her to know that her kindness was unnecessary and that Megan isn't going to die. I just wished they would tell me what's happened to her.

'Megan's all right,' Jane said. 'She wasn't badly burned. You did a good job in protecting her.'

I should've found this reassuring, but, oddly, I didn't. 'Has she gone home then?'

Jane hesitated. 'No. They've kept her here a bit longer. She doesn't want to go home.'

'I could have told you that.'

'Her mother and father are very concerned.'

'Stepfather,' I said.

'Yes,' said Jane.

And that was it. No further explanations. 'She can't be all right,' I said. 'Children don't normally start fires all over the place.'

I've told Jane about the other fires, about her unwillingness to go home. She accepts what I say without question.

'The police will have to bring charges against you,' she says one day. 'We'll have to hope that the judge will be lenient in view of the circumstances.'

'What circumstances?'

'You saved Megan's life.'

This sounds ridiculous now. All my actions seem to have been entirely selfish and I feel a fraud. I can't bring back the sense of power I felt, the feeling that I was finally doing something of value for someone else.

'But I stole her,' I say.

'Yes, they can't ignore that.'

'Can I see her?'

'No,' says Jane, 'I don't think that would be appropriate.'

I look at the picture behind her head, a landscape by Van Gogh, with a blue, blue sky and orange and yellow fields.

Adrian has been to see me several times. He comes alone, guiltily, as if he shouldn't be here. He brings me books, flowers, chocolates, cards. He never comes empty-handed, but he doesn't bring Emily or Rosie. I long to see them again.

'How are the girls?' I ask.

'Fine,' he says. 'Fine.' He doesn't tell me that Lesley doesn't want them to come, that she's afraid to let them out of her sight. But I know I'm Kitty the baby-stealer, Kitty the child-stealer. I can never be trusted again. Sometimes in the middle of the night, I cry about this. I put my head under the blanket and choke silently into my pillow.

'We should have told you,' says Adrian one day.

'Told me what?' There can't be more secrets, surely.

'About Dinah.'

Dinah, my mother. Someone is actually going to talk about my mother. I think of the terrible betrayal I felt when Margaret appeared. 'You all lied to me.'

He drops his eyes. He looks embarrassed. 'It didn't seem like lying. You were only little when you turned up. Dad suggested it would be easier to make you a little sister – that at least you would grow up feeling you were part of a proper family.'

'A family that hid the truth.'

He flushes. 'It wasn't like that. We wanted to protect you.'

'From what?'

'I don't know, it seems rather foolish now. At the time, we agreed. I suppose we thought Dad would tell you when you were older. Then it became a habit – too difficult to break.'

'So you never thought I ought to know?'

He hesitates. 'I did, actually, when I was researching my book. I began to realize that you needed to know.'

'But you didn't tell me.'

'No. You'd lost the baby. It didn't seem the right time.'

When is the right time to tell someone they're not who they think they are? 'I'm surprised Martin didn't tell me. He was no good at secrets.'

He nods. 'I thought he'd have told you years ago, but maybe he forgot.'

'You don't forget something like that.'

'But I think he really did. We all did. You stop thinking about these things in the end, and your memory becomes unreliable. You start to believe things that never happened.'

Miss Newman again. She crops up everywhere.

'When I wrote my book, I found I remembered very little about Dinah.'

'You didn't think about talking it over with the others? Sharing opinions?'

He looks startled. 'Well – no.'

'Not much good writing things down if you can't talk to your own family.'

'I know it's not much of a defence. I can see that now.'

I move restlessly in my bed. 'We're useless. Other families do things together.'

He looks at the floor. 'We all loved you, Kitty. You were important to us.'

'Oh, Adrian.' I never thought I would hear him say that.

'We were wrong. I see that now. You had a right to your own history.'

'Do you miss Martin?' I want him to acknowledge his own loss.

But he hesitates. 'I don't know. I feel that I hardly knew him. Or Jake, or Paul. You were our link, Kitty. Without you, we might never have connected at all.'

Tears drip again. Where does all the liquid come from? 'I miss Martin,' I say. I'm not afraid to say it.

We sit in silence for some time.

'I'm going to do an American tour soon,' says Adrian after a while. 'For six weeks.' He sounds unhappy, as if he doesn't want to go.

'Great,' I say. 'It's been a long time since you last went.'

'I've been putting it off.'

'Why?'

He sighs. 'I don't know. Lots of things. I wanted you to be out of hospital before I left.'

'No problem. I'll be home before you come back. Bring me a jug from San Francisco.'

'Yes.' He pauses. It's not like Adrian to hesitate. 'When I get back, I thought I might go and visit Margaret –'

'In Norfolk?'

'Yes.'

'In her caravan by the sea?'

'Yes.'

I wait for him to continue, but he doesn't. 'She's real then?' I say. 'I wasn't quite sure.'

He smiles. He is very handsome when he smiles. I wonder why he doesn't smile for the photographs on the back of his books. His publishers seem to like the brooding, anguished look of genius, but lots of people would prefer an amiable, handsome man. Besides which, he might well not be a genius.

'Well, it would be worth finding out more details, wouldn't it?' he says.

He's not committing himself. Apparently, after the funeral, she gave him an address and left. Without a backwards glance, according to my father. 'Didn't you believe her, then?' I say.

He pauses. 'I'm sure she was – is – Margaret – I don't know about her life, though, or her motives.'

He's preparing himself for disappointment. He's nearly fifty, and still searching for the mother who deserted him, but he doesn't expect to find her.

320

'So she didn't come back the next day, or make arrangements to meet you all again?'

'No,' he says. 'I was disappointed, I admit. I'd spent such a long time looking for her. When I was doing my research, finding her became very important to me. That's when I realized that you needed to know about Dinah.'

I've been thinking about Margaret, and I've decided that she didn't tell us the complete truth. No wonder everyone else was so good at lying. It must run through the genes. I'm convinced she didn't contact her parents after she left. They had no idea she was alive. She lied about that, so how could we believe anything else she said?

I want this mother to be real for Adrian. I don't want his need for her to be unfulfilled. But I'm afraid of what he will find out.

None of us saw Margaret through unprejudiced eyes. In the memories of my brothers, she is a warm but remote mother, romanticized by the thirty-year gap. My memories are equally agreeable, but they're not of her.

'Go and find out,' I say. 'It can't do any harm.'

Adrian gets up to leave.

For a brief moment I worry about him. 'You will be careful in America?' I say. 'Mugging and things.'

He looks astonished, then touched. 'Of course,' he says.

I don't want any more lost boys.

'Can I write to the girls?' I say quickly.

He pauses, looks at me. 'I don't really see why not,' he says.

Paul comes to see me at strange times. I sometimes wake up from a doze and he's sitting beside the bed, writing out mathematical formulae, or doing the *Times* crossword. He has an amazing ability to concentrate wherever he is.

One day, he walks in breezily and finds me awake. 'I have good news,' he says.

321

He's engaged, I think. To one of the thin women in tasteful suits. 'Congratulations,' I say.

He looks confused. 'You know already?'

'Go on,' I say. 'Tell me.'

'I've got a job.'

This takes me by surprise.

'Aren't you going to ask me what it is?'

'Yes, of course. What is it?'

'They've offered me a full-time job at the university as a lecturer.'

'But you don't like teaching.'

'Doesn't matter. I've applied, had the interview and been offered the job.'

I stare at him. 'Do they pay enough?'

'It's enough, Kitty. I need to settle down.'

Now it all fits. 'You're getting married.'

He looks amazed. 'How did you know that?'

'Who is she?'

'Well, she doesn't know yet –'

The job is impressive. He must be serious. I wonder if his change of direction has come about as a result of finding his mother again.

'Are you in contact with Margaret? Will you invite her to the wedding?' I say.

'No,' he says. 'Well . . .' He doesn't know, isn't ready to think about it. He's never been good at personal questions.

Martin's death has changed him, though. I'm not sure he knows this himself, but he's lost that boyish charm. There is something graver in his face. He needed to be shocked out of his lack of commitment. He's far too old to go on being irresponsible. He's nearly bald, for goodness sake.

Next time he comes, he brings Lydia with him. She is small, with Pre-Raphaelite hair, curly and tangled, never tidy. She has huge round glasses and a floppy cardigan. I stare at her. I think he's brought the wrong girl by mistake.

But she grins and gives me a kiss, and she is warm and funny and lovely. Well, I think. A sensible decision from Paul.

Jake and Suzy always come together, presenting a united front in case I start talking about babies. But I'm not going to. I talk about babies to Jane, so Jake and Suzy are quite safe. Jake seems unconcerned about Margaret, apparently not minding if she comes back into his life or not. I'm not sure if I entirely believe this.

One day he brings his violin, and gets it out of the case without telling anyone. He plays Massenet's *Meditation*, and the music is so piercing that I wonder if Massenet ever lost a child. Two nurses come in hurriedly, but stop to listen and forget what they came for.

I watch Suzy: she's quiet, contained, with her hands in her lap, but I see something in her that I have never seen before. She's happy. She and Jake approach each other from different poles and somehow meet exactly in the middle. Jake lives in a crazy, unpredictable world of music and non-conformism. Suzy steps out of her successful, sophisticated world and they slot together so well that you can't see the join.

I wonder why I've never seen this before. It seems so blindingly obvious and yet I had no idea.

Jake puts his bow down into silence. Seeing the nurses and the other patients, he grins, then leaps into a hornpipe, fast and furious, and I see how he almost breathes through the music. With an audience, he sparkles and glistens and gives off spectacular displays of light and sound, lit by an inner energy and excitement.

My talented brothers (who are really my uncles). And the one without a talent, but the one I loved the most, is dead.

'You've lost a twin,' I say to Jake when he's finished playing and the audience dispersed.

'I hardly ever thought of him when he was alive,' he says, looking out of the window. 'Now I can't forget him.'

'Adrian thinks we should meet up more,' Suzy says. 'I think it's a good idea. I could never understand why you were all so remote from each other.'

They've come in Suzy's lunch hour and she has to go back. She says goodbye and goes to the door. Wait, I want to call out. If you're pregnant again, can I have the baby?

But I don't.

I don't ask Jake about Dinah either. They didn't feel they were lying – they were just muddled.

'I don't think I've grown up,' I say to Jane. 'I don't feel important enough.'

'What do you think makes someone grown-up?'

'I don't know.'

'Then perhaps it doesn't matter.'

I wake quietly from a drugged dream to see my father sitting beside me. He hasn't brought anything to read, he's just sitting, and this is astonishing, because there are no twitching fingers, no jiggling leg, no restless energy waiting to be released. He looks like the father I saw at the funeral, desolate, old, shrinking fast. Is he happy? What would make him happy? What has he wanted from his life for himself? Even his paintings are not his reason for living: if he puts a hole in them – or they are burnt – it doesn't matter, he paints them again. Does he love us, his sons and me?

I wonder if he feels guilty because Martin died and he didn't. Perhaps he remembers his plane going down, his lost crew. There's a sadness in him that wasn't there before.

He brought us up on his own – accepted the challenge, even if he didn't have a choice. He's always pleased to see me when I go home, and I'm always pleased to see him. Is that his reward?

He moves slightly and sees that I'm awake. He smiles,

sits up straight and starts talking. He's the same as ever, alive, frenetic, exhausting.

'I know I should have told you about Dinah,' he says into the silence, as if we have been discussing her, 'but when you came, it was like a second chance. You were special – you gave me a sense of purpose.'

I saw my mother die. Sometimes while I lie awake in a silent ward, I go over it in my mind. I think I can see it again. The bright colours of the skirt, her scream, my scream. But I'm not sure if I can remember the feeling. Going over it, replaying it, freezing the image, I try to grasp the terror, but I can't quite. I'm sure it's there, somewhere inside me. I want to find it because I think it would help me sort it out. I want to recapture my last memory of my mother and frame it. It's the only part of her I have left.

In between crying for Martin, I have started to cry for myself, for the small child on a mountain in Austria, who watched her mother die.

James is with me. He's always here. Sometimes he talks, sometimes he reads, sometimes he just sits. When he's not with me physically, he's in my head. I tidy the blankets for him, rearrange the flowers, but he still finds something to do. My books need to be facing the same direction, he wants to straighten the pillows. He tries to be frivolous. One day he brings a tiny clockwork frog, and we watch it whizzing across the top of my water jug. Ninety-five per cent for effort. But I put it safely away when he comes again. I can see it disturbs him.

He has changed. I'm afraid that he likes me as a child, so he can look after me, and when I grow up, he might become redundant.

A letter arrives from Smith, Horrocks and Smith, solicitors. The Peter Smith on my answer machine. He should have written in the first place, then we might have sorted things out earlier, although I would probably have thrown it away unread. Granny and Grandpa have left me their house in Lyme Regis. I am greatly moved by this. No strangers will be moving through their dust, sweeping it away, modernizing it.

'What about Margaret?' I say to James. 'Shouldn't they leave it to her?'

'You're named in the will. There's no provision for Margaret.'

'She didn't telephone them, I'm sure. That was a lie.'

James shrugged. 'Does it matter? They wanted you to have the house.'

So many things we don't know. We think we know them, but we're wrong. We think we remember things, but the memories aren't reliable.

'Should we go and live there permanently?' says James.

'I don't know,' I say, thinking about our separate flats. Why does it matter that you live next door to each other? Dr Cross said. You can make your own rules. 'We could just use it for holidays.'

He seems pleased. He doesn't want to lose the bare empty air in his flat. 'That's a good idea.'

'Then we can have holidays whenever we want to without going on an aeroplane.' He smiles. 'Once they let me out of prison.'

He stops smiling. 'Don't say that.'

'But it might happen.' I want him to be prepared.

'Let's worry about that when we need to. Not now.'

We sit in one of our silences.

'I've been to see Dr Cross,' he says very quickly. 'She's arranging for me to see a counsellor. There's a long waiting list, though.'

I open my mouth to speak, then shut it again. I want to ask him what he said, what she said, how it went, whether he likes her. Then I see that he can't tell me. This is the man who can't cope with a brightly coloured rug.

'Should I try to find my real father?' I say one day.

He watches me. He is careful. 'What do you think?'

'Maybe, maybe not.'

'Maybe, then.'

So maybe I will go backwards. It might be possible. There must be people who remember the hippies in the pink van. I have the sense that I'm catching up with myself at last, after all those dreams of chasing my own skirt through empty rooms, all the wandering in circles, the trips round the number 11 bus route.

'James . . .'

He waits. He knows what I'm going to say.

I can't go on.

One of us has to say it. 'We won't be able to have children,' he says.

'No,' I say in a low voice. 'No forwards.'

'We can do other things.'

Yes. Have a cat, a dog.

'There are lots of people who don't have children,' says James.

'Yes,' I say.

The silence hangs around us.

'We have to manage without – make a life that doesn't involve children, doing things we want to do.'

I find it hard to speak. I look at the ceiling and see a tiny spider rushing along with an appearance of purpose. Does it know where it's going? I think. Or where it's come from?

'Yes,' I say.

Read on for an extract from Clare Morrall's new novel,
to be published by Sceptre in 2014.

AFTER THE BOMBING

On the night of May 3rd, 1942, fifteen-year-old Alma
Braithwaite and her fellow boarders at Goldwyn's school
huddle in an air-raid shelter as bombs rain down on Exeter in
one of the Baedeker raids. By the time the girls emerge, half the
school is in ruins and the city centre has been destroyed.

Twenty-one years on, Alma lives alone in the family house and
teaches music at her old school. She's moderately content, until
the death of the long-serving headmistress brings a new broom
in the form of the steely, modernizing Miss Yates. A new
student starts too – the daughter of a man Alma hasn't seen
since 1942, when he played a pivotal role in her life. Suddenly,
Alma is taken back to the summer that followed the raids, a
summer of numbing loss yet also of youthful exuberance,
friendship and dancing . . .

In this enthralling novel, Clare Morrall captures the impact of
the Second World War on those at home, particularly the ones
too young to take part, and poignantly conveys its
consequences for the generation of girls who grew up
to find there weren't enough men to go round.

Prologue

28 March 1942

A full moon. Lübeck, a Hanseatic city on the shores of the Baltic Sea, is in the grip of a hoar frost. Clear cold air drifts into the streets, forming white ice crystals as it touches colder surfaces. Feathers spread their delicate tendrils on window panes; trees become white-haired, wise and dignified, as snow-like deposits coat their branches; telegraph wires are streaked with silver, dipping under the icy burden; a translucent sheen blankets the pavements. The hand of cold squeezes and everything compresses, huddles together for comfort. The sky is deep and black, with a limitless vista of space. The moon, a vast, shining orb, with edges as sharp and defined as if it has been drawn with a draughtsman's precision, is reflected in the still waters of the canals.

A distant murmur grows into a drone, a rumble, an ever-increasing wall of sound. At eighteen minutes past eleven, the first 234 Wellington and Stirling bombers descend out of the blackness of the sky to two thousand feet and drop their bombs. They are like swarming locusts, intent on devouring everything in their path, expecting to leave bare bones in their wake.

Heavy bombs break open the brick and copper roofs of the medieval buildings and incendiary bombs set them on fire. Timber-frame houses burn easily. The RAF leaves a corridor of destruction three hundred metres wide. Hundreds die; thousands lose their homes. The city is transformed into a skeleton.

Nobody believes Lübeck or Rostock (bombed at the same time) are important strategic cities, but at the heart of the decision to bomb is the discovery that what people care about most is losing their homes. Demoralisation is as devastating as bombing. The authorities have studied the effect of the blanket bombing of Coventry.

Hitler's secret weapon of retaliation is a tourist guide that fits comfortably into the hand. It has a clean, sophisticated design and is bound in red, with embossed horizontal lines across the front. Baedeker's *Great Britain*. It's good at its job, highlighting the most beautiful and historic cities of England. Hitler chooses Exeter, Bath, Norwich, York and Canterbury.

4 May 1942

Alma Braithwaite is dreaming of her brother, Duncan. His face is just below her own. He's picked her up in his strong, safe hands and is whizzing her through the air as if she's still only three years old. He's looking up at her, his eyes narrowed against the brightness of the sky, his teeth white and pointed in his open, laughing mouth. She can hear her own giggles, rippling through the calm of the summer garden.

Duncan's hands tighten on her waist. Urgency seems to be creeping into the situation.

'Alma, Alma!' It isn't the giggles that are making her shake, it's someone leaning over her, rocking her backwards and forwards. What's going on? Duncan isn't usually so violent. 'Wake up!'

A thin, harsh wail finally penetrates the dream, dragging her back into the present as it intensifies into an ear-splitting shriek. The air-raid siren! Curls – Jane Curley (whose hair is so straight you could darn stockings with a single strand) – is almost on top of her, pulling at her shoulder. 'Wake up! They're coming! The enemy's at the gate!'

'All right, I can hear you,' she says, sitting up and pushing Curls away. 'Get off!'

'They're going to hit us!' screams a voice from the other end of the room.

'Don't be stupid!' shouts someone else. 'They're not interested in us. Why would anyone want to bomb a girls' school on the edge of Exeter?'

'It's obvious,' says Curls, who's now leaning over the end of her bed, rummaging in the pile of her possessions on the floor.

'They've always known about our existence. Goldwyn's girls and Goldwyn's brains are a major threat to their future plans.'

A switch is clicked on and light floods the room, dazzling Alma. A high-pitched, reedy voice calls from near the door, 'Hurry, girls! Hurry!' It's Olive Oyl, Miss Rupin, the housemistress, all tight and flustered. A long plait hangs down her back over her dressing-gown.

After the first serious bombing raid ten days ago, all the beds in Merrivale, the boarding house, were brought downstairs to the large hallway, close to the front door, so the girls would be ready for a quick exit. There are nineteen of them, and they've been squeezed in, side by side, the headboards backing up against the walls. You can do somersaults over the beds, from one end to the other, without touching the floor. The girls thought it great fun at first – there were bets on for the fastest round – but as the days have dragged on, and they've had to remake their beds every night, struggling to tuck in the sheets, finding shoe polish on their pillows, they've started to guard their individual spaces more jealously.

Still half blind from the sudden light, Alma crawls to the end of her bed, aware of urgent movements around her as everyone jerks into confused action. There should be a pile of sweaters, shoes and gas masks at the end of every bed, ready for emergencies, but not everyone has been conscientious about checking them regularly.

As the wail of the siren fades it's replaced by the sound of engines. The approaching aircraft are low in the sky – they must have come in beneath the radar, which explains why the siren was so late – a low grey mumble that increases steadily, expanding into the dark spaces of the night, reverberating through Alma's bones.

'They're going to pass right over us.' Miss Daniels, the matron, appears behind Miss Rupin, wearing a black Burberry coat over her pyjamas and tartan slippers. 'Follow me, girls. Quickly!'

Alma crams her bare feet into her outdoor shoes and shoves her head into her sweater. She can't find the sleeves. Where's the hole for her head? Where should her arms go? Nothing is in the right place. She can't co-ordinate her movements. She's in darkness again. She can't find the way out. Her stomach, her breathing, the air around her are vibrating with terror.

'We're running out of time, girls!' shouts Miss Rupin. 'Just grab anything you can!'

Alma's head finally emerges and she forces herself to breathe normally. She twists the sweater round and slides her arms into the sleeves.

Miss Rupin has her hand on the front-door handle, turning it—

'No!' shrieks Miss Daniels. 'The light.'

'I nearly forgot!' Miss Rupin's voice is cracked with panic. She switches off the main light, plunging them all into darkness again, and opens the door. Everyone scrambles for the exit, falling over each other in the confusion, tumbling out in a disorganised mass.

Alma's friends, Curls, Giraffe (more conventionally known as Marjorie) and Natalie, are waiting for her. They make a dash for the door, the last to leave, but Natalie suddenly stops, her eyes round in the white of her face, her red hair, black in the darkness, standing up as if she has had an electric shock. 'My gas mask!'

'Leave it,' snaps Miss Rupin.

But Curls, who never obeys rules on principle, darts away. 'I'll get it!'

'No!' screams Miss Rupin. She's too late. Curls has gone.

'We can't wait,' calls Miss Daniels. 'You'll have to catch us up.' She leads the other girls down the steps to the garden. Alma, Giraffe and Natalie hover uncertainly by the door, not sure whether to obey Miss Daniels or wait for Curls. Alma puts her hands over her ears and shuts her eyes, visualising the bombs falling through the darkness above her, but then changes her mind and removes her hands, afraid that she will miss the whistle of their downward flight and not know where they're falling.

The air around them is thick with the sound of Luftwaffe engines and Luftwaffe propellers, hiding the sound of the Luftwaffe bomb-bay doors opening.

She can hear cries of terror from the girls ahead of them, cut off abruptly as if someone is afraid the noise will betray their position. As if the Germans above them have some kind of radar that can pick up human voices.

'I've got it,' yells Curls, a few seconds later, and she's there beside them in the dark.

'You foolish girl,' snaps Miss Rupin, who has waited for them.

Alma can feel Curls at her side, her head close, fizzing with suppressed excitement.

'Olive's scared,' shouts Curls into Alma's ear.

So am I, thinks Alma, thinking of her mother and father, probably at home, sleeping an exhausted sleep before setting off very early in the morning for the hospital. Will they wake up and hear the sirens? Will they make it to their shelter?

Also by Clare Morrall

Natural Flights of the Human Mind

'A powerful reflection on shame, revenge and the consequences
of our actions. Like a latter-day George Eliot, Morrall has a gift
for creating a moving story out of potentially unpromising
material . . . she confirms herself as a writer of real talent'
Sophie Ratcliffe, *Daily Mail*

'Absorbing and beautifully written, these two oddballs and
their plights make fascinating reading'
Angela Cooke, *Daily Express*

'Gripping . . . She maintains the tension throughout the twists
and flashbacks of the plot, constantly springing surprises . . .
The resolution she offers her protagonists in this haunting book,
acceptance rather than absolution, is unusual but convincing.'
Sarah Curtis, *Times Literary Supplement*

The Man Who Disappeared

'A wise, intelligent and surprising novel, in which – as in life –
nothing is simple' Kate Saunders, *The Times*

'Down at the core, beneath its several layers, *The Man Who
Disappeared* is a well-crafted suspense story . . . Morrall digs beneath
the surface to mine psychological nuggets, some of them gold.'
Rachel Hore, *Independent on Sunday*

'A highly achieved, engrossing read . . . Superbly imagined, it
reads like documentary truth.' Tom Adair, *Scotsman*

The Language of Others

'It's the warmth and roundedness of her characters that give Morrall's novels their appeal . . . A suspenseful tale with a taut, spare style and real emotional impact'
Rachel Hore, *Guardian*

'A story of self-discovery, of difficult family relationships and redemptive friendships that slips between past and present and unfolds not so much a coming-of-age as a coming-to-understanding . . . An enjoyable, engrossing read'
Lisa Gee, *Independent*

'A writer with a phenomenal imagination and power with words' Fiona Atherton, *Scotsman*

The Roundabout Man

'Quinn is quietly fascinating . . . his fumblings towards an understanding that can only ever be partial are brilliantly achieved.' Suzi Feay, *Literary Review*

'Any novelist who can make the life of a service station warm and touching is bringing off a pretty remarkable piece of writing . . . an extremely interesting novel. Beneath the reality of the story set in the present, its characters brought vividly to life, there is another and deeply unsettling world'
William Palmer, *Independent*

'Morrall writes with poise and delicacy, and her subjects are delightfully offbeat.' Lucy Atkins, *The Sunday Times*